Duncan Campbell is a senio[...] *Guardian*, where he has worked as the paper's crime correspondent and Los Angeles correspondent. Born in Edinburgh, he has written five non-fiction books. He previously worked for LBC Radio, *Time Out*, *City Limits* and contributed to *Oz*, *IT* and *The Rising Nepal*. His first novel *The Paradise Trail* was highly praised and is also available from Headline Review.

Praise for *If It Bleeds*:

'A hilarious romp, full of in-jokes and bad jokes, that skewers the sick nostalgia for goons like the Krays and the stupidities of the modern media . . . the conversation crackles. It is a joy to read' *Scotsman*

'A gritty, drug-filled London gangland novel. ****' *Zoo*

'Amid the bad jokes (deliberate), pub-quiz trivia (extensive) and newsroom satire (pleasingly close to the bone), the plot feels almost incidental. That's half the fun' *Guardian*

'Campbell's second stab at fiction is full of bonhomie . . . [He] more than knows his patch' *Mirror*

'Full of great wit (mostly of the dark variety) and intrigue' *Newcastle Herald (Australia)*

By Duncan Campbell and available from Headline Review

The Paradise Trail
If It Bleeds

IF IT BLEEDS

DUNCAN CAMPBELL

headline
review

First published in 2009 by REVIEW
An imprint of HEADLINE PUBLISHING GROUP

First published in paperback in 2009 by REVIEW
An imprint of HEADLINE PUBLISHING GROUP

1

Cataloguing in Publication Data is available from the British Library

ISBN 978 0 7553 4250 1

Typeset in Hoefler by Avon DataSet Ltd,
Bidford-on-Avon, Warwickshire

Printed in the UK by CPI Mackays, Chatham, ME5 8TD

Headline's policy is to use papers that are natural, renewable and
recyclable products and made from wood grown in sustainable forests.
The logging and manufacturing processes are expected to conform
to the environmental regulations of the country of origin.

HEADLINE PUBLISHING GROUP
An Hachette UK Company
338 Euston Road
London NW1 3BH

www.headline.co.uk
www.hachette.co.uk

Chapter One

LAURIE RECOGNISED THE voice at once, although the only two words he had ever heard him utter were 'not' and 'guilty'.

Now that same, silky, north London baritone was on the other end of the telephone.

'Hello,' it said. 'My name is . . . Charles Hook.'

That would be, as the usher in court one of the Old Bailey had announced him all those years ago, Charles Edward Kitchener Hook. Charged with murder on that occasion but, over the years, with everything from demanding money with menaces to conspiracy to import cocaine. Charlie Hook or, as he was invariably described in the press, the Last of the London Godfathers.

'Am I speaking to Laurence Lane . . . crime correspondent?'

No one, apart from his poor, late father and a few half-remembered schoolteachers, ever called him Laurence.

'Yes, this is Laurence . . . er . . . Laurie Lane,' he said. 'Can I help you?'

'I wonder if we might have a – little chat?'

'Er . . . a little chat?'

A whoosh of aftershave and a shadow across the screen of his computer told Laurie that his news editor, Stark, was close by. What did they put in that stuff? Monkey glands, was it? God, it was strong. He felt a tap on his shoulder and turned to see Stark, all white shirt and shiny smile, gesturing at him, pointing towards his little glass-fronted office. Laurie gestured back, pointing at the telephone, in case Stark thought that he was only holding the receiver to his ear as an ergonomics exercise for his left forearm. Stark flashed his spray-on smile at him once more and was gone. There was the voice again.

'Yes, I wanted to put a little – proposition to you.'

'A proposition?' Laurie heard himself saying.

'That's right,' said the voice. 'Something to our mutual advantage. But I think it would be best if we were to make a meet.'

Couldn't he have just said 'best if we were to meet'? You had 'a meet' if you were planning a robbery or to dispose of a body.

'Er . . . OK. Where do you want to . . . er . . . meet?'

Laurie could remember the sniggers in court when the police surveillance team had read out their records of a week spent following Charlie Hook across London: Simpson's for breakfast, Café Royal for lunch, Sheekeys for dinner, Crockfords for late-night chemin de fer. What stamina, Laurie and his fellow reporters on the press benches had thought. That trial must have been twenty-five years ago now and Hook had not been a young man even then. After all, he'd been a driver for the Krays back in the sixties. What would he be now? Pushing eighty?

'Do you know Clissold Park, Laurence?'

Clissold Park. Did he really mean that flat, unprepossessing, north London park with its tatty aviary and cramped deer park? Of course Laurie knew Clissold Park. He had taken his daughter, Violet, there when she was a toddler, a perfect place for a surreptitious fag and a read of the papers while he pretended to be performing his fatherly duties.

'There's a little cafeteria there, Laurence,' said the voice. 'They make a nice cup of tea. I'll see you there in – what's the time now? – I'll see you at two o'clock. You know what I look like, don't you, Laurence?'

Oh, yes. The aquiline nose, the suspiciously black hair, the hooded eyes and those big, trigger-happy hands. I think I will recognise you.

Chapter Two

STARK WAS NOT impressed when Laurie told him that he had to nip out to see someone about a possible story.

'We do need to talk,' said Stark. And there was something almost as ominous in Stark's tone as in Charlie Hook's. Why did everyone need to talk to him? 'We need to talk.' That was what Caz had said to him before she skipped off for her gig yesterday. Why did people do that? 'We need to talk.'

He did not want to tell Stark that he was meeting Charlie Hook. Stark would get over-excited at the fact that his crime correspondent had been summoned to the court of Old Man Hook, the notoriously tight-lipped Old Man Hook, whom the police had been circling for so many years. Hook did not talk much. One of the old school gangsters, enigmatic, disdainfully referring to his lawyers all questions fired at him by reporters as he left the Old Bailey, looking at the agency photographers as though they were something to be scraped off his black brogues before he climbed into the cream Mercedes pulling up outside to take him away from the little minor inconvenience of a court appearance on a murder charge. Nothing to say.

'I shouldn't be long,' said Laurie. He turned his back on

Stark and almost bumped into Eva-Marie, the newly appointed young picture editor. She touched his arm.

'Oh, hi, Laurie, I was looking for you,' she said. Did she give everyone that full-on smile? Of course she did. She was twenty years younger than him. Bound to have a boyfriend. Or a girlfriend. Maybe she was married. Which reminded him. He had forgotten to get the strings for Caz's guitar when he was in Denmark Street. Shit. She always said that he didn't listen to what she was saying. Could he zip into Soho en route to see Old Man Hook? Not enough time. Couldn't keep Hook waiting. He would tell Caz they were out of stock. But what if she rang the shop?

'Why were you looking for me?' he asked Eva-Marie. She was half-something, wasn't she? Was it half-Portuguese or half-Brazilian? That long, very black hair.

'Oh, I'm always looking for you, Laurie . . . Are you doing the story about the missing lecturer in Brighton?'

I am now, thought Laurie. She touched his arm again. He would not let his eyes drift downwards towards the hint of scarlet bra beneath her pink denim shirt. 'Yeah, but I have to see someone now.' Busy man. Important assignment. 'I'll pop up as soon as I get back.'

'Don't keep me hanging on.' She smiled. Long eyelashes. Were they real? Caz had left one of hers in the bath yesterday. He had made a joke about it which she had thought was a put-down.

'Don't worry, I won't.'

He skipped down the stairs and out into the street. Taxi. The driver wanted to tell him about his recent vasectomy and his views on cyclists. Blank receipt.

It was a weekday. Laurie had only ever been to Clissold Park on a weekend. It was different today. Fewer diffident, frisbee-playing lefties from Stoke Newington, fewer pick-up games of football between portly Turks in replica Galatasaray football shirts, fewer picnic birthday parties with crying toddlers and frazzled late parents drinking warm white wine. Laurie had not been there for probably a dozen years. He would take Violet round the deer park and try to explain why the birds were contained in a big cage. What are they doing, Daddy? Life, he had wanted to say, but she wouldn't have got the joke. Playing, darling, he said. Now she was doing her A levels. Today there were just a couple of young mothers in hijabs; a bench-load of winos, offering broken-toothed smiles; a lonely-looking eastern European woman, staring onto Green Lanes. The sound of a siren. Wah-wah! Wah-wah! Police? Ambulance? Fire engine? As the sound of that siren faded, it was replaced by another, travelling in the opposite direction. The whole city seemed in a constant state of self-induced near-panic these days.

Old Man Hook was on time. He was easy to spot, sitting outside on a white plastic seat beneath a cheap parasol. The bearing was military, although Laurie knew that Hook's time in uniform had consisted of a couple of months in the glasshouse before a dishonourable discharge from the Coldstream Guards for smacking a couple of military policemen during a brief period of national service; Hook had been just too young to fight in the Second World War and clearly had not fancied making any significant sacrifice over Korea. Although it was summer and warm, Hook looked as though he was dressed for a boardroom meeting: pinstriped suit, pale blue shirt, regimental-style tie, neatly polished shoes, the effect only slightly spoiled by one lace being undone.

'Hi, I'm Laurie Lane.'

Hook nodded at him, as though he had just said, 'Good morning, I am the chief steward, I hope to make your voyage as pleasant as possible.' He cast his eyes towards the café, which was up a small flight of steps, with an unspoken command.

'Tea?' asked Laurie. 'Coffee?'

'Tea,' said Hook. 'Two sugars.'

Laurie negotiated his way down the steps with a cup in each hand. Hook looked at Laurie's cappuccino.

'Did you know that Charles the Second once banned coffee drinking? Didn't succeed, did he?'

'Clearly not,' said Laurie. You haven't brought me here to pass on titbits of social history, have you?

Hook looked around to see who was within earshot. He leant towards Laurie.

'OK,' he said. 'Down to business. I have heard that a little toerag from one of the papers is planning to write a book about me. You know the kind of thing: the Last of the Godfathers. Captain Hook. That kind of crap.'

'Which paper?'

'I dunno which one, do I? . . . Could have been the *Sketch*.'

The *Sketch*?

'Er . . . the *Sketch* hasn't been coming out for years, Mr Hook. It ceased publication in the seventies.'

'I didn't mean the fucking *Sketch*. Anyway, one of those papers. It'll be a load of lies, fed to them by the Old Bill. So here's my idea. I do my own one. Right? Get it out first. It's all up here.' He tapped his majestic forehead. 'I know you need photos. I've got them. Me with Ronnie and Reggie. Me with that Maserati I drove them around in. Me and Billy Hill in Tangier. Me and Taters Chatham outside Bow Street magistrates' court. You must have been to Bow Street a few times, Larry?'

'Over the years, yes. It's not a magistrates' court any more, you know, it's been sold and turned into a boutique hotel.'

Hook stared at him. 'A fucking boutique!'

'No, a hotel.'

'I thought you said a boutique.' Hook's eyes – a pale, watery blue – fixed on him, challengingly.

'It's a . . . turn of phrase . . . just means a little, fancy hotel.' Hook's eyes left him and carried out a swift surveillance sweep. A couple, the man in a bomber jacket and jeans, the woman in a grey trouser suit and white blouse, sat down at a table behind them and appeared to be engrossed together in a newspaper sudoku puzzle.

'Anyway, Larry, here's where you come in.'

Do I correct him? wondered Laurie. Probably better not. 'Yes?'

'I need someone to write it. I didn't finish school. Not like my boys. You know my boys?' Hook pulled a wallet from his jacket pocket and opened it on the table. There were the boys in a snapshot. Crispin and Ashley. Public-school-educated slicksters. Handsome young men. Now very much part of the family firm. Laurie had come across Crispin a couple of times. Had covered his trial on a cocaine conspiracy, of which he had been acquitted. Had even been introduced to him

9

once in Xanadu, the club he ran in Islington, part of the Hook empire. Ashley had not been so lucky and had done time. There was Mrs Hook, too. Polly. Pale face, dark ringlets, a black-and-white snap from years ago. And two young girls dressed as cheerleaders, smiling at the camera. Grand-daughters, presumably. Hook closed his wallet. 'So – what do you think?'

Oh, God, thought Laurie. I could do with the money. Clear the mortgage. Pay off the last of his father's debts. Take Caz and Violet for that holiday in Turkey he had always promised them. But what is Hook going to be like to work with? Will he take offence if I say no?

'What . . . er . . . what would you be saying in the book? Would it be like a memoir or a . . .' He wanted to say the word 'confessional' but he knew that might ring the wrong bells with Hook. 'I mean, would you go into some of the things you have been accused of? Like Barney Quick's murder?'

The eyes swung round again.

'Barney Quick was a little rat. He deserved everything he got.'

And he certainly got a lot. Grabbed outside the gym where he used to train on his way to becoming British and Commonwealth welterweight champion. Shoved into the boot of a car. Hands severed with a meat cleaver while he was still alive. Petrol poured over him and set on fire in the basement of a deserted house in Catford. Died a lingering death, lingering just long enough to scream out the name of Charlie Hook to a horrified passer-by who heard his dying cries. Laurie could still picture Quick's sister outside the Old Bailey, carrying a placard with the words 'Justice for Barney' on it and being moved on by the police, bellowing in outrage at the not guilty verdict.

'Sure,' said Laurie, as though it was accepted that Quick had only got his just deserts. 'But I think people would be interested in your . . . er . . . relationship with him.'

'My brother Ernie, God rest his soul, made Quick everything he was. He trained him, he managed him, he paid for his lodgings, he even taught him how to use a knife and fork properly. And what thanks did he get? Soon as Barney's making it in the big time, getting the big pay nights, he fucks off, doesn't he, with that . . . what's his fucking name? That fucking impresario, or so he likes to think himself. And then Quick wants to clean the slate and talk to the Old Bill. Fucking grass. No, we don't need to waste too much time on Quick. Slag.'

Laurie paused. Was it his imagination or had the couple doing the sudoku puzzle moved one table closer to them? One of them appeared to be on the phone.

'The thing is, if a publisher's going to buy your . . . er . . . autobiography, I think they'll want all that sort of thing covered.'

'Oh, I'll cover it all right. I'll cover it. The point is, Larry, everyone's done it, haven't they? Look at all the books about the twins. And Frank Fraser's done his book. And Freddie Foreman. And Bobby's just done his book, what was it called? *Born to Blag*! Fucking hell. The public love it, don't they? And there's not many of us left. Most of the chaps have gone now. Billy Hill and Taters and Jack Spot and Ron and Reg and Joey Pyle. They're all going, aren't they? There's good money in this.'

You don't need the money, Laurie wanted to say.

'So . . . what you're suggesting is . . .'

'You're a writer, aren't you? That's your job. I need someone just to put it all in words. My education . . . you know, Borstal, didn't pay that much attention to writing and stuff. That's why I wanted my children to have what I didn't.'

'Couldn't one of them help you with it?'

'Oh, no, they don't like the idea, do they? They say keep schtum, Dad. But if I don't do it, this toerag will and then it'll be too late, won't it? I can tell a few stories, Larry. Me and the twins. We didn't have bathrooms in those days, Larry, and me and the twins used to go down the Cheshire Street baths together. You never had to queue if you were with the twins. One time there was a fucking grass down there and we had just come in from being out in the clubs all night. I had a cigar cutter with me – you know what a cigar cutter is, do you, Larry? And—' A low-flying pigeon flopped down on the next table and distracted Hook's attention.

'Where was I?'

'With the Krays.'

'Yeah . . . Good days. I was with Jack the Hat the night before he was killed. I bet you didn't know that. Nice bloke but a chancer. Went to the twins' club with a bayonet in his hand and wearing a pair of those – what do you call them? Bahamas shorts?'

'Bermuda shorts.'

'That's what I fucking said. He arrives at their club in his hat and Bermuda shorts. No respect. I could tell you about that. He put up quite a fight, did Jack, when they killed him. Ronnie got a nasty cut when he stabbed him, you know. Got a great bandage on his hand afterwards. "What you done to your hand, Ron?" people would ask. "Gardenin'," Ronnie would say. "Gardenin'." ' Hook cackled and scanned the horizon.

'And judges I've been in front of. I was up in front of Lord Goddard once, Larry. Hanging Judge Goddard. Heard of him? Course you bloody have. Did you know that, when he sentenced someone to death, he ejaculated in his trousers? His clerk had to take a spare pair of trousers to court on days when he was sentencing. Ejaculated. How do you like that? Ejaculated!' Hook almost spat out the word and Laurie noticed a young mother hurrying her toddler past on the riverside path, beneath the chestnut trees, casting an anxious glance over her shoulder. Was that a soup stain on Hook's regimental tie? Or gravy? Blood, perhaps.

'I can tell you about all the briefs I had, too. I had the best. Georgie Carman. He defended me a couple of times. You should have heard him summing up for the jury. He was so good I almost believed him myself!' Hook cackled and spilled his tea. He leant towards Laurie. His breath was bad. 'Great days, Larry. And it's all changing now. All the families are out of it now. Except for us. They done the Krays, they done the Richardsons, they done the Arifs and the Adams. Now it's all Russians and Turks and the Albanians and all those other countries that didn't even fucking exist before. The Lithuanians and the . . . I don't know what's . . . There's no code any more, Larry. No respect. It's a fucking jungle out there now.'

A pigeon waddled beneath their table, pecking at flakes of a discarded currant bun on the ground. Hook lashed out with his foot and the pigeon scampered off. Out of the corner of his eye, Laurie could see two young men in lightweight suits striding purposefully up the steps of the café and between the pillars of what had presumably once been the heart of an estate, a century or two ago. No sirens or frisbees or hijabs in those days.

'They used to graze sheep here a hundred years ago,' said Hook, as if reading his thoughts. 'My grandfather could remember when there was sheep here.'

'Really? I used to come here ages ago with my daughter, when she was small.'

'How old is she now?'

'Seventeen.'

'Lovely age,' said Hook, softening for a moment, 'lovely age.' He frowned and shot Laurie a glance. 'I mean – lovely age to be. Although, when I was seventeen, I was in Borstal, Larry. I didn't have the chances your girl has. Anyway, there'll be a drink in this for you. I've had a publisher fellow on to me already. And I can tell you a thing or two, I can promise. No harm talking about some of the things I got up to with the twins because they're long gone now. They wouldn't mind. I can give the name of the one they never caught on the Great Train Robbery. And I know where Frank Mitchell's buried. You know him? The Mad Axeman.' Hook chuckled. 'And what really happened to Freddie Mills. OK? And maybe people would like to know about some of the other things I've done that they don't know about.'

'Famous . . . er . . . heists?' Maybe Hook was the one who got away in the Baker Street bank job?

'Are you fucking mad?' said Hook. 'No – my charity work.'

Oh, yes, thought Laurie, people would be really fascinated by that. Helping the blind kiddies, was it? He felt an ingratiating smile cross his face. Maybe you can put us in touch with all the old women you helped to cross the road.

'What's funny?' said Hook, suspicious again.

'Nothing . . . nothing. Would you . . . er . . . talk about the police at all? I'm sure your views on the police would be of interest.'

For years it had been suggested that the Hook family had a well-placed police source at Scotland Yard, one of the Met's most experienced officers, who had only recently retired having survived two corruption inquiries at different stages of his long career.

'You mean would I fucking spill the beans on Ginger Mulgrew?'

'Well . . .'

Hook threw back his head and laughed. 'Look, I don't know exactly what I'm going to tell you yet, Larry, but . . .' He leant close to Laurie again. What was preferable – Hook's halitosis or Stark's aftershave?

The two young men in lightweight suits had emerged from the café and were striding down the steps towards Laurie and Hook. They had the cocky look of lawyers in a slick American television series. The couple playing sudoku exchanged glances and carried on their game with a greater intensity.

'Hello, Dad,' said the two young men in unison as they arrived at the table. 'Are you going to introduce us to your new friend?'

Chapter Three

'I THOUGHT WE NEEDED to talk.'

First Hook. Now Stark. Do I tell Stark that Hook has just asked me to be his Boswell? Probably not.

'So you said.'

The smell of the aftershave was overpowering. When Gavin Stark had been appointed news editor a few months ago, Laurie had seen him unloading his personal items into his desk: a fat desk diary that looked like one of those plush, padded menus you were handed by waistcoated waiters in suburban steakhouses; that bottle of Homme Sauvage aftershave, which he slapped on so recklessly after he had been to the gym at lunchtime; photos of his wife and his two children, all beaming wholesomely at the camera. Laurie was sure that Stark had a 'baby on board' sign in the back of his . . . what would it be? BMW, surely.

Stark was giving him his sleeves-rolled-up, can-do, spray-on smile now. Laurie wanted to smack him in the face but he knew that would just hurt his fingers because he had never smacked anyone in the face before and he was aware that it was not as easy as it looked in films.

'What's happened on the missing lecturer story?'

'She's still missing.' Laurie had been working on this story for a week now. Attractive young anthropology lecturer at Sussex University had gone missing. Her boyfriend, a politics lecturer with floppy hair, had made an appeal on television asking her to let everyone know she was all right. Laurie's only contact in Sussex police, a world-weary detective sergeant, had assured him that the boyfriend had done it and would soon crack.

'Has her boyfriend bumped her off?'

'That's what the cops think.'

'And you – what do you think?'

Can't we just get on with whatever you want to see me about? thought Laurie.

'Probably he did. Most murders are committed by people who know their victims.'

'Interesting,' said Stark. Meaning either 'I know that' or 'I couldn't care less'. He gave Laurie his firm-but-fair look and licked his lips. Why was it that when women licked their lips it was sexy but when men did they looked like Hannibal Lecter?

'Now, I've been meaning to have this little chat for a week or two . . .' Laurie noticed that Stark was fiddling with a blue folder.

'Mmm,' said Laurie.

'It's just, as you know, with all of the challenges we now face in—'

'An integrated, multimedia, internet world . . .'

'That sort of thing . . . Well, I don't know how long you've been on the crime beat, as it were . . .'

'Twenty-two years – as it were.'

'Right. Well, it's just that, with things changing so fast on that front – you know, cyber fraud, computer crime, identity theft, intellectual property stuff, corporate shenanigans, cross-border trafficking – the old bang-bang coverage of crime is maybe getting a bit dated. I mean, there aren't that many bank robberies any more. It's all being done on the internet. Well, it seems that we may need a new sort of approach . . .'

The two men stared at each other.

'Another thing is, Laurie,' Stark continued, 'we do really need people who are happy to make full use of all the new tools at our disposal. You know, pod-casting and blogging, taking the old camera out on a job . . . As you say, the integrated, multimedia, internet world. Look, to cut to the chase: we just feel that maybe now there's a window of opportunity both for you and for someone perhaps more digitally, you know, savvy . . .'

'Sounds more like a defenestration than a window of opportunity,' said Laurie. Did Stark know what defenestration meant? 'Are you sacking me? Making me redundant? What is it you're trying to say?'

'Good heavens, no,' said Stark, waving someone away who was hovering at the glass door of his tiny office. Laurie turned round to look. It was the newsdesk secretary, Linda, who had been at the paper on and off for more than thirty years, once married to the paper's now dead and departed Los Angeles correspondent and now nicknamed the Merry Widow because she had had flings with a couple of the younger, hipper reporters. She did not catch his eye. 'No, no. We are just looking at moving some of the pieces on the chessboard.'

'So I swap from being a bishop to a pawn, do I?'

'Not at all. Anyway, I would have said that the crime reporter's job was a knight, rather than a bishop, no? No, what we were thinking is, how does motoring correspondent sound?'

'You are kidding. I don't even have a bloody car.'

'You're not banned, are you?' A flicker of dismay crossed Stark's unlined face. Laurie wanted to ask him if he used a moisturiser.

'Not at all. Clean licence. I just got fed up with the local toerags breaking in every six weeks and stealing my *A-Z* and my Lucinda Williams tapes.' Stark did not know who Lucinda Williams was. Not many people did.

'Well, the great thing about this job is that you will always – always – have a car at your disposal. And a nice new one at that, room for all the . . . you're married, aren't you?'

'I was when I left home this morning, certainly.'

'You see, things are so competitive now. And, well, to be blunt, you haven't been bringing in a lot of front-page stuff recently. Talking-point stuff . . .'

Should he tell him that Hook wanted to unburden himself? But the younger Hooks had not seemed that thrilled at the prospect. Would they persuade the old man not to go ahead? Better not mention it at all.

'Look, I know fuck-all about cars.'

'That might be just the sort of thing the readers would like – a motoring correspondent who's on their side, doesn't hide behind all the jargon, just gives it to them straight.' Stark gave him his head-prefect-meeting-the-member-of-the-royal-family smile. Maybe if I hit him with the side of the fist, like they did in *The Sopranos*, it won't damage my fingers, thought Laurie.

'And what if I refuse to move? You know, you could say this was . . . well, it's constructive dismissal, trying to make someone do a job they're not equipped to do.'

Laurie watched Stark's glance shift to the blue folder.

'Well, there was one other thing I wanted to talk to you about . . . Um, expenses.' Stark opened the folder and slid out what Laurie recognised as months of past expenses forms and receipts. Stark continued, picking his words carefully, forensically.

'The audit people . . . um, they found one or two . . . um . . . anomalies in your expenses, er, Laurie,' said Stark. He waved away another hovering shadow at the door. This time Laurie did not turn round to see who was there.

'There's a receipt for a meal at the . . . er . . . Badger's Den in Limehouse on February the fifteenth . . . one hundred and twenty pounds . . . But then you were at a Police Federation special conference in Scarborough on the same date. Then there's a taxi fare from Scotland Yard to the office supposedly, for fifteen pounds, and another taxi receipt which seems to have come from the same book of receipts . . . Now, of course, no one's accusing you of . . . fiddling expenses. That would be a very . . . damaging accusation. But, as I say, the audit people have brought it up and we are obliged – by law, I think – to check this through.'

Laurie and Stark exchanged a long stare.

'What I think you're saying is, if I refuse to go quietly, you'll make sure you find something shady in my exes and that everyone in the business will know that I'm being investigated for defrauding the company. But if I give up being crime correspondent and start writing about gear boxes – do they still have gear boxes? – then any "anomalies" will be quietly shelved.'

There was a second exchange of stares. Stark shifted his gaze only when there was a rattle at the door. Laurie used the moment to get up. 'Can I think about it overnight?' he said as he stood by the door.

Stark nodded happily.

Laurie wandered back to his desk, switched on his screen and scrolled through his emails. An Ethiopian prince wanted to offer him £10 million for doing nothing but sharing the details of his bank account. Leaving-party invitation from one of a wave of redundant colleagues. Insult from reader. Pedantic point from reader. Pedantic point from colleague. Request for loan from Nigerian diplomat temporarily discommoded. Russian woman seeks husband. Ukrainian woman seeks husband. Press release from the Association of Chief Police Officers.

His office neighbour – was there some word for that? Cell mate, perhaps? – appeared. Guy, the environment correspondent, a young man with short dark hair, the beginnings of a beard and startling blue eyes. There was something odd about his appearance.

'Is tweed jacket and tracksuit bottoms a new look or are you doing this for a bet?' asked Laurie.

Guy shot him a wounded look.

'What's happened?' Laurie persisted. 'Where're your trousers?'

Guy looked round to see if they were being overheard.

'Look, don't tell anyone this but – I went out for a run at lunchtime, changed in the gents, you know, in the shower room. Came back after my run and – someone had flushed my trousers down the lavatory.'

'What?' Laurie could not stop himself laughing. 'A whole pair of trousers? It wouldn't go down, would it?'

'They didn't go down all the way, they got stuck . . . Anyway, trousers are plural not singular.'

'Eh?'

'You said "it" wouldn't go down. Trousers are plural.'

'I think you'll find that they're singular on top and plural below. I said a "pair of trousers". That's singular . . . anyway.'

'What are you guys talking about?'

Laurie and Guy turned round to see Linda, the newsdesk secretary.

'Someone's flushed Guy's trousers down the loo . . . Don't laugh!'

It was too late.

'God, I told you not to tell anyone.'

'Well, I think you should try and find out who did it, Laurie,' said Linda. 'If you're a proper crime correspondent . . .'

'Ah, there you have struck a nerve, but yes, you're right. We should try and solve this . . . flush out the miscreant.' Laurie sniggered. 'Maybe it can be my last case.'

'What do you mean?' asked Guy.

'I think this is a conversation for the pub.'

Linda shot him a sympathetic look.

'What are you on about?' said Guy.

'I'll tell you about it. It'll put your trousers into perspective, I promise you. Got time for a pint?'

'I guess so. I'll go and see if my trousers are dry. I put them on the radiator.'

'I'm not having a drink with you if you're wearing trousers that have been round the U-bend, for God's sake.'

'All right, all right, I'll leave them here overnight. Are you coming too, Linda?'

'Not tonight, thanks.' She smiled. 'Got a date.'

Laurie and Guy headed down the corridor towards the lifts. As one lift opened, Eva-Marie, the picture editor, stepped out. That smile again. Laurie watched as she walked off down the corridor and tried to look as though he was not gazing at her legs.

Chapter Four

'QUESTION NUMBER EIGHTEEN: which President of the United States was never elected to that office? I'll repeat that. Which President of the United States was never elected to that office?'

'I know,' said Laurie.

'Keep your voice down then,' said Mick.

'Gerald Ford,' said Laurie in a stage whisper.

'You sure?' said Mick.

'Yeah . . . well, sure-ish.'

It was Thursday so it must be Quiz Night in the Dirty Dog. For the last two years, whenever he was not out of town working or away on holiday or watching Caz perform, Laurie had been part of a quiz team with Mick, Vic and Mary. Mick, big, bulky, solid, amiable, in leather jacket and jeans with thick, greying hair, and Vic, slim, handsome, dark haired, thin lipped, nervous, eyes constantly flicking from side to side, in suit and tie, were both former bank robbers. Laurie had met them many years earlier when writing an article about prisoners who had achieved Open University degrees. They had become friends. Mick had invited him to his wedding, when he married Mary, the manager of a bookies in Mile End, a tall, droll, knowing woman, blond, always immaculately dressed, as though on her way to a wedding. One evening, the four of them had been drinking in the Dirty Dog on what turned out to be Quiz Night. They had won, to the dismay of a team of local teachers at the next table, and this had set up a rolling rivalry between the two sides which continued to this day. Laurie, secretly and to his shame, kept a mental note of who was ahead in the victory stakes; he had calculated that their team, Long Lartin Old Boys, as they called themselves, had won twenty while the teachers' team, School's Out, had won twenty-two with various other, less dedicated, sides winning every third or fourth week. Caz went to Spanish classes on a Thursday night, if she didn't have a gig – and there seemed to be fewer and fewer of these – and Violet, their daughter, was happy to have the flat to herself, so the arrangement suited everyone. There had been some tension on Quiz Night recently, with accusations that the teachers' team had drafted in some ringers with specialist knowledge. Vic had studied English literature and philosophy, Mick had degrees in history and geography, thanks to the ten years he had had to spend in prison for a Midland Bank robbery, and Mary had an encyclopaedic knowledge of the hit parade from the seventies to the present day, as well as the equivalent of a masters in soaps. Laurie's contribution was politics, current affairs and sport.

'Question number nineteen: who had a hit with "Needles and Pins" in nineteen sixty-five?'

'Oh, I was just starting secondary school then,' said Laurie. 'I remember it. That was the Seekers, wasn't it?'

'I thought it was the Troggs,' said Mick.

'God, no, it was the Searchers – and I wasn't even alive then,' said Mary.

'I think she's right,' said Laurie.

'And finally,' said the MC, an unashamedly spotty young barman called Cliff, for whom Quiz Night was clearly the highlight of the week, 'who wrote *The Ancient Mariner*?'

'Getting a bit bloody intellectual, aren't we?' said Mick sarcastically.

'Samuel Taylor Coleridge,' said Vic.

'You don't say,' said Mick.

The quiz teams exchanged their answer sheets for marking. Vic went to the bar to buy a round. He was teetotal and always drank ginger ale, no ice. Laurie and Mick were on their third pints of Adnams and Mary on her third spritzer.

'You all right?' asked Mick.

'Why do you ask?'

'I can spot when someone's low – I was a "listener" in Dartmoor.'

'A what?'

'Someone who keeps an eye on people in the nick who they think may be about to top themselves.'

'Blimey. Do I look that bad?'

'Well . . .'

Vic returned with a tray of drinks. 'What's up?'

'We think the boy has something on his mind,' said Mick.

'Out with it,' said Mary.

'Well,' said Laurie, drinking about an eighth of his pint, 'I've just been told that I'm being sacked.'

'Sacked?' said Mick.

'Well, not exactly sacked. They want me to give up being

the crime correspondent and become the motoring correspondent.'

'What's wrong with that?' said Mick. 'Then you wouldn't have to hang around with all the pond life and you get a nice motor into the bargain. And that's making you all moody?'

'I don't want to be a motoring correspondent. Can you imagine me at all those trade things?'

'They still pay you the same, do they?'

'Yeah, I guess so.'

'Then what are you fussing about? Anyway, why don't they want you doing crime any more?' asked Mick.

'I'm not bringing in the stories, they say.'

'Poor lamb,' said Mary. 'Surely you boys can find him something, can't you?'

'I've no idea what's going on these days,' said Vic defensively. 'It's all crack and credit cards.'

'Yeah, but you still know all the chaps, don't you? You're always round at the Hooks' club, aren't you? The Hooks are all still at it, aren't they?'

'Well, here's the thing,' said Laurie. 'Right out of the blue, guess who rings me up today?'

'Desmond Tutu,' said Mick.

'No, seriously,' said Laurie. 'Old Man Hook. Wants me to ghost his autobiography.'

'Fucking hell,' said Mick. 'You're not going to touch it, are you? He's a fucking psychopath.'

'Well, apparently there's a publisher wants to do him – you know, Britain's *capo di tutti capi* . . .'

'Capo di tutti frutti, more like,' said Mick.

'But why would he want to do a book, for heaven's sake?'

said Laurie. 'That's what I couldn't work out. Then just as it was getting interesting, the boys arrive.'

'Who?' said Mick. 'Crispin and Ashley? I bet they marked your card. I don't know about the old man, though. I saw him at the boxing the other night. It was like he was on medication.'

'Skunk – the younger Hooks have moved into skunk, they've set up a whole lot of Vietnamese in empty properties in Leytonstone,' said Vic, 'producing this really strong hydroponic stuff . . . God, why do they have to have the music so fucking loud here? Can't hear yourself think.'

'Anyway,' said Laurie. 'Crispin and Ashley didn't seem too happy to see the old boy chatting to me. They more or less told me to Foxtrot Oscar. Very politely, of course.'

Cliff, the spotty barman, was about to read out the answers. The music was turned down, to applause from Vic. The School's Out team had got the date for a Bananarama hit wrong and had, inexplicably, written 'Gerard' instead of 'Gerald' Ford. Long Lartin Old Boys had triumphed. Mary went and collected the £40 prize money and handed each of them £10.

'See, if you do get the sack, you can always make a living in a quiz team, can't you?' said Mick, now in a boisterous, fourth pint mood.

It was raining slightly as the pub closed. It had been a long day, thought Laurie. The meeting with Hook. The talk with Stark. The quiz. They parted in the drizzle. Mick, one arm round Mary, patted him on the shoulder. 'Don't get involved with the Hooks, Laurie,' he said. 'They don't make spoons long enough to sup with that lot.'

Laurie walked the short distance home. Caz should be back from her gig by now – or was it her Spanish class? – and Violet would be doing her A-level revision, which seemed to consist of eating cartons of low-fat yoghurt in front of the television.

There were no lights on in the house when he put his key in the door. He heard a siren in the distance.

Chapter Five

LAURIE STRETCHED HIS arm out under the duvet. Hmm. Something odd. Nobody there. Where was Caz? She was normally fast asleep when Laurie woke at his usual 7 a.m. and switched on the *Today* programme.

'Caz?' Louder. 'Caz?'

He got up. He slept in an old T-shirt and pyjama shorts. He pulled on his dressing gown, the rather dashing, houndstooth, David Niven one that Caz had given him two Christmases ago. He headed downstairs. There was no sign that anyone else was up. Caz had not been home by the time he went to bed but that was not unusual. She sometimes went for a drink with the other students after her Spanish classes. Or maybe she had had a gig after all and had stayed behind with other musicians.

'Caz?'

Could she have had an accident? Had she told him she was going away to her brother's for the weekend? But wasn't that next weekend?

'Caz?'

A stirring upstairs, but from Violet's room. Had Caz spent the night there? She had done that once before, after a row.

Sleepy feet coming slowly downstairs. Violet was in her Arsenal pyjamas. She had inherited her mother's long, gangly limbs, wide mouth and tousled fair hair.

'Hi.'

'Good morning, Violet. Where's your mum?'

'You mean you didn't read her letter? She spent ages trying to get it right.'

'What letter?'

'There it is, on the table. Didn't you even see it?'

'I got in a bit late, I was very tired and—'

'Pissed, you mean.'

'Maybe, but also tired.'

Laurie opened the letter, written in her clear, almost childlike, handwriting.

'Dear Laurie,' it said. 'I'm so sorry to do it like this but I think it's kinder all round. I've met someone else and I'm moving in with him. There. I thought it best to be blunt, as you always say. Thanks for all the lovely times. I will call in a few days. Caz xx.'

'Blimey,' said Laurie. 'Is she serious? Was it something I said?' He felt his legs turn to ice.

Violet was putting on the electric kettle. 'I'll make a cup of tea.'

'When in doubt, make a cup of tea . . . "I'm a little teapot, short and stout/Lift me up and—"'

'Dad!' said Violet. 'I think you've got post-traumatic stress—'

'I think that comes later, dear.'

'Couldn't you tell? I can always tell when I'm about to be dumped.'

'It's so long since it happened to me – hey, I don't take sugar. Your mum and I have been together for about twenty years, you know. So, what is it? It's not another bass player, is it? Or did she meet some handsome young bloke doing her Spanish course?'

'No, he's older than you. He's the lecturer.'

'The lecturer? God, I thought that was illegal these days. Isn't that like a doctor sleeping with his patient? Won't he get struck off?'

'Drink your tea.' Violet placed a motherly arm around his shoulder. 'Maybe they'll give you some days off for compassionate leave.'

'Oh, God, don't bring that up – I'd stopped thinking about work for a minute . . . This is all very weird. Is she serious? It's not a joke, is it?'

Violet shook her head.

'So you're staying here, are you?' he asked.

'Well, Godfrey's just got a studio flat.'

'Godfrey! He's not even Spanish. What a poncey name.'

'Shall I make you a nice breakfast? Yes, I'm staying here because his place is miles from school and Mum thought I should stay with you at least until I go to university.'

'In case I top myself?'

'No, just to make sure you eat properly and everything.'

'Eat properly? It's your mother who's responsible for all the bloody pizzas and spare ribs that come into this house.'

There was a sound at the front door. A key in the lock? She was coming back? It was all a joke? The paper flopped through the letterbox. Violet fetched it from the mat. She opened it.

'Oo, look, there's that poor man whose girlfriend's gone missing.'

'Poor man, my arse.' Laurie had had to file five hundred words in a hurry on the story of the missing lecturer. 'Bloody murderer probably. Whenever a boyfriend or husband makes a plea for a woman to come back, you can tell they've killed her.'

'Is that what the police told you to print?'

'Oh, come on, Violet.'

'Well, our media studies teacher said that often journalists writing about crime just print what they're told by police. But I know you're different. He looks quite fit.'

Laurie gazed at the photo. 'Jasper Hatfield,' said the caption, 'who yesterday appealed for news of his fiancée, Sophie de Chair.' Laurie looked round the kitchen. What was missing?

'Has your mum . . . taken things from here?'

'Oh, only things of hers, things you didn't like.'

'I liked the toaster. We were very close.'

'Well, you were always making jokes about the Chinese bowls – she's taken them.'

'What about the CDs?'

'Well, I'm sure she's only taken what were hers. I would have thought you were more worried about her not being here rather than your – I dunno, your Townes Van Thingy.'

'Townes Van Zandt.'

'Well, at least now you'll be able to play all those morose songs and really identify with them.'

'Thanks a lot. You're a great comfort.'

'More tea? Oh, there's your mobile going.'

'Christ, I didn't hear it. I must be going deaf. Where is it?'

'On top of the fridge. I'll get it for you. Now, I'd better get ready for school. Are you going to be all right?'

'If I decide to slit my veins, I'll make sure I do it in the bath with the water running.' He stopped *The Sopranos* theme tune in mid-bar. It was Stark calling. Half past bloody seven in the morning and the news editor was on the blower. 'Hullllooo!'

Stark's voice was an octave higher than normal. He was excited. Laurie was not sure he had heard him right.

'It's not a great line. Have I got this right? Old Man Hook has had his brains blown out in his Highgate mansion. Fucking hell. I'll be on it right away . . . I'll call when I get there . . . yes, I think I know where it is. I had to doorstep it when it looked like they were going to reopen the Barney Quick case.'

He bumped into Violet as he ran upstairs two steps at a time.

'Was that Mum?' asked Violet.

'No, it was the newsdesk. Old Man Hook, the last of the Mohicans, has been shot dead in his own manor. And, what do you know, Violet – yesterday he asked me to ghost his bloody autobiography for him. I'd better dash.'

'Mum always said you were happier covering a murder than going for a picnic with us.'

'She never could make a decent sandwich . . . I'll see you later, sweet pea.'

He closed the front door behind him, and felt suddenly lonely.

Chapter Six

THE MINICAB DRIVER who picked up Laurie ten minutes after his call was an Afghan, Noor, who had arrived in London from Kabul the previous year. He was a serious young man with a pencil moustache and a snappier dress style than the other, mainly Turkish, drivers in the twenty-four hour firm on Green Lanes that Laurie patronised. They had once had a conversation about opium crop replacement on a speedy dash to the Old Bailey for a verdict.

'Where to, boss?'

Laurie wished he wouldn't call him boss. 'Call me Laurie,' he had said when it first happened but Noor had either misunderstood or felt more comfortable with 'boss'.

'We're going to Highgate, just up from the cemetery.'

'On job, boss?'

'Yes, there's been a murder.'

'Not so many murders here, boss.'

'I guess not compared to Kabul and . . .' he struggled for the name of the place where there was a lot of fighting going on, his brain in Quiz Night mode. 'Ah, Helmand. This one is a famous gangster . . . You know, "gangster"?'

'Sure, boss. Gangster – bang bang. Lots of gangsters here in

Hackney, too. Turkish gangsters, Kurdish gangsters, Russian gangsters.'

'Well, this one was an English gangster, last of a dying breed.' Would Noor know what he meant by 'breed'?

Classic FM was playing on the radio but not loud enough to drown the static from the cab radio. '. . . Pick up at Mercer Road bzzzz . . . fmmmpppp . . . Did you get that, Mehmet, over? Fucking . . . fzzzz . . . Camden Road jammed bzzz and fzzz over . . .' Or loud enough to drown out the thoughts rattling round Laurie's head about Caz.

Is this a temporary thing? Like with the moody young bass player? Will she ring me at the weekend and suggest we go to counselling? What had he done – or not done? He felt his Internal Prosecuting Counsel slipping into action.

'Perhaps you could tell the court, Mr Lane, when you last had what could be considered a "proper conversation" with Ms Caz Dupree?'

'Well . . . we talk all the time – you know, about what's happened during the day and how Violet is getting on at school . . .'

'We have already heard from Ms Dupree that, in her words, "he never listens to a word I say". She claims that on one occasion last week you fell asleep while she was talking to you about her concerns about your relationship.'

'But it was late at night and I was tired—'

'Please wait until I have finished asking the question, Mr Lane. As I say, she alleged that, not only did you fall asleep during the conversation but that you started snoring.'

'I apologised for that.'

'And is it not the case that you also pretended that you had been listening and when she asked what she had just said you were unable to tell her? Is that the case? Please answer the question, Mr Lane.'

'I . . . yes, yes, I suppose you're right but I thought everything was OK. I've always been a bit like that and she knew that when she married me.'

'You also said, I think, that you would make an effort to change. That you would seek to address her concerns. I put it to you, Mr Lane, that no such effort was made and that on a number of recent occasions you have come back late from work, drink having been taken, missing important family appointments and being cavalier in your responses to her. Is that not the case? Please tell the court, Mr Lane . . .'

They had stopped at the lights just after the Whittington Hospital.

'You OK, boss?'

'Yes, yes, fine . . . sorry, wasn't concentrating . . . Go up to the top of the hill and turn left, it's after that, sort of between the cemetery and the village. I'll recognise it when I get there.'

As they neared Old Man Hook's mansion, Laurie could see the familiar signs of a breaking story: the satellite television dishes, the blue-and-white police tape, taxis being paid off by young men in neat raincoats, carrying microphones or notebooks, the curious passers-by, the uniformed coppers, the cocky young snappers comparing equipment.

'Anywhere here is fine, thanks. What's the damage?'

Noor shot him a puzzled look.

'What do I owe you?'

'Twelve pounds, boss.'

'There. Can you give me a receipt for fourteen, please.'

The mention of receipts brought the previous day's conversation about expenses forms swimming back. His IPC was on his feet again.

'Do you mean to tell the court that you were dining in London on the very same evening that you were dining in Scarborough? Were you time-travelling, Mr Lane? Perhaps the jury would like to have a look at the two receipts . . .'

He accepted the change from Noor. He felt something hard in the small of his back.

'Don't turn around, sunshine, or I'll blow your fucking kidneys across the street.'

Chapter Seven

'THE KIDNEY WOULD BE about six inches higher up, Vicar,' said Laurie. It was Ron, of course, or the Vicar, as his colleagues knew him because he had once famously put on a dog collar in order to enter the home of the family of a murdered girl, posing as a comforting local priest. He must be in his seventies now, one of the oldest crime reporters on the beat, but he still often behaved like a twelve-year-old boy.

Laurie turned to face him. The unkempt, straggly white hair, the thin rescue-greyhound face, the complexion like an old tobacco pouch that had been left on a park bench. He was wearing his usual clashing shirt and tie ensemble. A shiny pink tie that looked like the wallpaper in a downmarket Indian restaurant was offset by a maroon shirt with a white collar. Nobody had worn white collars and maroon shirts since . . . since . . .

'Blimey, what an outfit. Have they made you a bishop?'

'Another leaving do tonight, another redundo,' said the Vicar. 'I always like to dress up for them. It's like a funeral, isn't it? I bet they're trying to get rid of you, too.'

'You must be psychic,' said Laurie. 'Now, what's happening here?'

Old Man Hook's mansion was guarded by two separate armies: uniformed police were in the finishing stages of attaching tape to lamp posts and letterboxes, and the Hooks' retainers, in their own uniform of Hugo Boss suits, dark shirts and micro mobile phones, were trying to assert their authority by chasing off photographers and reporters as different branches of the Hook family arrived.

There were four Hook children, the two boys, Crispin and Ashley, whom Laurie had seen only the day before in Clissold Park, and two girls, all of whom had gone into the family firm in one form or another. Crispin, the eldest, controlled the clubs business; Ashley supposedly ran the hydroponic cannabis enterprise, while one daughter, Camilla, a qualified accountant, organised the family's finances, and the other, Miranda, handled the escort business and hired the lap dancers who worked at Xanadu. Laurie remembered reading that both girls had been educated at Roedean.

There were grandchildren, too, some of whom had already diversified into legitimate worlds, one a rising tennis star. They were arriving now, young men with protective arms round the shoulders of their tearful mothers. Teenage girls dabbing at their streaming mascara. No sign of Hook's widow, the loyal Polly. Barred from entering the house because it was now a crime scene, they huddled together with their backs to the reporters.

'So who did it?' Laurie asked the Vicar. Not because he thought the Vicar would know but because he would always offer an opinion.

'Turf war,' said the Vicar convincingly. 'Probably the Turks.'

'Don't be daft,' said Laurie. 'Half of his people are Turkish.'

'Could be an old score being settled,' said the Vicar, blowing a puff of his first Hamlet of the day into Laurie's face. 'Remember he got acquitted of the Barney Quick murder? Quick's people never forgave him for that. And Old Man Hook made a lot of enemies in the old days. There's always been a feeling that he helped the Old Bill out with the Krays, you know. He was a driver for them in the early days.'

'So forty years later, Ronnie and Reggie rise from the grave and take their revenge?'

'Where was he shot?' asked the Vicar.

'In the sitting room, I think.'

'No, where on the body?'

'Head, I guess.'

'Doctor comes into emergency and says to the patient, "Where are you bleeding from?" Patient says—'

' "I'm from bleedin' Romford." God, how many times have you told that one?'

'So what's your suggestion?'

'The hardest three words for a journalist to say – I don't know.'

Another car spilled out its passengers on to the pavement.

'Morning, gentlemen,' said Daffyd Corr. The number two in the Scotland Yard press bureau had arrived.

'Nice of you to come,' said the Vicar.

Corr, tall, thin and thirtyish, was in tweed jacket and grey flannels. He cast his eyes over the assembled press throng. He nodded at Laurie and the Vicar and the other familiar faces from the press pack. 'Hello, Vicar, good to see you. Just come from a *GQ* fashion shoot, have you?'

'So whodunit then, smartypants?' said the Vicar.

'You're the guys who know, aren't you? I'll read about it in the paper tomorrow, won't I?'

Laurie tried to keep up with Corr as he strode to the police line.

'What's the score, Daffyd? Do we know how many shots? What kind of weapon?'

'I've just arrived, Laurie. I know as much as you. I gather that it's a pretty messy scene inside, though. Blood and hair on the walls. I think the aim is to make a statement with the family on the understanding that you will all then Foxtrot Oscar. I'll see you later.' Laurie watched him sweep past the police lines and beyond the reach of the mere press.

'What did he say?' asked the Vicar.

'Al-Qaida did it. Osama bin Laden didn't like Old Man Hook expanding his casino business in Morocco.'

'Could have been an angry husband,' said the Vicar, re-lighting his Hamlet. 'He was a randy old goat, you know. He had an affair with that pop star – what was her name? Can't bloody remember – the one with the curly hair.'

'Jealous boyfriend, eh?'

'You think I'm joking? I saw him in Stringfellows last year with a dolly bird on each arm. And he's been married to Polly for about a hundred years. Since she was a Tiller Girl.'

'They don't have "dolly birds" any more, Ron, they disappeared in the mists of the early seventies,' said Laurie. 'Anywhere to get a coffee round here?'

'What do they have?'

'I dunno. Slappers, I suppose.'

'There's a place over there. Can you get me a cappuccino?'

Crispin Hook was speaking to one of the uniformed

officers. Laurie wondered if he would acknowledge him after their brief meeting the day before. He did. He beckoned Laurie over with a tilt of his head.

'Tell you what,' said Laurie to the Vicar. 'You get the coffees and I'll tell you what's on the Dauphin's mind.'

'Whose mind?'

'Never mind. Latte. No sugar.'

Crispin Hook shook Laurie's hand and looked him straight in the eye.

'Sorry about your father,' said Laurie.

'Somebody will be,' said Crispin. He had his father's prominent nose but a weaker jaw and mouth, as though the family mould had been degraded. He was slimmer, shorter, less substantial.

'It seems extraordinary that only yesterday we were . . . he was . . .'

'He was talking to you about doing a book, wasn't he? Well, obviously that's a dead duck.'

Laurie nodded.

'You're Vic's friend, aren't you?' said Crispin. 'Still at the same paper, are you? Have you got a number? I might need to talk to you about what the old man was saying.'

Laurie handed him his card and caught the gaze of the huddle of detectives standing at the entrance to the mansion. He recognised Detective Chief Inspector Sandra King. She must be in charge. Her father had been killed in mysterious circumstances in India back in the seventies and he had written a couple of times about her attempts to find out what had happened to him. He turned his attention back to Crispin Hook.

'Had your . . . er . . . father had any threats?' asked Laurie. Not the smartest of questions but he had to keep the conversation going.

'I'll call you later,' said Crispin, taking the arm of the woman beside him, a tall, slightly bored-looking blonde – must be the wife – and whispering something into her ear.

The Vicar had returned with two Styrofoam cups of coffee and a bunch of flowers.

'My fingers are burning. Do they make coffee hotter these days? So what did Hook Junior have to say for himself?'

'It's all hush-hush.' Laurie surveyed the neighbouring homes, with their prominent burglar alarms, fixed self-importantly amidst the ivy, and their stern, wrought-iron gates. How had someone entered the Hooks' house so easily?

'Come on, you owe me one. I told you that tosser in Brighton was going to make an appeal yesterday. You would have missed it. Now, which one is the cappuccino and which one the – what's wrong with just a bloody coffee? Want to hear a joke?'

'Not if it's one of yours. What are the flowers for?'

The Vicar adopted an expression of exaggerated doleful-ness, handed Laurie his cup and made his way towards the house, sombrely, flowers held up before him. A uniformed policewoman spotted him, shook her head wearily and headed him off before he could breach the front gate. He returned and dumped the flowers on the bonnet of the nearest parked car. He smiled at Laurie.

'Worth a try, eh?'

A man in cardigan and cavalry twills approached them.

'Are you with the press?' he asked.

'No, I'm with the Woolwich,' said the Vicar.

'Yes, we are,' said Laurie. 'Are you a neighbour? Did you know Mr Hook?'

'We live in that house just there,' said the man. Laurie saw the Vicar jettison his coffee cup and whip his notebook out of his pocket. 'And something very odd happened last night.'

Am I having a heart attack? wondered Laurie. He felt that trembling feeling again. Caz would be sorry, she would feel it was her fault. He pictured her briefly at his graveside but the image he conjured up of her dabbing her eyes was spoiled by the intrusion of a man – a man older than Laurie, for God's sake – holding her elbow supportively. Oh, God, of course, it was his mobile phone on vibrate. It was Stark.

'Hello, yes, yes. I'm here at the murder scene right now . . . I'll call you straight back. Yes, yes, loads of leads,' he lied. The cardigan and twills had started to retreat, snubbed. 'Sorry, sir, you were saying?'

'You're not safe in your home any more,' said the cardigan. 'Bloody burglars.'

'I'm not sure if it was a burglary, sir,' said Laurie. 'Did you . . . er . . . know Mr Hook, the deceased?'

'Sounded like a burglary to me – heard the bang, thought it was fireworks or whatever and then, what, half an hour later, car driving off at a hell of a lick. Hook must have surprised them . . . Did I know him? Yes, charming man. He was having a party next week. Very insistent we should come to it – popped round a couple of times to remind us.'

'Did he ever talk about his . . . work?'

'He was in the entertainment business, he said. Clubs and

that sort of thing. Not really my cup of tea but he was a great supporter of Neighbourhood Watch, offered to take over as the coordinator from me until his wife told him he didn't have the time. See there, he's got the stickers up in the window . . . Why are there so many press here?'

'Well, I think people reckon it's probably not a burglary gone wrong, you know.'

Laurie noticed Daffyd, the police press officer, assembling people. He asked for and received the cardigan's name and telephone number.

Daffyd was wearing his 'sorry-folks-I've-got-nothing-to-tell-you' expression. The television crews switched on their lights. The crime-reporting old guard – the Vicar, Laurie, Mo Muskett, who was the new chairman, as she insisted on being called, of the Crime Reporters Association, Kevin Yu, Jeff and Mike and John and Justin and Martin and Jimmy Nicholson, the only other reporter as old as the Vicar and also with a nickname (the Prince of Darkness, something to do with his long black coat) – exchanged glances. The younger reporters opened their notebooks expectantly, like baby starlings waiting to be fed. Daffyd cleared his throat.

'This is, as some of you know, Detective Chief Inspector King, who is in charge of the murder investigation. At the moment, we just have a few details for you. Detective Chief Inspector King.'

'Thank you,' she said. Laurie tried to catch her eye. Remember me? She looked right through him. Had he changed that much in the last five years? Caz was always going on at him about the extra weight he had put on round his waist but his dark hair was still more black than grey, just. Just. DCI

King looked much the same. Short fair hair, freckles, a big, wide, humorous mouth.

'At six thirteen a.m., we received a call reporting an incident here in Buzzard's Close. Two officers from Kentish Town police station visited the address and found that the back entrance was open and appeared to have been forced. Inside they found the body of a man who has been identified as Charles Hook, aged seventy-eight. He had suffered a gunshot wound to the head. No weapons have been found on the premises and we would like to ask members of the public who may have heard anything suspicious during the night to call us on – have we got the number, Daffyd? Obviously, this is a very sad day for members of Mr Hook's family and we would ask that you respect their privacy. That is all we have to say on the incident at present and if there are any further developments they will be passed to the bureau.'

Another camera crew arrived, its breathless reporter pink in the face.

'Terribly sorry, but could you say all that again, please?'

Daffyd shrugged and Sandra King repeated her appeal verbatim, deadpan. A volley of questions was fired in her direction.

'Was there a struggle?'

'Does it look like a burglary or a hitman?'

'Has anything been stolen?'

'Who reported it?'

'Are any of the family going to say anything?'

'Have you got a first name, please?'

'Yes. Have you?' said DCI King. 'Sandra. Do I need to spell that?'

Laurie liked her style. He felt the throbbing by his heart. Bloody Stark again. He ignored it.

Sandra King gazed impassively over the heads of her questioners. She had obviously done a media-training course. Tell them nothing that might affect a future trial.

Laurie shouldered his way past the camera crews to talk to her as she repeated her appeal for the third time. He located the Sky News camera and positioned himself in its frame. Stark watched Sky News on the newsdesk television and would see him. For what that was worth. Detective Chief Inspector King was heading back into the Hooks' house.

'Hi,' said Laurie. 'I don't know if you remember me . . . Laurie Lane . . .'

'Yes, you did that piece on women in the police,' she said briskly. 'Misquoted me.'

'Sorry about that. Er, does this look like a . . . er . . . gangland thing or a burglary gone wrong?'

'Your guess is as good as mine. We only got here about an hour ago. If we have anything, we'll give it to the bureau.'

'Can I give you my card?'

Laurie had for years had a touching faith that, if he handed his card to enough people, someone would eventually come up with some information for him. It never worked. His heart trembled again.

Chapter Eight

EVA-MARIE, THE PICTURE editor, was in the canteen getting herself a cranberry and banana smoothie as Laurie returned to the office. She beamed at him. Her teeth were even, like an American's. Maybe she was half-Brazilian, rather than half-Portuguese. Who had the better teeth?

'Hi,' she said. 'So what's with this godfather being shot? Did you know him?'

'Funnily enough,' said Laurie, 'I had tea with him yesterday.'

'Wow! What is it, a gangland feud? That's what they said on the radio this morning.'

'Could be. Have you got any pictures of Old Man Hook? There should be some from the time he was arrested with the Krays in the sixties and when he was on trial for killing someone called Barney Quick. And I think there should be some recent ones of him at Joey Pyle's funeral.'

'Yes, I've seen a couple. He was quite handsome, wasn't he?'

'I suppose so.'

'Perhaps you could pop up later and I'll show you what we've got – some of them I'm not sure if it really is him. He seemed to have grey hair a while ago and then black hair a few years later.'

'I think it's called hair dye.'

'Live and let dye,' said Guy who was standing at the canteen counter beside them. 'Stark was asking where you were. Was it a hitman?'

'Don't mention Stark and hitmen in the same sentence, it might give me ideas.'

Eva-Marie clutched her smoothie and hovered in pre-departure mode. 'See you later, then, Laurie.'

'Yeah . . .' He and Guy watched her depart. When people used your first name, were they trying to indicate something? Or was that a trick you learned on management courses? Guy observed Laurie observing the picture editor.

'Anything going on that I should know about?'

'No such luck.'

'Hey, you're a happily married man.'

'I think only the last word in that phrase is accurate as of today.'

'What are you telling me? You and Caz—'

'I'll tell you about it later. Have you found out who tried to drown your trousers?'

'I thought you were meant to be investigating that. Any suspects yet?'

'On the trouser front or the gangland killing front?'

'On the big story – the trousers.'

'Well, know anyone who's got a grudge against you here?'

'God, loads of people. Henderson was pissed off I got the job instead of him but I can't see him resorting to that kind of stuff, can you? Stark thinks I'm always taking the piss but—'

The mobile vibrated in Laurie's pocket.

'Oh, God, it's Stark again. He has ADD.'

'Tell me about it.'

It was mid-afternoon in the newsroom. Stark was stroking his chin. Reporters were being quizzed about the strength of their stories. A small party of schoolchildren was being given a tour of the newspaper. They seemed unimpressed, in a fourteen-year-old sort of way.

'So, what do we have, Laurie?' said Stark.

'Looks like a hit – could be the tail end of an old feud, could be to do with what's happening now. The Hooks have still got a lot of the drugs and clubs market although I thought Old Man Hook had handed on most of that to his sons and daughters. Everyone says he was semi-retired – place in Capri, bit of golf, cruises.'

'Yes, that's what's on the wires. Do we have anything different?'

'Well, I'm still waiting for a couple of calls. Could be an old grudge. Something personal. There was a murder he was acquitted of – boxer called Barney Quick – that everyone thought he did. And an Asian minicab driver who got shot dead, mistaken identity, I think, that everyone said was the Hooks' fault but there weren't even any arrests on that. Suggestion that he was a little too close to someone at the Yard and might have been planning to spill the beans. I should have something by the end of the day . . .' He was not going to tell Stark about Hook's planned autobiography. Not yet, anyway.

'I hope so,' said Stark.

Behind Stark's back, Linda, the newsdesk secretary, raised

her eyebrows sympathetically. Laurie had travelled with her and a couple of others to the funeral in Hove of her ex-husband when he had died a few years earlier. She had not seemed overcome by grief, complaining on the journey about how little provision he had made for his two monotonal sons who sat beside them at the crematorium.

Laurie made his way back to his desk. The two assistant news editors, both in their twenties, were having a row. Did he hear one ask the other, 'Who's doing the paedo in the Speedo story?' His coffee was nearly cold. He skimmed through the wires. Detective Chief Inspector Sandra King was featuring a lot. He caught a glimpse of her on the television as Sky News flickered by. He started tapping at his keyboard.

'One of London gangland's best-known figures, Charlie Hook, 78, was yesterday found shot dead at his mansion in Highgate, north London,' he wrote. 'Police were last night searching for the murder weapon and investigating whether the shooting heralded a new round in the festering wars between the last of the old London gangs.'

Should he ring Caz? Was that what one did? He tried to remember when he had last been dumped. Oh, yes, Gloria. More than twenty years ago now. Flaming row in a pub. Everyone looking. But that had been a bit of a relief, if he was honest. Caz was different.

'You OK?' said Guy.

'Not exactly,' said Laurie. The second paragraph wouldn't come. His IPC was clearing his throat.

'Do you mean to tell me, Mr Lane, that you made no attempt whatsoever to contact Miss . . . er . . . Dupree? Please answer the question.'

'I was busy at work, my lord.'

'You're talking to yourself,' said Guy. 'Shall I get matron?'

'Fuck off.'

He forced himself on to the second paragraph. The phone rang.

'Hi, it's Vic here,' said the voice.

'Oh, hello. By the way, Mick was right about the longest river in Asia. I Googled it.'

'Look, I may have something for you on Old Man Hook. I don't want to come into your office but can I see you in ten minutes in that coffee bar opposite, the Penguin, is it?'

'Pelican.'

Vic was always prompt. All those years in institutions had given him an almost military obsession about neatness and punctuality.

'Can't stay long but I thought you might be interested to know what's on the grapevine.'

'I thought you were out of the loop now, that's what you always tell me whenever I ask for your help.'

'Well, for what it's worth – and this is coming from, well, the horse's mouth, more or less . . .'

'Yeeees?'

'This was a Russian hit.'

'You're kidding me.'

'No, seems like they wanted a bit of the action from the Hooks and the old man wanted to keep it in-house, as it were.'

'The Russians? Any particular ones?'

'The main guy – the guy they reckon may have been pissed off with Old Man Hook – is called Petrov. Vladimir Petrov. He's got a gaff off the Heath.'

'Not the one who was in the Rich List? Who's trying to buy nightclubs here? Ex-KGB? Looks like Gerard Depardieu? What was the nickname they gave him – the Tsar of Hampstead Heath?'

'That's the guy.'

'Blimey. How certain are they about this?'

'Well, he didn't leave his card there but that's what all the chaps reckon. They haven't told the police, of course, because they want to carry out their own inquiries first. They don't want to rock the boat too much until they're a hundred per cent certain. But I thought – well, you were saying that they're always on at you to get scoops and all, so – for what it's worth. The Old Bill will be knocking on a few Russian doors quite soon anyway. You might as well be ahead of the pack. Anyway, I must be getting off. I promised Mick I'd meet him at the Tate Modern for the Louise Bourgeois exhibition.'

'Thanks a lot, Vic. I appreciate that. See you next Thursday.'

'Oh, right. By the way, it was the Sioux Indians – that question, the one nobody got – not the Navajo.'

Stark was looking for Laurie by the time he returned to the office.

'We really need copy, by the way. How's it going?'

'Great! I've found out who did it.'

'So who did it?' Stark looked sceptical.

Maybe if I hit him with the side of my hand to his ear, it won't cause too much damage to my fingers, thought Laurie. Would that count as actual bodily harm or grievous bodily harm? Didn't skin have to be broken for grievous? But what if no skin was broken but brain damage was caused?

'Did you hear what I said?' asked Stark.

'Say it again.'

'So who did it?'

'Ah. A Russian gang led by a bloke who lives in a five-million-pound house off Hampstead Heath. He wants to get some of the Hooks' business. Old Man Hook refused, supposedly, words exchanged, didn't think they were serious. So – bang bang.'

'Is this kosher?'

'No, Russian Orthodox.'

Stark gave him a don't-take-the-piss-out-of-me look.

'Can we stand this up?' said Stark.

'You mean, can I get him to confess in the next half-hour?'

'No, I don't mean that. Will the police confirm it?'

Eva-Marie – this was not his imagination – was hovering at the newsdesk with a sheaf of old black-and-white photos in her hand.

'Sorry to butt in,' she said. That smile again. 'Can I just check that these are . . . Hook?'

Laurie examined them. There was Hook all right. A dashing, youthful Hook, wearing a suit and a slim jim tie, in a nightclub with Ronnie Kray and Lord Boothby, back in what must have been the sixties. Hook on the beach somewhere in old-fashioned woolly swimming trunks sagging at the crotch. Hook going into the Old Bailey with a snarl on his face and his wife Polly on his arm. Hook coming out of the Old Bailey, looking cool in dark glasses after being cleared of killing the boxer, Barney Quick. Hook in a wedding group. Was it his imagination or did Eva-Marie touch his arm again and squeeze it?

'Great pix,' Laurie said to her. She grinned back at him.

Stark was getting irritated. 'Can we splash on this – Russian Mafia Kill London Godfather? Something like that?' Stark often spoke in headlines at this stage in the afternoon. Laurie felt slightly light headed. Was it that he did not care any more? That Caz's departure had made his job seem less important?

'Sure,' he said. 'That's what I understand. Russian Mafia Kill London Godfather. But better put a "claim" in there somewhere.'

Chapter Nine

THROUGH HALF-OPENED EYES, Laurie watched as the door handle of his bedroom turned. Had Caz come back?

'Cup of tea?' said Violet as she came in with a mug. 'You weren't planning on sleeping in, were you?'

'Mmm,' said Laurie. 'Any word from your mum?'

'Haven't you tried to talk to her?'

'I had to do that story about Old Man Hook being shot yesterday,' he said. 'I didn't have time until it was too late to ring her.'

'That's the whole problem, your work was always more important than she was.'

'That's just not true.'

'Here's the paper,' said Violet, slinging it on to the duvet.

Laurie noted with a mixture of pride and foreboding that the headline was 'Russian Mafia "Kills London Godfather".' He leant over and turned on the digital radio he had given Caz for Christmas and which he had still not mastered. She had not taken it with her. The *Today* programme was on. A priest with a Highland accent was completing his Thought for the Day.

'Shouldn't you be at school?'

'Home revision day.'

'Really?'

'Why don't you ring Mrs Rolfe and ask her if you don't believe me?' Violet swept out.

The weatherwoman had news of scattered showers. The first news item was the cabinet reshuffle. The second, Old Man Hook's murder. The reporter said that the police were still searching for a murder weapon and motive.

'A senior police source said that suggestions that the Russian Mafia were involved were "extremely fanciful",' said the BBC reporter in what Laurie considered to be an unnecessarily smug tone. He got up and did a few half-hearted stretching exercises. He flossed his teeth and looked at himself in the mirror. Dental floss was not as cool as a toothpick. He tried to imagine Humphrey Bogart or Robert Mitchum flossing. He was shaving when Stark rang. 'Hulllllooooo.' He wished he had Stark's throat to hand. He wished he had a cut-throat razor instead of the silly two-blade or three-blade disposable nonsense. He nicked himself quite badly just below the nose. It bled. Damn.

'Did you hear that the Yard are rubbishing the Russian angle?'

Was it as easy to cut someone's throat as it looked in the films? Did the jugular always spurt forwards?

'Well, they would, wouldn't they?'

'Why would they?'

Laurie couldn't think.

'I'll be in shortly.'

'Yes . . . We need to talk.'

What, again? Laurie slapped on some of the Bay Rum aftershave that Caz had brought back from her Caribbean cruise, playing country classics to pensioners on board an elderly liner. He felt forlorn. His face looked puffy in the shaving mirror. The blood from his cut had dried just below his nose.

Violet was reading the television review in the paper and eating some improbably flavoured yoghurt from a tiny container.

'I read your story,' she said. 'You don't really think it was the Russians, do you? That's such a cliché. It's all because of that film with the stabbing in the Turkish baths, isn't it? Oooo, what have you done to your face?'

'It's a shaving cut.'

'Oooo, it's dried in a horrible way. It makes you look like Hitler.'

'Oh, shut up. You didn't finish the oatcakes, did you?'

'I don't eat gluten any more.'

'Your mother must have taken them with her.'

'You know that's not true.'

'Well, maybe her fancy man . . .'

'Godfrey. His name's Godfrey. You shouldn't be in the denial stage still. But really, the Russians – that's just what everyone says. The Russians are buying up Mayfair, the Russians are bringing in drugs, the Russians—'

'Sometimes clichés are true. God, the bloody marmalade is finished. I was told by someone—'

'Yeah, probably one of your bank robbers' old boys' club people. Who was it? Mick? Vic? I bet it was one of them.'

'I never disclose my sources. And shouldn't you be

doing home revision rather than reading the television page?'

'It's for media studies.'

'Of course it is. Look, Vic never tells me stuff he doesn't believe himself.'

'But don't you see that you're criminalising a whole community? We have this Russian girl at school and she's really nice and she says that everyone thinks she's very rich and her dad must be in the Mafia but he's a doctor at Great Ormond Street Hospital for Sick Children.'

'Good for him.' Laurie made himself a pot of tea. 'The thing is—' His mobile phone rang. *The Sopranos* theme by the Alabama 3. 'Oh, shit . . . Hello . . . yes . . . Really? When? . . . OK . . . Yeah. No problem. No, I'll do them both . . . Right. See you.'

'Work?' said Violet.

'No. Penelope Cruz saying she'd heard I was available.'

He kissed Violet on the cheek and ran his hand down the side of her face, the way he had done so often with her mother. She squeezed his hand, stood up and gave him a hug. His mobile rang again.

'I'm going to have to get you a new ring tone for that. *The Sopranos* is so dated, man.'

'It's comforting. What does Godfrey have on his? "Una Paloma Blanca"?'

'Please!'

When Laurie arrived in the office, forty minutes and a stressful bendy-bus journey later, Stark was already waiting for him. He flashed Laurie his can-do smile.

'Little chat?' said Stark.

In Stark's office, Laurie noticed a new photo of the Stark family. It had obviously been taken on a skiing holiday.

'Right,' said Stark, pressing his palms together as if in prayer that Laurie would take what was about to be said in a mature fashion. 'I really just wondered if you had had a chance to have another little think about the motoring correspondent's job?'

'I had a very little think and realised I couldn't do it. I would let the paper down.'

'I'm sure you wouldn't.'

There was a pause.

'The thing is, you saying the Russians were behind the murder has backfired a bit. Scotland Yard have pretty much poo-pooed it and all the other papers are having a bit of a laugh at our expense on their websites. They made a joke about it on *Five Live*. And the Russian Embassy have been on to us complaining and asking where the evidence is. Anyway, if you're dead set against the motoring correspondent's job, we wondered if you fancied a roving feature writer's role. There's a couple of slots in Section Two that need someone with a light touch. There's a new series starting called "Me and My Luggage" which they need someone good to write.'

'You are kidding.'

'No. It's been tested, it got a very good response. You know the sort of thing – round-the-world yachtsman and his favourite haversack, theatrical dame and the suitcase she's had since her days in rep, Keith Richards and his Louis Vuitton. I think the marketing people reckon there are a lot of tie-in possibilities and it would run on the website for readers to respond to with comments on their own favourite pieces of luggage. I think you could bring something to it.'

'What, like a hitman and his favourite body bag?'

Stark gave him a weaker smile.

'Laurie, I'm trying to help here, although I know you don't think I am. We're living in a changing world. We all have to adapt, work for the paper and the web . . . learn new skills. I know you and . . . some of your colleagues . . . see yourselves as the old cowboys battling bravely against the arrival of the steam train and so on but these days you only find cowboys now in the movies and on dude ranches, don't you? Life moves on. Anyway, think about it.'

Laurie's throat felt dry. Don't say anything you may regret, he thought. Be dignified. Talk to the mother of the chapel. Be icy. He got to his feet and turned sharply to make an abrupt exit. As he did so, he felt his knee – injured in a grudge football match against *The Times* some twenty years ago and a source of regular discomfort – lock. Agony.

'Shit!'

'I don't think there's any need for that sort of reaction,' said Stark, looking startled.

'Oh . . . never mind,' said Laurie, gaining his composure as he reached the door handle. He hobbled back to his desk. Guy was sitting close by, looking crestfallen. As Laurie passed by him, he noticed that he was wearing a shirt and V-neck sweater – and a pair of running shorts.

'God, Guy, what's happened? The phantom trouser-strangler hasn't struck again, has he?'

'I thought you were going to do something about it.'

'"Had I but time enough . . . and . . ." How does it go?'

Chapter Ten

'DON'T MOVE, SUNSHINE, unless you like the taste of hot lead in the base of your spine,' said the voice behind Laurie as he stood at the urinals in the Bow Street Runner.

'I don't think I've ever tasted hot lead, Ron. What's it like?' said Laurie as he zipped himself up. 'And I don't think you should be pressing up against men in the gents.' He turned round to see the Vicar washing his hands and straightening his curry-spattered Paisley tie in the mirror.

'Woman walks into a bar, says to the barman, "Can I have a double entendre?" So the barman gives her one.'

Laurie laughed. 'That's actually quite funny, for a change, and I've only heard it about three times before. So, are we going to be told anything today about who killed Old Man Hook?'

It was the last Tuesday in the month, four days now after Old Man Hook had been shot, and every last Tuesday in the month the couple of dozen members of the Crime Reporters Association met at the Bow Street Runner, just around the corner from Scotland Yard in St James, and received an off-the-record briefing from someone in the police, the intelligence services or Customs. Today, it was the Deputy Assistant Commissioner of the Metropolitan Police, an ambitious man in his early forties, called Gonzales, with responsibility for organised crime. He was not known for being indiscreet.

'I don't think Speedy is going to tell us anything,' said the Vicar. 'I thought you knew anyway – didn't you say it was all the Ruskies' fault?'

'Yeah, I did,' said Laurie, feeling suddenly weary.

'Well, you can ask Speedy to confirm it, can't you?'

The door of the gents swung open and Deputy Assistant Commissioner Gonzales and his staff officer entered in mid-conversation. They looked at Laurie and the Vicar warily.

'Hello, Mr Gonzales,' said the Vicar. 'Hope you've got something tasty to tell us today. Is there going to be a gangland war in London, like the old days?'

'Is that what you'd like?'

'Absolutely. Wouldn't you? Make a change from all these low-life toerags stabbing each other on buses, wouldn't it?'

The Vicar had finished washing his hands and was looking for a towel.

'I hate these bloody blow-dryers,' he said, banging his fist to start the machine.

'They're much healthier,' said DAC Gonzales, in a be-friendly-to-the-media voice, as he took his place at the urinals.

'Actually,' said Laurie, 'I just read a piece by our health editor which said that's a myth – that, in fact, hand-dryers blow faecal spores across the room at forty miles an hour and thus spread germs and cause food poisoning.'

'Bloody hell!' said the Vicar on his way out of the gents.

'We're just about to have our bloody lunch. See you at the bar, playmates.'

Laurie and the Vicar joined the other crime reporters in the bar of the 'functions room' where an impassive eastern European waitress was proving unresponsive to the approaches being made to her by two of the younger reporters. One of them, Bradley, broke off when he saw Laurie.

'The Russians are coming! The Russians are coming!' he chanted.

'Fuck off,' said Laurie.

'Look, we all had our newsdesks ringing up asking why we didn't know it was the Russian Mafia. Did you just make it up?'

'Oh, sure. Have you got a better idea?'

'I've heard that Old Man Hook was a bit of a randy devil and it's to do with a slapper from one of his clubs,' said Bradley.

'He was seventy-eight,' said Mo, one of the two women in the association and its chairman. She was not the first woman to hold the post – Sylvia Jones of the *Mirror* had beaten her to that title by a few years – but she was the first black woman. 'I don't think he was really *crime passionel* material. Much more likely to be an old grudge.'

'Haven't you heard of Viagra, Mo?' said the Vicar.

'Is that a threat or a promise?' asked Mo. 'Excuse me, can I get another red wine, please?'

DAC Gonzales had joined them now and Mo started to gather the reporters together and tell them to take their seats at the long table laid out neatly with cheap cutlery and red paper napkins. There were little printed menus. Oxtail soup, lamb cutlets or fried squid, lime pie. Laurie felt his spirits sink further. He found himself sitting between DAC Gonzales and Bradley. Gonzales graced him with a rictus grin.

'Haven't been to one of these events before,' he said. 'What's the form?'

'Well, we have lunch, then we put on our aprons, bare our breasts and take the oath.'

He saw a moment of alarm flicker across Gonzales' face. Better not to play the giddy goat all the time, as his father used to say. Poor Dad, the giddiest goat of all. A failed business wherever he went. Still, it had meant that Laurie and his brothers were familiar with almost every small town in Britain, which had often been helpful when covering crimes in obscure places.

'No, it's all pretty low-key. When we get our coffee, if you have something you want to bring up, then that's fine. Otherwise we just fire questions at you. You'll probably be asked about . . . um . . . Old Man Hook.'

He saw Gonzales and the staff officer exchange conspiratorial smiles and nod at each other. Oh, God, thought Laurie, they know who the killer is already. My humiliation will be complete. I will be talking to famous dog trainers about their favourite dog baskets by the end of the month. He had lost his wife and his job within a week. Don't these things come in threes? What else do I have to lose? Was his heart beating uncommonly fast or – no, he had his phone on vibrate. It would be Stark again. 'Hullllllooooo.' Could he sue him for constructive dismissal?

'I'm with the Deputy Assistant Commissioner,' he muttered into the phone. Stark seemed unimpressed or perhaps he had not heard properly. He was not going to repeat it. 'I will call you when I am free.' He snapped the phone shut and concentrated on trying to ingratiate himself with Gonzales. He looked round the table. There was quite a good turnout today, probably prompted by the desire to find out something – anything – about Old Man Hook that they could take back to their newsdesks, tails wagging, and deposit at the feet of their news editors.

The Vicar was failing to impress Bradley with his joke about the double entendre. The soup was tepid. Mo and DAC Gonzales were tiptoeing around each other on the matter of the murders of black men and the availability of firearms. Gonzales was using the word 'holistic'. Laurie had ordered the squid but wished he had chosen the lamb. Why did they come here? Just because it was round the corner from the Yard.

'How can you eat that bloody squid?' asked the Vicar. 'Tastes like knicker elastic.'

'How do you know?' said Laurie.

Weak coffee was served and Mo called them to order. Everyone looked surreptitiously at their watches. Deadlines approached faster than ever now. The old days of moseying back to the office and filing for the first edition at around 6 p.m. and then heading off for a pint had ended with the internet. Now the beast had to be fed constantly, great shovelfuls of information, much of it undigested, was dropped into a voracious gullet.

Mo was on her feet introducing DAC Gonzales. She had done her homework. Who knew that Gonzales had a first in classics and had played badminton for Oxford? Gonzales took the floor. He looked pleased with himself. The Vicar had moved his seat so that he was at Laurie's elbow. He nodded towards Gonzales and his shiny young staff officer.

'He looks like he's fucked the bride,' said the Vicar. 'Why is he so fucking pleased with himself? And his catamite looks fucking smug as well. What's going on?'

'When did catamite become part of your vocabulary?'

'You forget I was with the *News of the World* in the fifties, baby.'

Gonzales flexed his neatly manicured fingers.

'Right, can I just thank Mo for her very kind invitation to address you. I know that many distinguished former guests have had the privilege to talk to this body in its more than fifty years of –'

Get on with it, for God's sake, thought Laurie.

'– sterling service of informing the public. But I know the last thing you want is to hear some bromides from me and what you would most like is some information on the story of the day. We will be announcing this later today but we thought that this distinguished company should be the first to be appraised of the situation.'

'Bloody hell,' said the Vicar. 'He's actually going to give us something.'

'I can tell you that this morning we have recovered the firearm that was used in the murder of Mr Charles Hook on the premises of a house in Hampstead, north London. We are now seeking to talk to the owner of the house, Mr Vladimir Petrov – do you want me to spell that?'

Spell it? thought Laurie. Why don't you bloody sing it? He flashed Mo a smile and she winked back at him. As DAC

Gonzales spelt out the name, Laurie allowed himself the pleasure of watching Bradley and Kevin Yu scribble it down and try to avoid his look. 'As I say, we are now seeking to talk to Mr Petrov and we would ask members of the public not to approach him but to contact the police . . .'

Chapter Eleven

AURIE SHARED THE taxi to Hampstead with the Vicar, Kevin Yu and Mo Muskett. The sun seemed brighter, Kevin less irritating and world-weary than usual. Laurie was even able to smile indulgently when the Vicar told Mo the story about the man driving down the M4 whose car was stopped by the police. '"Excuse me, sir, did you know that your wife and son fell out of the back door of your vehicle a mile ago?" says the policeman. The chap smiles. "God, that's a relief – I thought I was going deaf!"' The Vicar chortled as he delivered the punchline, a strange sound that Laurie imagined was what a death rattle would be like. Mo rolled her eyes and looked out of the window.

They had been beaten to the house by a couple of agency photographers in motorcycle leathers. Already neighbours were peering from windows and doorways, wondering what was going on.

Laurie waved away his fellow passengers as they offered to pay the fat cab fee. Noblesse obliges.

'What's going on?' asked a truculent elderly woman, wearing her territorial entitlement like a wide-brimmed straw hat.

'There's been a triple murder, dear, and we've come to pick up the torsos – the only thing the fiend left behind him,' said the Vicar.

The chance to see the woman's reaction was stolen from Laurie by the sudden arrival of the Sky News satellite van which parked itself directly in front of him. By the time he had rejoined the Vicar, Mo and Kevin, the woman had fled.

The Scotland Yard press officer, Daffyd, had arrived and was chatting earnestly to Detective Chief Inspector Sandra King, who flashed a chilly smile in their direction.

'Be still, my beating heart,' muttered the Vicar under his breath. 'I bet she's a tiger in bed.'

'Is he with you?' asked Mo wearily.

'Couldn't get him off my shoe,' said Laurie. He approached the police team. 'Where was the gun found?'

DCI King and Daffyd exchanged glances.

'Er . . . I am not sure if we are going to go into details, are we?' Daffyd asked her. 'Detective Chief Inspector King is not going to be giving a press conference. A statement will be made available later today.'

'Bloody 'ell,' said the Vicar. 'Why can't they tell us something? Drag us all the way up to bloody Hampstead Heath . . .'

'No one said there was going to be a presser, Ron,' said Daffyd, amiably enough. 'All we are saying is that we are anxious to talk to Mr Petrov following the discovery in his premises, in the wake of information received, of the weapon used in the murder of Mr Hook.'

'Who was this information received from?' asked the Vicar.

Press officer and detective inspector exchanged glances again.

'Obviously we can't say, for operational reasons,' said Daffyd.

'Bit bloody convenient, isn't it?' said the Vicar. 'Someone tells you where the weapon is and it just happens to be in the back garden of a bloke from Leningrad with a dodgy record.'

'St Petersburg, actually,' said Laurie.

'Christ, just because you got your O levels. I can remember it when it was bloody Stalingrad,' said the Vicar.

'It never was Stalingrad,' muttered Laurie.

'I bet you it was.'

'Wasn't.'

'Boys, boys,' said Mo.

'Can you tell me,' said the Vicar, addressing Sandra King, 'did I miss something or do murderers these days keep the murder weapon in a handy place where the police can find it? I thought that rule one in the murderer's handbook was get rid of the bloody weapon.'

'If every murderer followed the rule book we'd never catch any of them, would we?' replied Sandra King. She graced Laurie with a smile. She did, didn't she? His IPC kicked in.

'Do you mean to tell the court, Mr Lane, that you believed that Detective Chief Inspector King gave you the impression that she would welcome an approach from you?'

'I wouldn't say that for a moment. It was just that, perhaps, my lord, I was feeling a little lonely on account of the fact that my wife had recently run off with an older man and—'

'With an older man?'

'Yes, my lord, an older man.'

There was a tugging at his arm.

'Are you still with us?' asked the Vicar.

'Sorry, thinking of something else,' said Laurie. 'What's happening?'

'Kevin has bunged the neighbour a pony to let us look from the top of her house into Boris's garden.'

'It's not Boris, it's Vladimir.'

'I know, I know. Come on.'

The neighbour who had succumbed rather too swiftly to Kevin's proposition was obviously already regretting her decision as half a dozen journalists and photographers clumped through her front door and made their way to the roof terrace that overlooked the house and garden of the man the police now believed could help them with their inquiries.

'Where's the bloody swimming pool?' asked the Vicar.

'Nice lawn,' said Kevin Yu. 'Is that a croquet mallet there, leaning against the tree?'

'Another potential murder weapon,' said Laurie. 'In fact, I think it's just a spade.'

'Equally suspicious,' said Mo, winking at Laurie.

'Well, we'd better decide,' said Kevin. 'What's it going to be, a croquet lawn or a potential burial ground?'

'How about, "Leaning against an oak tree in the garden of Vladimir Petrov's luxury north London mansion was a spade" stop,' said the Vicar. ' "A pile of freshly turned earth was only partially hidden in the thick undergrowth—" '

'That's not an oak tree,' said Mo.

'What is it then?'

'A beech, I think.'

'It's got to be oak,' said the Vicar.

'How about poison oak?' said Kevin Yu.

'You're learning, lad, you're learning.'

'Where's the freshly turned earth?' asked Laurie.

'Use your bloody imagination.'

'I prefer the croquet lawn,' said Kevin Yu. 'Like, "The neatly manicured croquet lawn in the back garden of Vladimir Petrov's luxurious house has yet to yield up its secrets—" '

'Mansion,' said the Vicar. 'This is a mansion, lad, not a house. No serious criminals live in houses, do they, Laurie? Remember when we went after Ronnie Knight down on the Costa del Crime in – where was it? Estepona? Puerto Banus? – and we came across one of the silver bullion guys living in a horrible little bungalow. By the time we were finished with him, he was in a Roman-style villa with a breathtaking view across the turquoise waters of the Mediterranean.'

'You should have been an estate agent, not a crime reporter, Ron,' said Mo.

A genteel throat was cleared.

'Can I get any of you a cup of tea?' said the owner of the house who had been standing at the door, transfixed.

'That would be lovely, darling,' said the Vicar. 'Three sugars in mine.'

'So is it a croquet lawn or a burial site?'

'Can't it be both?' said the Vicar. 'Did you see the people next door much, love? You didn't see them digging ever, did you?'

'They used to sunbathe sometimes,' volunteered the owner, who was looking nervously at Kevin, clearly wondering whether the promised £25 was going to be forthcoming.

'In the nude?' said the Vicar.

'No, I don't think so . . . In their swimming costumes.'

'Semi-nude,' muttered the Vicar out of the corner of his mouth. Mo rolled her eyes again.

'What was he like as a neighbour?' asked Kevin Yu.

'Well, he didn't recycle at all,' said the house-owner. 'But I know they had lots of bottles because you used to see them being delivered from Oddbins.'

'Lot of drinking, was there?' said Kevin Yu.

'I should say,' said the house-owner.

' "Neighbours spoke," ' muttered the Vicar, ' "of semi-nude orgies in the Roman-style villa of Russian billionaire and distant descendant of dictator Joseph Stalin . . ." '

'Blimey, where did Stalin come from?'

'I thought you said he came from Stalingrad, he's bound to be related in some way. We're all in line to the throne . . . He's not going to bloody sue, is he? He's done a runner.'

'Do they not mind on your newsdesk if it all turns out to be bollocks the following day?'

'Not at all, as long as it's a good read. They like stories about wicked eastern Europeans these days, haven't you noticed? And this bloke's obviously got his cock in the custard, hasn't he? You must remember Bill Driscoll, Mo, don't you? Lovely bloke. Dead now, like all the good guys. He got sacked from the *Express* for over-egging it a bit. He started off one story about some little toerag who had murdered somebody in the Midlands – "They called him the golden-haired Adonis of the Market Harborough smart set." Beat that. That's bloody poetry . . . Hang on, there's someone moving behind that tree.'

'Old Man Hook's ghost,' said Laurie. 'It's just the bloody

wind.' His heart fluttered. Or rather his mobile phone vibrated against his heart.

'Who's got wind?' asked the Vicar.

'Yes?' said Laurie into the phone after he had heard the first 'Hulllloooo' from Stark. 'We're at his house now. Where is he? Well, amazingly he has omitted to leave a forwarding address on his front door. That's Russians for you.'

He switched the phone off and it rang again at once. He glanced at the screen. He recognised Caz's number. This time it really is my heart that is fluttering, he thought.

Chapter Twelve

NO GLOATING. IN VICTORY, magnanimity. No dragging the bodies round the battlements. Calm, serene even. Above it all. Laurie prepared himself for his entrance to the office as he hopped out of the taxi and pocketed the blank receipt offered to him by the driver.

'Hello, Laurie,' said the security officer at the front desk.

'Hello, Barry,' Laurie replied. Was it his imagination or did he hear the words, 'Actually, it's Brian,' as he headed up the stairs? No matter. He ignored the lifts and ran up the steps two at a time. He was puffing by the time he reached the newsdesk. Stark gave him his spray-on smile.

'So . . . it was the Russians after all,' he said. 'Can you give us about seven hundred words – and perhaps a sidebar on Russians in London? We've got an agency pic of Petrov and we can use stills from *Eastern Promises* – is that what that film was called, the one where the Russian bloke gets cut up in the sauna?'

Laurie nodded. Firm but fair, that was what he was trying to project. He looked at the two assistant news editors, imagining that there would be some hint of recognition of his little scoop but there was nothing. They were already on to the next story, their eyes flickering between their screens, their phones, their BlackBerries. One flashed him a grin and was about to say something when his phone rang and the moment passed. Laurie paused at the trolley to buy a tea and took it to his desk. In the distance, he spotted Eva-Marie, the picture editor. She waved at him. He smiled back. Guy was at work, staring at his computer screen. He did not acknowledge Laurie.

'What's up with you?'

'Nothing.'

'Come on, I can tell when you are pissed off about something,' said Laurie. He glanced down at Guy and did an exaggerated double-take.

'I hate to be the person to tell you this but you've forgotten to put your trousers on.'

'I'm wearing shorts.'

'Shorts and a tweed jacket?'

'It's happened again.'

'What has?'

'Some bastard flushed my trousers down the loo again. It's not funny.'

'I'm sorry but – that's three times now, isn't it?'

'How would you like it if every time you go for a run at lunchtime someone takes your trousers out of the shower and flushes them down the loo? It's not funny, for God's sake. If it had happened to you you'd be calling up one of your criminal friends to do something about it.'

'But why on earth do you leave your trousers there in the first place?'

'I didn't think it could ever happen again. I thought before it might have been an accident or something.'

'But now it looks like there's . . . a serial trouser-flusher. Amazing. Which trousers were they?'

'The red ones. And it's NOT FUNNY.'

Their neighbours in the office were starting to look over, anxious for some distraction. Above Guy's head, Sky News flickered on the television. There was Breaking News. RUSSIAN SOUGHT FOR GANGLAND MURDER . . .

'Any suspects yet?'

'No. I can't think who the hell would want to do that. Someone must really hate me.'

'What about Conrad Henderson? You said he thought he should have had your job? This is definitely a two-pipe problem, Watson.'

'And it is not funny.'

Laurie delicately removed the tea bag from his paper cup and deposited it in the rubbish bin.

'Why don't you have a bloody mug instead of using those bloody things?'

'God, even without his pants on he is still in full environmental mode. I saw you with one of these yesterday, you hypocritical bastard. Look, I think you are going to have to either rig up a CCTV camera in there or, let's see, I could hide in one of the cubicles, perched on the seat of the toilet so that my feet would not be seen under the door, and you could attach, say, a bell – like a cat's bell – to the trousers. When it rings, I spring out and—'

Stark was hovering.

'We need the copy pretty quickly. What's happening here?'

'Guy was just helping me with some Russian contacts of his.'

'Oh. And after you've filed, the people in accounts want to see you about . . . you know . . .' Stark flashed his smile again and was gone.

'What's that about?' said Guy.

'Stark's accusing me of fiddling my exes.'

'Did you?'

'On the advice of my lawyer, I am saying nothing . . . There, does that put the lost trousers into perspective? Oh, yeah, I knew there was something else. Caz has definitely left me. Is that worse than wet trousers?'

'God, I'm sorry. Is it, like, a trial separation, or . . .'

'She's met some other bloke.'

'Gosh, I'm sorry. I'm not sure what to say.'

'It is a tricky social problem, certainly. You could say, "I never liked her," but then, if we get back together next month, you'll feel awkward. Or you could say, "I know someone who really fancies you." By the way, what's the magic word this week?'

Guy, Laurie and a number of other reporters played a newspaper game that had first become popular with bored reporters in the seventies whereby they all tried to get an agreed uncommon word or phrase into the paper by slipping it into a story. 'Gallimaufry' had been one. 'Antimacassar' another. The winner was the first person to get the word successfully into the paper. A reporter on the *Daily Mail*'s diary was famous for meeting the challenge of 'moist gusset' by introducing a Eurotrash character called Moi St Gusset into a tale.

'It's "engorged", I think, but the desk may be wise to it.'

Laurie nodded. He rang the Russian Embassy and asked a press attaché how many of his countrymen and women there were in Britain.

Chapter Thirteen

THE HOOK MANSION looked different on a damp day and without the flurry of journalists outside it. Smaller, less significant. The rain was getting heavier. Depressing. A week since the murder now and time for a return visit. Laurie felt that familiar feeling of dread that came when he rang on the door of a murder victim's house. What would he say to whichever of the Hooks answered the bell?

'So the dog barks and the caravan moves on,' said a voice behind him.

He turned. For a couple of seconds he could not place the face. It was the neighbour. The chap in cardigan and cavalry twills who had buttonholed them on the day after the murder. He was taking his golf clubs out of the back of his grey Discovery. If Laurie had been describing the car in a news story he would have called it 'battleship grey' because he knew that in news stories all greys, from clouds at funerals to walls outside murder victims' homes, were battleship grey. Why? It sounded serious and sombre. But, for the purpose of his current thoughts, grey would do.

'Hello,' said Laurie. 'I think we met briefly on the day after Mr Hook was killed.'

'You left a dreadful mess behind you,' said the neighbour, hauling the golf bag out. 'Not you personally, I suppose, but all you reporters and people. Dreadful mess.'

'I'm sorry about that.'

'Bloody paper cups and cigarette packets everywhere – although somebody came and cleared it all up later. So what do you want now?'

'I was trying to find out a little more about what happened that night. Thought some of the Hooks might be around. You said you'd heard a bang, didn't you?'

'I've told all this stuff to the police, you know. Which paper are you with?'

Laurie told him.

'Never read it,' said the man. 'My wife gets it sometimes.'

'Have you lived here long?'

'Twenty years now. The Hooks moved in about five years ago. We had no idea that they were – that he was – you know . . .'

'A master criminal?'

'Yes. We always thought he was in the entertainment game. He told us he had clubs and that sort of thing. Always said we were welcome. Not really my sort of scene. But they obviously weren't short of a few bob. New cars all the time. Decorators always coming in. Money no object.'

'Behind every great fortune is a great crime,' said Laurie.

'Is that so?'

Laurie nodded in what he hoped was a sage fashion. He didn't want to have to tell him that the line was Balzac's and the only reason he knew it was that Vic had identified it one recent Quiz Night at the Dirty Dog. It was raining more heavily.

'Getting a bit wet, isn't it?' said Laurie. 'Is there anywhere I could buy you a drink or a coffee or something near here?'

The neighbour looked at him as though he had asked him if he fancied some oral sex.

'I beg your pardon?'

'I just wondered if we could have a very brief chat – I'm under a bit of pressure at work to come up with more stuff on this murder and I don't really know what sort of a life Old Man Hook led over the last few years.'

'I don't suppose you're one of those reporters with a chequebook, are you?'

'Afraid not. It's more luncheon voucher journalism at our place.'

'Oh, well, look, you might as well come in and have a cup of tea. Can't hear yourself think in the bloody pubs round here.' The neighbour shouldered his golf bag and pulled his keys out of his cavalry twills.

The house was untidier than Laurie expected. There was a pile of bottles and magazines by the door.

'My wife is into all this recycling thing . . . What did you say your name was? I'm Michael Plimsoll.'

Laurie lowered himself into an uncomfortable floral armchair.

'Tea? Coffee? Beer?'

'Coffee would be fine, thanks.'

As Plimsoll busied himself in the kitchen, Laurie checked out the sitting room. An ugly oil painting of – what? The sea? Mountains? Who knew? – hung over the fireplace. Two lampstands of nymphs in diaphanous gowns which Laurie found disturbingly erotic. A wicker basket with neatly chopped logs. A drinks cabinet with some impressive malts and a chipped decanter. Plimsoll, surprisingly light on his toes, was back in the room with a mug in each hand.

'So, you remember when the Hooks arrived?'

'Oh, yes. You should have seen the amount of furniture they brought with them. Van after van. Then they threw a party for the neighbours in their back garden. Barbecue affair. No expense spared. Roast pig. Proper bubbly – none of that imitation Spanish crap that gives you a headache.'

'Can I ask how much – roughly – they might have paid for the house?'

'Yes, you can ask and I can tell you: two and a half million. Be worth four by now.'

'Did they have a lot of visitors?'

'Not many during the day. I'm retired so I'm around quite a bit, but at night there used to be a fair old bit of activity.'

'What sort of activity?'

'God, you're like the bloody coppers, aren't you? That's what they wanted to know.'

'Well, all crime reporters would secretly like to be either detectives or bank robbers – but we don't have the height or the nerve.'

'Is that a fact?'

'So, who was arriving late at night?'

'Well, I'm a bit of an insomniac, as my wife would tell you, so I paddle downstairs and watch the telly to get to sleep. Quite often, around – what? – three in the morning, these cars would drive up and out would hop these young women.

Usually the driver was a big, beefy fellow, and the girls, they looked foreign.'

'In what way?'

'Well, you know, in the summer the windows would be open, you could hear them chattering away. Polish, Russian, Czech, one of those eastern European languages. Can't tell the difference. They dress differently, too, don't they? The beefy fellow would wait for them in the car. Then after a while, beefy was replaced by a tall thin streak of a chap and he must have been one of them because he spoke whatever it was they were speaking. I'm having a second cup of tea. More coffee? No?'

The coffee was disgusting. He had not had such bad instant stuff since last year's Police Federation conference in Blackpool. That reminded him: next week was the ACPO drugs conference.

'As I was saying, we didn't really know them too well but last summer, one Saturday night, they had a party. We weren't invited but it got so noisy that eventually my wife went over to say something to them. They were very apologetic, she said, and she ended up having a drink with them all and staying on for a while. So she used to pop in a bit after that. She would have a chat with Polly – Mrs Hook. Then, the last Saturday before Hook was shot, another party, more bloody noise, Beth had to go over again but there was no problem, very apologetic again.'

'And on the night he was shot. What happened then?' Laurie's eyes strayed to the nymphs.

'Like my nymphs, do you? Saucy little minxes. Oh, that night. Yes. I was in bed, heard what I thought was a shout.

Then a bang, like a gunshot. Then silence. I almost got up but then I thought—'

'Car backfiring?'

'Yes, that's right. Or firework or something.'

'Firework? At that time of the morning?'

'You'd be surprised. Bloody fireworks going off all the time these days. Once upon a time, it was for a week or two before Guy Fawkes night, now it's the whole bloody time, isn't it? Anyway. Neither my wife nor my daughter, who's staying with us at the moment – marriage problems, I'm afraid – woke up. So I left it. Dozed off. Then, must have been about half an hour later, there's this car which shoots off at speed, tyres squealing and so on. That woke Beth up.'

'Getaway driver, d'you think?'

'Yes, like a getaway driver. Bloody noisy. And then . . .' Plimsoll cocked his head. There was the sound of a key turning in the lock. Laurie turned towards the door. There was a muffled bark, then a woman's voice. 'Tyson! Tyson, get down.'

The door opened and a Chihuahua scampered in followed by the owner of the voice.

'Hello, darling, have we got company?'

The woman standing by the door with two large shopping bags – Agnes B, said one of them – looked about thirty-five. Light brown hair, with blond streaks, immaculately combed, looked like a shampoo advertisement. Big jaw. White polo-neck jersey, a little tight. Jeans, ditto. Fawn suede coat, belt hanging loose. She gave Laurie what he would have described as a 'who-the-fuck-are-you?' look. This must be the daughter with the marriage problems. Marriage problems. An image of Caz, standing naked in their bedroom, drying her hair with a towel, flitted briefly and tantalisingly into his head.

'Oh, darling, this is Laurie . . . What did you say your last name was?'

'Lane.'

She gathered up her purchases. 'Laurie Lane? Really? Sounds like something on the North Circular.'

'Funny you should say that,' said Plimsoll. 'I was sure there was an actress, sort of pin-up, I think, called Laurie Lane. God, what was that film she was in? *Sing You Sinners*? Something like that.'

Laurie sighed inwardly. He remembered when the knowledge of an American actress called Laurie Lane had been brought to his attention shortly after he had arrived at yet another new school in – was it Nottingham or Welshpool? – and he had had to put up with the sniggers for weeks. 'I'm just going to put these away,' said Beth. 'Can you fix me a drink?'

'Wine?' asked Plimsoll.

'Yes, there should be some of the Pinot Noir left from last night.'

Plimsoll went off to the kitchen and there were sounds of corks and glasses. The woman came back into the room, minus her coat. Laurie got to his feet. Always stand up when a woman comes into the room, was one of the lessons his father had taught him. What else? Not too much. Never run for a bus. Gentlemen lift the seat? No, that was what it used to say in the lavatories on trains.

'I'm sorry – I'm a journalist. I was just asking your father—'

'That's not my father, that's my husband.'

The last remark was delivered just as Michael Plimsoll came back into the room carrying a very large glass of wine. One that would cost four quid in a pub. He arrived in time to hear his wife say 'that's my husband.'

Shit, thought Laurie. One of those moments. ('And when is the baby due?' he had asked the newsdesk temp, knowing, within a nanosecond of the remark and just before her face went pink and her eyes moist, that she was not pregnant but, well, overweight.)

Plimsoll looked distinctly cooler. He handed his wife the wine.

'There you are, Beth. This gentleman wants to know about the Hooks.'

'Oh, he does, does he? You think you're going to solve the murder on your own, do you? I thought the police knew who it was. Russian chap, isn't it? It was on the news.'

'I was just trying to build up a bit of a picture of them. What kind of life they lived, whether they mixed much. Is there anyone in the house at the moment?'

'No,' said Beth, savouring the wine a little too greedily. I could do with a drink myself, thought Laurie. She caught his look. 'Polly's staying with one of the children, I think. She wasn't there on the night . . . on the night it happened. Do you want some wine too?'

'Er . . . no, thanks.'

'Not on duty?'

'Sort of.'

'You married?'

'Er . . . sort of.'

'Reporters always hate people asking them questions, don't they? They don't like it up 'em, do they, darling?'

Plimsoll nodded. He seemed ill at ease. Not as ill at ease as me, thought Laurie.

'I should be going,' said Laurie. 'I'll leave my card, if I may. But your . . . er . . .'

'Husband.'

'Your husband said that the Saturday before Mr Hook was killed, you had to go over to get them to turn the noise down. I wondered if . . .'

Beth Plimsoll shot her husband a dark look. He almost seemed to flinch.

'Oh, I just popped my head round the door. They had the music on too loud. Windows open, summer night. I didn't see anyone with a machine gun there, if that's what you were wondering. I was only there a minute or two.'

Laurie got to his feet. 'You wouldn't be able to tell what nationality the people who were there at the time were, would you?'

'You're absolutely right, Mr Lane, I wouldn't.'

'Just family, was it?'

'I'm afraid the only people I spoke to were Mr and Mrs Hook. I think you'll find they're English.'

'Right, well, mustn't dawdle.' Now that he was standing, he could feel his damp trousers sticking to his calves, like a wet hand grasping him from the grave. 'Have any of the Hooks been around at the house since the shooting?'

'Not to stay,' said Plimsoll. 'Crispin and Ashley showed up once. I suppose the police forensic chaps wanted the run of it and I heard there was, you know, blood on the walls. Polly's staying with one of the boys, certainly until after the funeral on Friday.'

'Oh, yes, of course, and that's going to be at the Wanstead cemetery, isn't it?'

'No,' said Plimsoll. 'Chingford Mount. Service at St M's round the corner from here first.' His wife shot him another look.

'I think you'll find it's private,' said Beth Plimsoll sharply.

Laurie smiled at her. 'I'll let myself out. Thanks for all your help, Mr Plimsoll.'

Laurie closed the door and looked across at the Hook mansion. As he did so a strangely familiar figure in a shabby white raincoat scurried away with something in his hand.

Chapter Fourteen

MICK, VIC AND Mary were already hunched over their quiz sheets at the Dirty Dog when Laurie arrived.

'Where have you been?' said Vic. 'They're just about to start. God, look at Cliff – he must've fallen asleep under his sun lamp.'

'They want more on the Old Man Hook murder. I went up to his gaff today and—'

'Good evening, ladies and gentlemen, and welcome to Quiz Night at the Dirty Dog,' said Cliff, whose normally pallid and spotty complexion had been replaced by what appeared to be an uneven coat of caramel paint. 'Nice to see some of our regulars here tonight . . .' he nodded at their table, 'and to welcome some new friends . . .' he smiled at the table of young Polish decorators, white paint still drying on their forearms, who had, to Cliff's surprise, asked for quiz forms as they sipped their lagers. 'Our prize tonight is a fantabuloso eighty pounds. So, sharpen your minds and your pencils because here is our first question of the night and it's an easy one: what is the capital of Malaysia?'

'Kuala Lumpur,' muttered Laurie.

'You don't say,' said Mick, as he always did when someone announced the answer to a question which he deemed too easy to bother uttering out loud. School's Out, the teachers' team, were at full strength and even had an additional, new member with them. Mick eyed them.

'If they spent as much effort on teaching kids how to read and write as they do on this bloody quiz, this country wouldn't be in such a bloody mess,' he said.

'You sound like the *Daily Mail*,' said Mary.

'Are you chewing gum and drinking, Mary?' asked Vic.

'Nicorettes,' said Mick. 'She's never adjusted to the smoking ban, have you, darling? So, Laurie, you find out anything about Old Man Hook?'

'I met his neighbour – the first time I've ever met a neighbour on a story who doesn't say about a murder victim that "he kept himself to himself". Oh, and his neighbour's wife. Boy, she was a piece of work.'

'Thou shalt not covet Old Man Hook's neighbour's wife,' said Mick.

'Who said I fancied her?'

'We can tell,' said Mick.

'Why would he fancy her when he's got a lovely girl like Caz?' said Mary.

'Had,' said Laurie. 'Past tense.'

'You're not serious?' said Mary. 'When did this happen?'

There were noises of interference coming from Cliff's microphone. Laurie shook his head to signify that he did not want to talk about it.

'What is the number of the psalm that begins "The lord is my shepherd"?' asked Cliff, employing his best if-there-is-an-agent-out-there-looking-for-new-television-talent-I'm-it voice. 'What – is – the – number – of – the – psalm – that – begins "The lord is my shepherd"?'

'That's not very fair on the Muslims, is it?' asked Mick, scrawling 23 down on their pad.

'Not very fair on us Buddhists, either,' said Vic, sipping his ginger beer.

' "King David and King Solomon led merry, merry lives, running round the tabernacles with other people's wives. But later in the evening, when their conscience gave them qualms, Solomon wrote the proverbs and David wrote the psalms," ' said Mick.

'Very, very clever,' said Vic.

'And when did you become a Buddhist?' asked Laurie.

'At Highpoint. We all did,' said Mick. 'Yoga, too.'

'You lot weren't Buddhists, you were just doing it for the parole board,' said Vic.

'Bollocks,' said Mick.

'A Buddhist wouldn't say bollocks,' said Vic.

'Bollocks,' said Mick.

'And the next question is, who wished that the Roman people had only one neck?'

'You should know that, Mick, you're the fucking history professor,' said Vic.

'Caligula,' said Mary.

'How do you know that?' asked Vic.

'She watched that saucy film,' said Mick. 'And keep your voices down, the teachers haven't got it yet.'

'Anything new on the grapevine about Hook?' asked Laurie.

'Just that it's looking a hundred per cent it was the

Russians,' said Vic. 'They wanted in to the clubs. Old Man Hook didn't want them. They warned him apparently, used Petrov as their front man. They don't take any prisoners, those guys. I'll get another round in.'

'I'm sorry about Caz,' said Mary. 'D'you not want to talk about it, Laurie?'

'Not right now,' said Laurie.

'Question number four: in what year did a British team win the European Cup for the first time?' said Cliff.

'Manchester United, wasn't it?' said Mary. 'George Best. When would that be? About nineteen sixty-eight.'

'No, it was Celtic,' said Laurie. 'The year before.'

'He's right,' said Vic, returning to the table with a tray. 'I remember it. I was in Brixton. Funnily enough, so was Old Man Hook.'

'What was he in for?'

'It was that time he was awaiting trial on some GBH thing,' said Mick. 'He wasn't that bothered. It was like he knew he was going to get off. I remember his old lady used to come to visit him and bring little Crispin with her. In those days, you were allowed to bring in fags and food and everything. She used to get a right earful if she didn't bring nice ripe fruit in. He was very, very picky.'

'D'you really think the Russians would bother with him?' asked Mary. 'He looked like a sad old man the last time I saw him at Xanadu.'

'And question number five, QUESTION NUMBER FIVE,' Cliff was having to raise his voice to make himself heard above the hubbub. The Polish decorators were having an animated argument about the European Cup and Cliff was making polite gestures to get them to quieten down. 'Who won an Oscar for her performance in *Boys Don't Cry?*'

'Hilary someone,' said Vic. 'Skank, something like that.'

'Swank,' said Mary. 'They're a bit easy, this week. See, the teachers have got that one, all right. They're looking really smug. They were well pissed off the last time we beat them. I heard the two women in the loo – they were even saying that they thought Cliff tipped us off with the questions beforehand, cheeky cows. I thought the Russians wanted to keep their heads down after the Litvinwhatsit business anyway. Why would they get into a fight with the Hooks? Oh, bloody hell, I've bit my bloody tongue. These Nicorettes are a bloody nuisance.'

'Some people are putting it about that Hook was thinking of going over to the other side and telling the Old Bill exactly what the Russians were up to,' said Vic. 'They were wanting in on some of the Hooks' business – not just the clubs, but some of the skunk and some of the action in Ibiza where Crispin's got his club. So Old Man Hook reckons it would be easy to stitch them up, get them out of the way early on, get some of them deported. Apparently, he had the business on them. You know how the Hooks always get wired up and record people they think are a bit iffy? And then play back the tapes in front of everybody? He was a sly old bugger.'

'Crispin's just the same, I've heard,' said Mick. 'Maybe someone didn't like the idea of him doing a book with you, Laurie. Let too many cats out of the bag.'

A waitress with her light brown hair in a ponytail asked if they were finished with their glasses. Mick helped her and she flashed him a grateful smile.

'So where are you from?' he asked her. 'Sydney or Melbourne?'

'Brisbane.'

'My favourite Australian city,' said Mick.

'Just ignore him, dear,' said Mary. 'He's never been west of Benidorm.' The waitress shrugged and sashayed back to the bar.

'I was just being friendly with her,' said Mick. 'She was nice, wasn't she? You should take a couple of tips, Laurie, now that you're a single man again.'

'Take no notice of him, Laurie,' said Mary. 'I can't see Old Man Hook grassing anyone, even the Russians. He was always really old school.'

'That's what they used to say about Bertie Smalls,' said Vic. 'Anyway, someone may have been putting the word out about him just to wind up the Russians so that they would do something like that. And the Old Bill hasn't a clue about them yet. They've got about ten years before they get infiltrated and before the Yard has got its Russian graduates in there. I'm going for a piss. Come and get me if the next question is anything about Virginia Woolf.'

Cliff was tapping the microphone. The noise in the Dirty Dog was growing. The teachers' team appeared to be two short as a couple of the side had slipped outside for a cigarette. On hearing the sound of the microphone, they both hurried back in, bringing with them the strong whiff of tobacco.

'Disgusting habit, isn't it?' said Mick. 'You're right, Mary. I don't think Old Man Hook would have done that. If it had ever got out, he would have looked like a right pratt. I'm not sure about all this Russian stuff. All a bit neat, isn't it? Hook had a lot of other enemies. He used to have a bloke in the Yard – what was his name? Ginger . . . Ginger Mulgrew – he used to feed him people and in exchange Mulgrew would drop him out of things. Mulgrew must be retired now. Maybe he wanted a little pension from the Hooks and was pissed off with them. He would have known where that Russian bloke lived, wouldn't he?'

'QUESTION NUMBER SIX!' Cliff was doing his best. There was a brief lull. 'Question number six: who, in the summer of two thousand and seven, had a hit with the song "Big Girls Don't Cry"?'

'That's Fergie,' said Mary.

'Keep your voice down, don't let the teachers hear,' said Mick.

'They know anyway,' said Mary.

'Yeah,' said Vic, rejoining them. 'It's probably a set text for A levels these days.'

'You all sound like the bloody *Daily Mail* these days,' said Mary. 'And your flies are undone.'

Laurie went to the gents. A new condom machine had just been installed, offering a variety of different flavours, colours and exotic ridge formations. Did someone test these? he wondered. Probably students would do it to pay off their grants. When was the last time he had used a condom? Before he met Caz, so that would be more than twenty years ago. Would he have to start buying them again now? Would he be laughed at if he produced the ridged ones? His mobile phone rang. There was a silence at the other end. One of the teachers' team walked in and saw him on the phone.

'Not calling a special friend to see who sang "Big Girls Don't Cry", are we?'

'I don't have any special friends,' said Laurie.

'I wouldn't be surprised if it was his old lady had him bumped off,' said Mary, after Laurie had returned to the table. 'In the old days, he was always having it off with someone else and flaunting it in front of her. Didn't you say that, Vic?'

Vic shrugged.

'I bet she's glad he's gone now,' said Mary. 'She put up with a lot, what with him and Crispin and Ashley. Spent half her time sorting bail out and going off to Parkhurst or Durham. I feel sorry for her.'

'What, you reckon Polly whacked him and then dumped the shooter in the back garden of the Russian geezer?' said Vic.

'I've no idea. But often those things that the papers say are gangland hits – no disrespect, Laurie – turn out to be a bit of domestic. Don't you remember him at Xanadu when it first opened? He always had his hands on someone's knee.'

'Did he ever try it on with you, darling?' said Mick.

'Course not, he knew I was with you. But I bet there are a few faces who were inside then who found out what he'd been up to with their old ladies when they came out. He could be a real groper. Shall I get some more in? Another ginger ale, Vic?'

The teachers' table had ordered a plate of nachos and salsa, the Dirty Dog's concession to world cuisine.

'They've definitely got a ringer there,' said Mick. 'I bet he's someone from *Mastermind* or *University Challenge* or something.'

'You know I saw a bloke on *University Challenge*, from Oxford, he was,' said Vic, 'and Paxman asked him what was the name of the American general who took the surrender from the Japanese and d'you know what he said?'

'You're going to tell us,' said Laurie.

'General Custer.'

'He must have been having a laugh,' said Mick. 'Hey, Laurie, here's that barmaid again. Say something sensitive.'

'Leave him alone,' said Mary.

Cliff had moved from the British pop charts to what jockeys meant by the joystick and the artist who painted the Hay Wain by the time Mary returned to the table.

'In Greek mythology,' said Cliff, 'to whom did Zeus reveal himself as a bull?'

'Europa, mother of Minos, King of Crete,' muttered Vic.

'Pardon my fucking Greek, but I'm impressed,' said Mick.

Chapter Fifteen

THE TEACHERS WERE celebrating their victory noisily. The failure of the Long Lartin Old Boys to identify the year in which Bobby Darin had had a hit with 'Mack the Knife' had only compounded their inability to come up with the name of the male tennis player who had won Wimbledon most often. It did not help that the teachers were now in full triumphalist mode, singing out, 'Pretty teeth, dear!' to each other and, as Laurie and his companions headed for the door, 'Someone sneaking round the corner . . .'

'Don't tell me it's only a game,' said Mick as they huddled outside on the street in the light drizzle. 'I thought you were meant to be our sports expert, Laurie.'

'Come on, come on,' said Mary. 'D'you want a lift home, Laurie?'

'No, it's OK. Back to my empty-bed blues.'

'Oh, I am sorry about that,' said Mary. 'I'm sure she'll be back, Laurie. You know what it's like in the world she's in. Sure you don't want to come back with us for a nightcap?'

'No, I'd better get home. Violet will still be up.'

The lights in the house, blazing from every room, assured him that she was. He sighed as he fumbled with the key in the lock. How many pints had it been? Five? What was that in units?

'How much have you had to drink?' were Violet's first words of greeting, although her eyes did not stray from the television.

'Oh, don't you start.'

'Did you win the quiz?'

'No. The bloody teachers did. They brought along a sports nerd as a ringer. Bloody cheats. No wonder kids today have no sense of morality – apart from you, of course. Is there anything in the fridge?'

'Not unless you're interested in archaeology,' said Violet.

'Very droll,' said Laurie. He opened the fridge. It was empty apart from an egg of doubtful age, a few slices of sweating salami and a half-empty bottle of tomato ketchup. 'Isn't there anything to eat at all? How's the revision going, by the way?'

'There's some pasta you could heat up.'

'Any news from your mum?'

'Why? D'you think she's going to ring up and say it's all been a terrible mistake? I had lunch with her and she seemed happier than she has been for years.'

The bathroom looked different. As he peed, for what seemed like a quarter of an hour, Laurie cast his eye round the room. Something was missing. There had been some change. He went downstairs to where Violet, now in her Arsenal pyjamas, which seemed to be her default mode of dress these days, was back watching television with a cranberry juice in one hand and the remote in the other.

'What's happened to the bathroom?' he asked Violet.

'Oh, Mum took some things – hot water bottle and her bubble bath stuff, I think.'

'She's been here on a raid, has she? Anything else gone? Apart, of course, from my faith in humanity.'

'Oh, God, you're not going into one, are you? Oh, by the way, the night newsdesk rang for you. The bloke with the Geordie accent. They said they couldn't reach you on your mobile phone. I told them you were probably undercover and couldn't have it on for security reasons.'

Laurie had switched it off after he came out of the pub loo after being accused by the teacher – only partially in jest – of cheating and had forgotten to switch it back on. He rang in.

'Hi, I gather you called.'

'Just thought I'd let you know that the *Mirror* is running a story that the lecturer – what's his name? – the one whose girlfriend is missing, has been taken to hospital. Looks like he slashed his wrists.'

'Guilt,' said Laurie, gesturing to Violet to turn the television down.

'Not grief?'

'Guilt and grief,' said Laurie. 'Often the two can go together. No sign of a body yet?'

Violet shot him a look.

'Do you want to do anything with it?' the night news editor was asking. 'We can run a NIB, just take it from the wires.'

'Yeah, if you don't mind. I think a NIB is all it needs. Interesting that he's slashed his wrists. If it was you, would you go for that or sleeping pills? Or the old noose? You'd probably jump off the Humber Bridge, wouldn't you? Is it high enough?'

'Morbid,' said Violet, when he had rung off. 'What's a nib?'

'News in brief. Little story.'

'You're not thinking of doing yourself in, are you?'

'So that your mum could sing sad songs about me and take dead flowers to my grave? What do you think?'

'I don't think you'd have the nerve, would you? There's a girl in my class who's always doing it.'

'Doing what?'

'Committing suicide.'

'Well, she can't be always doing it.'

'You know what I mean. Always trying to do herself in.'

'And why is that?'

'Attention-seeking.'

'Maybe she's just lonely. Are you nice to her?'

'Oh, Dad, for heaven's sake . . . I'm trying to watch this,' said Violet, gesturing with her cranberry juice at the television screen. 'Are you going to get a new girlfriend?'

'Isn't it a little early for that? "Ere yet the salt of most unrighteous tears . . ." '

'OK. We did *Hamlet* for GCSE.'

'I did it for O level. Those were in the days when people still had to pass exams through their efforts and studies rather than just having to show up.'

'I'm serious. I don't think Mum is coming back. Do you not think you're ready yet for a new relationship?'

'Bloody hell, it's only been – what? – a week? I'm still in mourning. I see that bottle of vintage cider is missing. I suppose your mum took that – for sentimental reasons.'

'We did mourning in our citizenship class. Apparently there are seven stages: shock, denial, grief, guilt, anger . . . I can't remember the others.'

'Which one do you think I'm in?' said Laurie from the kitchen, helping himself to a Ben and Jerry's Bohemian Raspberry which he had found almost stuck at the back of the freezer.

'Probably denial. That's why you feel you have to make a joke about it, like Mum was always complaining – you could never take anything seriously, it always had to be a joke.'

Laurie dug a spoon into the frozen ice cream and watched it buckle slightly.

'Look, you won't remember this because you were not yet in existence but your mother used to say that was why she went out with me in the first place.'

'What, for a laugh?'

'In a way, yes, although I'm not quite sure about the way you put it.'

Violet watched Laurie eating the ice cream.

'You won't get any new girlfriends if you go on an eating binge.'

'I'm not on a bloody eating binge. I haven't had any supper and you know what a fuss you make if I bring in a kebab.'

Violet used her two forefingers to make the sign of the cross at the mention of kebabs. 'Oooo, we learned about doner kebab meat. You know what happens to it?'

'I don't wish to know that. And how is school anyway? Isn't it parents' night some time soon?'

'Oh, I get it, you fancy Miss Ransome, don't you? You can do the deserted dad thing, can't you? But I think she's got a bloke now anyway. I saw her getting on the back of a motorbike after the sixth form play rehearsals last week.'

'Well, I can't compete with a motorbike, can I?'

'You could learn. Did that bloke who cut his wrists kill his girlfriend then? You're not going to finish that, are you? That's disgusting.'

'I think he probably did but they haven't found a body. I think if you reckon your girlfriend's run off with someone else you don't kill yourself these days unless you're only sixteen. But if you've killed somebody and you're going to jail for the next twenty years you might. D'you think I should make an attention-seeking gesture to get your mum back?'

'Oh, I think you've gone straight from shock to anger and you've missed out those ones in between – what is it? Guilt? If you are going to do yourself in, then can you wait until I'm just about to start my A levels because they take it into account? Jasmine's dad died of a heart attack last year and they bumped her up at least one grade. In fact, I think she got an A in history which she was definitely, definitely going to fail.'

'I think I'll go back to denial and then to bed.'

'Is it a bit weird not having someone in the same bed as you?'

'Not really. Amazingly enough, I used to sleep alone when I was growing up, you know. Anyway, there are compensations: no one beside you listening to Cajun music with their headphones on.'

'Mum said you had offered to have a nose op because you snored so loudly. What happened to that?'

'Give us a kiss. Goodnight.'

'Goodnight, Dad. Don't kill yourself during the night because I'm going to KOKO with Niyaz and Jo tomorrow and I would have to cancel.'

'I promise. If you promise that, when that tosser on the

telly has finished speaking, you will turn off the bloody machine and go to bed and get some sleep. I'll shout when I'm out of the bathroom.'

As Laurie lay in bed, he heard his daughter turning off the television, opening and shutting the fridge and making a telephone call. He could still hear her responses – 'No, he didn't! Bless! No, I won't tell him' – in the background as he drifted off to sleep. He was woken a few hours later by the high-pitched squeal of foxes rutting in a neighbour's garden.

Chapter Sixteen

'**W**HY ARE YOU dressed like that?' asked Violet. 'You look as though you're going to a funeral.'

'How very, very perceptive of you, Violet,' said Laurie, as he wondered why the collar of his white shirt had shrunk and how long the crumpled handkerchief in the suit pocket had been there. Could they get DNA from snot? Why did he have such unedifying thoughts? 'It is because I am, in fact, going to a funeral.'

'Anyone I know?'

'Old Man Hook.'

'Oh, that'll be great, won't it? Will it be like one of the Mafia funerals with lots of women in black veils?'

'Show a little respect for the dead. Anyway, I shouldn't be too late tonight. D'you want to go out for a meal? The Thai place? Or Bella Napoli? See old Giovanni.'

'Bella Napoli's been closed for two years now, Dad, and Giovanni died ages ago. And we're not going to the Dirty Dog because their burgers are undercooked. I saw them preparing them.'

'When?'

'Oh, last week. I went for an interview there. They're

Duncan Campbell

looking for barmaids for the summer when all the Australian girls go round Europe.'

'God, I'm not sure I want you working there, counting my pints . . . Well, think of somewhere for tonight. See you later.'

There was a slow drizzle in the air as Laurie arrived at the church in Highgate. The pack had already arrived. After the deaths of the Krays, there had been a dwindling interest in the coverage of criminals' funerals. Joey Pyle had had a good send-off in Sutton, with a big turnout of old faces, a former boxing champion, a snooker star and that singer – Kenny something – who'd had a couple of hits in the sixties or seventies. But the big villains these days were largely unknown, too savvy to want to have their photo taken by David Bailey or to seek the sort of profile enjoyed by the old gangs. Old Man Hook represented the end of the era. Periodically, a foolhardy young television journalist would do a programme on 'Britain's Number One Crime Family' and there would be archive footage of Hook in grainy black and white being taken, handcuffed, out of a police van. Now came his funeral, and the satellite dishes, the jostle of photographers and reporters, the passers-by asking what was going on indicated that his final hours above the surface of the earth would also be recorded for posterity.

Laurie felt a squeeze on his arm. 'Hello, mister,' said a familiar voice. There was Eva-Marie, camera round her neck, neat little backpack of equipment over her shoulder. She was dressed in white jeans and a blue polka-dot blouse.

'What are you doing here?' he asked. 'I thought you were meant to be the boss now?'

'Well, they want a nice moody shot over two pages and

everyone's either out on jobs or ill so I said I'd do it.' She smiled. 'Got to keep our hands in, haven't we?'

'Well, I'm glad to see you're dressed for a funeral anyway.'

'I know,' she said, glancing down at the white jeans. 'It's embarrassing, isn't it? But I didn't know I was going to be sent on this.'

She was carrying, as were some of her fellow photographers, a small fold-up ladder so that she could get a decent view over people's heads. She shrugged away his offer to carry it.

'I'm going to have to go into the church to hear the service,' said Laurie. 'You know the actual burial is way out in east London, don't you? I think you'll get better pictures there. Graveside stuff.'

He spotted the Vicar, Mo Muskett and Kevin Yu spilling out of a taxi and the Vicar having an argument with the driver over how many blank receipts were required. A posse of young men in dark blue suits, wearing dark glasses and gazing around them with a vaguely menacing look, had taken up a position at the entrance and were flexing their fingers. The trio of fellow crime reporters spotted Laurie and joined him. He introduced them to Eva-Marie.

'Have you done a lot of these?' asked Eva-Marie of the Vicar.

'I've done every villain's funeral since Judas,' said the Vicar. 'Ronnie's was a good one, wasn't it, Laurie? Except I nearly had my foot run over by a bloody stretch limo.'

'I remember that service. What were the songs they had? They had "My Way", of course. Oh, and "I Will Always Love You". And then, what was the reading?'

' "Invictus",' said the Vicar. 'W.E. Henley:

> It matters not how strait the gate,
> How charged with punishments the scroll,
> I am the master of my fate;
> I am the captain of my soul.

'Master of my fate? Captain of my . . .? Poor old Ronnie wasn't even the captain of the Broadmoor tiddlywinks team by the end. I remember going and seeing him one time. He was still kitted out like a gent, silver sixpence cufflinks, nicely ironed white shirt, polished shoes – oh, look, here comes the Old Bill. There, that bloke who's walking like he's just cacked in his pants. They think no one will recognise them. They might as well wear T-shirts with "Undercover Old Bill" on them . . . Morning, officer, how's tricks? Keeping an eye out for the odd absconder? Do you think the bloke who killed him will come and do a lap of honour round the coffin? As it says in the Scriptures, as the dog returneth to its vomit . . .'

The Vicar's patter was rewarded with watery smiles from the couple watching the mourners arrive. They were smartly dressed. Where had Laurie seen them before? Ah, outside the cafe in Clissold Park, in jeans and bomber jacket and trouser suit. Pretending to do a sudoku puzzle together.

'Now when the Krays' mum died – when was that, Laurie? Back in the seventies, I think – they let the twins out for the funeral but handcuffed them to the tallest bloody prison officers they could find so they would really look small and insignificant because they were only, what, about five foot nine. But when Ronnie died and they let Reggie out of nick for the funeral, they handcuffed him to a woman prison officer – that was really rubbing it in.'

'And she let him give sugar lumps to the horses that pulled the coffin into the cemetery, didn't she?' said Kevin.

As if on cue, the hearse came into view, drawing an audible gasp from the growing crowd of mourners and passers-by. Old Man Hook's coffin was draped in flowers. One wreath said 'The Guvnor'. Another 'Grandad'.

'Oh, by the way, Laurie, you'll enjoy this – I just had Drake Publishing on to me last night, they want me to ask Polly Hook if I can ghost her autobiography – *A Wife of Crime, From Tiller Girl to Queen of the Underworld*. What do you think? Thirty grand they're offering.'

'Maybe right now is not the perfect moment to ask her,' said Laurie.

Eva-Marie was snapping away at speed as the cortège wound its way towards the church. The limousine immediately behind the coffin contained Polly, the widow, looking remarkably composed, steely even, thought Laurie, and the two Hook sons, Crispin and Ashley, and their wives, all self-consciously elegant in black. Successful criminals get good-looking wives. Two identical cars carried what appeared to be the remaining members of the clan, from the two Hook daughters and their husbands through to what Laurie presumed were the youngest of the grandchildren, teenage boys wearing an air of haughty privilege. Some he recognised from the scenes outside the Hook mansion on the day of the murder. With their snappy suits, white shirts and slim ties, they looked like a school production of *Reservoir Dogs*. One of the girls was in tears.

'Point out anyone I should get,' said Eva-Marie.

'Get the brothers,' said Laurie, as the cortège drew to a halt outside the church and a young rosy-cheeked vicar came forward, wearing his condolences on his cassock sleeve, to take Polly Hook by the hand. Crispin and Ashley Hook were standing by their mother, looking like secret service agents guarding a first lady. Their eyes slid over the gathering, taking in the first of the mourners. An occasional nod of recognition. Crispin caught sight of Laurie and tilted his head in acknowledgement. The family entered the chapel and the other mourners started to follow them.

'There's Bruce Reynolds, the great train robber,' said Laurie to Eva-Marie. 'Get a nice picture of him . . . There's Peter Scott, the one in the blazer, with the limp, king of the cat-burglars . . . There's that boxer, God, I can't remember his name, Joe McSomething – he became the welterweight champion after Barney Quick was killed, I think. And the bloke who used to be in *EastEnders* . . . can't remember his name either.'

Eva-Marie snapped away, nodding as he identified faces.

'I'm going in now or I won't get a seat,' said Laurie. 'I don't think they're allowing snappers inside. I'll see you afterwards.'

How many funerals have I been to? wondered Laurie, as he took the order of service from one of the young ushers – had he seen him once in the dock in Snaresbrook? He squeezed himself into a back row pew. The most recent had been Caz's mother's last year. Caz had sobbed throughout. No Caz to report news of this to at the end of the day. That was what he missed already. Someone who knew the narrative of your life and with whom you could reflect on its little triumphs and catastrophes. No Caz. Had she been waiting for her mother to die before she did a runner? Death had that effect on some people, a sudden feeling that, if you don't follow your instincts, change things fast, you, too, will end up at the embalmer's with nothing but your shroud and your regrets.

'We are gathered here today to remember the life of Charles Edward Kitchener Hook,' said the vicar, who had a public schoolboy's manner and accent. Laurie recognised the vowels. He had had two brief terms at private school before his father's debtors came calling and he had been removed. Did the vicar come with the church or had he been hired by the Hooks?

'I had the great privilege of knowing Mr Hook as the chaplain of the school attended by both his sons and his grandsons,' said the vicar, helpfully answering Laurie's unspoken question. 'I know that he was a man who was, above all, a loving husband and father, a man who was true to himself and loyal to his family and friends.'

'And a savage bastard to his enemies,' muttered a voice beside him. The Vicar with a capital V had squeezed in beside him.

'Why don't you do the service?' asked Laurie, under his breath.

'There's Mad Frankie Fraser over there,' said the Vicar, ignoring him.

The real vicar was moving on to the lessons from the bible.

'I bet he's going to do the bit about the two blokes beside Jesus on the cross both being thieves,' said the Vicar.

'And lo, Jesus said, my God, my God, why hast thou forsaken me?' said the vicar, on cue and over-dramatically.

Laurie saw Mrs Hook's shoulders go up and down. Was she sighing or crying? Who knows, maybe chuckling. The vicar moved on speedily to casting the first stone. Laurie watched the Hook brothers. They were still acting like secret service agents, their eyes never still.

'And the first hymn on your sheet, "To Be a Pilgrim . . ."'

> He who would valiant be
> 'Gainst all disaster,
> Let him in constancy
> Follow the master.

Surprisingly, the Vicar had quite a sweet singing voice, mulled by years of Senior Service and Guinness. Laurie glanced round as some late arrivals were being shoehorned into the back row. It was the Plimsolls. Beth Plimsoll looked as though she was dressed for Ascot. She wore a wide-brimmed straw hat and a cream dress with a plunging neckline. They swapped nods.

> Then fancies flee away
> I'll fear not what men say,
> I'll labour night and day
> To be a pilgrim.

The vicar bade the congregation be seated. Laurie noted that the two detectives had squeezed their way into the back of the chapel and were now trying to make themselves look as small as possible as the rest of the mourners sat down.

'Charles Hook was a man who had faced those twin

impostors, triumph and disaster,' said the vicar.

'Oh, God, he's not going to read us "If", is he?' muttered the Vicar.

'My favourite poem,' said Kevin Yu, who had slid into the end of the pew.

'It would be,' said the Vicar.

'What's yours?' asked Laurie. 'The Ancient Bloody Mariner?'

'Shhh,' said a voice behind them. Laurie turned and saw the figure of Horace, one of the Xanadu bouncers and a former boxer, standing behind them. Horace smiled politely at him and put a stagy finger to his lips.

'. . . he would have been the first to acknowledge that, on the long and complex journey through life, he had taken some wrong turns.' The shoulders of Crispin Hook seemed to square back at the vicar's words. 'But, as we all know, we do not enter this world with our own in-built satnav.' Polite titters from some of the mourners. 'What matters is whether or not we recognise what errors we have made and adjust the compass of our life accordingly.'

'Where the fuck is this going?' muttered the Vicar.

'I'm just counting the extended metaphors,' whispered Laurie.

'SHHHH!' came the ominous sound from Horace.

'His generosity was legendary,' said the vicar, 'and many beneficiaries of it are here today, whether they are young men who were able to pursue their love of the martial arts through the Ravenscroft Boys' Boxing Club or young women who learned the often underestimated skills of the cheerleader through the Mile End Majorettes, and also . . .'

'Aye-aye,' said the Vicar. 'When did Old Man Hook get into sponsoring cheerleaders?'

Laurie, recalling dimly that Horace had once nearly taken on Lennox Lewis for one of the versions of the British heavyweight title, dug the Vicar hard in the ribs.

'. . . many others who have cause to remember acts of personal kindness. Above all, was his deep generosity of spirit . . .'

'He's making him sound like Mother Bloody Teresa,' said the Vicar. 'Old Man Hook must have got this preacher off some kiddie-fiddling charge and . . .' he tailed off as the sound of Horace taking a deep breath could be heard above the eulogy.

'. . . and I would ask you to remain in your seats while Mr Hook's old friend, Kris Kurtis, sings his favourite . . .'

'Please God, not "My Way",' Laurie could not stop himself from saying. 'Or "I Fought the Law and the Law Won".'

Kris Kurtis, whom Laurie had thought was long dead, approached the microphone. He had had brief fame in the late fifties and early sixties before the arrival of the Beatles and the Stones. A contemporary of Tommy Steele and Marty Wilde, he had had a couple of hits and a few appearances on *Juke Box Jury* and *Six Five Special*. Laurie had seen some ancient publicity shots of him: hair combed into a quiff, blazer, narrow tie with a cheap jewel in its centre. Then there had been some problems with amphetamines and an attempt to regain past glories with a dreadful cover version of 'Hi Ho Silver Lining' before disappearance into the obscurity of cruises and holiday camps.

'I thought he was dead,' said Laurie under his breath.

'You will be if you don't shut it,' said the Vicar, turning in the pew to smile at Horace.

Kurtis was frowning and holding the microphone close to his face, staring at it as though it was an ice-cream cone and he had just spotted a dog turd in it. The frown, Laurie supposed, was to suggest grief and gravitas.

'For my dear friend, Charles Hook, I would like to dedicate this song by Bobby Darin which Charles loved and which is called . . .'

'Christ, he's not going to sing "Mack the Knife", is he?' said the Vicar.

' "The Curtain Falls".'

Kurtis squeezed every drop from the lyrics, even managing a half-sob in his voice for the line about the music softly dying. The official vicar and Kurtis embraced in a stiff, ecumenical hug and Kurtis ostentatiously took a large white handkerchief out of his pocket and wiped his eyes. Would he be paid for this performance, wondered Laurie, or is he paying off some old debt?

There was another prayer. Laurie looked round to see whose eyes were closed and who was kneeling. He caught the eye of one of the detectives who gave him the flicker of a smile. The Vicar said an overloud 'amen'. The congregation were invited to attend the burial at Chingford Mount cemetery and those without transport were informed that there were four minibuses available outside. Mrs Hook, with Crispin and Ashley each holding one of her arms, as though taking her into custody, led the mourners out of the church.

Eva-Marie had her car with her and gave a lift to Laurie, the Vicar and Mo Muskett. The traffic was heavy and the day was hot. The journey took nearly an hour. Six black-plumed horses, sleek and elegant, were waiting patiently outside the cemetery to take the coffin on its final journey.

'Top pedigree horses,' said the Vicar.

'What do you know about horses?' said Mo Muskett. 'I bet that's the first time you've seen one without a little man in a cap sitting on it.'

'My uncle was in livestock,' lied the Vicar.

The grave had been dug deep. There was a pile of flowers, chrysanthemums and poppies, roses and lilies, arranged respectfully beside the mound of fresh earth. Eva-Marie had already positioned herself on her little stepladder and turned and smiled over her shoulder at Laurie. Laurie smiled back and tried to pretend he had not been looking at her bottom. He checked out the dedications on the wreaths. 'The Guvnor' and 'Grandad' had pride of place. 'To Hooky, a gent to the last, the Boys on B Wing.' 'Goodbye, old friend, see you on the Other Side, Mikey.' 'To the Boss, Rest In Peace, Matty N.'

The coffin was carried towards the grave by Ashley and Crispin, with the help of two sons-in-law and Brian 'Bodger' Boone, and James 'Little Legs' Vine, both old villains who had been part of the Hook empire.

As they approached the grave and paused on the artificial grass around its edge, there was the sound of a microphone being tested.

'Bloody 'ell,' said the Vicar. 'They're going to put a mike in the grave with him so he can haunt his enemies.'

'It's worse than that,' said Laurie. 'Kris Kurtis is doing an encore.'

And, as the coffin was lowered into the grave, Kris Kurtis,

frowning yet more deeply and with one arm operatically outstretched, sang 'Ave Maria'. As he hit the top note – or almost hit the top note – he was nearly drowned out by the sound of a half-suppressed sob from what Laurie took to be one of the granddaughters, a teenager dressed in an incongruous mix of funeral formal and nightclub Goth: black velvet dress, unfeasibly high heels, morgue-white make-up. Horace dabbed his eyes.

The Vicar nudged Laurie and gestured over his shoulder. 'Where have I seen that bird over there before? Does she know she's at a funeral? Look at that cleavage – you could park a bendy bus down there!'

Laurie followed his gaze and found himself staring straight at Beth Plimsoll who was watching the ceremony stony-faced. She returned his gaze, unblinking. Laurie spotted a few more faces: the King of the Jury Nobblers was there and two of the surviving members of the Barnet Bullion gang, one with a silver-handled cane. Probably a sword-stick. There were even a couple of exiles from the Costa del Crime, their Sexy Beast tans highlighted by their white shirts and blow-dried silver hair. And was that Vic? Had he not said that he never went to funerals?

'Ashes to ashes,' intoned the vicar, 'dust to dust.'

A photographer whom Laurie did not recognise had strayed a little too close to the grave, clearly trying to get a shot of the widow. Horace laid a mighty hand on his shoulder and the snapper unwisely shook it off.

Each member of the Hook family scattered a handful of earth on the coffin lid. The grave diggers started their work as the family moved towards the place where the cars were parked. Laurie lingered. He noted a self-confident young man who looked eastern European – something about the unfamiliar cut of the suit and the Slavic cheekbones – laying a wreath down with the others. As the young man moved away, Laurie went over to see what the inscription was. It was in Russian. Eva-Marie joined him.

'I wonder who that was,' he said. 'You don't read Russian, do you?'

'Did it for A level,' said Eva-Marie matter-of-factly, bending over to look at the inscription. She shook her head.

'What does it say?' asked Laurie. In the distance, he could see Horace with the pushy photographer. There was a brief scuffle and the young man departed. Laurie made out the odd muttered word from him as he left – '. . . our lawyers . . . haven't heard the last of this . . .'

Eva-Marie was frowning as she looked at the inscription.

'So, what does it say? You're going to tell me that these are words you didn't get taught for A level.'

'No . . . It's just that, well . . .' Laurie studied her face in what he hoped would appear to be a concerned way, 'it's not very nice.'

'Just give me the translation.'

Eva-Marie lowered her voice. 'I think it says, "I urinate on your grave".'

Chapter Seventeen

'NICE FUNERAL, WAS it?' asked Guy, as he looked at the photos from the whole page dedicated to Old Man Hook's farewell.

'As funerals go,' said Laurie. 'Sweet of you to ask.' He was in the office carrying out his morning cull of overnight emails and fiddling his way despondently through the post. *Police Review*. Press release from Transform about the rise in jail sentences for cannabis use. Details of the ACPO conference. Book launch invitation. Letter from Parkhurst jail on lined paper.

'So do the sons take over the empire now?' said Guy, stroking his slight beard.

'They pretty much have anyway, although I think they want to go legit as soon as possible. You can make almost as much money from legal betting and property deals these days. The old family firms are dying out. The multinationals are taking over.'

'Happy with the pictures?' It was Eva-Marie.

'Um . . . yeah. Nice shot of the horses.'

Why was Eva-Marie smiling at him? Was she trying to tell him something? She looked over his shoulder at the screen, resting her hand on his arm as she did so.

'God, you get a lot of emails from Russian women seeking husbands, don't you? Do you know who left that message on the grave yesterday?'

'No idea,' said Laurie. '"I urinate on your grave." Do you think that's more aggressive than "I spit on your grave"?'

'Interesting thought – depends what you've been drinking, I suppose,' said Guy.

'We're putting a whole lot of the pictures on the website,' said Eva-Marie, whose eyes, Laurie noted, were of different colours. 'Could you pop up and help me label them? I wasn't sure who everyone was.' She tapped his arm again, flashed a smile and turned to go. 'Some time before one, if that's OK? It's the women's lunch today.'

'The women's lunch?'

'Yes, all the women in editorial who are around meet for lunch once a month. It's open to everyone – if they're women, of course.'

'What about a woman trapped in a man's body?'

Eva-Marie rolled her eyes, gave him another smile and was gone.

'Any . . . um . . . er . . . word from Caz?' asked Guy.

'Well, strangely enough, she just texted me today to tell me that she's playing at the Goblin tonight and I should come along and we could "have a chat" afterwards. At least, I think that's what she meant. It said "hv cht". Do you think it could mean something else?'

Guy shrugged. He had turned the page and was studying a feature in that day's paper, a questionnaire entitled Are You A Secret Alcoholic? He read the questions out aloud. 'Number one, do you have a drink first thing in the morning?'

'Sure. Cup of tea.'

'They mean alcoholic drink, clever dick. Number two, have you ever missed a day's work because of your drinking?'

'Oh, that time last month after Stewart's redundo leaving do on the Thames. But I don't think leaving dos count, do they? By the way, there's another leaving do on Thursday. Half of the home subs are taking redundo. Soon there won't be anyone bloody left to bring out the paper.'

'We're not a paper, we are a multimedia information provider. Don't you read your corporate emails? Are you ever unable to remember what happened the previous night as a result of your drinking?'

'I've forgotten what the question was.'

'Ho-ho, kindly leave the stage.'

'Busy, chaps?'

The whiff of Homme Sauvage told Laurie that Stark had arrived.

'Pretty busy,' said Guy. 'There's a new survey on global warming in *Nature*. D'you want something on it?'

'We're all doomed,' said Laurie.

'Great,' said Stark. 'Yes, let's have a look at that. Any word on the Hook murder, Laurie? Or the lecturer? Is he likely to make it? Any sign of the missing fiancée?'

'Oh, I'm sure he will make it,' said Laurie. 'I don't think he hit an artery. Cry for help. No sign of her, though. And as for old Hook, the DCI has promised us all a briefing soon.'

'Any word about the Russian chappie? Extradition proceedings?'

'They don't know where he is yet,' said Laurie. 'In order to start extradition proceedings, you have to have a country to extradite someone from.'

Stark gave him a stony look. 'Hmmm. And, oh yes, have you seen accounts yet? We want to get all that cleared up, don't we?'

Stark spotted someone else at the end of the newsroom. He switched from stony look to spray-on smile and was off.

'You're quite a crawler, aren't you?' said Laurie. 'All this chat about global warming. What was the next question?'

'Do you ever drink more than ten units at a time?'

'How much is a bottle of wine?'

'About seven or eight, I think.'

'And a pint?'

'Two.'

'The answer is yes.'

Laurie rang Daffyd, the press officer at Scotland Yard.

'What's happening? Any news about Vlad the Impaler?'

'If there was, it would be on the website.'

'Next year it would . . . Seriously, I'm being leant on to come up with something.'

'Love to help, Laurie. Enjoy the funeral yesterday? It looked fun.'

'Yes, it was. Some of your team were there as well. Did they see anyone they weren't expecting?'

'If they did, they didn't share it with me. That's my other phone, Laurie. See you at the next CRA meeting.'

Laurie idly checked the Sussex police website on his screen.

'MISSING LECTURER BODY FOUND.' Laurie stood up.

'Question four,' said Guy. 'Has a family member or friend suggested that you are drinking too much?'

'Violet is always saying that I am but Caz used to complain that I didn't drink enough. She used to have a brandy and an espresso first thing when I first met her. Do you think that cancels out? Hang on, I've just got to tell the newsdesk something.'

'I don't think so, I'm afraid. What's made you so cheerful?'

'They've found the body of that woman, Sophie whatsername, the missing lecturer, in Putney, in the garden shed of her fiancé's parents' house. I knew he'd killed her.'

'That cheers you up?'

As Laurie hurried to tell the newsdesk of the new development before they found out about it for themselves, his Internal Prosecuting Counsel cleared his throat.

'Perhaps you could tell us, Mr Lane, why you take pleasure from the misfortune of others?'

'I don't take pleasure from their misfortune, my lord, but I have to admit that the fact I have a big fat story to report that does not involve a great amount of work is sometimes a relief in this highly competitive world of journalism.'

'Do you mean to tell the jury that, at your age, with – what? – more than thirty years in the trade, you put the chance of a by-line higher than the happiness of strangers?'

'I'm not sure I can answer that.'

'Yes?' Stark was saying. 'Yes?'

Laurie realised that Stark must have already asked him a question.

'They've found the body. In Putney.'

Stark seemed to be ignoring him.

'Did you hear what I said? They've found the body.'

'Yes, we heard already. It's on PA. We've sent Rosie down there.'

'But . . . but . . . it's kind of my story.'

'We thought you should be concentrating on getting something more on Hook. And Rosie's going to pod-cast and blog on it, too. And then you have to see accounts, don't you?'

Laurie turned on his heel. The two young male assistant news editors, both staring at their newsdesk screens, were running through the news list.

'Is Paul doing a story about women in sports?' asked one. 'Or is it women in shorts?'

'Grow up,' Linda, the news desk secretary, told them.

As Laurie retreated to his desk, he bumped into Geraldo, the cleaner, removing all the plastic cups from beside the water-cooler. They exchanged world-weary shrugs.

'Question five,' said Guy. 'Do you ever hide bottles from your family?'

'Only from Violet when she has her friends over after that business when they finished half a bloody bottle of Famous Grouse. That doesn't count, does it?'

Laurie's desk phone rang. It was Barry – or was it Brian? – the security guard in reception. He had a visitor. He could tell from the tone of voice that it was a 'visitor' – someone about whom there was a tiny doubt. It usually meant that the person was suffering from some form of mental illness, someone who believed, perhaps, that a monitoring device had been implanted in their palate or that messages were being transmitted to them via their television set. They would have two large plastic bags full of scrawled evidence and display a weary resignation when Laurie explained that he did not think he would be able to help.

But the figure in the shabby white raincoat who greeted him in reception was a familiar one: Gustafson. No one knew his first name but Gustafson made his living by going through the bins of the famous or notorious and selling to newspapers and television companies whatever clues to their lives he found there. He was not the only person in the field – Benji the Binman was better known – but Gustafson's strength was that he apparently had no scruples. He liked to call himself a 'neo-archaeologist', arguing that he was doing the same work as archaeologists but more speedily. He had had a couple of memorable hits: pregnancy test kits found in the bin bags of a teenage soap star, Rizla rolling papers and the fag ends of joints exhumed from the rubbish of a famously proper newsreader. But people had become aware of Gustafson's activities after a Channel 4 documentary about him and the resulting caution amongst the famous and the increased popularity of the shredder had confined him to the occasional hit on an unwary *Big Brother* contestant or footballing wastrel.

Laurie had had dealings with Gustafson only once, when he had arrived at the offices one morning, with two plastic bags full of material which he had removed from the rubbish of a Home Counties chief constable, who was suing Laurie for libel for an article he had written about his behaviour towards a woman officer. The news editor of the time had decided against using the collection of spanking and sado-masochist literature that Gustafson had unearthed, although it appeared over two pages in a Sunday paper a week later and the libel case quietly expired. Laurie had felt in Gustafson's debt ever since.

'Can we talk somewhere?' said Gustafson.

He was dressed in his trademark brogues, tracksuit bottoms, beret and shabby white raincoat. Now it clicked. Gustafson had been that half-familiar figure outside Hook's house the previous week. Gustafson had been cleaning out the Hook family bins.

In the canteen, over a camomile tea for Gustafson – a man of mystery in every way, thought Laurie – and a too-frothy cappuccino for Laurie, Gustafson delved into one of his overflowing plastic bags and produced his findings with the quiet pride of a participant in *Antiques Roadshow* presenting a great-aunt's Georgian carriage clock that had lain forgotten in an attic for fifty years. Over his shoulder, Laurie spotted Eva-Marie at the counter. Did she live off fruit smoothies? Should he get a photo taken of Gustafson's hoard?

Spread out before Laurie on the canteen table were brochures for investment opportunities in real estate in St Petersburg, some of them with question marks scribbled on them, six packets of condoms, an empty packet of Jaffa cakes, two packets of peroxide, an empty bottle of Lyr vodka and perhaps thirty empty bottles of Listerine mouthwash.

'Well, he seems to have liked the peppermint flavour best,' said Laurie eventually. 'This is . . . er . . . interesting stuff, but, well, what do you make of it? Old Man Hook had bad breath – it's going to be kind of hard to make a six hundred-word story out of that. The Russian stuff is certainly very interesting, though. It could suggest that he and Petrov had been doing some business together. Perhaps Old Man Hook was considering investing in real estate in St Petersburg. Eastern European property is still pretty cheap compared to here so perhaps it was a sign that the Hooks were moving their assets out of Britain because it was getting too hot for them here. Maybe Petrov was offering them a way out and, in exchange, he could get the clubs and the casinos . . . Sorry, I'm just thinking aloud. If it had been forty years ago, mind you, we could have suggested he was working for the Soviet Union and then we'd have had an even bigger story. Don't you miss the Cold War?'

'But that peroxide. There are bomb-making recipes on the internet that suggest that you can use peroxide to make explosives and—'

'I've never heard of mouthwash being used to make a bomb. When did you get this stuff?'

'Just after he died and before the rubbish had been cleared away.'

'This is a bit of a change of pace for you, isn't it? Old villains' bins?'

'Business is not so good at the moment. *Big Brother* is off the air. In fact, I don't do much of this any more but he lived just round the corner from my girlfriend and it seemed like too good to miss.'

Eva-Marie, smoothie in hand, was looking curiously at what Gustafson had spread out on the table. Laurie started busily scribbling in his notebook. He found it hard to believe that Gustafson had a girlfriend and wanted to ask about her. He wondered what she looked like. Did they go through bins together? Did she say anything when he brought home piles of potato peelings and used tissues? Did he wash his hands before they had sex?

'Hadn't the police been through them?'

'I don't think they realised they were his. They have to put them at the end of the alleyway and none of them looked like they had been touched. Oh, and there's something else.'

Gustafson rummaged to the bottom of the bag.

'There – thought that might be of interest.'

Laurie spread out the crumpled page of a magazine. It was an old black-and-white photo of a boxer, stripped for action, shoulders forward. Laurie recognised it as Barney Quick, the man of whose murder Hook had been acquitted.

Scrawled across it, in shaky ballpoint pen, were the words: 'Remember me, Charlie? Box on!'

Chapter Eighteen

THE GOBLIN WAS only half full when Laurie arrived at 9.30 p.m. A middle-aged trio of men in faded denim and grey T-shirts, which did nothing for their bellies, was on stage performing a sluggish version of 'Wheels'. Give me bloody wheels, thought Laurie, and take this boy away. Why did I come? He had not been to the Goblin for years, not since he and Caz had come to watch Hank Wangford play. 'Jogging With Jesus' – was that what Hank had sung that night? The place had recently been taken over by a new owner and had been expensively refurbished. There were moody framed photos on the walls, featuring men who looked like the Marlboro cowboy. It had lost its old smoky, beer-soaked charm. Laurie recognised no one; in the days when he had been courting Caz twenty years ago and attending her every show, he had known most of the other singers and promoters on the circuit. Where was she? She had said she had a 'guest spot' for half an hour at ten o'clock. Were they meant to have their 'cht' before or after she sang? He ordered a pint of beer.

'Four pounds? Bloody hell, does that come with a cherry and a cocktail umbrella?'

'We can do that if you want, sir,' said the barmaid, with a

helpful smile and a – Polish? Czech? Lithuanian? – accent.

As he turned away from the bar, he saw her. She was standing by the entrance to the ladies with her guitar slung over her shoulder and, as she tossed her hair away from her face in that familiar way, that heart-stopping way, he caught her smile and felt the same, breathless longing and beguilement that he had experienced all those years ago. What is it about someone flicking the hair back from their face that makes them so desirable? She acknowledged him and approached.

'Hello, stranger, how are you doing?' she said, pecking him on the cheek. He looked over her shoulder and then round the bar. 'It's all right. I'm alone.'

'Did you think I'd take a swing at him?'

'I didn't think you would but maybe one of your heavy friends might.'

'They're outside in the Lagonda with their starting handles up their sleeves just waiting for a nod from me.'

'Always the clown, Laurie.'

'Would you rather I was weepy?'

'That would be a nice change. So how have you been?'

'I miss you.'

'Oh, Laurie, it just wasn't working out. You know that as well as I do.'

'I thought it was quite perfect.'

'No, you didn't. How's work?'

The trio were singing 'Mama Hated Diesel So Bad'.

'They're trying to get rid of me. They've accused me of fiddling my expenses and they want me to become the motoring correspondent. They think I should solve the murder of Old Man Hook on my own. They sense that I am a wounded beast so, like a pack of jackals, they are trying to finish me off.'

'Are you serious? I thought you always said everyone fiddled their expenses. And can you get me a half of cider? I've only got a fifty-pound note.'

'Oh. That should just about cover it . . . Yes, I'm serious.'

'So did you?'

'Did I what?'

'Fiddle your expenses.'

'I'm not going to answer that without my lawyer being present.'

'Look, I've got to do four songs with the boys and then we can have a proper chat. I just thought that it would be easier here rather than back at the house – and I didn't think you would want to come round to Godfrey's place.'

Laurie stared at her.

'He wants to meet you,' she said. 'I know it sounds odd but – you'd like him.'

'Oh, I'm sure I would.'

'By the way, you know I asked you to get me some strings in Denmark Street—'

'Oh, God, yes, they were out of stock, I meant to tell you.'

Caz paused. 'I tried to get hold of you to tell you not to worry – the shop closed last year.' They looked at each other.

The singer from the trio on stage had taken over the microphone and was shielding his eyes from the overhead lights to scan the auditorium.

'I hope she's out there somewhere!' said the singer. 'Our guest tonight needs no introduction, I am sure, to many of you here tonight. A long-time favourite of the Goblin, a former member of the Restless Idlers and the Companions of the Rosy Hours – ladies and gents, please put your hands together for Mizzzz Cazzzz Dupreeeeee!'

Laurie smiled. Her real name was Carol Biggins but her first agent had insisted that she was unbookable on the country circuit under that name. She kissed him on the cheek and was off towards the stage. He wondered how many people noticed her limp, the result of an old motorbike accident long before they had met, which had messed up her knee and hip and which she disguised with a sort of rolling cowboy swagger as she walked. She whispered something to the singer, who nodded and passed it on to the other two on stage, brushed the hair away from her face – a gesture that made his heart skip a beat again – adjusted the strings on her guitar and launched into her version of 'Silver Threads And Golden Needles'. Was it his imagination or did she stare at him as she tightened the strings? She was wearing a silver top he hadn't seen before. Was that Godfrey's idea? Had he bought it for her? When had Laurie last bought her something to wear? He looked round at the audience who were not paying her much attention. The days had passed when, a few drinks down, he would go up to people and tell them to be quiet while she was singing or, if he was with Mick and Vic, tell them to piss off out of it if they didn't want to hear the music – but he found himself still feeling protective towards her.

After two pints, four songs ('Water Into Wine', 'I Made My Excuses and Stayed', 'Ain't We Got Love?' and 'The Streets of Baltimore') and an appeal to buy the CD, he was making room for her at the bar and ordering her another cider. A large fan loomed over them with an ancient LP cover that he wanted her to sign and then they were alone together as the trio cleared the stage in preparation for the main act of the night, a Cajun band from Canada that had had a modest success at Glastonbury the previous year.

'Violet tells me that you're in denial,' said Caz.

'What am I meant to be in?' said Laurie. 'Am I meant to have "moved on" and "drawn a line under it" and reached "closure"?'

'Don't be so angry, Laurie.'

'Why not? I thought you were always wanting me to show my emotions more.'

'I know, I know . . . I'm sorry. It's just, well, I just felt that what we had wasn't going anywhere and – I'm sure you'll find someone too, Laurie.'

'What – speed dating?'

'Well, why not? You like quizzes, don't you? You look pretty good still – I think sadness suits you, you look a bit more drawn and interesting. Why not try a little bit of dye round the old sideburns? Get yourself a haircut, get rid of those shoes. Plus there's a great shortage of halfway decent men in their forties and fifties. You know that. All my girlfriends are saying—'

'Look, Caz, can't we have another go? I'll try and spend more time at home and—'

'Give up your job?'

'I can't do that.'

'Why not?'

'What would I do?'

'Find out about yourself? Do something different? Teach?

We don't need that much money now. Violet's almost grown up.'

The new band were testing out the microphones. The smokers were coming in from the street trailing the whiff of tobacco and traffic.

'Are you saying that, if I get another job, we could get back together again?'

'I think it's a little early for that, Laurie, and I was thinking more of you than, well, of us. But it might be worth thinking about it, mightn't it? You don't want to be defined entirely by your work, do you? Particularly if they don't want you any more.'

'You know how to wound a guy, don't you?'

'Of course I do, I'm a country singer. Is Violet doing her revision?'

'Well, if revision involves lying on the sofa doing infantile phone-in quiz games on the telly, she is. Couldn't you have waited till she'd finished her A levels?'

'It was her that suggested I should go, she said it was too stressful me being there and us not getting on.'

'Weren't we getting on?'

'Oh, Laurie . . . Anyway, is work OK, apart from all the expenses thing? Are you doing the story about that old gangster who got shot?'

'Obviously you study the paper closely.'

'Godfrey gets all his news off the internet so we don't have any papers in the house. Less of a carbon footprint, he says.'

'Good for Godfrey. That's why our circulation is going down. No one is forking out for a paper. Who does he think is going to pay for us to go out on stories? The tooth fairy? Another cider?'

'Sure. Violet can stay with us, you know, but I thought it would be nicer for you to have her.'

'I like having her – she reminds me of you.'

'Oh, God, Laurie, you sound like a bad Porter Wagoner song.'

'You do know how to wound. What's happening to your career, if you don't mind my asking?'

'Couple of gigs in Denmark next month, so I'm trying to see if we can get some more work in Scandinavia. Godfrey's never been there and he's keen to see it.'

'What, before he dies?'

'What?'

'Well, Violet said he was . . . older.'

'He's only a couple of years older than you and he's very fit. He did the London marathon last year.'

'Marvellous. Did he dress up as something? A rabbit or a marrow or something?'

'Bitterness does not become you.'

'Now you sound like Tammy Wynette.'

Caz laughed and, in doing so, spilled some of her cider over Laurie's trousers, just at crotch level. This made her laugh more and she leant her head on his shoulder. For a moment their cheeks touched. He found himself looking at her with sudden desire. The band were singing 'Malheureuse'.

'Oh, another thing that happened at work – someone keeps throwing Guy's trousers into the loos.'

'God, that's weird,' said Caz, dabbing at his trousers with the bar towel. 'What's that all about?'

'Who knows, just one of the many mysteries I must solve. Look, can't we go for a Thai or something now? Do you have to get back?'

Caz looked at her watch. 'I guess I could give Godfrey a ring. Let me go and get my stuff and see if the bastards here are going to pay me.'

She slipped off the bar stool. Laurie turned his attention to the Canadian band as Caz headed for what he remembered as a tiny dressing room. The fiddle player was good, the lead singer a little uncharismatic, the bass too loud but the audience, now almost filling the Goblin, were enjoying it. Never underestimate the power of the fiddle to touch the soul of man. Who had told him that? Some old boy in a bar in Austin, Texas, during the early days, when Caz had thought that the big time beckoned. So long ago now.

A few moments later, leather hat at jaunty angle on her head and guitar slung over shoulder like a rifle, she flashed him that smile again, pausing for a chat with a couple of fans at a table. As she did so, Laurie felt the throb in his pocket. The damn phone. It was a text message.

'Gt 2 Xndu urgt.' It was from Vic. He sighed. He was still shaking his head when Caz joined him.

'Surprise me,' she said. 'I know that look so well. "Something came up" and you have to go.' Before he could answer, she had kissed him lightly on the cheek and was cowboying it out of the bar with just a toss of her hair in farewell.

Chapter Nineteen

F HORACE RECOGNISED Laurie from the funeral, he showed no sign of it. He gave him the same curt nod of admission when he arrived at the door of Xanadu in the Angel. There was, Laurie knew from his previous visit, a 'smart-casual' dress code that forbade trainers, scruffy jeans, singlets and underpants that showed above the waistband. Laurie felt Horace's eyes flicking over his clothes with all the disdain of a fashion editor. He knew his seersucker jacket was too crumpled, his trousers unironed, his office Doc Martens down-at-heel. He headed for the gents.

Once again, he was amazed at the sheer choice of condoms. Whoever had ordered the machine at Xanadu clearly took the same sort of pride in their job as would an organic delicatessen owner. There were condoms flavoured in blackberry and crème de menthe, tangerine and – surely not? – Angostura bitters. They were double ribbed and came in sizes listed as Commando, Cavalry and Special Forces. Which were bigger? he wondered. Probably Special Forces. Was there an SAS version? A policeman had told him once that men arrested for domestic violence often claimed to have been in the SAS but rarely had been. All of which made him think once more, as he stood, involuntarily breathing in the abrasive smell of some strange, fizzing, powder-blue ball in the base of the urinal, of Caz and her sudden departure. How well she knew him. Should he have run after her? Begged her to stay? Ignored Vic's message?

'Do you mean to tell the court, Mr Lane,' said his Internal Prosecuting Counsel, 'that you regarded the possibility of a story through a meeting with a former criminal in an establishment known as a meeting place of other members of the criminal classes as more important than the opportunity of rebuilding a relationship with your wife and the mother of your child?'

'Well, she didn't even give me a chance to talk to her . . .'

'Do you mean to tell this court that, if she had not left, you would have gone for a meal at . . . here I must consult my notes, my lord, I think it is in the blue bundle . . . yes, at the Mar-dun Thai restaurant in Tufnell Park? I would remind you, before you answer, Mr Lane, that you are under oath.'

'Well, I—'

'Please just answer the question, Mr Lane.'

He realised he was standing alone at the urinal and had long since finished his pee. The line about Michael Corleone in *The Godfather* flashed into his head. What was it? Something about not leaving him standing there with his dick in his hand. He wondered if anyone had ever hidden a gun behind the water cistern in the toilet of Xanadu. He looked round. There was only one other person in the gents, a young man with his wide-collared shirt open almost to his waist. Laurie did not catch his eye. He zipped up, washed his hands and held them beneath the electric dryer. Did these dryers really send out emissions of faecal spores? What would a spore look like? Did it matter? Would it have been a good name for a punk band? What had happened to the punk bands that used to play in the Goblin before it went country? Where was Vic?

Outside the gents, he studied the arrows pointing to the various attractions that Xanadu had on offer. Downstairs was dancing. Upstairs, in the Pleasure Dome, was where the lap dancers worked. Along the corridor was Alph's Place, a quieter bar. A smaller arrow pointed to the Kubla Khan room which was for invited guests only. Vic would be in Alph's, he guessed. He was right.

'You OK?' said Vic as he gestured him towards a bar stool.

'Yeah, yeah.'

'Caz?'

'Don't ask.'

He did not ask Vic about his love life either. There was an unhappy ex-wife, he knew, and a couple of grown-up children but his girlfriends always looked much younger than him, were usually middle-class and rarely seemed to be long on the scene. Vic was alone at the bar, nursing his ginger ale.

'You called,' said Laurie.

'That's right,' said Vic. 'Someone wants to see you.'

'That sounds ominous. Have I been seen running in the school corridors?'

'I'm trying to help you out, Laurie. I thought you were in a bit of bother at work.'

'I appreciate it, I really do. Did you enjoy the funeral?'

'I don't think a funeral's a funeral unless there's bagpipes myself.' Vic allowed his handsome, matinee-idol face to break into a smile. 'What are you having to drink?'

Laurie had just put his hand round a bottle of Peroni beer – £5? they must be joking – when Vic jogged his elbow.

Two women, wearing nothing but red thongs and matching high heels, strode in. One had a little pink towel slung over her shoulder, the other was looking for her cigarettes in her handbag. They were both blondes. One was nearly six foot tall, with low-slung breasts that swung as she walked, the other, almost flat chested, about a foot shorter. Laurie caught the eye of the taller of the pair. A phrase shot into Laurie's head. Breasts like hunting horns. Where had he read that?

The women seemed completely at ease, as though strolling almost naked through a roomful of men was the most natural thing in the world. In a way, it is, thought Laurie. Man is born naked but everywhere is in vest and pants, as Guy liked to say when he came back from his runs. The taller one flashed a smile in Laurie's direction. What is the etiquette with naked strangers? wondered Laurie. Do you look them in the eye? The woman approached. They were obviously eastern European.

'Any chance of a drink?' asked the taller one. She was Scottish.

'Er . . .' Laurie knew he had a fixed grin on his face.

'Don't worry,' said the woman. 'We're not working. You don't have to pay to get us a drink. Crispin sent us down to say he'd be here in a minute.'

'I was just going to say that I was sure you were from eastern Europe,' he said limply.

'Near enough. East Fife – Kingsbarns. And mine's a vodka tonic,' said the woman. She nodded at her shorter companion. 'Valentina'll have a rum and Coke. A large one.'

'Is she from eastern—'

'Sunderland,' said the shorter friend. 'Is that east enough for you?'

'Things busy?' asked Laurie. It was what he always asked minicab drivers as an ice-breaker.

'Aye,' said the Scot. 'Bunch of Chelsea fans in. What a crowd of wankers. You a reporter?'

'Er . . . yes,' said Laurie.

'Can you get my picture in the papers?'

'Er . . . it's not really that sort of—'

'Only kidding. What's your name?'

'Laurie. And yours?'

'Desdemona?'

'Really?'

'What d'you think?' With her towel, she wiped a mist of sweat from her breasts. Laurie followed her gesture and she caught his glance and shrugged.

'What d'you need to be a reporter?'

'A lack of scruples and a fertile imagination,' said Vic, who had swivelled round on his bar stool. The two women smiled and moved closer towards them. The Scotswoman bent towards Laurie as if to whisper something to him. Her breast touched his chest. There was a flash. Someone had taken a photo with their phone. He cast his gaze round the room but was distracted by a hand squeezing his upper arm.

'Hello, Laurie. Good to see you at the funeral,' said Crispin. 'The family liked the write-up you did in the paper. Not like that crap in some of the rubbish papers. Do you want to come into the Kubla Khan room? Thanks, girls.'

The two women melted away. Laurie caught their back views as they headed for the door. A male hand reached out to pat the Scotswoman's bottom and she slapped it away without looking round at the groper, like a thoroughbred swishing its tail at a horsefly.

There was a slightly smaller version of Horace standing outside the entrance to the Kubla Khan room. Laurie had noticed a sign to it on previous visits but had never been invited inside before. There were two large white leather sofas with a low glass table between them. Crispin gestured to Vic and Laurie to take a seat and went to the bar. 'Famous Grouse, isn't it, Laurie?' How does he know that? wondered Laurie. He also seemed to know that Vic was a teetotaller. Laurie watched to see what Crispin poured for himself. It looked like vodka. What was he putting in it? Cranberry juice? Laurie was starving. Would it be rude to ask if there was any chance of a sandwich? Crisps even. Maybe it would. There was a moody black-and-white framed photo of Old Man Hook above the bar. Bailey? Donovan? He was about to ask but thought better of it.

'Vic tells me that you are interested in helping to bring the people who murdered our father' – Laurie knew he was speaking for the family but 'our father' still gave the dead gangster an almost biblical quality – 'to justice. We are not sure that the police are one hundred per cent committed to finding the . . .' Was he going to say evil-doer? Or bastard? '. . . perpetrator so we have been carrying out our own inquiries. Now, I know as well as anyone that you are innocent until proved guilty and, obviously, if we are seen in certain places, it will look like we are taking the law into our own hands. But . . .' Crispin paused to sip his vodka and whatever, 'what I wanted to know was whether or not you might be in a position to go to the place where we believe my father's killer is. It would be quite a story, wouldn't it? Showing that you had tracked him down while the Old Bill were dragging their feet?' He paused and raised an elegant eyebrow – did he pluck them? – at Laurie.

What am I meant to do now? wondered Laurie. Say that, of course, I would happily go and confront the gang who bumped off your old man? That would certainly take his mind off Caz and Stark and the job. He wanted to say, 'I would love to help but my daughter is about to do her A levels and I should really make sure she does her revision.' But the words didn't come out. Instead: 'Sure, I would be interested in doing that. Obviously, I will have to check at work.'

'Of course,' said Crispin, warming now to his theme. 'You see, we're already hearing on the grapevine . . . You're an educated man, Laurie, where does that expression "on the grapevine" come from?'

This is like pub quiz night, thought Laurie. He looked towards Vic for assistance.

'Funny you should ask,' said Vic. 'I do know. There was this linguistics academic from Cambridge who was in Wandsworth with me on some iffy indecent exposure thing . . . I think he said that it comes from the States and that the original telegraph wires there in the nineteenth century—'

There was a slight tap at the door and Horace junior poked his head round.

'Sorry to interrupt, Crispin,' he said.

'The man from Porlock,' said Vic. Crispin shot him a puzzled look.

'We'll be another five minutes, Phil,' said Crispin. He was

no longer concerned about the origins of the grapevine expression. 'The thing is this. We have people . . . acting for us. In a few days, we should be able to tell you something that I think you and your paper will find quite interesting. What I wanted to find out is whether or not you would be up for that, whether you might be able to go somewhere . . . Really, we wanted to know if you were – serious.'

Oh, God, thought Laurie, what does that mean? He tried to catch Vic's eye again but Vic was studying the label of his ginger ale bottle as though it was one of the Dead Sea Scrolls. He tried a hearty smile but then realised that that was not appropriate. His eye flashed to the photo of Old Man Hook in the silver frame above the bar. It was between two paintings, which looked like recent purchases as both had red spots on them. The photo must have been taken a few years ago, probably when Old Man Hook was in his early sixties. He was handsome still, with his big aquiline nose, his thick, wavy grey hair and his sulky lips.

'Bailey,' said Crispin, catching his smile. 'Good, isn't it?'

'And the paintings?'

'Boshier,' said Crispin. 'Derek Boshier, contemporary of Hockney. Saw them in a gallery in Hoxton last month and bought them on a whim.' He delivered the word 'whim' with a little spin to it, as if to let Laurie know that a 'whim' was something that he could act on very easily and that a 'whim' was something that might cut both ways. 'Do you collect art, Laurie?'

'No, not really,' said Laurie. What was there hanging in the house? He tried to remember. Something Violet had painted at school during an earnest, fourteen-year-old phase. Had Caz taken the only valuable painting, the little Paula Rego that her uncle had given them for a wedding present? How much was it worth now? From the club's bowels came an urgent bass beat. When did I last have a dance? he thought. Concentrate, concentrate.

'So,' said Laurie. 'What you're saying is that you think the people responsible for this . . .'

'We know who's responsible, Laurie,' said Crispin. 'But they are slippery customers and we don't want them to get away with it. The Old Bill – well, you saw some of them at the funeral, didn't you? I think you were having a word with them. The Old Bill aren't too bothered. As far as they are concerned this is a slag-on-slag killing, that's what they used to call it, didn't they, but slag means something a bit different nowadays, doesn't it? Yes, as long as it's villains taking lumps out of each other or black-on-black killings, they're not too troubled. They are quite happy for Mr Petrov and his chums to be off the scene for the time being. But for the family, for my mother, there's a bit more in this. I don't want to see, in ten years' time, some tosser on a telly series about great unsolved crimes putting his snout into my dad's grave. Do you follow? By the way, what did the old boy have to say to you when you were having tea together?'

'Oh, we hadn't really got to that stage,' said Laurie. 'It was just, you know, would I be able to work with him on a book. Very vague really.'

'Is that so?' said Crispin. 'He didn't say he wanted to chat about the Krays or Ginger Mulgrew or Barney Quick or the old days?'

'No, I don't think that came up,' said Laurie. 'He was just

chatting a bit about the old days and his charity work and—'

'His charity work?' said Crispin, raising an eyebrow. 'He told us that you'd been pumping him about bent cops and all of that sort of stuff. I wonder why he said that. Anyway, fancy another Famous Grouse?'

'Er . . . yes, thanks. How did you know that was what I drank?'

'On the grapevine, Laurie. On the grapevine.'

There was another tap on the door. Crispin pushed back the cuff of his dark suit and examined his watch. He was short sighted, thought Laurie, but too vain to wear specs. Crispin shrugged and looked at Vic who shrugged back at him.

'Come in, it's not locked,' said Crispin.

The door was thrown open and there, in scarlet dress with plunging neckline, hint of black lace bra, a forearm's worth of matching scarlet bangles, hands on hips and seductively quizzical smile, stood Mrs Plimsoll.

'Hello, dear,' said Crispin. 'Dressed to kill, are you?'

Chapter Twenty

VIOLET WAS STILL up when Laurie arrived home. The television was on. Some seventies film, to judge by the haircuts and the suit lapels. There was a glass in front of her. She was angry with him.

'That was very smart, wasn't it?'

'What was?'

'Meeting up with Mum and then running off on some silly story, just like you always did.'

'So I've been convicted without my brief being allowed to make a speech in my defence, have I? What's that you're drinking?'

'Lime cordial, since you ask. More to the point, what have you been drinking? You smell like one of those blokes on the Green.'

'I had one whisky – and don't roll your eyes. I'm not doing A levels in the morning.'

'Liar. Nor am I.'

'I thought it was tomorrow.'

'If you listened, you would know it's on Friday and, yes, I have been revising although that was interrupted by my mother ringing me to tell me that my father had invited her for dinner and then stood her up.'

'It wasn't quite like that. Look, it wasn't me that ran off with another woman.'

'Well, you've been around someone who wears a lot of perfume tonight. Where have you been?'

Laurie inhaled. She was right. There was a vague whiff of whatever Beth Plimsoll had been wearing.

'Xanadu.'

'You must be joking!'

'No. Vic rang me about a story and that's where he wanted to meet.'

'That is so SAD. A man of your age going to Xanadu. That's where all the girls at school who want to pull blokes from the City go. They think it's trendy. Were you in the Pleasure Dome? I can't believe it. I hope none of my friends were there. Were people doing lots of coke in the bathroom?'

Laurie sat down on the sofa beside her. She had been crying. He moved to put his arm round her shoulder but she pulled away.

'No, and I wasn't dancing, you'll be relieved to hear. I had a drink with Vic and someone else.'

'The Hooks own it, don't they? Was it about that murder? Who cares if he got killed, he's had lots of other people killed. You think they're so romantic, don't you, but they're just businessmen with guns.'

'Look, I—'

'You're not going to say "I'm only doing my job", are you?'

'Probably I was. Look, about your mum. She was very adamant that she didn't want to get back together. You know that. What am I meant to do? Come on, there're plenty of times when she got work and it scuppered everything. Remember when we were going to Italy on holiday and we had to cancel because she got offered two nights at Dingwalls and then it never happened? I didn't make a fuss about that.'

'No, you're only bringing it up again after ten years. Why is it so important that you find out what happened to Hook, anyway? Can't the police do that?'

'Probably not. The Hooks seem to think that the guy who did it is out of the country now and they think they know where he is. It's just that they want to get rid of me at work so I am trying to show them that I am indispensable.'

'That's pathetic. Why don't you do something different anyway?'

'Like what?'

'I dunno. You don't have many skills, do you.' It was a statement, not a question.

'So how're things going with revision? Shouldn't you be getting your sleep in?'

'Don't change the subject. It's OK. I know I'm going to fail.'

'I didn't think anyone failed A levels any more. We always seem to have a picture of happy girls in V-necked pullovers jumping in the air when the results are announced. Doesn't everybody get something?'

'God, you're not going to do that "it's so much easier than when I did it" stuff, are you?'

'No, I'm sure it's not: Well, I'm knackered and I'm going to hit the sack. What time shall I wake you up?'

'I don't feel like getting up.'

'Oh, Violet, I know it's hard. You have to just try and

concentrate on the exams, try and only think of them for the next two weeks. Then it'll be holidays and summer and everything will look different.'

The tears were rolling down Violet's face. Laurie put his arm round her again. This time she leaned her head against his shoulder. They stared at the television together. A man with an Afro and wearing a yellow suit with flared trousers was running after two men in dark glasses. There were sounds of gunshots. A woman screamed.

'Isn't there anything else on?' Laurie asked after a few minutes.

Violet was fast asleep.

Chapter Twenty-one

THE MEETING WAS in the Human Resources office on the tenth floor. Human Resources, or HR, as they referred to themselves, had taken over from Personnel five years ago and had flourished since, increasing in size from two middle-aged women who pruned job applications to a team of eight who sent out regular reports of their activities, with titles like Meeting the Corporate Challenge and Towards Excellence. One of them, a young woman called Marcia, was already in their meeting room when Laurie and Rosie, a thirtyish reporter who was his National Union of Journalists representative, arrived for his appointment to discuss 'issues regarding expenses' with the accounts department and Stark. He was glad Rosie was there. She seemed undaunted by authority.

Laurie was tired. He had not slept well, had had a row with Violet before he left for work and she for school and had cut himself shaving. Again. There was an irritating spot of dry blood on the collar of his light-blue shirt.

'Right,' said Marcia from HR, with what was clearly intended to be a conciliatory smile. 'Perhaps the best idea would be if we were to all introduce ourselves and to mutually agree on the ground rules.'

And see how many infinitives you can split in one sentence, thought Laurie. His Internal Prosecuting Counsel kicked in: 'Do you really think that splitting the infinitive matters at all any more?'

'My name is Marcia and I'm a senior human resources consultant,' she said, with a sweet smile at the young man from accounts who looked as though he would rather not be there.

'My name is John and I am the assistant executive manager, expenses.'

Marcia nodded at Stark.

'My name is Gavin Stark and I am the executive news editor.'

'My name is Rosie and I am the chapel representative for home news.' The slowly widening beam that was Marcia's smile shone on Laurie.

'My name is Laurie and I am an alcoholic . . . Oh, sorry, wrong meeting. I am a crime correspondent.'

The joke had not gone down well. Stark was already playing with his BlackBerry but glanced up long enough to shoot a look that, if it would not quite kill, would inflict internal bleeding. The man from accounts looked at his watch. Marcia took control.

'Now, the important thing to remember is that this is a pre-resolution strategy meeting which means that everyone can say what they want, without prejudice, with the intention of seeking a solution agreeable to all parties and before a representative from the NUJ is involved at national level. Perhaps John could kick things off.'

John, looking even more as though he would rather be

anywhere else in the world, took a pile of receipts and forms from a folder and started running through them, mumbling almost inaudibly. Laurie vaguely recognised his own scrawled handwriting. Stark cast a suspicious eye over the paperwork. He saw what he was looking for.

'Ah, this is a receipt for "meal with senior police contacts",' said Stark, dealing a bill from Zetters across the table as if it was the ace of spades. 'But I think I'm right in saying that, on the same day, you were supposedly in Blackpool at a Police Federation conference.'

'Transmigration of souls,' said Laurie. He vaguely remembered the meal. It had been with Vic and Mick. How many bottles of wine had it been? Had there been brandies?

Marcia intervened. 'Now, perhaps I should spell out the parameters within which the company is required to act under the Companies Act,' she said. 'As we have to submit these receipts to the tax inspectorate, any incorrect information included could leave us liable, as a company, to the charge of fraud. That is why –' she flashed a toothpaste commercial smile at Laurie – 'we have to be completely frank. Now, Laurie, has there possibly been something of a misunderstanding . . .'

'You don't have to answer that, Laurie,' said Rosie.

'Look, I had hoped that I had made this clear,' said Marcia. 'This is still an informal process.'

'Then why are you tape-recording it?' asked Rosie.

Marcia paused for just the hint of a beat. 'Purely as an aide memoire. I am more than happy to give you the tape after the meeting so that everything is transparent.'

The word 'transparent' made Laurie think involuntarily of

what Eva-Marie had been wearing when he saw her in the lift. That blouse. Had she noticed his glance?

'Look, can I just explain something in general terms,' said Laurie. 'Often I don't fill in the expenses until ages after the event. I forget the exact date but I know that you –' he nodded at John, the blushing young man from the expenses department – 'I know that you have to have one so I always put one down. It may be wrong. That's what has happened here. No intention to deceive.'

Stark could not contain himself any longer. 'If a chief constable had used that as an excuse for fiddling his expenses, how understanding do you think we would be?'

'Well, a chief constable would be on about twice my salary and would have a full-time secretary to process all that information so I don't think that would apply,' said Laurie. He could tell from the frown on Rosie's face that she did not regard this as a fruitful defence. Clearly, neither did Stark.

'What you're saying is that people who are paid less than a hundred thousand a year are entitled to fiddle their exes? Is that right?'

'He didn't say that at all,' said Rosie. Her chin jutted out. Laurie wanted to tell her that he liked the cut of her jib but he knew Rosie might tell him to piss off. Guy, whose own marriage had ended a year or so ago, had asked him once if Rosie was single.

Marcia's smile beamed around the table, a benign searchlight.

'Now, I think we're all getting a little ahead of ourselves,' she said. 'Perhaps if John could be allowed to explain the areas where there is some . . . confusion . . . we can clear things up here and now. If, of course,' she fixed her smile on Laurie, 'if there is goodwill all round.'

Laurie's head was throbbing. Stark seemed to have double-dosed on the Homme Sauvage this morning. The smell was intense. Did some people really like it? If Laurie wore it, would it help him meet someone new? Would he want to meet someone who was attracted to that smell? Would Caz ever come back? His head was exploding.

'Look, this is all bollocks,' said Laurie. 'If you think I've fiddled my expenses, say so and we'll fight it out but spare us all this fucking pussy-footing around. And let's have full disclosure. Can we see exactly what Stark – what Gavin – has claimed in terms of expenses over the last five years and can we submit that to the same scrutiny on the understanding that whoever has fiddled more will resign on the spot? I would be happy for that.'

There was a long silence, broken eventually by a gentle sigh from Rosie.

'Just tell me,' said Rosie, as they walked down the stairs to the newsroom together after the meeting had reached its abrupt end, 'did you intend to do that right from the start or did you just have a rush of blood to the head?'

'The latter,' said Laurie. 'I've been having a lot of rushes of blood to different parts of the body over the last week, Rosie, as I watch my life slowly fall apart.'

'Let's not go there,' said Rosie. 'And just remember, there is nothing women find less appealing than a man who feels sorry for himself.'

'I'm sorry I said that stuff upstairs but Stark was just getting right up my nose. This is all about trying to get rid of me. If I was one of the blue-eyed boys, I could have charged for a night at Stringfellows and he would have been perfectly happy.'

Rosie patted his arm as they reached the newsroom's floor. 'I know. And I enjoyed the intervention. I had to look away in case Laughing-boy saw me smiling. But you have to watch your back, Laurie. You're just giving them loads of ammunition. Let's talk later.' She patted him on the arm again and headed for her desk, her screen, her ringing phone.

'How did it go?' asked Guy.

'There was a full and frank exchange of views,' said Laurie.

'That bad? Should I start the collection for your going-away present? I've just heard that half the obits department are taking redundo – you could have a joint going-away do with them.'

'Not a bad idea. But don't get me one of those big shiny embossed cards with "We're Gonna Miss You!" on it. And do make a note of how much everyone gives. By the way, has there been any more . . . er . . . trouser activity?'

'I haven't been for a run this week. I thought you were going to solve this anyway. Haven't you made any inquiries? You're not taking it seriously anyway, I know.'

'First they came for the red trouser-wearers and I did nothing because I did not wear red trousers . . . Look, I've been busy solving murders,' said Laurie. 'But I did think of introducing a sort of Trouserhood Watch, you know, asking people to report suspicious behaviour. You don't look too convinced.'

'Go on. Treat it as a joke.'

'I know, Guy, but it's like that Graham Greene story, the

one about the little English boy whose father is killed in Naples when a pig falls off a balcony on top of him. You don't know it? What was it called? "A Shocking Accident", I think. Anyway, the little boy is at prep school in England – I think that's right – and his headmaster calls him into his room to break the news of his father's death and he tells the little boy that his father has been killed in Naples. And the little boy says, "Was he shot, sir?" and the headmaster says, "No," but when he tries to tell him exactly what happened, he can't stop laughing. And the little boy goes through life having to deal with the fact that, whenever he tells anyone how his father died, whether it's girls he fancies or whatever, they can't stop themselves giggling about it, however badly they feel about it.'

'And your point is?'

'Well, Guy, I can't help it. If someone had nicked your wallet in the showers, then people would be righteously pissed off on your behalf, but can't you just change in the gents and bring all your stuff back and shove it under your desk? Do you have to leave your trousers hanging up in the shower cubicle?'

'I just feel that that would be to concede to them.'

'You mean that that would mean the trouser-flushers had won?'

'There you go again. It's all a joke to you.'

'Look, Guy, I've been deserted by my wife, I'm about to be sacked, I'm meant to solve a gangland murder and you want me to feel your pain over a pair of damp red flannels. You shouldn't wear red trousers anyway. Only nobs with names like Peregrine wear red trousers.'

'They're not flannels, they're moleskin,' said Guy, draining his cappuccino, 'but I take your point. No word from Caz, is there? I saw a picture of her in *Time Out* – she looked great.'

'Probably an old photo.'

'Probably. Did Rosie represent you in the meeting?'

'Yeah, she did. She's good.'

'I know. Is she a Trot, d'you think? Who d'you think make the best union representatives – Trots, Tankies or liberals?'

Laurie shook his head at him and started flicking through his emails. Russian Lady Seeks British Man Friend, leaving do, Crime Reporters Association annual general meeting, Viagra, Congratulations – You Have Won £500,000. ACPO briefing. Latvian woman seeks sincere friendship. Who replied to these? he wondered. Someone must. Just as someone must get suckered in by all the Nigerian scams that offered a share of the £50 million that was just seeking a home in someone's British bank account. What was it like for the Russians and the Latvians and the Lithuanians? Did they ever find love? Or was it all another scam, a ploy to take advantage of lonely middle-aged men in car coats and tasselled shoes? What did they do on a first date? What if the Russian economy really boomed? Would there be English women and Welsh women advertising themselves in *Pravda*? He clicked through the offers. Guy tapped him on the shoulder, wondering if he wanted a coffee from the trolley. Laurie declined the coffee and clicked on. He knew it was unwise to open attachments but he did not feel in a wise mood. Was this a human trafficking scam? That would make a story.

The Latvian woman attachment scrolled its way open on his screen. It showed a couple of women in basques, pouting at the camera. He realised that someone was standing at his shoulder, also looking at the screen. It was Eva-Marie.

'Oh, sorry,' she said. 'Am I interrupting something?'

'Let me explain,' he said. But before he could, his phone rang. He did not recognise the voice immediately. Was the caller saying they were called Chris? He asked them to repeat themselves. It was Crispin.

'How's things?' said Crispin.

'Oh . . . just fine and dandy,' said Laurie.

'Got an up-to-date passport?'

Chapter Twenty-two

'THEY SEEM TO make the distance between the seats shorter every time I fly,' said Laurie to the woman sitting next to him. He said the same thing to whomever he sat beside on a plane. When he had first flown abroad for the paper, nearly twenty years ago, on what turned out to be an inevitably fruitless search for Lord Lucan in Kampala, he had travelled first class. But those days had long gone, the victim of the scrutiny of people like John in accounts. Reporters flew economy. It was nearly a week since the meeting over the expenses and the memory of it made Laurie shudder.

'Too cold for you?' said his neighbour. She looked Asian, about forty. Big smile, long red nails. Dark red nails. Burgundy nails, he decided. She had a Yorkshire accent. 'Shall I turn it down?' She indicated the little air-conditioning nozzle above them.

'No, I'm fine, thanks,' said Laurie. 'I was shuddering about something completely different.'

'You running away from something too?' she said.

It was the 'too' that made Laurie warm towards her. Was he running away? Well, not exactly. He was heading for Bangkok. He had £1,000 in expenses in his pocket, signed over to him by a very wary-looking John, a *Rough Guide to Thailand* tucked into his laptop case. His suncream had been confiscated by security at the airport.

'In a way, yes,' said Laurie, giving her what he hoped was his enigmatic smile.

'Me, too,' said the woman. 'I got back with my ex-husband after ten years away and it was a bloody disaster. We both realised after about a week in the house together that it was a big mistake so this is me giving myself a holiday to celebrate getting divorced twice from the same bloke. Been to Thailand before?'

'No, never have, never been anywhere in Asia,' said Laurie. 'But my daughter came here last year with some friends so she gave me some tips.'

'I bet she did,' said the woman. 'I'm Flo, by the way. I work in social services in Sheffield.'

Do I tell her what I do? Is this not meant to be a secret assignment? What if the other papers found out where he was?

'Don't worry, darling, I'm not going to ask you what you do,' she said. 'I've been up since four a.m. so I'm going to kip now. Wake me up when they bring the meal, would you? And if I talk in my sleep, just give me an elbow. That was what my husband said was the breaking point for him. For me, it was him snoring. Why do men have to snore so bloody loudly?'

'I think it's something to do with our different nasal-larynx passages or something like that,' said Laurie. The paper had run a whole-page piece on it the other day, complete with ten possible cures for snoring. What were they? There was an operation you could have, apparently, and a plaster you could attach to your nose, a clamp you could put between your teeth, like the gum shields rugby players and boxers wore, or you could abandon your pillows and sleep flat and then . . . He was about to share this with Flo when he heard her deep breathing. She was already fast asleep. It was a gentle, comforting sound and reminded him of Caz. He checked to see what new films were available on the tiny screen. None were ones he wanted to see and he was not sure he could be bothered watching *The Graduate* again. The photographer who had been assigned to accompany him was CJ, a tall, middle-aged south Londoner with a face like a horse – a nice, slightly startled, about-to-bolt horse – who suffered from depression and a bad back but was good in tight corners. He had installed himself in an aisle seat far from Laurie.

Crispin Hook had been very explicit. Vladimir Petrov, the man who had killed his father, was holed up in Pattaya, in Thailand. He even gave him the name of the bar where he would be found. Why are you telling me this? Laurie asked himself. Why don't you just hire a hitman out there? Or, if you want him to stand trial, why don't you get someone to tip off Scotland Yard anonymously? Pattaya was the new Costa del Crime, the place where British criminals on the run went to hide out. There was an extradition treaty with Britain but the process was slow and in an emergency you could always slip across the border to Cambodia, where there was none. It was one of the easiest places in the world to get a new identity. Fresh passport, £600. Any nationality. Even a US passport. Most of the British criminals avoided drug-dealing, too great a risk of spending time in jail, but there were plenty of ways to make an honest dishonest living: selling fake replica football shirts and Gucci handbags online, handling the security for a little beachfront bar, property deals with the Russians and Arabs who were moving into the region. Just as the British criminals who, if not on the run, were travelling at jogging pace, were settling in to Pattaya and Phuket, the more adventurous in Chiang Mai, so, too, were other villains from different parts of Europe. Russians, Bulgarians, Romanians now all had their little Asian bolt-holes.

After Crispin's call, Laurie had been in a quandary. Should he tell Stark that he could locate the man that the police wanted to trace? Crispin had been very specific: this was information for him only, he did not want it passed on to Scotland Yard. Why? Laurie asked himself again. But if he told Stark, would he insist that they tell the police? The spectre of the Ronnie Biggs fiasco hovered in the air: a reporter from the *Daily Express* had been offered an interview with the fugitive train robber Biggs in Brazil and had then tipped off the police, who duly tried to arrest him in Rio de Janeiro. An ill-fated move. While most attention had focused on Jack Slipper, the detective who had failed to bring Biggs home, the behaviour of the *Daily Express* had confirmed the view of the criminal fraternity that reporters were little more than coppers with notebooks and not to be trusted. And would Stark instruct him to get on the next plane out? What about Violet's A levels? But what if he didn't go and the story appeared somewhere else, when he was meant to be the reporter with the inside track? He had sat on it overnight, kept Crispin at bay by telling him that they were having difficulty getting a flight and then finally told Stark, who seemed remarkably keen on the idea. This in itself made Laurie suspicious. Did he want him to fly to Thailand and fail to come up with anything? Or was this his big chance to redeem himself? We Find the Man Wanted for Gangland Murder. Or perhaps Stark secretly hoped he would get himself killed.

Stark had been anxious that he should get on the first plane out. Violet had been very understanding. Caz had said she would, if necessary, come back and stay in the house until Violet's exams were over. Would the hated Godfrey come too, he had wanted to ask but had managed not to. In his bedroom? Was he meant to have any vaccinations? Who cared? Might as well die of malaria or cholera. Then Caz would really be sorry. How many words of obituary would he get from the paper? Six hundred, if he was lucky. An old, unflattering black-and-white photo, possibly, from the time when he first joined the paper and before his hair had started to turn from black to grey. But with that bad moustache. A couple of probably inaccurate anecdotes, a mention of the time he had been nominated for, but had not won, the reporter of the year award some fifteen or sixteen years ago; that night when there had been a fight between a drunk reporter and the news editor of another paper. Broken glasses, blood on white shirts, embarrassment, recriminations in the gents. Some tosser had won the award for a story about Princess Diana.

The drinks trolley had come and gone and the pilot, a droll Scot, was informing them of their altitude. Laurie glanced across at the central aisle. One man was gesturing frantically for a steward. What was it about long flights that infantilises people, Laurie wondered, so that they have to ask constantly for blankets and pillows and glasses of water? Flo had woken up.

'So is this a holiday for you?' she asked.

'Not exactly.'

'Hoping to meet some ladies, are you?'

'No, no, that's not on the agenda,' he said. Did I really say that? he asked himself. Did I really say 'that's not on the agenda'?

'Oh, I see,' she said.

'Oh, no, it's not like that either, I'm not . . . I'm, you know . . .'

'You're trying to say that you're not a paedophile, is that right? Oh, there's the hostess or whatever they call themselves nowadays. Can you catch her eye? I missed the drinks and I'm dying for a G and T. It's all right, love, I didn't think you were a paedo and you don't have to tell me what you're doing. I was just being nosy. What part are you going to? Phuket?'

Should he tell her? Thousands of people went to Pattaya but, if he said Pattaya, wouldn't that mean that he was admitting that he was on the hunt for bar girls? He could say that he was going to Chiang Mai and explain that he was interested in Mon and Karen artefacts. Or he could pretend to be asleep so that he would avoid her cross-examination. But he did not want to miss lunch.

'I haven't quite decided yet,' he said. Spread some mystery around. 'I want to explore a bit.'

'Of course you do, love,' said Flo. She had her gin and tonic now and was sucking on the lemon. She had a big wide smile. I am technically single now, thought Laurie.

Just before they were due to come in to land, CJ came down the aisle to say he felt unwell.

Laurie introduced him to Flo as 'my colleague'. Would she

think they were both sex tourists? Thailand had the highest ratio of single men holidaymakers of any country in the world, or so the travel editor had informed him when he borrowed his *Rough Guide*. CJ had made a couple of oblique references when they were checking in. 'Will there be time for a little social recreation?' he had asked. Laurie hoped CJ would not hit one of his lows during the trip. He pushed the thought away, it was unworthy of him; CJ had once rescued him from an angry Moss Side crowd who thought Laurie was a cop, when they were covering a story of drive-by shootings in Manchester. He had gone to the picture desk to see Eva-Marie and to explain that he would need a photographer to come to Thailand with him. Eva-Marie was as friendly as ever. She had even said, 'I wish I could come myself. We would have fun.' What could that mean? CJ's depressions had the upside that he did not care if he lived or died and was thus fearless and did not panic in a crisis. If they had a confrontation with Vladimir Petrov, that could be very handy.

But what if they never found Vlad? Would Stark hold it against him? Was this the whole point of the trip, so that he would mess up at great expense and Stark would be able to say 'I told you so'? Even Violet had thought the whole idea was crazy.

'What are you going to do if you see him? Go "tig"?' she had asked him. 'Aren't you worried that he'll shoot you too?'

'Well, if he shoots me, won't that more or less guarantee you get through your A levels on compassionate grounds?' he told her. 'And imagine your street credibility rating. "Dad shot dead by gangster" – it'll go through the roof.'

The Scottish pilot was informing his passengers of their

imminent arrival at Bangkok airport and asking them to return to their seats in tones of mild condescension.

'I'll see you in the baggage reclaim place,' said CJ as he left them.

'We really are colleagues, by the way,' said Laurie to Flo. 'We haven't come for sex.'

'Whatever you say, pet,' said Flo, arching one eyebrow. 'Now fasten your seat belt like the nice man said.'

Chapter Twenty-three

THE AIM WAS to take a wander down the main tourist streets of Pattaya, as if they were tourists, to carry out their reconnaissance. Laurie put on the shorts that Caz had bought for him when they had been on holiday in Corsica the previous year. His legs looked pearly white and was that the hint of varicosity in the vein on his left calf?

It was only 10 a.m. and already it was hot. What time was it in England? He should ring Violet to wish her well in her exams. He should have arranged for Interflora to send her good-luck flowers. No, she would have thought that lame. He pulled on a plain black T-shirt and a pair of sandals from that same over-priced beach shop in Corsica and walked along the corridor of the Pattaya Lux Resort hotel to tap on CJ's door.

CJ was already assembling his camera equipment and was dressed in a pair of baggy battledress trousers with lots of pockets down the side and a khaki T-shirt.

'Dressed for action?' he asked.

CJ gave him a brief 'whatever' shrug.

'I was just going to take a small camera with me this time, in case we spot him,' said CJ. 'I know you don't want to alert him so I could just hang it round my neck like a tourist. Do you know what you're going to do if you see him?'

'Good question.'

'So you haven't thought about it.' CJ shook his head. 'No probs. I'd rather spend a few days here than be taking pictures of pricks outside Parliament or flood victims in Dorset. Take as long as you like.'

'I wish I could.'

They went through Mike's Shopping Mall and strolled along Walking Street. Most of the bars were still empty. A few Europeans were emerging from their hotel rooms and service flats and ordering Full English Breakfasts from the bars and cafés, copies of British newspapers spread in front of them, beside the HP Sauce and tomato ketchup. A bar girl or two in high heels, denim shorts and crop-tops leant lazily against the serving counters. Pop music – George Michael, Bruce Springsteen and sounds that Laurie did not recognise – echoed from the kitchens.

'Is that place really called the Dog's Bollocks?' asked CJ, nodding at one of the bars.

'Sure,' said Laurie. 'You'll probably find that half of the Thai restaurants in Britain which we think have rather cute Thai names are really called something like the Shitty Fat Bastard.' They peered inside. Behind the bar were T-shirts on sale bearing the legend 'Lager Louts Welcome – No Japs, No Arabs, No Backpackers'.

'Shall I get you one as a souvenir?' said Laurie, following CJ's gaze. 'You could wear it when you next have to go down to cover a Stop the War demo.'

They stopped at a bar called Guts for Garters.

'Full English for me,' said CJ, ignoring him. 'No tomatoes, though.'

'Can I just have a mushroom omelette?' said Laurie.

'You can't have a mushroom omelette,' said CJ. 'It will draw attention to us.'

Laurie looked round the bar. There were a couple of men who looked English, sitting separately, one wearing a red bandanna round his head, no top, and shorts with lots of zips, the other in an unflattering purple shell suit.

'Tea or coffee?' asked the waitress.

'Tea for me,' said Laurie.

'Coffee for me,' said CJ.

By the time Laurie looked up again, the man in the red bandanna had gone. Shell Suit smiled at him. Laurie smiled back.

'Press, are you?' asked Shell Suit.

'What makes you think that?' asked Laurie.

'You don't look like a lager lout or a Chelsea fan or an expat and most of the other British people who come in this bar are either police or press, wanting to make trouble. Wankers.'

'I agree,' said CJ, a little too heartily. 'Journalists are a bunch of wankers who know fuck-all.'

Shell Suit now seemed slightly taken aback.

'You new here?' he asked.

'Yeah,' said Laurie. Who was this bloke? Had their cover been rumbled already? Would they alert Vlad that there were British reporters already out here and on his case?

'Well, if you're looking for accommodation,' he produced a card from his pocket, 'let me know. The Russians are moving in here fast. Buying up places like there's no tomorrow. They'll rip you off. I won't – at least, not as much!' He was called 'Ronnie Lowe, Estate Agent to the Expat Gentry' and he had a local address and one in Bangkok. 'Must dash – the grandchildren arrive this afternoon. Mind how you go.'

'Right,' said Laurie to CJ. 'So, if we never find Vlad and I decide I can never go back to England again, at least I'll be able to find somewhere to stay here.' A sign above the bar said 'No darts, no quizzes'. He thought again of Vic and Mick and Mary. Would they co-opt someone else into the team? The phone rang in his pocket. It was Stark. 'Hullllooooo.' Laurie looked round. Should he go out into the street or would that look suspicious? Perhaps it would. Don't call attention to yourself.

'Hello,' he answered softly into the mouthpiece. 'Yes, yes, you have got the right number. Can I ring you back? Yes, we are here. What time is it with you?' Stark must have a real problem to be calling this early. 'You what? Look, I'm in Pattaya and I have no idea why a taxi fare from the High Court to Tintagel House would have cost sixteen pounds when it's less than a mile. Are you really ringing me up to ask me that?'

CJ was asking him if he wanted all his toast. Stark wanted to know what was happening.

'I'm having breakfast with CJ. Is that all right? I'll get a receipt and work out how many baht there are to the pound. We are planning our day. Look, as soon as I have anything I'll let you know . . . Yes . . . yes.' He switched the phone off.

A couple of pounds heavier, they wandered down Soi Yamato. The bar where Crispin had claimed that Vlad hung out was called Henri's and was in the parallel street. The aim was to walk slowly past it and see if there appeared to be any gathering of Russians in it. They would also see if they could find a good vantage point where CJ could use a telephoto lens without being spotted.

On one side of Henri's was a clothes shop, selling Versace and Gucci knock-offs and T-shirts that announced that 'Good Guys Go To Heaven, Bad Guys Go to Pattaya'. On the other side was a restaurant called Balti More offering 'Pattaya's Tastiest Curries'. Cooking had obviously started and the whiff of cardamom and coriander was drifting across the street. Directly opposite was St Trinans – spelled wrongly and notable for its young Thai waitresses in school uniforms and stockings with suspenders and for a sign outside that said 'Study Hard!' It offered an eclectic menu of roast beef and Yorkshire pudding, chicken tandoori and noodles. Two young men with pink, sunburned noses and camouflage sun hats were already examining a menu with the help of a bored waitress who had a 'prefect' badge pinned to her light blue tunic. In the distance, Laurie saw the first jet-skiers of the day scything their way across the bay.

'Wouldn't it be nice if we didn't have to do any work?' Laurie asked CJ.

'Getting nervous, are you?'

'A bit.'

A tall woman with short blond hair was sitting on a wicker chair on the patio outside Henri's as they walked past. Russian? She could be. Her eyes followed them.

'Well, that's the place,' said Laurie.

'What do we do now?'

'Come back later, I guess. They seemed to be pretty

adamant that he showed up there every evening. Any other suggestions?'

'Well, that St Trinian's place is my best bet for hanging out in, on that sort of patio outside. Are you going to try to talk to him?'

'I think the idea is that, if I see him, I go up to him and introduce myself and ask if he wants to put his side of the story.'

'You will recognise him, won't you? Is he going to have a lot of heavies round him?'

'Could do. And, yes, I think I'll recognise him if he looks anything like his photos.' Laurie's heart sank. What if he ended up at the bottom of the bay, a victim of some waterskiing or windsurfing 'accident'? Would Stark send anyone out to investigate that?

'Do you think he'll want to talk to you? What's in it for him?'

'Well, if he's not involved, he's got a chance to say that it's all been a terrible misunderstanding, that he's been stitched up.'

'How likely is that?'

They had reached the end of the street and were back on the front amidst the tourist shops and burger bars. It was nearly noon and hotter than ever. The beach was filling up and the pavement was crowded with mainly large, ungainly white people. A small, pretty Thai woman in a lemon T-shirt declaring 'No Money, No Honey' sauntered past.

'Not too likely, I guess,' said Laurie, feeling a wave of weariness. 'Look, here's the plan. We'll go back to the hotel, have a bit of a lie-down – or I will – have a swim in the hotel pool so that, at least, if nothing happens with Vlad, our journey won't have been entirely pointless, then come back in the early evening and stake the place out for a couple of hours at St Trinian's.'

'That should look good on your expenses.'

'God, do you know about that as well?'

'Eva-Marie told me.'

'What did she say?'

'That you were being framed by small-minded pricks on the newsdesk.'

'Did she really say that?'

'Something like that. Although I don't think that Eva-Marie uses a word like "prick", does she?'

'Maybe not.'

They were almost back at the Pattaya Lux Resort, the little boutique hotel that the paper's travel agency had recommended. The very young manager, who had greeted him and CJ with a cocktail on their arrival, looked Indian but had a laidback American accent, a pierced tongue and was called Clara. Through the lobby, Laurie could see bodies plunging off the diving board and into the pool. He decided he would follow them. 'OK, CJ, let's meet down here at six and hope that the gods are with us tonight.'

After ten lengths, he was already aching and heading for his room. He lay naked on his bed, too tired to feel dread. When he woke, he rang CJ on his mobile and found that he was already out and round at Guts for Garters where he had left his sunglasses that morning. Laurie joined him there and ordered a pint of lager.

'Drinking on duty?' asked CJ.

'Just trying to blend in,' said Laurie. 'Shall we head off round the corner and try and get Petrov after this?'

His mobile rang. The line was bad. The numbers indicated that it was a call from London.

'Hello, who is that? I'm sorry I can't hear you. Who? Where am I? Guts for Garters, since you ask . . . I'm sorry I can hardly hear anything . . . Who is it calling? Mrs Rolfe. Oh, Mrs Rolfe! What? You say that Violet did not arrive for her A level exams . . . Um, no, I'm in Thailand, I'm afraid. No, no, for work. For WORK. Look, I'll call her mother and ring you back.' He rang Caz but her phone was only taking messages. He told her voicemail about Violet's non-appearance and asked her to ring him. He sighed.

'Let's go to St Trins,' said CJ.

Three hours, four drinks and two nasi gorengs later, the sky had darkened and the bar was crowded. The US Navy appeared to be in town and there was a raucous table of dashing young sailors, egging each other on to make approaches to the waitresses, who chatted to each other indifferently, switching on bright smiles only when a customer waved at them.

'Look at all these guys who've come in to see women dressed as schoolgirls,' said CJ as a trio of middle-aged Englishmen, in belly-hugging T-shirts and bad shorts, came in and scanned the bar girls, like greedy uncles at Christmas, fingers hovering over the Milk Tray selection as they decided whether to take the caramel or the hazelnut. 'I bet if you accused them of being paedophiles they would bop you one.'

Laurie nodded in agreement and contemplated another lager.

Henri's appeared to be the least popular bar on the street. A sign apologised for the fact that the kitchen was closed. Apart from the brief visit of what looked like a stag party, the only patron seemed to be the tall Slavic-looking woman from the morning. Then, just as Laurie was about to suggest packing it in for the night and just after he had turned down the offer of a 'treesome' for the second time, a grey – 'battleship grey', of course, he told himself – Toyota SUV with darkened windows drew up outside. The driver, a short bald man, jumped out and cased the street for a moment. He opened the passenger door and out stepped an imposing figure, his pale blue blazer jacket on his thumb over his shoulder, like a casual boulevardier out for an evening in the tropics. In the neon light of the street, Laurie could make out the handsome features of Vladimir Petrov.

Chapter Twenty-four

'THAT'S HIM,' SAID Laurie. 'That's our guy.'

CJ already had his camera out.

'Shit, he's inside already,' he said.

A waitress in a schoolgirl uniform saw CJ with the camera and approached the table smiling.

'You like me take photo of you both?'

'Er . . . no . . . no, thanks,' said Laurie.

'Actually,' said CJ, 'that's not such a bad idea. If we give you ten dollars would you mind taking a picture of us in that bar across the road?'

'In Henri's?' said the girl. 'Oh no, Henri's don't like people taking photos.' She shook her head at them and departed for the table of American sailors.

'How are we going to do this?' asked CJ.

'Well, I guess what the paper wants most is a pic of Vlad. If we can get that without him taking your camera off you then all I need to say is, "Excuse me, I'm a member of Her Majesty's press, I wonder if you would care to put the record straight or alternatively confess to the murder of Old Man Hook and accompany me back to London and a trial at the Old Bailey to be followed by my book which will top the non-fiction best-selling lists at Christmas".'

'How much have you had to drink?'

'Not much. It's just the fear talking.'

The street was crowded and noisy now. What would Caz have thought of all this? Laurie wondered, as he watched the bar girls curling elegant fingers towards the groups of men and giggling with their colleagues as the men, flattered that someone seemed to find them desirable, responded. Come to think of it, why hadn't Caz phoned back? Why hadn't he phoned Violet again? Had she run away? Bad dad. A man with a shaven head and an XL T-shirt labelled Beer Monster waddled past, a paper cup in one hand and a chicken leg in the other. Competing music – hip-hop and Thai pop and Elvis – blared out from the bars and tourist shops.

'I guess,' said Laurie, his heart sinking, as Elvis sang 'The Wonder of You' in the background, 'I guess we have to go over there and . . . well, maybe you can make it look like you are just trying to take a picture of me on my hols . . .'

'With a telephoto lens?'

'People have telephoto lenses on wildlife holidays, don't they? We can pretend to be a bit drunk.'

'Pretend?'

'Look, what's the alternative? Wait until he comes out? He might be there all night and go out the back way and we may never see him again. It could be our only chance.'

Laurie waved their waitress over and paid the bill. He ignored the knowing look towards him and CJ from one of the trio of Englishmen who were in the process of negotiating a 'bar fine' with the manager and indicating the three waitresses they would like to join them.

Across the road in Henri's, Vlad was standing temptingly at the bar with the short, bald man. His eyes brushed over them as they took a small wicker table and two stools in the corner. CJ slowly slid his camera out.

'If you move your seat round ever so slightly to your left,' he said, 'I can get a shot of him and make it look like I'm taking one of you. Try and smile and look like you're on holiday rather than on Death Row.'

'Like this?' Laurie flashed a bogus smile at him as he shifted his seat round.

'You need to move a little further . . . About three inches . . .'

Laurie raised both thumbs in the air and gave him a further manic grin.

'How's that?'

He watched CJ's expression change as he posed again. Too late, he realised that someone was approaching them. It was Petrov who laid a hand on his shoulder and smiled. It was a warm smile, not sinister at all. Laurie felt his heart beating. Maybe I am having a heart attack. Which arm is it that goes stiff? Guy would have been able to tell him. Guy was always self-diagnosing on the internet, checking whether the pain in his hip was cancer or the stiffness in his fingers was arthritis or repetitive strain injury. Certainly his heart was seriously pounding. Would they leave him to die in the bar? Or dump him on the beach? Still, better than having the heart attack in St Trinans. An image of Alistair Sim in drag as the headmistress in the old St Trinian's films floated in front of him in black and white. I am dying, he thought. Maybe all the films of one's childhood rush past you rather than everything that happened to you. Will I see *Lassie* and *Ivanhoe* and *The Sound of Music*? Stark would be sorry now. No, in fact, he wouldn't. Stark would only be sorry that he hadn't died in St Trinans, in a lap-dancing bar. It would suit Stark very well. He would probably speak at his funeral. The thought of it sobered Laurie up.

'We need to have little chat,' said Petrov. Not another. That's what Stark had said to him. And Caz. His world was now defined by people who wanted to have a little chat with him. There was no escape from them. Even Violet's teacher wanted to have a little chat with him. CJ had disappeared.

With a nod of his head, Petrov bade him follow and led the way with an athletic, rolling stride.

The room at the top of the stairs was neat and characterless, like a hotel room. It did not look as if anyone lived or relaxed there. There was a bowl of fruit. Kumquats? wondered Laurie. And then wondered why he was wondering about identifying species of fruit at a time like this. He realised he needed a pee but felt that to ask for one was a poor negotiating move. Prostate? Why not? He tried to remember the Ten Warning Signs For Prostate Cancer that the paper had helpfully run and he had casually ignored only two weeks earlier. Vlad seemed both relaxed and amused.

'We've not met,' said Vlad, offering a firm handshake. 'I remember when I first arrive in England from St Petersburg being told by old friend who had been in London for a few years that British press were much more efficient than KGB in finding things out about people and destroying them. But I have to say that KGB that I knew would have been a little – what shall I say? – more . . . subtle about its surveillance techniques. Still, perhaps you are jet-lagged. Can I get you something to drink? To eat? I am afraid kitchen is closed but place next door does rather good satay.'

'I'm OK, thanks,' said Laurie. He felt a stream of sweat slipping down his spine.

'Should I put air conditioning up? No?'

'I'm fine, thanks,' said Laurie, trying to be casual.

'Anyway, I read piece you wrote about me when Mr Hook was shot and I don't think I would have to take too many guesses to find out who told you that. What I was more puzzled about was how Scotland Yard were prepared to go along with idea.'

The door opened again and the tall Slavic woman whom Laurie had seen earlier came in. She exchanged a few words in Russian with Vlad and left with a slight smile on her face.

'Er . . . my colleague . . .' mumbled Laurie.

'Oh, he has already been taken to work as sex slave – "sex slave" is right? – in one of our brothels,' said Vlad with a smile.

Laurie's heart pumped again. Vlad laughed. 'He's fine, he's having drink downstairs. We just wanted to check on what photos he was taking. I don't want to annoy Thai police and there's nothing annoys them more than when foreigners with business interests here get into trouble. I'm sure you can understand that.'

'Yes,' nodded Laurie. He watched as Vlad opened a cold Chang and thought, oh, I would like one of those. He gazed at the elephants on the label. But to ask for a beer would be a surrender, would it not? Vlad had slung his blazer on a chair. His shirt was open three buttons down. A gold crucifix dangled over his chest. Was he a Christian? There was a gold ring on the little finger of his left hand and a small star-shaped tattoo at the base of the thumb. His shoes were snappy, alligator skin, perhaps.

'Now, I don't know exactly what you intended to accomplish by coming here, presumably something along lines of "We Find Gangland Hitman Suspect In Asian Brothel", no? Yes, I study British media closely. One day maybe start paper in St Petersburg. You think you're very brave in England, no? In Russia, journalists who fight bosses and government, they get killed. In England, they get little pat on back, no? You think you are all very anti-establishment, yes? You march to sound of different drum and all that. In fact, you march to sound of same drum, you even look side to side to make sure you all in step. Never mind. That is your way. But when I hear that someone hanging around St Trinans – as do many of your countrymen, I might add. What is that schoolgirl thing English men have? – I thought best clear all this up very quickly. Then you can tell your paper real story or you can have yourself little holiday here. Basically story is this: I have absolutely – absolutely – nothing to do with murder of Mr Hook. I promise you. You have lie detector test, I take it. OK? Now . . . perhaps you know this verse:

> Hear me, auld Hangie, for a wee,
> An' let poor, damned bodies be;
> I'm sure small pleasure it can gie;
> Ev'n to a deil,
> To skelp an' scaud poor dogs like me,
> An' hear us squeel.

'No? You don't recognise it?'

'Er . . . it's Robert Burns, isn't it? I can't remember which one.' During his shiftily peripatetic father's brief and unhappy sojourn in Oban, Laurie had studied Burns for a year.

'Yes, of course, Burns. Address to the deil. Is that how you pronounce it? Deil? Address to the devil, yes? So why you all want to hurt poor dogs like me? You like hear us squeal?' Vlad paused and shrugged at Laurie.

'It really amaze me when I arrive in Britain how little people knew about their culture,' he continued. 'You must know that Burns very popular in Russia? Working-class poet? Yes? My father was president of Leningrad Burns Society. Every January – what was it? Twenty-fifth, yes? Pretty good memory, yes? – we have dinner to celebrate. They get haggis, even – yes, haggis – which cousin bring back from Harrods in diplomatic bag. Maybe Burns not so popular in new Russia. But me and my brothers, we were expected to learn one poem and recite it every year. It was burden for young boy who would rather be playing ice hockey or football but now, well, Burns is great philosopher. "The Address to the Unco Guid" – is that how you pronounce it? – full of wisdom. You see what has happened here is that you and Scotland Yard have very definitely passed Wisdom's door and entered Folly's portals. Very silly. Think about it for a moment. Why would I, Russian businessman with two successful restaurants in London, want to expose myself to anger not only of London's most – what shall we say? Angry? – gang but also irritate Scotland Yard? Think about it. What did you say your name was?'

'Laurie.' It did not come out with the self-assurance he had intended.

'Lorry? Like truck? OK. You sure you won't have beer? I am not going to tie electrodes to your genitals, I assure you – at least not here.'

'Yeah . . . OK, that would be good,' said Laurie, affecting a we're-just-a-couple-of-blokes-having-a-chat mode. The bald man handed him a Chang and Laurie swigged it back. I should have just sipped it, thought Laurie. That would have looked a little more self-confident, wouldn't it?

'You see some people have own reasons for not wanting me in London,' said Vlad. 'Difficult to explain. So when someone kills Mr Hook, is perfect chance for them to try and suggest it is me. Yes, I knew Hook, I did not like him but I am not stupid. He was going to invest in some of my property in Russia. He tell me to bring friends to his house for parties. You think I drive out to where he lives and shoot him in middle of night? Like dog? And then bury gun in my garden? Please!'

Laurie placed the Chang delicately on the edge of the table. 'I don't think it was suggested that you had . . . er . . . personally . . .'

'They think I hire a hitman? Where do I hire hitman? Yellow Pages? And then ask him to put gun in my garden? What do you think?'

Should I ask if CJ could be allowed to join us now? wondered Laurie. Vlad leant forward and stared at him intensely.

'Look, my friend,' he said. 'Who tells you that I am responsible for this?'

'I don't think . . . I . . . well, the police said that they were looking for you . . .'

'Yes, I know that but, day before police announce my

name, in your paper you say they are looking for Russian man with home by Hampstead Heath, yes? Who tells you this? Policeman? Or someone else? You don't want to say, no? You see, when I realise that police want to talk to me about this I know what can happen. That is why I leave country and tell my lawyers to explain that I only come back when I know I am not going to be made – what? Scapegoat? Perfect to have Russian. Russians now big criminals in London, yes? Once it was Jews, yes? And Chinese? And Pakistanis, no? We get some peace when bombs go off because everyone is looking for Muslims but now is Russians again. You think all Russians are criminals? My sister, she lives in England, she surgeon. My niece, she is what you call? Beautician. Makes two hundred pounds a week and tips. My cousin, not so bright, he works in old persons' home, wipe arses of old British people. But no, that does not fit our image, does it? Now just like your old James Bond films. Now is *Eastern Promises*. Russians in gangs, Russians with tattoos, Russian oligarchs – you like oligarchs, don't you? You think Britain has no oligarchs? Russian kleptocrats. Where you think British get nice big country houses? By work hard? Oh, sure. So, are you going to write story? What is it? We Find Evil Gang Killer In Thai Bar? Yes? No? That is why I don't want photos. Now, I have people to see who have come long way but – where you stay?'

'The Pattaya Lux Resort.'

'Nice hotel. OK. We talk later and I tell you who really responsible for this. OK? But no photos, OK?'

Vlad stood up. He was in good shape. The crucifix stopped dangling. Laurie stood up too and they shook hands.

Downstairs CJ was sitting with the tall Slavic woman. He

had been given his cameras back but, to judge by the crestfallen look on his face, all traces of Vlad had been wiped from them. They walked back together to their hotel without speaking.

'So what are we going to do?'

'Well, he denies it all, of course and since we don't have any photos now – not your fault, I know – I'm not sure what we can do,' said Laurie. 'I think we need a drink.' He felt a sudden throbbing in his thigh. Thrombosis? Was that how it started? Was it prompted by tension? Of course, the long-haul flight! This would be deep vein thrombosis. Was it a painful end? It seemed to have a rhythm of its own. Was he ready to die? He should have apologised properly to Caz. And told Violet he loved her. And given more money to that homeless man who sold the *Big Issue* near the office. Too late. Too late.

'What makes you think we haven't got a photo?' asked CJ.

'Well, didn't they get hold of your camera?'

His leg was still throbbing. Stay calm. Should he tell CJ?

'Yeah, but . . .'

'But what?'

'Perhaps I already had one taken.'

'And where would it be?'

Throbbing still.

'Well, Laurie, the great thing about digital photography is that you can shove what you have just taken with a digit into a place where no one is going to look. So if you want to wait while I pay a visit . . . By the way, your phone's ringing.'

Chapter Twenty-five

I T WAS STARK. OF course. The 'Hulllooooo' seemed
longer than usual. Laurie pictured him in the office, eyes
darting like a lizard's tongue from screen to BlackBerry
to the door of the editor's office, white shirt sleeves rolled
up just enough to show the dark hair on his arms and his
fat watch. Was he hoping that Laurie had messed up? Or
that he had found Vlad? Probably a bit of both, his brain
tussling its way between a desire to see Laurie humiliated and
a chance to tell the editor that he had the following day's
splash. Or perhaps I am being unkind, he thought. Maybe
Stark has hidden pains. A lurking depressive illness kept at bay
by drugs? A wife who no longer cares for him? A damaged
child?

'Yeah, we found him,' said Laurie, trying to make his voice
sound as casual as possible. As if not finding him had been 'not
an option', as Stark would put it. 'He denies any involvement,
of course.'

Was that a hint of disappointment in Stark's voice? Did he
expect that Vlad would have rolled over and admitted it all,
like the guilty man in a bad television detective drama set in
the Cotswolds? 'Yes, yes, I did it but I'm glad, I tell you

GLAD . . . Now, if you'll excuse me, inspector, I will throw myself out of the window.'

Stark wanted to know where the pictures were. Was there a possibility of hinting at Russian government involvement in Vlad's flight? Could Vlad be called an oligarch? How soon could he file? Had he spoken to Scotland Yard? Stark was obsessed with work. Did he have no hinterland? Laurie had discussed this once with Guy but they had been unable to agree on what a hinterland actually was. Was hill-walking and singing in a choir a hinterland? Or was it having had a nervous breakdown and knowing all of Proust? Laurie raised his eyebrows at CJ as he listened to the requests.

'Look, I'm going to have to go to my room and file something,' said Laurie eventually. 'Can you let them have the photo?'

He rang Violet from his hotel room.

'Hey, how are you? I got a call from Mrs Rolfe—'

'Don't panic, Dad,' said the distant voice. 'She thought I was meant to be sitting physics but I'm not. She got me mixed up with another Violet. Everything's cool.'

'How many Violets are there?'

'Four. And two Daisys and two Irises and a Lily.'

'Sounds like one of your mum's songs. Is she there, by the way?'

'Yeah. Hang on. Godfrey! Are you both in the bath? Can you tell Mum that Dad's on the phone.'

Laurie contemplated ringing off. But that would be petty, would it not?

'Hello, Laurie,' said the second faraway voice. Had the tone changed ever so slightly? Was there a distance to it, a distance beyond the thousands of miles between Pattaya and London? 'How's it going? Are you going to name the guilty man?'

'That's the problem,' said Laurie. 'I'm not sure any more if he's guilty but they still want a story in about ten minutes' time.'

'Got to sing for your supper?'

'You're meant to be the one singing for your supper, aren't you? I'm sorry I had to go the other night . . . I thought you were great, by the way.'

'Oh, Laurie, don't worry, that's all water under the bridge now. Look, I've got to go. I've got to see someone about the Denmark tour. Take care. Bye.'

Denmark. Would Godfrey go with her? Would they have the sort of time together that Laurie had had with Caz when they first met and she was playing in clubs in Amsterdam and Rotterdam? What did she sing then? 'Fountain of Sorrow'? Or was it 'Needle of Death'? He unfolded his laptop and started writing. When in doubt, write. Someone had told him that. Who? Some early news editor. It had all been so simple in those days.

'The man police are seeking in connection with the murder of the head of Britain's best-known . . .' Hmm, better make that 'notorious'. 'Britain's most notorious criminal family is enjoying the good life in a Thai tourist resort.'

No, that didn't sound too exciting. He could imagine Stark spicing it up. What had Vlad actually said to him? He had not taken any notes. There was a tap at the door. It was CJ.

'Hi,' said Laurie. 'How did the picture come out? Have you sent it?'

'I don't know how to say this,' said CJ. 'Maybe one day we

will look back at this moment and smile.' His sad horse face looked inconsolable.

'It didn't come out?'

'Who knows? I shoved it up my arse so they wouldn't find it and when I got back to my room I got the runs and – it was just at that very moment when I flushed the toilet that I remembered.'

'Fucking hell.'

'Don't tell anyone, will you?'

Laurie was already rehearsing how he would recount it. He pictured himself in the pub with, well, Eva-Marie and Guy and Rosie, milking the story for all it was worth. The Vicar would love it too. He could picture him chortling. So would Violet. Sorry, CJ, he said silently to himself. Too good to keep quiet. How would he explain to Stark that there was no photo?

'Of course not. I don't know what kind of story I'm going to do anyway. He seemed like quite a reasonable bloke.'

'Probably Fred West and the Boston Strangler did too. I had to take Henry Kissinger's photo once and he was really funny and nice. Did you expect him to beat you up?'

'That would have made a better story.'

Laurie tapped away. He read out what he had written to CJ.

'"We have traced the man sought by the police for the murder of London gang leader, Charlie Hook. He is in Pattaya in Thailand and is denying any involvement in the shooting of Britain's most notorious career criminal." How does that sound?'

'Was he really the most notorious criminal?' asked CJ, perching on the edge of the bed. 'More notorious than Fred

West and – what's the Moors murderer called? Brady? Or the bloke who killed the two little girls?'

'Well, Fred West is dead.'

'So is Old Man Hook, isn't he?'

'Yes but "career criminal" is different. Murderers tend not to be career criminals. The only murders that Hook organised were business rather than personal. Fred West and Brady and Huntley carried out their murders for kicks.'

'Does that make them worse?'

'Course it does. And most of the people that Hook is meant to have bumped off were in the same game, really.'

'Do you think that made it easier for the relatives of the people he killed? Who was that boxer he had done over? Barney Quick. His family were well pissed off. I remember I took photos of them outside the Old Bailey when Hook was acquitted. I was with PA in those days. And wasn't there an Asian minicab driver his lot did over by mistake?'

Laurie tapped on. He knew that Stark would ratchet the story up when he got it and he was glad that he would not be in the office to watch the process.

'I'm going to lie down,' said CJ. 'I feel crap. The travel department want me to do some film for the website. Three minutes of life in Pattaya. They can whistle for it.'

'You could film the Dog's Bollocks and Guts for Garters.'

'Maybe not. I think it's meant to be windsurfing and food stalls.'

Laurie felt a wave of weariness washing over him. The sky was darkening outside. He finished his story, trying to keep it as ambiguous as possible, and watched on his screen as it landed safely at the newsdesk in London six thousand miles away. He phoned to ensure that someone had noticed its arrival, told them he would have his mobile close to his heart and left the hotel. Fortunately, no one asked him about the absence of a photo. He needed to get out of his hotel room.

'Hello, dark-ling,' called out a bar girl as he walked past. Laurie sighed. What was it that someone had written, that at a certain time in one's life you realise that your physical appearance no longer 'snags' a member of the opposite sex as they go past; you have become part of that amorphous mass of clothed flesh bumbling along life's promenade. Certainly no one's darling.

'Hello, my Adonis,' shouted another bar girl. Who had taught her that, for heaven's sake? He could not help but smile and she took this as a breakthrough, running after him and slipping her arm through his. He apologised and slowly extricated himself. He was just about to return to the hotel when he felt a tug at his elbow. It was Petrov's bald companion.

'Having a nice walk?' he asked.

'Sure,' said Laurie. 'How about you?'

'Vlad would like to see you in the morning,' said the man. He had a Russian accent. 'Maybe talk some more. Good idea. We come pick you up. Don't worry. No troubles.' And he was gone.

As Laurie rounded the corner, he heard a woman's voice calling out to him from a passing cab. Who the hell else knew he was here? As he turned, the cab executed an elegant U-turn and its driver delivered a beaming Flo, his companion on the flight to Bangkok.

'Hello, sailor,' she said.

Chapter Twenty-six

HOW MANY TIGERS had he wrestled with? Or, to be more accurate, how many Tigers had he wrestled with drunk? Or to be even more accurate, how many Tigers had he drunk? Eight? Ten? What did it matter? They had the nicest label of any beer in the world. No wonder Anthony Burgess had used it on the cover of his Malaysian Trilogy. And there had been a couple of Changs, too. Tigers and elephants. No wonder he felt ropey. It had been that joint that had done it, though. He could picture it – fat and leaking leaves. But where had they been? On a balcony. Whose balcony? He was not going to ask himself 'Where am I?' because he knew he was in Thailand somewhere. This room seemed strange but familiar. Someone else's luggage was in the room. Where were his clothes? There was a scratch on his arm. Perhaps he was in hospital? Maybe he had had a breakdown and collapsed in the street. Would Caz come and collect him? This would certainly help Violet towards some more compassionate upgrading in her A levels.

Then he heard a soft and just – only just – familiar sound beside him. Deep breathing. A tiny mumble. He was not alone!

Without lifting his head from the pillow, he swivelled his eyes to the side. There was long dark hair on the pillow. Whose? Had he picked up a lady-boy? Had he had a good time? Was this a crossroads in his life? Had they had sex? If not, why were they in bed together? What would Violet think? Would she think it cool? They would be unable to sack him now because it would amount to discrimination. Had he been passive or active?

Where was his phone? His wallet? Had he been slipped a Mickey Finn by Vlad? Did people still talk about Mickey Finns? What was the difference between a Mickey Finn and a date rape drug? Why did one sound benign and the other egregious? Could he get the word 'egregious' into his story? His companion of the night was still breathing deeply. Laurie's head was too heavy to raise from the pillow. He tried to lift it again but it would not move. Maybe it had been attached to the pillow with some hidden fiendish bondage. Vlad! Had that urbane approach all been a smokescreen?

His Internal Prosecuting Counsel was clearing his virtual throat and getting to his feet, adjusting his wig at a surprisingly jaunty virtual angle.

'Are you really telling the court, Mr Lane, that until you woke up you were completely unaware that you had spent a night of sexual activity with the witness, whose very disturbing testimony we have just heard? Are you claiming that someone "spiked" your drink? I'm sorry, Mr Lane, you're going to have to speak very clearly so that his lordship and the jury can hear you.'

He slipped his hand down his side. Yes, he was completely naked. He shifted his hand slowly to his left. Yes, the person beside him was naked too. The flesh was soft. Did this mean the sleeper was a woman? Maybe a very soft man. Maybe men had become quite soft and he was unaware of the fact because he had never woken up beside a naked one. He tried to shift himself slowly on to his hip so that he could—

'Hi, there,' said a husky voice. 'I thought you were never going to wake up.'

A long brown arm with a bracelet on it and with red – no, burgundy! – nails moved in slow motion across the sheet and swept away the dark hair to reveal Flo, his neighbour on the plane trip to Bangkok.

'Hi . . . er . . .'

'Flo,' she said. 'I'm sure you've forgotten although you called me that enough times last night. I guess you haven't had too much sex recently.'

'How did you guess?'

She ignored his question and shifted herself so she was leaning on an elbow and surveying him. Her breasts reminded him of something.

'You look like a Gaugin painting,' he said.

'You mean my breasts are brown and floppy. Is that the best you can do for compliments?'

'Give me a minute.'

'That's what you kept saying last night.'

'God, was it that bad?'

She laughed and rolled on top of him, her breasts pressed against his chest, her hand brushing her hair away from his face. She grinned and shook her head at him. He traced the lines on each side of her lips with his finger and looked into her eyes.

'What are you going to say – no one laughs that much?'

'No, I was going to say what a nice way to wake up in a strange place. But I wish my damn head didn't ache so much.'

'I know. I didn't know how strong that stuff was. I just bought it from a kid on the street. I thought it would be pretty weak. The last weed I had was from one of my clients and it was nothing. Now you're going to tell me that you have to get to work, are you? That's what you were going on about last night. I think you must have grown up in a very puritanical home.'

He pushed her gently up by her shoulders and cupped one of her breasts in his hand.

'Puritanical was not the word I would choose. My dad was . . . well, never mind.'

'Sounds like my dad.'

'Where . . . where was he from?'

'You mean which half of me is from the northern hemisphere and which from the south? Dad from Orissa and Mum from Bradford. Now you see why I have a sense of humour.'

'And your husband – your ex-husband?'

'Bloody Leeds. There was one before him who was from your way, from London, but—'

'What, you've been divorced three times then?'

'First one . . . well, he's not with us any more. He was from Orissa originally too, distant relative . . . But never mind.'

'I think you're the first social services outreach worker from Yorkshire I've even been to bed with.'

'Do I get a medal?'

'Where would I pin it?'

He pushed himself up from the pillow and kissed her on the lips, then on each breast. She kissed him back, leant back on her haunches and pushed her hair back again over her shoulders.

'What time is it?' Laurie asked.

She looked at her watch.

'What time would you like it to be?'

'Can you organise that?'

'Oh, sure.'

'How about making it about ten years ago.'

'Ooo, we're not going to have a conversation about how everything was going so well ten years ago and now it's not, are we? Don't look back. You may be working, pet, but I'm on holiday. Shall we go and get some breakfast?'

'Sure. Where?'

'Well, just round the corner from here there are about a dozen places offering a full English breakfast complete with black pudding and a pint of lager.'

'Oh, I feel ill again.'

'Come on, it's just what you need.'

She stood up and starting combing her hair in front of the mirror. She caught his gaze in the mirror.

'Don't stare at my bottom. It's not my best feature.'

'Looks pretty good to me.' He leant forward and kissed it.

'You should have seen it ten years ago.'

'Don't look back.'

She turned and smiled at him.

'Come back to bed,' he said. He slid to the bottom of the bed and she sat astride him on his lap. They made love.

'You're watching me in the mirror, aren't you?' She laughed. 'You little perv.'

Flo's mobile phone rang.

'Hello, pet, how are you? How's work? Great . . . Yes, I'm fine. Mmm, just exploring a bit – looking at some of the ancient monuments. Yes, OK. Going to your dad's tonight, are you?' Flo nibbled his left ear abstractedly as she spoke to – whom? It sounded like her son or daughter. 'I'll ring you tomorrow, pet. Love you! Yeah, don't worry. I haven't forgotten. Bye.' They disentangled themselves. Laurie stood beside her. He was a head taller than her. He encircled her waist with his arms and slipped one hand between her legs. She wriggled away from him, grabbed a towel and headed for the shower.

'I don't even know where we are,' said Laurie as he joined her in the shower. 'I take it this is your hotel?' They dried each other with the depressingly threadbare towels. It must be a cheap hotel, thought Laurie. He pulled on his jeans. Flo stood naked and still, looking out of the window.

'Mmm,' she said. She pulled the curtain aside further and frowned.

'What are you looking at?' asked Laurie.

She did not answer him at first.

'What is out there?' asked Laurie, tucking his shirt in. His head hurt.

She beckoned him over with an elegant, burgundy-nailed index finger. He followed her gaze out into the street which was already full of Pattaya's morning bustle.

'See that guy over there?' she asked.

'There's dozens of guys over there.'

'Come on, concentrate. The bald guy in the red and white striped shirt.'

'Yeah . . .'

'He was walking behind us when we got into the hotel last night.'

'He's not your ex-husband, is he?'

Flo shook her head and looked away.

'So maybe he's just an admirer,' said Laurie. 'Oh, hang on. I know that guy. It's Petrov's mate. Come on, get your clothes on and come down with me. If he wants to see any-one, it's me, and I'm sure the chances of him doing anything to me will be substantially reduced if you are there as a witness.'

'Thanks very much.'

'Not at all – and breakfast is on me.'

'You're too kind.'

He rang the Pattaya Lux Resort and asked for CJ. A groan answered the phone.

'Are you OK?' asked Laurie.

'Bloody guts. I think it was the smoked salmon on the plane,' said CJ. 'Do you need me?'

'Um, not quite sure. Let me find out. D'you want me to get you anything?'

There was a feebler groan and the phone went dead.

'What's up?' said Flo.

'My snapper is indisposed.'

'I can take pictures,' said Flo, gesturing at her little Olympus. Laurie smiled back at her.

As they left the hotel, the bald man approached. He smiled broadly at them and extended his hand to be shaken.

'Hello,' he said. 'I have message. Vladimir would very much like it if you were to come visit with him.'

'Visit him?'

'Yes, visit with him.'

'Visit him is fine – you don't need the extra preposition,' said Laurie.

'Don't be such a pedantic snob,' said Flo. 'I bet you were a little prig at school.'

'No, I wasn't. That came later. I was just trying to be helpful.'

The bald man looked bemused.

'You are coming visit, yes?'

'Sure, sure.' Laurie looked at his watch. Nearly ten in the morning. That meant only five in the morning in London. But his story from the night before would already be in the online edition. Had Vladimir seen it? Was he angry? Stark had ramped it up and made it into a sensational, braggartly piece. We Find Britain's Most Wanted. Could he offer him the chance to 'set the record straight' again? Or did Vladimir Petrov have something new that he wanted to tell him? His mouth felt dry.

'Look, can we just grab a very quick bite and then I'll come with you, OK? By the way, I don't know your name.'

'Lev,' said the man.

'Oh, like Lev—'

'Yes, like Lev Yashin, Russian goalkeeper. British people know five Russians – Stalin, Lenin, Putin, Abramovich and Yashin . . . Yes, I join you.'

'What about Gagarin and all the tennis ladies?' said Flo. 'And how many Indians and Yorkshiremen do you know? And are you still going to treat me to a nice breakfast, Laurie?'

'I said breakfast, I didn't say it was going to be a nice one,' said Laurie. He scanned the street, saw a sign offering Full English Breakfast and headed for it.

'Large Diet Coke, no ice,' he ordered as the three of them were shown to a freshly wiped table. An elderly couple, newly arrived British, to judge by their pallor, were sitting in the corner reading the previous day's *Daily Express*.

'Very bad for you, these breakfasts,' said Flo.

'Worse than ten beers and a spliff?'

Their companion raised his eyebrow almost imperceptibly. They ordered from a cheery waitress. Somewhere – on the radio? On a CD player? – Elton John was singing.

'Why is called full English breakfast?' asked Lev.

'Because only fools and Englishmen would eat something that would inevitably lead to a heart attack,' said Laurie, gesturing to the waitress for another Diet Coke.

'Can I ask,' said Flo, 'why you are having a Diet Coke when you are just about to eat two rashers of bacon, baked beans, two sausages, two fried eggs and four slices of toast? Do you think that will magically keep you nice and slim?'

'Much too early in the morning for such tricky questions.'

Lev shifted his puzzled gaze between them, like someone watching a game of tennis for the first time.

'You are married?' he asked.

'Yes,' said Laurie. 'But not to each other.'

Lev smiled and nodded.

Three heavily freighted plates arrived, trailing smells of bacon fat. Laurie felt suddenly sick.

'Have you got any ketchup, love?' asked Flo of the waitress.

Lev tucked in. As he did so, his mobile phone rang with a delicate melody.

'What's that tune?' asked Flo. 'It's lovely.'

'Prokoviev,' said Lev as he put the telephone to his ear. 'Did you think it should be 'Lara's Theme'? Excuse me. Bad line.' He stepped outside the café.

'Is anyone going to tell me what's going on?' said Flo.

Laurie was just about to try and work out what he could tell her when Lev returned.

'I think maybe we finish breakfast and go now,' he said. He pulled out a wad of bhat notes from his pocket and slapped them on the table. Laurie stuffed a slice of undercooked bacon into his mouth, swigged down the glass of Diet Coke.

'Can I come too?' asked Flo.

Lev paused for a moment then shrugged and said, 'Why not?' He gestured towards his Toyota SUV.

Chapter Twenty-seven

L EV STEERED THROUGH the traffic on the road out of Pattaya towards Pluta Luang.

'Do I get to find out where we are going?' asked Flo.

'We go find Most Wanted Man In Britain,' said Lev, looking straight ahead.

'Really? Who's that?'

'Your friend will tell you.'

'Well . . . I think there's been a little bit of a misunderstanding,' said Laurie. The team with the pneumatic drill who had been at work spasmodically inside his head since he woke up had resumed. He could feel the beads of sweat assembling on his brow, ready to tombstone on to his lap.

'You see, Yev's—'

'Lev,' said Lev. 'My name is Lev.'

'That's what I meant. Lev's boss, Vladimir Petrov, got – how should I say it?'

'Try truth,' said Lev.

'Mr Petrov was named by the police as a person of interest in connection with the murder of an old London gangster called Charlie Hook and—'

'A person of interest, what does that mean?' asked Flo.

'It means police think maybe this person is killer,' said Lev, eyes on the road, 'or maybe not, but he is foreigner anyway so they tell press that he is person of interest and then everyone think he is killer.'

'As long as he's not one of those ones that the police say members of the public should not approach,' said Flo. 'What a beautiful day, isn't it? This is just what I need. I don't think the sun has shone properly on Sheffield since the year before last. So why do the police find your friend so interesting?'

'You ask your friend,' said Lev. 'He is first person to suggest him.'

Laurie's heart sank. How did he get out of this?

'Well, in fact, it was the police who named Mr Petrov.'

'Yes, but only after your paper had said Russian businessman with house near Hampstead Heath was suspect.'

'But there are lots of Russian businessmen with homes in Hampstead.'

Lev looked unconvinced.

'Anyway, there was this story that possibly – just possibly – a Russian might have been involved. Then the police came up with Mr Petrov's name and that was in all the papers, not just ours. Then I heard on the grapevine . . .'

Lev was listening carefully.

'Yes?' said Lev, head cocked. 'And what is grape vine?'

'Good question,' said Laurie, thankful for the distraction. 'I don't know why it's called the grapevine. One theory is that—'

Flo started singing 'Heard it Through the Grapevine' to Lev's obvious irritation. Lev started glancing through his CDs, eyes flicking up to the road and down to the little rack beside his CD player. He found what he was looking for and inserted it.

'George Orwell always used to say that you should never use a dead metaphor – I think he called them "dying metaphors" – you know, clichés, where everyone has forgotten what their origin was. Like the grapevine, I suppose.'

'Is that so?' asked Flo. Her lips were pursed. She was teasing him.

'I think the grapevine came about because early telegraph wires . . .' What was it Vic had said? 'Yes, telegraph wires in nineteenth-century America looked like grape vines . . . and vines would be very familiar to Italian-Americans and . . . maybe it's a Mafia thing . . .'

That was a mistake. He caught a flash of Lev's eyes as he spun the car round a corner and up a side road. He resumed his narrative. Lev turned up the music. Laurie could not place it.

'Anyway, I heard—'

'On grapevine,' said Lev.

'Yeah, on the grapevine, that Mr Petrov was now in Thailand and might be contactable at Henri's bar so . . . obviously, we wanted to get his side of the story. So here we are. I had a chat with him last night and now – do you know exactly what it is that he wants to discuss this morning, Lev?'

Lev shrugged.

'What's the music?' Laurie asked.

'Yegor Letov,' said Lev. 'Russian punk, OK?'

They were now travelling up a side road off a side road, climbing a modest hill. There was building work underway, what looked like a small apartment block being constructed. Holiday homes, perhaps. There was a sign in Russian by the side of the road. They had reached the top of the crest of the hill and beneath them, on a plateau, was a new, timbered, ranch-style building with its own eggshell-blue swimming pool, empty of water, and a garage with its swing doors open. Outside the main house was a Mercedes, its boot open as though someone was in the middle of unloading things and taking them into the house. Lev pulled in beside it and they all got out. Lev went inside while Laurie and Flo sat down gratefully on a hammock on the deck.

They could hear Lev speaking in Russian, first quietly, then gradually raising his voice. There was a slight breeze which stuck Laurie's shirt to his back with sweat. He sensed that some of Lev's cool and self-control was slipping. Laurie caught Flo's eye. He was glad she was here. He clutched his mobile phone. If anything happened to him, they would be able to trace him through his phone. He had covered a murder trial the previous year in Birmingham crown court in which it had emerged that the victim had been found in the quarry where his body had been dumped only through a signal on his mobile phone that placed him within five hundred yards of the spot. Or had it been five hundred metres? There were constant rows with the newsdesk now as to whether one used yards or metres. He was 1.79 metres tall. Which sounded ridiculous. A boy aspired to be a six footer, not a 1.82 metrer, didn't he? As if responding to the pressure of his hand, his phone rang. He looked at his watch. It would be 6 a.m. in Britain. Lev came out of the house and shot him a suspicious glance. He beckoned them to follow him and continued his search round the ranch with Flo and Laurie ambling behind him.

'Hi, Dad,' said the voice. 'I think I failed history.'

'History has failed everyone else, darling,' said Laurie, surprised at his own speedy response. 'I'm sure you haven't. Are you OK? What have you got today?'

'Spanish.'

'Well, you'll be fine with that.' Violet had spent a month in Seville the previous summer, supposedly buffing up her Spanish. There had been postcards with frequent references to 'Arnando' and then the references had stopped. Both Caz and he had imagined that she had lost her virginity to him but had never been certain. Arnando always lurked in the background in any discussion of how well Violet was doing in Spanish.

'Are you staying at your mother's?'

He listened uncomfortably to an account of what a fabulous time had been had by all the previous evening. He wanted to ask if she should not have been revising but felt that the moment was not right. Lev had now mounted a hillock just above the ranch and was staring down the valley towards the sea.

'Do you know what's happening?' asked Flo.

'Search me,' said Laurie.

'Are you with someone, Dad?'

'Er . . . yeah . . . sort of, yes . . .'

He caught a mildly contemptuous smile on Flo's face as she checked out her camera, as if in preparation for taking a snappy portrait of Vladimir Petrov.

'Look, Violet, I'll ring you back. *Buena* . . . er . . . *Buena fortuna* . . .'

'*Suerte* actually, Dad, but good try,' said the echoing voice. 'Is everything OK for you?'

'Er, I think so, sweetie. And, if it's not, just think of all those extra compassion points you can log up.' Lev was gesturing to them both now from his perch on the hillock. 'I promise I will call you later.' Lev's gestures were becoming more urgent.

Laurie and Flo hurried up the hillock. Lev pointed towards something twenty or thirty yards – metres – below them.

'Oh, my,' said Flo.

'Oh, fuck,' said Laurie.

Chapter Twenty-eight

'THAT'S . . . ER . . . QUITE a statement,' said Laurie.
'Statement?' said Lev. He was shaking. 'Statement? Is that what you call it?'

Vlad was lying on the grass wearing the same clothes he had been the previous night but there the similarity to the urbane eastern European, who had quoted Burns at Laurie, ended. The face was a bloody pulp, the savagery of the blows that had been delivered had transformed his elegant eyebrows into a collision of bone, hair and blood. His gold crucifix had been ripped from his throat, presumably in the struggle, and lay forlornly beside the body. The gold ring on his pinkie finger had also been half wrenched off and dried blood partially obscured the star-shaped tattoo below his thumb. Pinkie finger. Where did 'pinkie' come from? Better to use 'little finger' when he wrote the story. On the other hand, if he used 'pinkie', might that not give the tale some resonance of *Brighton Rock*? Why had Graham Greene chosen 'Pinkie' as a villain's name? Criminals usually had nicknames like Rocky or Mad or Scarface. How many Mads did he know? Mad Frank Fraser. Frank 'The Mad Axeman' Mitchell. Then there were all the nicknames about size – 'Little Legs' Larkin and 'Little

Legs' . . . Who were all the other Little Legs he had known? There was a 'Little Legs' Lloyd, for sure. Then there had been John 'The Target' Moriarty, so called because he had been hit so many times. Dead, now, wasn't he? Car crash in Spain, was it? Then there were all the names that criminals had assumed when they wrote their memoirs. The Guv'nor. The Enforcer. The Mean Machine. But Pinkie? It was like Pussy in *The Sopranos*. It worked because it was counter-intuitive. That was it, counter-intuitive. Did Vlad have a nickname? he wondered.

'Hello, are you still with us?' asked Flo, brow furrowed, eye cocked.

'Oh, yeah, sure,' said Laurie.

Lev had gone into the house and was still calling out in Russian. Who was he hoping to see there? Was the assailant still around? Laurie scanned the hillside. The blood on Vlad's face was drying and already attracting flies. He must have been there for a while. No attempt had been made to hide the body. Laurie felt strangely calm. Was it the reassuring presence of Flo, who was kneeling now by the body?

Laurie glanced round, a slow pan taking in the whole scene. Vlad, so handsome in life, was ugly in death, bloated perhaps by being left in the sweltering Thai sun. One of his smart alligator-skin shoes was lying beside him. Had he been trying to flee? There was his wallet, made from the skin of some other exotic creature, passport sticking out but the little plastic windows that housed credit cards had been ripped from the seam and there was no sign of any cash.

Flo, he was impressed to see, had realised that there was nothing to be done for Vlad and had taken out her camera and started shooting. He looked at the body again, trying to conjure up what kind of image she would be capturing. He recalled the favourite magazines of his boyhood, *True Detective* and *True Crime*, with their grainy black-and-white shots of bludgeoned bodies, bullet-ridden saloon cars and guilty dames. His mother had expressed concern to his father about his preference for such fare over *Eagle*, the more wholesome choices of his older brothers. Even *Hotspur* was seen as healthier for a twelve year old than all those riddled corpses, all that crimson prose. He would grow out of it, he had heard his father telling his mother as he lay, reading by torchlight under the sheets, of stranglers and garrotters, hitmen and dogged detectives in hats.

'I . . . er . . . suppose we should call the Old Bill,' said Laurie.

'Who?' said Lev, appearing on the deck of the house, mobile phone in hand. 'No, we call police.' He started dialling, failed to get a connection, cursed – Laurie assumed it was a curse, it could have been a prayer or anything – and dialled again.

Now what did Old Bill come from? That was a good point. Did that count as a cliché that one should know the origins of before using or—

'Laurie, are you OK?' said Flo. 'You seem to be a bit distracted.'

'Sorry. It's just, well, you know – this!' He gestured at Vlad. The flies were massing in the bloodied mop of his hair. His hair was still a fine auburn colour. Had he dyed it like Hook did? No. It was a brave thing for a man to do, thought Laurie. Not as brave as a toupee, of course, but still courageous to risk the mockery of your fellow males. He wished he had had the courage to do it. Too late now. There was one chief constable who dyed his hair; Laurie remembered sitting behind him at a boring talk about community policing at an ACPO conference and, as someone droned on about 'best practice', studying the just-perceptible borderline between dye and roots on the chief constable's neck. Did his officers think the less of him for it?

'I thought a big crime reporter would see this all the time,' said Flo, adjusting the camera once again and checking to see what she had already shot.

Laurie was unwilling to admit that the only bodies he had ever seen were his grandmother laid out at the undertaker's in Nottingham – he had kissed her forehead, cold as marble – and Lenin's, embalmed, on a school trip to Moscow that he remembered chiefly now because his father had not paid the school for it and there had been an embarrassing fuss afterwards. He had wanted to ask Vlad about Russian embalming, apparently the best in the world. Too late for that now.

'Yes, I guess so, but it still takes a bit of getting used to. You seem remarkably . . . er . . .'

'Cool? Is that the word you're looking for?' said Flo. 'You work in social services in Sheffield and you get used to this sort of thing. He's not the first murder victim I've seen.' Laurie shot her a glance. She paused. 'I was a nurse for nearly ten years. A body is a body.'

Lev was talking in slow English now. Laurie presumed he had made contact with the local police. Another phone call and now he was talking Russian. Was it Laurie's imagination or did Lev seem to give a short, snorted laugh? Should he phone the newsdesk and let them know that the Most Wanted Man

In Britain was now the Most Dead Man in Thailand? Would they be able to use Flo's photos? Or would they be deemed a little too gruesome for breakfast?

'Want to have a look?' said Flo, reading his thoughts. She handed him her camera. The pictures were hard to make out in the glare of the sun but they had a grim power.

'Yup,' said Laurie. 'I would say that you've got a real marmalade-dropper there.'

'I know you want me to ask what a real marmalade-dropper is so I'll ask. What is a real marmalade-dropper?'

'I don't know where the idea came from originally. I think it was someone at the *Daily Telegraph* who invented it but it's when there's a story or a photograph that is just so . . . so . . . weird that when you're reading it at breakfast and you're just about to eat your toast and marmalade—'

'The toast doesn't reach your mouth and the marmalade drops on the table.'

'I think you got it. You know how to send these things, these photos, do you?'

'Yeah, I do live in the twenty-first century.'

'Great.' What better excuse to phone Eva-Marie than this? He rehearsed the conversation. Casual. Self-confident. Man of the world. Foreign correspondent. 'Hi there, Eva-Marie, how are you?' he would say. Not too effusive. 'Got some photos I was going to dispatch. A colleague here – freelancer – Flo.' He did not know her last name. Now was perhaps not the time to ask. Would they be impressed that he had photos of the scene? Would Flo mind if he claimed to have taken the photos himself? Surely not. After all, she was not a professional and she was hardly going to change career on the basis of photos of a dead Russian. He would pay her, of course. He hoped her scoop would not get poor, sick CJ into trouble and deepen his depression. But Stark would surely be impressed when these exclusive snaps dropped at the other end. It would show how committed he was to the paper's new multimedia imperatives. Would Eva-Marie be impressed? Ah, but she would realise it was not his own work and she would not be impressed by his lying. Better to credit Flo. Perhaps he would bring Eva-Marie a small gift back from Thailand. Nothing too personal, of course. Would news of his ended marriage already have percolated right through the paper, where rumours spread as swiftly as flu on a 747?

Lev was giving directions to the house over the phone. He seemed calm, in control. Too calm? Was Laurie his alibi? The passing British journalist, with no previous convictions, who would swear that Lev had been in his company for the past few hours. Was that why he had been happy for Flo to tag along too? Another witness with no connections to him.

Lev joined them by the body.

'Are the police on their way?' Laurie asked.

'Ambulance and police, yes. I speak to Russian Embassy, Bangkok.'

'I think it's a little late for an ambulance,' said Flo.

Lev shrugged. 'Is necessary. Protocol.'

'I suppose there is nothing we can do. It seems a bit hard on Mr Petrov that we can't put a blanket or a sheet over him. It's so undignified.'

Lev shrugged again. His mobile phone rang and he walked back into the ranch, talking in Russian. Was he aware that the police could trace all this stuff nowadays? Every move you make, every phone call you take. Laurie presumed that they were safe. Lev would hardly have brought them along to act as his alibi witnesses if he was going to bump them off, would he? Ghosts from *True Crime* floated past. Mass murderers – the serial killer had not been a fashion in those days in the sixties – sometimes liked their victims to see other victims. Maybe Lev was planning some vast funeral pyre. That would solve everything. That would certainly mean that Laurie got more than six hundred words for his obituary. He moved closer to the body and reached into the back pocket of his jeans for his crumpled notebook. Must record the scene.

Face a bloody pulp. Wasn't there some less clichéd, more poetic way to put it? Face like a melon that had been dropped from the thirteenth floor of some godforsaken Deptford highrise. No, no, no. Too showy. Face like a tomato that had been run over in a supermarket car park? Tacky. And Vlad's people might not like that. An early news editor had told him never to write about a murder victim in such a way that you would be unable to justify your description to the parents of the dead person. Vlad might still have parents. He pictured two elderly Russians being visited at their humble dacha by – by whom? No more KGB – by whoever brought bad news. They probably had a liquor store on Long Island.

He heard his name being called and turned to see Lev. In the distance he could hear the sound of a siren, soon joined by the sounds of others. He and Flo followed Lev's beckoning arm. Was he going to plant weapons on them or something?

They joined Lev just round the corner of the house. He was pointing up a pathway to a gap that had been torn in the fence.

'That is where they must have come in.'

'They?' asked Flo.

'There must have been more than one person to kill Vlad. Strong man.'

They moved gingerly along the path. Laurie envisaged the murderer lying in wait for them, club in hand, ready to batter all three of them to death. Lev ushered him forward but he had not yet eliminated Lev from his inquiries and he did not want to be presenting his skull too temptingly for him. But he must not show fear. Was that the case with murderers? Or was that just grizzly bears? Maybe murderers liked to see a bit of fear.

'You know the way,' he said to Lev. 'I'll follow you.'

In the long grass near the gap in the fence was a flutter of dollar bills. There were dozens of them – $100 bills. Would it be very bad form to grab a couple? No one would notice half a dozen missing. Pay for Violet's first year at university. Probably stolen or the fruits of extortion anyway. Better that they should go into the British education system than some corrupt policeman's pocket. Or, worse, be blown away on the wind.

'Robbers must have left these as they ran away,' said Lev. Flo said nothing but gave Laurie an enigmatic look. The sirens were getting closer.

'I think we should go back to the house and wait for the police,' said Flo. 'We don't want to mess up the scene of the crime, do we?'

They retraced their steps, with Flo leading the way. As she turned back to where Vlad's body lay, Laurie saw her start and stiffen.

'What's up, Flo?'

'Wooo, gross,' said Flo, slipping the camera from her shoulder. 'Gross. Gross. Gross.'

Laurie joined her. They had a new companion. A brown and white Staffordshire bull terrier. It was eating Vlad's face. It seemed to be enjoying the lips.

Chapter Twenty-nine

FLO PEERED OVER Laurie's shoulder at the laptop. They were sitting together on the end of his bed in his hotel room. She was in a turquoise swimsuit. She was too old now for bikinis, she told Laurie. He told her she wasn't.

'So, is this how it's done? You write your name first. Is that the most important thing?'

'Well, it's the one thing I'm sure of. And it's reassuring. Laurie Lane in Pattaya. Has a ring to it, doesn't it? You can help me with this. How long have we got before we're meant to see the police again?'

Flo looked at her watch. 'We have a couple of hours.'

Laurie started tapping his story in.

'The Russian businessman sought in connection with the murder of London gangster Charlie Hook has been found murdered at a house outside the Thai resort of Pattaya. He had been bludgeoned to death in what police believe may have been an international gangland revenge killing.' Laurie paused.

'That's a bit flat, isn't it?' said Flo. 'Does this place do room service?'

'I expect so,' said Laurie. 'What do you want me to say?

I'll change "house" to "villa" or "ranch", if you like.'

'Well, you could make it a little more dramatic, couldn't you? Bloody hell, think of what he looked like when we found him. Like a bloody mashed turnip. Can I order some lunch? I'm starving. I never got to finish that breakfast you so kindly treated me to. Fancy some pad thai?'

'Sure, but I have to crank this out.'

Laurie started tapping out again.

'The murder came the day after we had tracked Vladimir Petrov down to his Thailand hideaway and—'

'I thought he tracked you down – it was him that asked you to go and visit, wasn't it?'

'Sure, but how do I express that? "The murder came the day after we had a friendly chat in a bar in Pattaya, after I'd got smashed on some Thai weed and had a hot night with a sexy social worker from . . ."'

'Sheffield.' She kissed the back of his neck and slipped her hand under his shirt. He could feel her nails on his back.

' "And after the murdered man had invited me to his house to talk . . ." Do you think we're suspects, Flo?'

'How could we be? We were with Lev.'

'D'you think Lev did it?'

'I thought you were meant to be the person who knows everything about crime.'

'Yeah, but you're meant to be a social worker, aren't you? Can't you tell when someone's trying to hide something from you?'

'Well, I would guess that Lev is up to something but whether or not he's actually killed his – is he his boss, the dead guy? – his boss or he's just up to some dodgy business, I have no idea. Anyway, hadn't you better get on with your pearls of wisdom?'

Laurie resumed. 'The murder came the day after Mr Petrov—'

'It's Mr Petrov, is it? Bit of respect for the dead?' asked Flo, leaning over him. Laurie could feel her breast pressing against his arm. Concentrate, concentrate.

'The rule is that the victim becomes a Mr or a Miss – or a Mrs – and the perpetrator loses his title.'

'How very moral. On you go.'

'Right. How does this sound? "The brutal murder—" '

'Aren't all murders brutal?'

'Not at all. If you just gave someone an overdose of sleeping pills and they died in bed without ever knowing anything about it, that wouldn't be brutal, would it? Or, I suppose, smothering someone with a pillow wouldn't be too brutal really, if they were too feeble to struggle. I think anything with a lot of blood spraying around or with any torture involved would count. For instance, if you used a chainsaw to lop someone's limbs off one by one or clipped off the tips of their fingers with secateurs and let them bleed to death—'

'OK, OK, I get the picture,' said Flo, moving away from him slightly. 'It's just whenever you see a story about a murder in a newspaper it always says "brutal" murder.'

'I know,' said Laurie. 'It's an obligatory adjective. You know, every suburb is leafy and—'

'Every woman with an opinion is feisty,' said Flo.

'And every journalist is always award-winning and every toff with a drug problem is troubled and—'

'Are you an award-winning journalist?'

'As soon as I said that I knew you were going to ask. And the answer is no. But nearly . . .'

'Well, maybe this will do it for you. You not only find old whatsisname but give them another murder – another "brutal" murder – into the bargain. You've sewn up the whole case, haven't you? Shouldn't that get you some honour?'

'Like an MBE, you mean?' He kissed her on her open lips. 'Look, order that pad thai and something sweet and fizzy for me because I must get this over before we have to see the police again.'

'I was once Employee of the Month, you know. In a previous life at Marks and Sparks, before I went into nursing.'

'I'm impressed. Now, tell me what you think of this bit. Have I got it right? "Detective Thaweesuk of the Pattaya police said that the killing appeared to have been a robbery gone wrong. International police sources however suggested last night that it had all the hallmarks of a 'tit-for-tat slaying'—"'

'Hey, hey, wait a minute,' said Flo, leaning forward and examining the story on the screen. 'When did these "international police sources" arrive on the scene?'

'Well, I know that there are coppers who would say that it looks like a tit-for-tat murder.'

'I thought it was a "slaying" now. When does a murder become a slaying?'

'Well, you can't keep using the same word over and over again so you come up with a synonym. "Slaying" is OK, isn't it? Or too noir for you?'

She shook her head mockingly at him.

'Is it too *noooiiiirrr* for you?' she said, imitating his voice.

'And where does this "last night" thing come from? There hasn't been a night since we saw the body, has there, so how can these non-existent copper pals of yours be commenting on something last night?'

'Look, this is just a convention. When people are reading their papers over breakfast—'

'This isn't more stuff about marmalade, is it?'

'I'm trying to explain the conventions.'

'Sounds more like a load of fancy bollocks for making things up. And I thought you said something about not using clichés unless you knew where the original phrase had come from?'

'And?'

'Well, are you going to explain where "tit-for-tat" comes from – without being a little boy about it?'

'Good question.'

'So you don't know the answer. You blokes are all the same.'

'That may be true but right now we have to finish this damn story or I'll get into trouble with someone much more ruthless and unforgiving than the Thai police. So what was it the policeman said?'

'Well, the main guy, the one not in uniform, who Lev seemed to know, said that it looked like – what did you say in your story? "Had the markings of"? Something like that.'

'Had all the hallmarks of.'

'What does that mean? What's a bloody hallmark when it's at home? Is that another one of your what-do-you-call-thems?'

'It is, it is. But what did he say?'

'He certainly didn't say anything about bloody hallmarks. He just said that it looked like a robbery. That Vlad – is that really his name? – that Vlad must have disturbed the robbers when they were breaking in and that there must have been a fight. And that they were looking for a group of men who could be European and – what is a hallmark anyway, smartypants?'

'I think it's something to do with silverware, isn't it? Did he really say they were looking for European men? I didn't hear that.'

'That was when you were giving your statement to the bloke in dark glasses,' said Flo. 'What he said was that they were looking for these Europeans and that they had been concerned that a – what did he say? – a criminal element from the United Kingdom had established itself in the area and that one line of inquiry would be amongst British expatriates in Pattaya.'

'Well, we're British expatriates in Pattaya, aren't we? Did he mean us?'

'Don't be silly. He means all those guys who we saw eating bacon and eggs and drinking lager. Talking of which, I could do with a drink right now. Do you want a beer?'

'I'm working, for heaven's sake.' Laurie tapped on. 'Mr Petrov had clearly fought his assailants hard. There were signs of a violent struggle with broken glass and upturned furniture in the villa near where his body was found. His gold ring had been half ripped from his little finger and his shoes – his alligator-skin shoes—'

The theme for *The Sopranos* rang out. Did the Alabama 3 get a royalty every time someone's ring-tone rang with their tune? Hardly. He used to have the first bars of 'Crazy' on his phone, 'Crazy' being the song that Caz had sung on the night that they met in the Goblin all those years ago. Crazy for trying. Crazy for crying.

'Hulllooooo.' Stark, of course.

'I'm glad you rang,' Laurie said. 'I'm in the police station being interrogated. I'll ring you back in an hour – is that about how long this will take, Inspector?' He nudged Flo into action.

'About one hour, yes,' Flo replied in a faux-deep voice. 'If you cooperate, Meester Lane . . .' She slipped her hand between his legs. Laurie put his hand over the phone. 'All right, all right,' he said and placed his finger over her lips. 'Sorry about that,' he told Stark. 'No, no, no need to get in touch with the consul, I can handle it fine, really. As I said, I'll file as soon as I'm out of the cop shop. What? A what? A podcast with the police? I don't think that will be allowed. Let me ask the inspector . . .' He placed his hand over the mouthpiece once more and tried to stop Flo from giggling. He paused and resumed his conversation.

'Unfortunately, the Thai police have very strict rules about talking on pod-casts – well, talking on the radio . . . yes, it is odd, isn't it, but there you go. Look, is Scotland Yard saying anything about this at all? No comment? Great. After we find their man for them you would have thought that the least they could do for us is—'

Stark wanted to know about photos.

'Yes, well, you know CJ is very, very ill – he may have to go to hospital – but we have some photos from the scene, of course . . . Yes, very good freelancer . . . What's his name? Shame on you. It's a she. She was at the scene. No, not agency, no one else will have it. I'll make sure we get an exclusive deal with her . . . No, I haven't spoken to the picture desk but why don't you put me through and then I'll send the story . . . What's the bottom line? Who did it? Well, an expat robber or a local crook or a Hook family avenger or someone from Vlad's KGB past or . . . No, I've no idea if he was in the KGB . . . Take your pick really . . . Yeah, yeah.'

Flo's pictures looked remarkably professional. There was Vlad sprawled on the ground, taken at a respectful distance but clearly showing a dead body, and a close-up of his face, too grim and gruesome to use in a family newspaper. Were there any newspapers that were not 'family' newspapers? Laurie wondered. What was the opposite of a 'family' newspaper? Or was there a 'single-parent family newspaper' that had lower standards? There was a landscape shot that showed the whole ranch with the body in the centre, which he imagined being used across half a page. There was a moody shot of Vlad's hand with the ring half ripped off the finger. There was a more discreet shot of the body from a side angle with the alligator-skin shoe to one side. There was even one of the Staffordshire bull terrier investigating Vlad's face, which was definitely not for even a dysfunctional family newspaper.

Did dogs really eat humans? Were we not too toxic for them? No. Laurie remembered, as a young reporter in Manchester, having to cover the death of an elderly woman who lived alone with her eight dogs and who had died unnoticed until the stench alerted the neighbours that something was up. Her dogs had more or less cleaned her down to the bones, something that his paper – being a real family newspaper – had delicately skirted around, although it had been the talk of the newsroom for days.

He was impressed by the speed with which Flo

downloaded the pictures and despatched them to the picture desk's email address. He rang the paper again to make sure the photos had arrived safely.

'Hello,' said Eva-Marie's voice at the other end. Was it his imagination or did it sound more mysterious, more intimate than usual? Maybe she just had a sore throat. 'I was just thinking about you, Laurie.' Was she really? 'Are you OK? It all sounds a bit hairy.'

'Oh, it's all cool,' said Laurie. He felt Flo's hand on his thigh. This was confusing. 'I just wanted to check that all the pictures of the murder scene in Thailand had arrived. Yes . . . Yeah. Flo. F for Freddie, L for Lima, O for the wings of a dove.' He felt Flo's nails digging into his leg as she kissed him on the neck. 'No, it's OK, just a bad line.' This was very, very confusing. Here was Eva-Marie being attentive and concerned and yet there was no way he could continue this conversation. 'Last name Dutta. D for Delta, U for me and me for you . . . just joking . . . T for two and A for 'orses . . . What, you've never heard that? You're so young.' It was hard to flirt at six thousand miles while someone else was squeezing your thigh.

'Yeah, they are a bit – what did you say? Explicit? Well, death is quite explicit, isn't it? Yes . . . OK. As long as they have arrived.' He rang off and he and Flo embraced, undressed each other swiftly and made love on the unmade bed.

As Flo smoked a duty-free Camel and lay propped up against a pillow, Laurie knocked off a farewell to Vlad, sitting again on the end of the bed with his warm laptop on his knees.

'Not since the death of Charlie Wilson,' he wrote, 'the great train robber, who was gunned down in Spain in 1990, has there been a foreign killing with such resonance for the London underworld. What remains unclear is whether this latest murder was carried out on the orders of associates of the Hook family or had some other motive. Meanwhile, last night Thailand's most senior detectives were trying to put together the many pieces of the jigsaw that was the life of Vladimir Petrov.'

Flo had leant forward and was looking over his shoulder at what he had written. He could feel her breasts against his back.

'Why have you put "last night" again?' she said. 'And how do you know the Thai police are trying to put any pieces together? Do you just make that stuff up?'

'Well, not exactly. As I was trying to explain earlier, it's more a convention. You could call it well-founded speculation, I think.'

'Well-founded la-di-da bollocks more like.'

Chapter Thirty

I T WAS THAT difficult Day Three. He could tell that the newsdesk was already losing interest. Other stories back home in Britain were taking over. A Premiership footballer had killed a pregnant woman in a hit-and-run accident. A shadow cabinet minister had admitted that, as a student, he had liked to cross-dress. An alleged al-Qaida cell, consisting of middle-class biology students, had been arrested in Stevenage. After the front-page splash, complete with Flo's photo of Vlad's corpse, and a follow-up the next day, there was not too much to say. Laurie had already phoned the Thai police and been told that there were no new developments, and the detective who had taken a statement from Flo and him was unhelpful. The Russian Embassy had no comment and a trawl of the bars, from the Dog's Bollocks to St Trinans, had yielded little in the way of information. Laurie felt torn between wanting to get back to London and being tempted to prolong this strange and delightful interlude with Flo, who was out shopping in the market. CJ was still ill and in bed. He would take one final stroll round the bars, see what the word was today and ring the newsdesk.

Lev was sitting calmly outside Henri's, sipping a cocktail

with an umbrella in it. Laurie remembered when cocktails had become fashionable – or become fashionable again – at the Dirty Dog and every drink had an irritating little umbrella stuck in it. The barmaid at the time – what had her name been? – had to consult a booklet of cocktail recipes to mix the drinks and, on seeing that some required a cocktail onion, had taken to hoisting a pickled onion from the jar on the bar and dumping it in the drink. What had been worse was that some of the patrons did not even notice, even appeared to like the combined taste of vinegar and Cinzano. If he caught the plane to London out of Bangkok airport tomorrow, he would be back in time for quiz night. Vic would be bound to have some inside gen on what the hell was going on, would he not? Surely he would.

'Hi,' he said to Lev, who nodded back at him. Lev seemed remarkably untroubled for someone whose buddy and partner had just been whacked to death and had his face eaten off by a Staffordshire bull terrier. It had been a Staffordshire bull terrier, hadn't it? There had been an email from a reader, querying this, on behalf of the Staffordshire Bull Terriers Owners Society, who said that it was impossible that the breed would be eating a human face. Laurie wondered about sending the reader some of Flo's more explicit photos or challenging them to lie supine on the ground with some gravy on their face beside the terrier concerned.

'Any news?' he asked. Lev put his drink down and beckoned him over. Laurie sat beside him. It was hot. He fancied a Chang or a Tiger but it was too early in the day and he still had to file.

'I have spoken to police this morning. They say they think it was British man who already left country.'

'Why didn't they stop him?'

'False passport.'

'False passport?'

'Is easy to get false passport in Pattaya. You want false passport?'

'The idea does appeal.'

That would solve everything, thought Laurie. New identity, new life. Reinvent yourself. Eliminate the design faults of the previous model. He would let Violet know, of course, but apart from her, no one, not even Guy or Vic, Mick and Mary. Certainly not Caz. She would wonder what had become of him, she would pine. But, in reality, Violet would tell her immediately and Caz would not pine at all but think that this would be a nice adventure for him. The fantasy of a new identity dissolved.

'But I think it would all be just a bit too complicated. Do the police have a theory as to why someone would do that? Do they really think it's just a straightforward robbery? There're easier ways to make money round here than bumping someone off for a few hundred dollars.'

'Safe was open,' said Lev. 'Nothing inside. Wallet empty. Credit card already used once in Bangkok. What your plan now?'

'Well, I've made my statement and the police said that I could return to England provided I tell them and the British Embassy how they can get hold of me. I think it helped that we ran a picture of the chief of police this morning.' It had not been Flo's most artistic achievement – the officer was blinking into the sunlight and his face was scrunched up – but it had occupied a single column and the chief had seemed gratified when Laurie pointed it out to him on the paper's website when he had been down at the Pattaya police station.

Lev seemed unbothered by Laurie's impending departure. Vlad's body was in the morgue in Pattaya, he said. His ex-wife was on the way to identify him formally. It would be flown back to St Petersburg for burial when all the tests had been carried out on it. The police were examining a baseball bat they had found discarded by the highway for any fingerprints or DNA traces. The Staffordshire bull terrier was in a kennels but had been offered a home by the owner of Guts for Garters. Laurie copied down Lev's mobile number and bade him farewell.

Back at the hotel, he went up to his room and filed his story. The room had been made up and his luggage was piled on a side table. The newsdesk had said that six hundred words would be sufficient so he quoted Lev as a 'close friend' who said that the safe and Vlad's wallet had been empty and sent the story on its way. Did they want him to stay on or should he head home? He received his marching orders, alerted a slowly recovering CJ, and rang British Airways to book their flights home. There was a tap at his door.

'Hello, sailor,' said Flo. 'Are you running out on me already?'

'No, I was going to come looking for you to say goodbye. Honest. But I have to get back.'

'The wife taking you back?'

'No chance, I don't think. How about you? Any second thoughts about your old man?'

'Third thoughts, they would be – but no. I don't blame your wife. You're all tied up in this work thing as though it's the most important thing in the world.'

'What should I be doing? Jet-skiing with you?'

'That would be a start. Don't worry. It's been fun – isn't that what men like, one of those no-strings numbers in a hot climate?'

'Come on, you don't get rid of me that easily. Can't I have a string attached? You're going to show me round Sheffield, aren't you? I haven't been there since that story about the police and the girl outside the nightclub. When are you off?'

'Do you mean, have we got time for one final . . . You're so, so predictable. D'you want a hand with your packing?'

'I don't have too much. See!' Laurie lifted his case, the one with little wheels that Caz had made him buy the last time he put his back out and had to go to the Chinese osteopath in Wembley. He thought a case with wheels was, well, demeaning for a grown, healthy man and she had mocked him for it. 'I'll get my trunks out – there's time for a final swim.' He reached into the case. His swimming trunks were at the bottom. And what was that underneath them? A pouch of some kind? His sponge bag? Why was it called a sponge bag when you never carried a sponge in it? No, it was not his sponge bag, which was still by the side of the basin. He pulled it out. It was an unfamiliar plastic zip-up container. Inside it was what, at a wild guess, was probably £50,000 worth of heroin.

Chapter Thirty-one

'AND QUESTION NUMBER three is, how many sides does a pentagram have? I'll repeat that: how many sides does a pentagram have?'

'These questions are getting too easy,' said Vic, sipping his ginger ale. 'I blame the dumbing down of the education system. They'll be asking us how many decks a double-decker bus has. Now, Laurie, when are you going to tell us what the fuck happened out there? If it was the Hooks who done him in, why did they want you out there to see it?'

'Don't you read his paper?' asked Mary. 'He's just like all the other journalists, he hasn't a fucking clue. No disrespect, Laurie.'

Laurie emptied his pint. His third? His fourth? The plane had been late and he had not escaped from Heathrow for nearly an hour. Customs had stopped him for a search for the first time since he had been a student and returning from a holiday in Peru. There had been a diligent perusal of his case first and then a polite request to come into the office for a body search.

'Did they find anything?' asked Mary.

'Well, this is the weird thing,' said Laurie. 'I was just going through my luggage before coming back from Thailand and someone had put a packet of heroin in my case.'

'You're kidding,' said Mick. 'Where is it now? Did you swallow it all? You are kidding, aren't you?'

'He's not,' said Mary. 'I can tell.'

'Who the fuck would do that?' asked Mick.

'God knows,' said Laurie. 'We dumped the heroin in a bin in Pattaya but whoever it was must have tipped off Customs at Heathrow because, sure as hell, they were expecting to find something. I mean, do I look like a drug smuggler?'

Mary surveyed him. 'I can see it,' she said. 'Slightly shifty, hair slightly too long, bloodshot eyes, little bit too much stubble.'

Laurie reached into his pocket for a £20 note to get in his round before the next question. Too late.

'Number four, question number four. What was the forty-ninth state of the United States?'

'I used to bloody know that,' said Mick. 'It's either Hawaii or—'

'No, it's not,' said Mary. 'I went there on a holiday – before I met you,' she said to Mick. 'Amazingly enough there was life on the planet before you came along and Hawaii is definitely – definitely – the fiftieth.'

'Well, that only leaves another forty-nine to go through.'

'Alaska,' said Mick. 'It must be Alaska.'

'Final answer?' said Mary.

'I'm a hundred per cent sure. When I did that four stretch in the Scrubs I learned all the names of the states by heart to get me to sleep at night because there was this nutter in the next cell who—'

'You can't say "nutter" any more,' said Vic.

'Why not?' said Mick.

'It's derogatory of people with mental problems. It's like saying "poof" or "Yid" or "wog".'

'Where did you get this from?'

'It was in Laurie's paper. Anyway, are we all agreed on Alaska? You're in trouble if it's wrong, Mick. I thought you had a bloody geography degree.'

Laurie checked the bar. It was too crowded to slip in a round before the next question would arrive. He would have to wait for the half-time break after ten questions.

'Go on about the search,' said Mary.

'Well, we get into this room and the Customs guy was really embarrassed – he was just young.'

'Did he bat for the other side?' asked Mick.

'That's just as offensive as "nutter",' said Vic.

'No, it's not. It's just two teams – the heteros and the homos,' said Mick. 'What's the matter with that?'

'Anyway,' said Laurie, 'he said, "I'm going to ask you to take off all your clothes and bend over and—"'

'Sounds like Mick on our first date,' said Mary.

'Question number five,' said Cliff, talking too close to the microphone. 'Over what country did King Zog reign? I'll repeat that. Over what country did King Zog reign?'

'Albania,' said Vic. 'I told you it was all getting too easy.'

'What d'you want them to ask?' asked Mary. 'How tall was Virginia Woolf?'

'What you on about?' asked Vic.

'Don't you want to hear the end of this?' said Laurie.

'Anyway, I take off all my clothes. Fortunately, I had put on clean underwear in Thailand and—'

'I bet he wears Calvin Klein,' said Vic.

'I bet he wears Y-fronts,' said Mick.

'Ignore them,' said Mary.

'Anyway,' said Laurie. 'I have to lie on my back so he can look between my toes. I have to bend over so that he can look up my arse.'

'Please, we haven't eaten yet,' said Mick.

'And he seemed really surprised and disappointed that he found nothing.'

'But whoever put the smack in your luggage would have thought that you'd be nicked at Bangkok airport and that you'd be going away for a twenty stretch in Thailand at least,' said Mick.

'Well, I didn't get searched on the way out of Bangkok. They're looking for stuff that people bring in, aren't they?'

'Are they? I thought that, when people were set up with drugs, the Thai police nabbed them on the way out. You're lucky you're not on Death Row in the Bangkok Hilton.'

'So, maybe, once they realised you were on the plane, they thought they'd missed it in Bangkok and they tipped off the Old Bill back here,' said Mary. 'Who would want you to get busted like that? Bastards. Anyway, you're here. We have to beat the School's Out team this week. We got clobbered last week. Vic forgot all his Shakespeare, didn't you?'

'Well, I was sure it was from *As You Like It*,' said Vic. 'They may not have been targeting Laurie at all. In Thailand, they get paid for tipping the Old Bill off about drug smugglers so someone may have just chosen Laurie because he was a foreigner who was getting packed up to go home, planted some smack on him and hoped to pick up the reward.'

The pub was crowded with the usual Thursday night quizzers and a couple of tables of young Poles, who were working on the renovation of the next door flats. Cliff had earlier announced, to cheers from the Poles, that Lech beer was now on draft.

'And the next question,' said Cliff. 'What is the name of the composer of "The Protecting Veil"?'

'Bloody hell, is that intellectual enough for you, Vic?' asked Mary. 'Whose round is it anyway?'

'Mine,' said Laurie.

'"The Protecting Veil"?' said Mick. 'Sounds like a make of condom.'

'Have you seen the selection in the gents these days?' asked Laurie. 'What does "Ribbed for her pleasure" mean?'

'Don't ask me,' said Mary.

'John Tavener,' said Vic. 'I've got the CD.'

'Get you,' said Mick. 'You're really upwardly fucking mobile, aren't you? Can I have all your old David Bowie records then?'

'But has there been any chat about what happened to Vlad?' said Laurie. 'What's up with the Hooks? Did they have anything to say about what happened to him?'

'You think they'd issue a press release welcoming the demise of the evil Russian who killed their old man thus robbing the world of a great philanthropist?' asked Mick.

'So everyone is still pretty sure that it was Vlad who killed Old Man Hook?'

'That's the word,' said Mick. 'Isn't it, Vic? You hang out

with that crowd still. I never reckoned them that much. Bunch of bullies. I still think it was one of Barney Quick's people.'

'What are the Old Bill saying, Laurie?' asked Vic.

'Well, they're just saying that they found the weapon at Vlad's place, that he did a runner and that we can draw our own conclusions,' said Laurie. 'But they haven't yet said that they aren't looking for anyone else in connection with the murder, which is their usual code for "we know who did it and he's dead".'

'Question number seven. In what year was Margaret Thatcher elected prime minister?' intoned Cliff. 'I'll repeat that. In what year was Margaret Thatcher elected prime minister?'

'I know that,' said Mary, writing '1979' on the answer pad.

'More bloody trivia,' said Vic. 'I can remember when this was one of the good quizzes, it didn't have lots of dates and stuff about *Big Brother*.'

'Just because they haven't got a question about Virginia Woolf for you to show off about,' said Mary. 'But, Laurie, don't any of your policemen friends think it's just a bit too convenient that the murder weapon turns up in the back garden of a dodgy Russian? And then – whoopee! – the Russian gets bumped off in Thailand, nice and far away and they can all suggest everything's hunky-dory and solved. I think it's all bloody iffy.'

'So have you got a better idea?' asked Vic.

'I dunno,' said Mary. 'But like I said before, Old Man Hook was a real groper. He seemed to think he was entitled to cop a feel of any girl around. He specially liked the really young ones and I'm sure he went much further than a grope. I should think lots of people would have liked to see him dead. He was a bully, like Mick said. I don't know why you hang around with them, Vic. Still, you did all right out of the Russian, Laurie, didn't you? You were all over the front pages. God, I could do with a fag. I suppose I'll have to wait till half-time because you sods won't be able to get any of the music answers without me.'

Laurie fiddled with an empty packet of spicy peanuts on the table.

'But if it wasn't Vlad who did it, why would anyone bother to kill him? That's the question, isn't it? If it was one of the Hooks' people in Thailand, why would they bother doing that if they weren't sure it was Vlad? After all, they don't want all the heat that a murder brings, even if it is thousands of miles away.'

Mary shook her head. She had her cigarettes and lighter out on the table and was fiddling with them.

'Well, maybe whoever did kill Charlie Hook wanted Vlad out of the way before he could prove it wasn't him. The other thing is that Dee – you remember her, Mick? – went out with one of the Hook boys when she worked at Stringfellows and she always said that they hated their dad. So—'

'Patricide,' said Vic. 'Which reminds me. I was right about Oedipus, that question last week. I knew I was.'

'So the boys bumped him off so they could inherit the empire and then fitted up a harmless Russian businessman?' asked Laurie.

'I'd keep that one to yourself if I were you,' said Mick.

'Number nine, question number nine: who won an Oscar for their performance in *Kiss of the Spiderwoman*?'

'God, I know that,' said Mary. 'Hey, look, is that one of the teachers texting someone? Do you think they've got people waiting at home with their computers on, ready to answer all the questions? Bastards.'

'Give him a break,' said Mick. 'He's probably texting his girlfriend to apologise for being such a sad sack as to be out playing pub quizzes.'

'Just because you couldn't remember the battle that Rommel was in last week,' said Vic. 'I thought you were meant to be our military expert.'

'I got bloody Thermopylae for you, didn't I?' said Mick. 'And Troy.'

'I got Troy as well,' said Mary. 'So who did win an Oscar for that?'

'John Hurt, wasn't it?' said Vic.

'No, it wasn't,' said Mary. 'Keep your voice down. They're trying to earwig us.'

'I think it was William Hurt,' said Laurie. 'In fact I'm sure it was. I remember watching it with Caz.'

There was a sympathetic silence at the table.

'Any news on that?' asked Mary.

'Well, I haven't seen her since I got back,' said Laurie.

'He'd rather be answering questions about the highest mountain in New Zealand with us than trying to patch his marriage up,' said Mick.

'Oh, leave him alone,' said Mary. 'You just have to give her a bit of time, Laurie. She was always a bit impetuous, wasn't she? Or otherwise she'd never have ended up going out with you, would she? I mean, she could really have her pick of the blokes, couldn't she?'

'Thanks a lot,' said Laurie.

'And the last question before the break is number ten and, yes, it's another one about number ten,' announced Cliff, trying to make himself heard above the noise. 'Who is the shortest serving British prime minister? I'll repeat that – the shortest serving British prime minister?'

'Must be Clem Attlee, he was only five foot six,' said Mick.

'He didn't say shortest, he said shortest serving,' said Vic.

'God, your radar's messed up these days, Vic,' said Mary. 'Did you think he was serious? So who is it, Laurie?'

'Um, Sir Alec Douglas-Home? I'm not sure.'

'Bloody media,' said Mick. 'They don't know anything any more. I reckon it was one of those obscure ones like – God, what was he called? – the one who got assassinated.'

'I don't think a British prime minister ever got assassinated,' said Mary.

'He did. I can't remember his name,' said Mick. 'I did him for A level when I was in Maidstone. I can still remember the politics teacher. She was a little fox. What was her name?'

'It wasn't the one that got assassinated,' said Vic. 'It was George Canning. He died of pneumonia. I remember that teacher. I tried to get hold of her when I got out but a bloke answered her phone and I don't think he passed on my number.'

'I can't think why,' said Mary. 'So are we definite it's George Canning? Can I go and have my ciggie now?'

'Yup,' said Vic.

'I've got a cigar,' said Laurie. 'Got it at the duty free in Bangkok. I'll join you.'

Outside, there was a small huddle of Poles, joking and smoking. Mary lit Laurie's cigar and her own cigarette.

'Look, I didn't mention it in front of the chaps,' said Mary, 'because they always say I should mind my own business but this Old Man Hook stuff, there is something very fishy going on because Dee, Ashley's ex, rang me wanting to know what you were saying about it all. I shouldn't really be telling you this but I don't think you sometimes realise what these guys are like. You think it's all like *Guys and Dolls* and everyone's a laugh and a rogue and a character but a lot of them are just vicious bullies. This lot are not straight-goers. Watch out that you don't get your fingers burned.'

One of the Poles, cigarette in hand, asked her for a light. She lit his cigarette and that of his companion. A third of their crew leant forward with a roll-up in his mouth.

'Third one, bad luck,' said Mary but held the guttering match forward for him.

'Like I say,' she said to Laurie. 'Watch out you don't get your fingers burned.'

Chapter Thirty-two

THE LIGHT IS on, thought Laurie. This means that either I forgot to switch it off or Violet is back. Or whoever is curious about what I know about Vlad's death and Old Man Hook's death has decided either to search my flat or is planning to garrotte me as I enter. He was too tired to bother with any precautions as he unlocked the front door.

'Did you win?' asked Violet when he came in. The television was on and she was halfway through a pizza the size of a satellite dish.

'Since you ask, no. The bloody teachers did. We didn't even come second. Some new team of young swots who, I think, are the local Green Party. Or the local Respect Party. Or, to judge by the way they sniggered at some of our answers when they were marking us, the local Disrespect Party.'

'Well, quizzes get harder as you get older,' said Violet, not taking her eyes away from the screen. 'Your memory starts going downhill from the age of seventeen. D'you realise that I'm in my decline now? Fifteen thousand brain cells die every day. Imagine. Fifteen thousand.'

'Really? So how did all the A levels go? I am so sorry I wasn't here. Did it all go OK in the end?'

'Not really, but it doesn't matter. How was your holiday in Thailand?'

'It wasn't a holiday, Violet. I only went because—'

'Yeah, yeah, your work. That's what Mum said.'

'Look, I'm in a bit of a jam at work at the moment. You don't want me to be unemployed, do you? Sitting around watching daytime TV. I wouldn't be able to help with your student loan.'

'What's wrong with daytime TV? I bet you've never watched it.'

Laurie ignored the invitation to argue. He wanted a drink but felt that that would give Violet the wrong impression.

'Well, I'm sorry I wasn't here.'

'I said it didn't matter. Have you solved the crime? I've forgotten what it was now. Was it that lecturer who killed his girlfriend?'

'No, the lecturer's already coughed, I think. It was the gangster guy, Old Man Hook.'

'Ohhhh, of course it was. Ah, now it all makes sense.'

Violet was devoting her attention to seeing whether she could lift her pizza from its container without breaking a long string of tenacious cheese which was attaching the crust umbilically to the cardboard. The cheese string broke and she frowned in frustration.

'What makes sense?' asked Laurie.

'The hook.'

'What hook?'

Violet raised a large triangle of pizza above her head, shaped it into a funnel and aimed it into her mouth as she enjoyed her father's attentive puzzlement.

'What hook, Violet?'

She savoured the pizza. Were those little circles of pepperoni swimming in the cheese? Had Violet forgotten the graphic description she had once given him, during her vegetarian phase, of how the pepperoni was made, what bits of the pig's trotters and discarded intestines were crushed and processed and re-cooked and coloured? Clearly she had.

Violet was enjoying her moment. She had watched enough American police procedurals on television during those long days of A-level revision to know how to tell a story that might intrigue a cop or a lawyer. Spin it out a little. Plenty of detail.

'Well, the bell rang late one night just after you went to Thailand. I was just here for an hour or so picking up some books to revise with as I was staying at Mum and Godfrey's – oh, did I tell you he's now got this really sweet little pug that Mum loves. I think he bought it for her. It's got a sweet little scrunched-up face.' Violet obligingly scrunched up her own face to illustrate the point. 'You know how she always said there was nothing she wanted more than a dog and how you went on and on about not wanting to start your day picking up dog shit with a plastic bag in the park and so she never did.'

Laurie decided he would need the drink. When I am properly grown up, he had often thought, I will have a drinks cabinet with bottles of interesting gins and rare single malts and conversation-starting vodkas but it had never quite happened. Whenever he had assembled a quorum of grown-up spirits, Caz would come back from a gig with a couple of members of the band and the entire spirit collection would be gone by dawn in a haze of 'Can I try this one, Laurie?' and 'OK if we just stretch out here on the sofa for the night?' and 'Let me play you this one track of this Iris de Ment/Jerry Jeff Walker and see what you think'. But there was a bottle of Budvar in the fridge and he gratefully popped its top with the opener that Caz had brought back from a gig in Albuquerque, in happier times, that played a little jingle advertising Corona beer when it was engaged. 'Ahhh, Corona,' said a Mexican voice. It was funny the first eight hundred times or so but now it was beginning to grate and also it reminded Laurie too much of Caz and carefree times. Should he offer Violet some? There was only one bottle left.

'You don't want any of this, do you?' he asked.

'Oh, yeah, that would be great. I haven't had anything to drink since yesterday.'

Laurie poured what he estimated to be around a third of the bottle into a glass for Violet. How different was this beer from Chang and Tiger? Would he see Flo again? Where had he put her telephone number?

'You were saying about how the doorbell rang when you were alone in the house.'

'Yeah.' Violet slugged back the beer rather too effortlessly for Laurie's liking. 'Yeah, the bell rang and I thought it might be Mum because she was going to drop by and pick me up—'

'But she's got her own keys still, hasn't she?'

'Yeah, but she didn't want to invade your space or something. Still, it wasn't her and when I got down there was just . . . let me get it.'

Violet deposited the remains of her pizza on the low table in front of the sofa that had accommodated as many fiddlers and mandolin players as a Nashville motel and skipped up to her room. She returned with an envelope from which she pulled a note, a shotgun cartridge and the sort of hook on which butchers hang their joints and chops.

'See,' she said triumphantly. 'How weird is this?'

'And was there anyone there? Did you see who left it?'

'Yeah, a guy about seven foot tall and wearing this weird iron mask and chains round his waist and carrying a scythe—'

'Violet, you're kidding.'

'God, you'd believe anything, wouldn't you? No wonder the papers are full of bullshit. No, there was no one there. But as I picked it up – and this is true – a car drove past and flashed its lights.'

'What kind of car?'

'You mean, I'd know the make of the car? It had four wheels, if that helps.'

'Very clever. Let me see the note.'

'Well, it's not exactly a note.'

Violet handed him a cutting from a newspaper. It was the first story Laurie had written about Hook's murder. Around it someone had written, in brown ink, '3/10 – must do better.'

Chapter Thirty-three

'**H**AVE YOU BEEN to the police about it?' asked Stark with almost – almost, but not quite – touching concern when Laurie told him about the hook and the cartridge the following day in the office.

Laurie licked the foam off the top of his cappuccino and contemplated how best to respond to this: reporter under threat of death but gallantly showing no concern for his own safety? Father worried only that his daughter should not get caught up in the dangerous games her dad was forced to play by the demands of his taxing job? Daredevil 'Bring-it-on!' derring-do dazzler who enjoys the whiff of danger in an all too mundane and safe world?

'What if it was the police who left it there?' said Laurie.

It did no harm to play with Stark for a moment or two, hint that they were dealing here with many unseen forces and risking a sudden end at every turn. If anything did happen to him, Caz would be around £250,000 richer as the paper provided a handsome parachute for the widows and widowers of any staff killed in the course of their duty. (The insurers had never actually had to pay out, although there was currently a protracted negotiation under way, on behalf of the late religious affairs correspondent who had fatally crashed his car on his way home from an inter-faith conference in Canterbury and had been found to be twice over the drink-drive limit; the insurance company insisted that this meant the nullification of their agreement, while the correspondent's widow claimed it was merely the result of extra strong Communion wine forced on him at the event. Would Caz spend it all on buying a love nest for her and her academic beardie somewhere in Umbria? Uggh.)

'Do you think they might have done it to warn you off getting too far ahead of them?'

This was a pleasant thought. Laurie smiled graciously at Stark across the chrome canteen table. Geraldo, the cleaner, was polishing the coffee bar counter and winked at him. Laurie could play this one for a little longer.

'It's a possibility,' said Laurie. 'I mean, it's a little embarrassing for them that they're looking for Vladimir Petrov and we find him and interview him even before they know where he is and then even more embarrassing that he winds up dead meat before they can get to him. I've got a message to call Sandra King, the detective in charge. I guess I should call her now that I'm back but I wanted to fill you in first.'

Crawl, slime, crawl. Stark smiled and nodded back. How much had Laurie now deposited in the credit bank? Two – no, three – splashes. Front pages of the paper appearing behind newsreaders on television bulletins, according to Guy. Great photos from Flo – he must pop up and see Eva-Marie and check that Flo would receive her reward – which had been syndicated around the world; he had seen one in the

International Herald Tribune at Bangkok airport and in one of those discarded free papers that now seemed to litter the London transport system. Was that the future? Free news. Did everyone now expect they should not have to pay for it because they could get it for nothing online? None of Violet's friends seemed to buy anything, not even the *NME* or whatever it was that teenagers should be reading. They turned up their noses at the idea of paying for CDs, far less a newspaper.

'When are you seeing the police?' asked Stark.

'I dunno. I expect they'll want me to come in and bring them up to date this afternoon,' said Laurie. Was it his imagination or was Stark using even more Homme Sauvage than usual? Stark rose from the table, indicating that the audience was at an end. He turned to go and then spun round on his heel.

'Oh, yes, should have brought this up earlier,' he said. 'Can you pop in and see the people in accounts? I think they were quite keen to see you. Today would probably be best.'

Guy was strolling past towards his desk. Stark spotted him.

'Ah, Guy, glad you're here. We've had a couple of calls about your climate change story this morning – a reader who's a climatologist wanted to know what an "engorged nimbo-stratus cloud" is.'

'It's a new theory from MIT,' said Guy. 'Most British scientists won't have heard of it yet. Put 'em through to me if they ring again.'

Guy and Laurie retreated to their desks.

'So you got "engorged" in but it sounds like you've been busted,' said Laurie.

'Fear not,' said Guy. 'Stark's attention span is low. By the way, Eva-Marie and that bloke from accounts have both been looking for you.'

'Did they say what they wanted?'

'Well, Eva-Marie seemed very excited that you were going to be back today and the chap from accounts was looking in your *Police Almanac* to get the address of the Fraud Squad – only joking, only joking.'

'Not funny. What else has been happening while I was away? Have your trousers been safe?'

'I haven't risked them in there. I was waiting for you to come back and solve it for me so that I could be present at the unmasking. I have two more suspects.'

'Oh, who?'

'Well, funnily enough, that bloke John from accounts. He questioned my exes on that trip to the Galapagos about the turtles and I took it up with the management and they found out I had undercharged – UNDERcharged – so they got him to write a note of apology to me.'

'You're kidding.'

'No, straight up. How's things on the . . . er . . . domestic front?'

'No better. Violet's messed up her A levels, I think, so she'll never be an atom scientist and Caz – well, I haven't heard from her at all.'

'There was a piece about her in the *Standard* the other day, her gig at the Mean Fiddler. Said she'd never been better and that her voice had a new resonant quality as though it had been released from bondage or something.'

'Oh, please.'

Laurie's phone rang. He picked it up as he scanned his emails. Dismissive reader. Penis enlargement. Meet Ukrainian beauties. Meet Uzbek beauties. Uzbek beauties? That was new, wasn't it? Viagra. ACPO briefing document. Make a million, thanks to Ghanaian princess. Press release from Strathclyde police. Meet Russian woman. Scathing reader. You have won a prize. Press release from Greater Manchester police. Leaving party. You have won another prize.

'Yes,' he said distractedly.

It was Eva-Marie. Yes, he might just be able to pop up for a chat. The voice had a twinkle in it. During a brief and unsuccessful period in BBC local radio in Cardiff at the start of his career he had been taught by an elderly producer how to talk on the radio 'with a smile in your voice'. Was Eva-Marie smiling as she spoke? Surely she was. By now, she must know that he was a single man. Deserted. Vulnerable. No longer prohibited by the chains of convention from a relationship. After the Thai trip, he was entitled to a few days' leave. How about lunch in Paris? A little place I know near the Gare du Nord. We can hop on the Eurostar at St Pancras. Maybe see something at the Beaubourg.

A trip to the gents to check that his hair was looking OK. Geraldo was in there and winked at him again. Someone was in one of the cubicles, noisily expelling whatever he had had for breakfast. Bran, no doubt, thought Laurie, when an elderly sub emerged and sheepishly washed his hands. As Laurie left the gents, he bumped into John from accounts, who almost jumped. John worked on a different floor. Why was he in that gents?

'Ah . . . er,' mumbled John. He obviously felt that he did not know Laurie well enough to call him by his first name and he knew unconsciously that to call him Mr Lane would be too formal, too like a police officer. 'Um . . . er . . . could we . . . perhaps . . . er . . . now?'

'Was there something you wanted to discuss?' said Laurie. Make the bastard suffer. Except that he probably wasn't a bastard, probably had to spend all his time being patronised by journalists over their all too obviously fiddled expenses when he had maybe once dreamed of – well, who knew what he had once dreamed of, certainly not checking scrawled receipts for taxi fares from Westminster to Blackfriars or deconstructing lunches at Moro or the Gay Hussar.

'Erm . . . couple of queries and . . . wanted to ask about . . . um . . . that text message,' blushed John.

'Well, let's get it over with,' said Laurie. What text message? he wondered. Was Eva-Marie waiting for him now? Would she take it as a sign of lack of interest if he did not immediately appear by her desk? Or playing hard to get? Or just busy, international kind of guy, lots of calls on his time?

John's office was a cubbyhole on the second floor. There was barely space for his desk and one small chair with just room on it for two unassuming buttocks. Laurie sat down while the still blushing John pulled a file from his top drawer. Laurie recognised his own signature at the bottom of a couple of expenses forms. His heart sank. The adrenaline created by sleeplessness and alcohol was starting to evaporate. John passed him the forms to which he had attached Stick-its of different colours. Were they colour coded? Yellow for a dubious claim. Blue for an excessive lunch. Red for a clear lie.

'There's a . . . well . . . er . . . um . . . a bit of a problem with these claims because they seem to have you in two different cities at once.'

'Sure,' said Laurie. 'I must have got a date wrong. That's all. Look, I'm sure there are odd inconsistencies because I fill all these in ages after they've happened. I thought I'd explained that.'

John seemed unmoved. He pushed some taxi receipts in front of him.

'This is for a journey from . . .' John peered at Laurie's scribbled note. 'It says Paddington to St James's Park and it's costed at twenty-six pounds. Now, we have spoken to the Taxi Drivers' Association about this and they say that the journey should be no more than fourteen pounds.'

'Well, we may have had to take a detour via . . . er . . . Bayswater, now I come to think of it and, God, you know what taxi drivers can be like, they enjoy an argument. I had one the other day who was adamant that Darwin's theory of evolution had been disproved by—'

'And this receipt here,' said John, no longer blushing but now playing the role of a prosecuting counsel hitting a wobbly defendant with a flurry of lethal blows, 'is from the same book of receipts which would indicate that the taxi driver provided two blank receipts and that they have both been completed in your handwriting.' John looked up at Laurie.

'Blimey, has all this been taken to the forensic science labs? What's that receipt for? Twelve quid? What's going on here? All these journeys are journeys I've taken and—'

'Our difficulty is,' said John, 'that these have to be submitted to the Inland Revenue and they now examine them in detail. We would have to admit that some of these must be inaccurate or are not genuine contemporaneous receipts and as such amount to an attempt to defraud the Exchequer.'

'Bloody hell. This is absurd. Let me have another look at them.'

Laurie's own Internal Prosecuting Counsel was taking over the case. 'Would not the simplest course for you be to admit your guilt, admit that you have forged and fabricated your way to your employer's funds, that you have committed a serious breach of trust and that the dignified action for a person of your age and background would be to offer an apology to the jury for wasting their time and to accept the inevitable punishment with grace?'

'No, no, no,' said Laurie.

'I'm sorry?' said John.

'Look, I think I'd better get a chapel representative in here if it's going to be silly buggers stuff.'

John frowned. There was something else he wanted to say, that clearly made him far angrier than any geographical debate about the Paddington-Bayswater-St James's Park triangle. He had picked up his mobile phone and was feverishly clicking through his text messages. Finally, he found what he was looking for.

'And there is this!'

Laurie peered at the message on the tiny screen. The words were just visible. 'GET A LIFE!' it said.

'So?' said Laurie.

'You sent me this.'

'No, I didn't. I haven't ever sent you a message.'

'Well, it's from your phone on . . .' he read out the time and date. Last Monday. Laurie had been in Pattaya then. It must have been late at night.

'Why would I have sent you a message from Thailand?'

'It was in immediate response to a message that I sent to you.' John scrolled down to show Laurie the original missive. It read: 'Sorry to bother you but can you explain why two lunches in Scarborough at Police Fed conference Sept 5?' 'The reply definitely came from your phone so, if you didn't send it, who did?'

Oh, God, thought Laurie. That little bleep that had come through while he lay, stoned, drunk, exhausted, sated, in bed with a naked Flo. 'Is that my phone?' he had asked through his haze. 'Don't worry,' Flo had responded with that grin of hers. 'I'll take care of it.' And she had, hadn't she? She really had. But how do I explain that to John? John's office phone rang. Now he was quite assertive for a young blusher.

'Maybe it is best if this is taken up through the proper channels,' he said, his hand covering the mouthpiece of his phone, dismissing Laurie from his cubbyhole. 'I will contact Human Resources to get them to arrange a final meeting.'

'Look,' said Laurie. 'I do promise you, word of honour, that I did not send that text.' John clearly did not believe him. 'I mean, you do have a life, don't you?' John blushed again. A deeper red, this time. 'Why would I say "get a life" when you have – I mean, I'm fifty-five and I don't even have my own office yet, like you do, and I'm sure . . .'

John averted his gaze. Laurie rose from the seat. Eva-Marie, Eva-Marie. After this disaster, the fates would surely deal him a fine hand. Three Jacks or at least a couple of pairs.

Eva-Marie greeted him with an undipped headlight smile.

He would remember this smile, he thought. In years to come as they lay in bed together, he would say, 'I didn't realise that you were serious until I saw that smile,' and she would nestle her head against his taut – gym, walks, weights, he would get down to them all at last – torso and flash that same smile again.

'Hi, Laurie,' she said. There was no one else on the desk. He looked past her at her screen with its menu of the day's stories in pictures: a demonstration in Burma, a mugshot of a boy band member busted for crack, the new Carmen at the Coliseum. Eva-Marie looked round as though she, too, wanted to make sure there was no one who would overhear them. She was wearing a pink shirt and black shorts. She gave that smile again. Full wattage. 'Oh, Laurie,' she said. 'I'm so glad you're back safely.'

He placed his hand gently on her arm and she reacted immediately with another dazzling smile. Clearly, she was not bothered by the age difference between them. They could shrug off the doubters who would say the gap was too wide. He smiled back at her. Who cared about what other people said or about silly expenses now?

'I don't know how else to say this,' she said. She seemed breathless. Was it just his imagination or was that music gently swelling too, somewhere in the background, maybe even in his subconscious? How was she going to put it? Something like, 'I can't help myself but I think I'm falling in love with you'? Or would it be something earthier, more physical? Or more poetic? He could not quite picture how that would go. He remembered in a brief, swiftly banished flash how Caz had made the first approach, late on the very first night they had been introduced by the paper's music critic at that gig at the Goblin and she had grinned at him, tossed her hair out of her eyes in that way and said, 'Fancy a fuck?'

Eva-Marie granted him a third, flirtatious smile. 'I feel very presumptuous saying this when we don't really know each other but . . .' Presume! Presume! urged Laurie silently. 'But I'm going to say it anyway. The thing is, Joe, my bloke – you'd really like him, I think he's like a young version of you – Joe has just finished his postgraduate media studies course at Goldsmiths and has been offered a traineeship here and he would be so, so, SO grateful if you would agree for him be attached to you as a trainee. Oh, Laurie, do say yes!'

Chapter Thirty-four

I T WAS NEARLY twenty-four hours later and Laurie still felt bruised. But relieved, too. Imagine if he had jumped in a moment too soon and said, 'No need for words, Eva-Marie, we're both grown-ups, even if there is a slight difference in age. Let's just grab a taxi, head for the Eurostar and spend the night in Paris under the stars.'

Since Laurie was in the Old Bailey now, sitting in the press room, in the bowels of the building, it was only natural that his Internal Prosecuting Counsel should kick in immediately.

'You said "a slight difference in age", Mr Lane. Is it not the case that there are twenty-six years difference in age? In fact, is it not true that you are almost double – yes, ladies and gentlemen of the jury – almost double the age of the young lady concerned?'

Laurie scanned the day's court listings on the sheet in front of him but his IPC was in full flow.

'And perhaps you will also tell the court if it is the case that you were quite prepared – the very day after you had returned from your assignment in Thailand – to abandon your vulnerable teenage daughter . . . excuse me, while I consult my notes . . . ah, yes, Violet . . . and run off to Paris with a woman to whom you were not married? Please speak up so that the jury can hear you, Mr Lane, and I do not think I have to remind you that you are under oath, do I?'

He was aware of a tap on his shoulder. He turned to see Kevin Yu, Mo Muskett, Bradley and the Vicar.

'Back from Thailand?' said the Vicar. 'Had your penicillin shots?'

'Give us a break,' said Laurie. 'I was working.'

'Yeah, saw the pieces you did. So do you really think it was the Hooks that bumped off poor old Vlad? They didn't impale him, did they?'

'I thought you said you read my story,' said Laurie.

The Vicar ignored him. He was staring over his head at a tall, cadaverous man in a horsehair barrister's wig and frayed black gown, who was hovering at the press-room entrance.

'Hello, Sir Stanley,' said the Vicar. 'You look more and more like Peter Cushing in *Dracula* every day.'

'Thank you, Ronald,' said Sir Stanley, pushing his wig forward. 'You look more and more like Miss Havisham in the black-and-white *Great Expectations*.' He was not quite the most senior of the prosecuting counsels active at the Old Bailey but close. Only Sir John Nutting was better known. 'I see there is now a prayer room where the old gents used to be.'

'Bloody ridiculous, isn't it?' said the Vicar. 'No one told us it was happening. I went in there for a piss and found two blokes on the floor on their knees.'

'Sounds like the gents in my local,' said Kevin.

'It's not funny,' said the Vicar. 'We have to go up two flights to have a bloody piss.'

'Well, it's a human right to be able to pray,' said Mo.

'It's a human right to have a piss,' said the Vicar. 'People were pissing for millions of years before they were praying. Isn't that right, Sir Stanley?'

'Indeed,' said Sir Stanley. 'But I gather you wanted to know whether any plea was going to be entered on Jasper Hatfield's behalf today and I understand, from his counsel, that the answer is no. We are months away from the trial proper but he will be making an appearance. We will just be fixing dates. Oh, hello, Laurie. How are you? Interesting stuff on Mr Hook's untimely demise. Very interesting.'

'How do I decode that?'

'As you wish, dear boy, as you wish. I think that if Mr – what was his name? The Russian gentleman.'

'Vladimir Petrov.'

'Yes, I think if I had been asked to prosecute Mr Petrov, I would have had a number of questions for the police on how many cases they knew of where the suspect helpfully buried the murder weapon in a shallow grave in his own back garden.'

'Murderers have done sillier things than that,' said Laurie. 'What about Hatfield? Hiding the body in his parents' house.'

'Well, obviously I cannot comment on Mr Hatfield's case but there are amateur criminals and there are professional criminals and I was under the impression that Mr Petrov was of the latter persuasion. However, no one is now going to be required to plead Mr Petrov's case.'

'Except, of course,' said Laurie, 'in a higher court on the final day of judgement . . .'

'When the problem will be finding enough briefs who have made it into heaven to defend anyone,' said Kevin Yu gloomily.

'Quite so,' said Sir Stanley, gathering his gown in his arms in a way that reminded Laurie of an old geography teacher in his school in – was it Welshpool or Nottingham? – who had fought a losing battle to pass on his knowledge of trade winds to ungrateful little sods in between flamboyantly wiping the blackboard. The Vicar had decided to ignore the conversation.

'Man walks into a bar with a crocodile,' said the Vicar, fixing Sir Stanley with a grin. 'Says to the barman, "Do you serve lawyers?" Barman says, "Sure, of course we serve lawyers." "OK," says the man. "I'll have a pint of lager for myself and a lawyer for my friend." '

'Very droll,' said Sir Stanley. He turned on his heel. 'I bid you all good morning.'

Something had caught the Vicar's eye in one of the newspapers laid out on the table.

'Blimey, look at this,' said the Vicar. 'It says here that semen is ejaculated at an average of twenty-nine mph. How the hell do they measure that, do you think?'

'Speed cameras,' suggested Mo.

'That would be some job, wouldn't it?' said the Vicar. 'Measuring the speed of sperm. Bloody hell. I wonder what the fastest is.'

There was an announcement over the public address system telling all those in the case of Hatfield to go to court ten.

'Guilty little shit,' said the Vicar. 'I knew that the minute I clapped eyes on him.'

'You've just got a prejudice against university lecturers,' said Kevin. 'Now, is it my imagination or has Stanley's wig—'

'SIR Stanley, please,' said the Vicar.

'OK, has Sir Stanley's wig got yellower? It's a sort of nicotine now, isn't it?'

'You're right, it looks as though it's been smoking Capstan Full Strength.'

'I was in one case last year – what was it? One of those terror ones, I think – and the judge, Norton-Beavis, I think it was, told the jury when they had all been sworn in that they should feel free to ask him any question they wanted; whatever they didn't understand, they should not hesitate to bring it up. So after about two days' worth of evidence, one of the jurors passes the judge a note. Silence in court. The judge reads it. One of the jurors wanted to know why Sir Stanley's wig was so much yellower than the other briefs'. True story.'

'What did the judge say?' asked Laurie.

'Said that this was a court of law not a palace of variety and they should restrict their queries to matters concerning the evidence. Anyway, how come the Thai police let you go so quickly? Aren't you a key witness to Petrov's murder? What are you doing back here when you could be lying on the beach with a bar girl under each arm?'

'Why should he want to have a bar girl under each arm when he has a lovely wife?' asked the Vicar. Although Laurie had known the Vicar for more than twenty years, they did not share the details of their lives. Laurie was vaguely aware that there was a Mrs Vicar somewhere and possibly at least two generations of Vicarettes but he knew nothing of their names, their jobs, their lives, their dreams. The Vicar, on the other hand, being a country fan, although of the more traditional kind of music than Caz played, could occasionally be seen in the pubs and clubs where she was performing. Was even known to shout a request – 'Nobody's Child' was his usual choice – from the bar. Caz had indulged him on a number of occasions. Afterwards, the Vicar would insist on kissing her hand and ordering her a double bourbon because he believed that that was what a country singer should be drinking. Laurie decided that this was not the occasion to explain to the Vicar that Caz had left him for another man. The Vicar blundered on.

'I saw her last week at the Goblin,' said the Vicar. 'Old Ginger Mulgrew insisted on taking me there – did you know he liked that kind of music, Laurie? Gave me a lift home. Said he had the entire works of Merle Haggard. Who would have thought it?'

'Who indeed?' said Laurie. What was Mulgrew doing at the Goblin?

'And she was with some old bloke with a beard,' said the Vicar. 'Who was he?'

'I think he plays the fiddle,' said Laurie. So he does have a beard.

'I'd watch him, if I were you, chum,' said the Vicar. 'He was getting a little too pally with her, I thought. He got quite sniffy when Mulgrew went up to have a word with her.'

'That's showbiz,' said Laurie. 'What did Mulgrew want to have a word with her about?'

'Well, you were in Thailand and I think he just wanted to make sure everything was OK. You know, that nothing suspicious was going on after you had run that story about the Russians. Some of them don't really play by the old rules, you know.'

'How very thoughtful of him.'

Mulgrew was a bent copper. He had retired a couple of years ago now. He was one of the Vicar's main contacts and had been for many years, happily slipping the Vicar tip-offs and background in exchange for a few hundred quid here and there. How he had survived in Scotland Yard was a puzzle to many as he had been the subject of at least two major corruption inquiries. He had been accused by one young detective of taking money from one of the Hook family's lawyers back in the eighties but the accusation had never stuck and the young detective who made the allegation had long since left the force and the country. Mulgrew was with a security company now. Laurie had never liked him. He remembered seeing him a few years ago having a drink with Sandra King when she must have still been a detective sergeant. He should ring her.

'How's er . . . ?' Laurie could not remember the Vicar's wife's name.

'Sheena's grand,' said the Vicar. 'Bit of a problem with her waterworks but nothing to trouble the scorers with.' Laurie noted Kevin Yu wrinkling his nose in the background.

'Which reminds me,' said the Vicar. 'There's this elderly couple in bed. He's in his flannel pyjamas. She's in a nightie.'

'Oh, no, not a nightie joke,' said Kevin.

'Shut up, Kevin, you haven't heard this one,' said the Vicar. 'Right, there's this couple in bed and the woman says to her husband, "Darling, if anything ever happened to me, do you think you'd remarry?" And the old bloke thinks for a while and says, "Well, I suppose, yes, I probably would." So the old woman says, "And do you think, if you did remarry, you would stay in this house?" And the chap says, "Yes, I suppose it would make sense, wouldn't it?" And the woman says, "And would she share this bed with you?" And the chap says, "Well, when you think about it, I suppose that would happen, yes." And the old woman says, "And would you give her my golf clubs?" And the chap says, "Oh, no, certainly not." And she says, "But why not?" And he says, "Because she's left-handed!"' Kevin snorted with laughter despite himself. 'Anyway,' said the Vicar, 'when is your missus going to be performing again?'

A further announcement – 'All those in Hatfield to court ten' – spared Laurie from further inquiries. They crowded into the court and slid into the two press benches. Laurie scanned the public gallery. There was an elderly couple, who looked uncomfortable and out of place, sitting in the front row, gazing forlornly at the dock. The murderer's parents, Laurie presumed. Lower middle-class, they looked. Confused by all the jokey, self-confident bustle of the barristers and solicitors in the court beneath them. They had probably thought that this was a scene they would only ever encounter on television, in some Sunday evening drama or an old episode of *Rumpole*. Now they were going to watch their son being brought in by two uniformed prison officers, charged with murdering a beautiful young woman whom they would have hoped might one day have been the mother of their grandchildren. What beckoned now for them were a series of prison visits to their son, probably until their deaths. What would he get? Crime of passion, his barrister would argue, never happen again. Full of remorse. Previous good character. Maybe they would dredge up a student or two whom he had helped. A family friend. Perhaps Hatfield would himself apologise, show contrition.

Weep. Hope to get a tariff of, say, fifteen years and be out while he was still able to pull.

'Court rise,' said the usher, looking round menacingly to see if anyone was going to ignore her command. The judge entered. It was Norton-Beavis, looking weary and irritated. He cast a passing glance at the public gallery. He must have known that the deferential pair up there were the parents.

Kevin Yu's mobile phone went off and he scrambled to silence it. Norton-Beavis appeared not to notice. He nodded to the usher, a signal to bring the defendant into the court. Laurie glanced round to see Hatfield emerge. There were bandages round each wrist, just visible below his shirt cuffs. At least, Laurie presumed they were bandages. He was hardly likely to need sweat bands in prison. Hatfield spotted his parents in the public gallery and gave them a nod and a smile. Maybe he was relieved at being arrested and charged. He must have known it would happen eventually. Few amateurs, unless they were psychopathic strangers, succeeded in getting away with murder. Or maybe he was well medicated. Sir Stanley rose.

'My lord, I have already consulted with my learned friend, Mr Beirce, who represents the defendant, Mr Hatfield, and I think we have been able to agree a satisfactory timetable,' said Sir Stanley, nodding at Bill Beirce, the diffident, somewhat shifty-looking defence counsel, who bobbed up and down a couple of times in agreement. The trial was set for the early new year. Sir Stanley estimated that three weeks would be sufficient.

Laurie slid a look in the direction of the dock and found his gaze returned by Hatfield who gave him a bright smile, the same anxious-to-please expression which he had given his parents a few moments earlier. Without thinking, Laurie smiled back.

'Setting up the first prison interview already?' asked the Vicar out of the corner of his mouth. 'When the poor lass's body is still warm in the grave.'

'Silence in the court,' said the usher fiercely.

'Silly old bat,' said the Vicar under his breath. 'By the way, are you coming to the Flying Squad bash tonight?'

Chapter Thirty-five

THERE WERE ALREADY a score or so of detectives and their guests in the lobby of the Grosvenor House Hotel when Laurie arrived. All of the Crime Reporters Association had been invited and Laurie could spot the Vicar and Mo in deep conversation with Detective Chief Inspector Sandra King, who was wearing a blue off-the-shoulder evening dress. It was the first time Laurie had seen her with make-up on.

There was to be a dinner during which half a dozen boxing bouts would take place. It was an old Flying Squad tradition. Usually, the contest was between a south London boxing club, consisting mainly of young black fighters, and the Metropolitan Police's boxing team. Laurie had been to the event twice before and the south London boxers clearly relished the chance to whack policemen without fearing the possibility of eight years in prison for so doing. Then there would be a couple of speeches and an auction in aid of the charity which ran the boys' clubs that the Flying Squad supported. Laurie dreaded the auction because the press were supposed to bid heavily and there was much heckling and barracking if any of them failed to display sufficient generosity. Tensions between the police and the press were always there beneath the surface and, after a few gallons of wine and gin had been consumed, they bubbled up. The previous year, Laurie had been buttonholed in the gents by an aggrieved detective sergeant who felt his role in the arrest and conviction of a kidnapper had been given insufficient recognition in Laurie's paper and who hovered by the urinals as Laurie peed, returning from washing his hands to issue a fresh barrage of anguished bile. Laurie had pretended to be still relieving himself long after he had finished because he knew that the detective sergeant, being very much of the old school, would eventually become uncomfortable at hanging around a man with his flies undone.

The tables were a mix of Flying Squad officers, their colleagues in other branches of the police, crime reporters and a few other guests. Laurie recognised a couple of forensic scientists and a few recently retired detectives, some wearing their squad ties. Ginger Mulgrew was at a far table. Well, well. A team of waiters, all of whom looked eastern European, were handing round drinks on silver trays. Laurie watched in admiration as the Vicar deftly hoisted a large glass of white wine from one tray and an identical glass from another, without either waiter being aware of it. He would have made a good shoplifter.

Laurie found himself sitting between Mo and a fresh-faced young detective who introduced himself.

'Who's going to win the boxing tonight?' asked Laurie.

'I'm not really much of a boxing man myself,' said the young DC.

'I've got my money on the south London team,' said Mo. She was not bothered about making small talk. 'So what's the word on the Hook murder?' she asked the DC. He feigned ignorance. Or maybe it was genuine.

'I think you probably know more about it than we do,' he said.

'That's what you always say,' said Mo.

The Vicar hovered past, elbows jutting out, a wine glass in each hand as though they were pistols and he was a cowboy entering a hostile saloon bar.

'Behold the Vicar,' said Mo as she watched him slide into a seat beside the head of the Flying Squad. 'How come he always gets to be on the table with the big cheeses? It's certainly not charm.'

'Just be grateful,' said Laurie. 'At least you won't be subjected to the latest wave of "man goes into a bar" jokes.'

'They can't be worse than the knock-knock ones. Or is it only me he tells them to because I is black?' she asked with a smile. The DC looked confused.

'Working on anything interesting at the moment?' Laurie asked him.

'Well, we just finished with the Rolls-Royce gang,' said the DC. This had been an entertaining case in which a small crew of young men from Shepherds Bush had stolen one of the local council's car recovery vehicles and had used it to lift Rolls-Royces that were parked in the streets of Knightsbridge and Belgravia. It had been a sure-proof method of theft. Passers-by imagined that men in orange fluorescent vests lifting cars onto flatbed lorries were acting lawfully and they were anyway often quietly pleased to see expensive vehicles being confiscated. When, however, the gang had eventually been cornered at a scrap metal dealer's yard in Battersea, there had been shots fired but no one hit. The trial had just concluded at Woolwich crown court with indefinite sentences handed down to the two gang members who had opened fire.

'Fair sentence, d'you reckon?' asked Mo.

'I think they know that, if they use firearms against us these days, they're not going to get too much change out of twenty-five,' said the DC, tucking into his avocado prawns.

The first fight was due to start. A young woman wearing shiny sequinned electric-blue shorts, white high heels and a very tight white T-shirt entered the ring carrying a large card with the figure One on it.

'Is this one of the Met's new equal ops initiatives?' asked Mo. The DC affected not to hear the question. A large man with curly black hair and thick grey sideburns, dressed in a dinner jacket, clambered under the ropes and into the ring.

'My lords, ladies and gentlemen,' he said. 'I would like to welcome you all here on behalf of all the members of the Flying Squad. I would particularly like to welcome our guests from the Police Service of Northern Ireland who are with us today from Belfast.' There was polite applause. Laurie could recall the time when they were still the Royal Ulster Constabulary and their members were being killed by the IRA on a regular basis; then the mere announcement of their name at these functions prompted a standing ovation from their fellow officers in the Met. But times had changed and they were now no longer seen as beleaguered soldiers on the front line but just as fellow officers from a different part of the country. 'We have an excellent evening of entertainment in front of us with some very fine fighters giving up their time for an excellent cause. We would also like to mention our good friends in the media and the ladies and gentlemen of the Crime Reporters Association who are here with us tonight.' There were a few boos, followed by laughter.

The matches started. True to form, the south London boxers won most of the bouts. There were a lot of clinches, many cries of 'Break!' and a little blood. Most of the diners seemed to be paying more attention to the wine waiter than the men in the ring. Laurie toyed with his steak and roast potatoes and excused himself to go to the gents. As he was heading back to the banqueting hall, he almost bumped into Detective Chief Inspector Sandra King.

'Hi,' she said. She gave him a dry look. Had she been drinking? She looked slightly flushed, slightly off-guard for someone who was usually so composed. He had never seen her in a dress before. It was usually a severe trouser suit. Normally, she would have nodded and moved on but she seemed anxious to linger, to talk.

'You don't smoke cigars, do you?' she asked.

'Occasionally,' said Laurie.

'Great,' she said. 'Our table has all been given a . . .' She fished in her handbag and pulled out a Romeo y Julieta, still in its cartridge. 'One of these by the sponsors. I don't know what to do with mine and I don't feel like giving it to my bosses after all the grief they've been giving me . . . By the way, can we have a word?'

'Sure,' said Laurie. Outside, there was a small huddle of smokers on the pavement. Laurie clipped the end of his cigar off with his nail. Hook had never finished that story about the cigar cutter and the grass in the public baths. Now he would never know what had happened. He bummed a light from another guest. There was a slight chill in the air but Laurie felt warm. He inhaled. He felt light headed. Was it the Cuban tobacco or the proximity of this newly exotic inspector?

'Did you ever smoke?' said Laurie.

'Couple of times when I was a kid. Doesn't really go with marathon running. Look, Laurie, I wanted to talk to you about the Hook business.'

'Yessss?'

'You were the last person to see Vladimir Petrov before he was killed. What did he have to say about it all?'

'Well, I put most of what he said in my story. He was really just saying that he hadn't had anything to do with it. Only dealings he's had with Hook was over property in Russia. He was going to tell me who he thought had done it and then he got whacked.'

'Did he say why he did a runner?'

'Said that after his experiences with the police in Russia, he couldn't be sure he would get a fair trial and he didn't want to waste a lot of time in jail while he proved that he had nothing to do with it. Said that he felt that everyone had a stereotyped view of Russians now – that they were all criminals and kleptocrats – and this would probably include English jurors.' Laurie tried unsuccessfully to blow a smoke ring. He suppressed a sudden desire to cough.

'Did you reckon he was telling the truth?'

'Well, what do I know? But, yes, I suppose he did seem quite plausible. But then I hardly expected he was going to fall at my feet and confess to removing one of the obstacles to his establishing a club and casino empire in London.'

'So who do you reckon killed him?'

'I thought that was your department.'

'Oh, do come on, Laurie.' She was being almost flirtatious now. 'You must have picked up something in the bars there. Did you not see any of the "chaps" there? Any of Hook's old chums.'

'Now, if I did, would I be fingering them at a Flying Squad boxing night do?'

Detective Chief Inspector King surveyed the cars driving past on Park Lane and returned her attention to Laurie.

'You've got some chums on the Hook team, haven't you?' she said.

'I have chums everywhere. That's the kind of guy I am.'

'So what do you reckon, Laurie? Do you really think that the Russians thought Hook was important enough, at his age, to kill and risk all that bother from us? Look, can I tell you something, if you agree not to use it yet?'

Laurie tried to smoke his cigar the way, well, the way – who would it be? George Raft? – would smoke it, rolling it round a little bit in his mouth. A flake of tobacco caught his tongue and spoiled the effect. Why was she telling him this? She had always been very cautious and tight lipped on their previous encounters. Maybe she was just drunk enough to spill some beans? People still said things in their cups that they regretted the morning after. He tried to act non-committal, as though senior detectives regularly made confessions of crucial investigative details to him.

'Sure,' said Laurie, gazing into the middle distance across the darkness of Hyde Park and trying not to choke on his latest over-hearty inhalation.

'Well, the forensics people say that the murder weapon, the gun found on Petrov's property, was the same weapon that was used to kill a minicab driver – you remember the case, that Asian guy that the Hooks were always suspected of? Never went to trial. Pissed-off widow always attacking the police for not doing enough to get a conviction.'

Laurie did remember it. It had seemed like a gangland hit at the time. He had written a brief story about it and spent another couple of days making desultory inquiries about the dead man and getting nowhere. The Hooks' name had been mentioned and there had been suggestions at the time that it was a case of mistaken identity but nothing had ever come of it.

'So,' said Laurie. 'What you're saying is that Hook's murder was probably carried out by one of Hook's own people.'

'No, I'm not saying that,' said Sandra.

'I wonder how you blow the perfect smoke ring,' he said. 'I've never quite mastered it.'

'You part your lips and you blow, Laurie,' she said.

'Oh, very good,' he said. 'So, if it wasn't one of the Hook clan, who would have got hold of that gun?'

'Well, you were at that superintendents' conference when they had the rundown on weapons, weren't you? The gun could have been hired out, sold on, stolen years ago. It doesn't prove anything. You could even say that Vladimir Petrov might have got hold of it when he arrived in London because only a stranger or an amateur would be so incautious about getting a weapon that must have done the rounds.'

She glanced over his shoulder, as if checking that there was no one listening to their conversation. There was a roar from inside the hotel. A knock-out?

'Anyway,' she continued. 'The other thing I'm curious about – and you must definitely keep this under your hat – is if you ever came across one of my former colleagues in the world of the Hooks.'

'Ginger Mulgrew?' asked Laurie.

'How did you guess?' She was not surprised.

'Why do you ask?'

'Well, you know about my dad . . .'

'Yeah. Lewis King, killed in Calcutta in the seventies.'

'Well, it turned out it was an accident, as it happens, but what I found out was that he was on to Mulgrew. Even then he knew Mulgrew was on the take. On the take from your lot but, more importantly, on the take from the Hooks. Anyway, Mulgrew was investigated, twice, but each time he got cleared. Now he's retired and I think he's getting a little careless. We think he thought Hook was about to spill the beans on him. Apparently, the old boy had been talking about writing his autobiography. Or getting it ghosted.'

She looked straight at him. He returned her gaze.

'You don't say,' said Laurie. 'What kind of a hack would take that job on?'

'Anyway, we've been checking Old Man Hook's mobile phone calls for the last few months of his life and we keep finding Mulgrew at the other end. And the odd journalist, Laurie. Now, we know Mulgrew was often paid by Hook for tipping them off before raids and there was a rumour that Old Man Hook was going to shop him finally because he took money from them and then wasn't able to get Ashley Hook out of trouble that time he was done for the coke and amphetamines. Hook was acting a bit out of character. He had the business on Mulgrew, I'm sure.'

'Have you spoken to him?'

What was that whiff of perfume?

She arched an eyebrow at him as if to say, 'What would be the point?'

'Nice perfume, by the way,' said Laurie.

'Is that your best shot?' She shook her head at him.

There was the sound of the revolving doors being pushed a little too fast. The Vicar emerged resplendent in dinner jacket with velvet lapels and shiny black patent-leather shoes.

'Hello, playmates,' he announced. 'How do you like my outfit? Do I look like a film star?'

'Yeah,' said Sandra King. 'Sid James.'

'Hey,' said the Vicar, lighting a cigarette. 'You should watch out for this guy, Sandra, he's single now. Watch his hands!'

The Vicar spotted a couple of paunchy retired Flying Squad friends and made off in their direction.

'Why is he called the Vicar?' asked Sandra.

'Don't you know? Ages ago, he impersonated a vicar to get into some murder victim's house and get the family photos off the mantelpiece and I guess it's stuck.'

Sandra watched him making the retired policemen laugh and shook her head. A young photographer, camera round his neck, was hovering close by. He approached them.

'Sorry to bother you,' he said. 'I'm from *Police Review*. Can I take a picture?'

'Rather not,' said Laurie. 'We're both undercover officers.'

'Oh, of course,' said the young man, retreating. 'Sorry to have bothered you.'

'You journalists are such tossers,' said Sandra. 'Anyway, if you hear anything about Mulgrew, let me know. I'll return the favour. Are you really a single man again?'

'I'm afraid so. How about you?'

'You're not going to tell me you've always fancied a girl in uniform, are you?' She mocked him with an exaggerated flutter of her eyebrows. 'How is your cigar?'

'Fantastico,' said Laurie.

'As I say,' said Sandra King. 'Keep all of this under your hat for the time being. It would be unhelpful if it got out now. I know the Hooks imagine that, with Mr Petrov being so handily whacked in Thailand, we will lose interest in it all and call off the dogs. Would you not think that's their game plan?'

Laurie shrugged. She must know that he had been in touch with Crispin Hook. They probably had someone watching to see who was going in and out of Xanadu. Maybe even someone working there. Was it his paranoia or might she be wired up? Not in that dress, surely. Might she be testing him out and then passing information back down to the line? To whom? To the rest of her team? To the Hooks even? There had always been a belief that the Hooks had a top man at the Yard but the suggestion had always been that the top man was indeed a man and was probably Mulgrew. What if Detective Inspector Sandra King was that 'top man', protected in her role by age-old assumptions about corrupt officers always being male?

A throat was cleared noisily.

'Hello,' said the Vicar, cigarette still in hand. 'I hate to intrude but the auction is about to start and I know Laurie wanted to bid for two tickets for the *Phantom of the Opera*.'

Laurie glowered at him. He exchanged glances with Sandra.

What does one do with a half-finished cigar that must be worth £30? he wondered. He checked that it was out, flicked the ash off its end and slipped it into his dinner-jacket pocket. Sandra nodded at him and headed back into the hotel in front of him. She turned and tugged at Laurie's sleeve.

'You have my mobile number,' she said. 'Give us a ring if something occurs to you. I would hate to think that anyone had . . . got their hooks into you.' She pulled herself up to her full height.

Two police cars, blue lights flashing, sirens blaring, shot down Park Lane. Laurie watched them disappear towards Marble Arch. Sandra did not spare them a glance.

'Is it always a thrill to be in a police car with the siren on or does that pass like every other excitement?' he asked.

Sandra shrugged.

'And is it my imagination or didn't I used to be taller than you?' asked Laurie.

'You could be again, Laurie, but you'll have to try wearing three-inch heels,' she said. 'And I don't think you've got the legs for it.'

Chapter Thirty-six

YEARS AGO, THOUGHT Laurie, as he stood in the queue at the office canteen the following day, years ago there was always talk about the 'canteen culture' within the police force. The idea was that, whatever honourable intentions the senior officers had, the chaps in the canteen would hold fast to the old style of policing. The mood in the canteen would be that the men and women in uniform, the ones who were despatched to break up riots or subdue knife-wielding crack-heads or drink-fuelled tossers, were badly led by 'politically correct' and effete superiors. In the canteen, they could talk honestly amongst themselves without having to watch their language or adjust their views for 'multicultural-ism'. It was this 'canteen culture' that kept alive the old habits of fitting people up, of tailoring the evidence, of protecting their mates in a conflict, even if it meant giving a sound beating to a couple of toerags. That was the theory, anyway. Who, he wondered, had first come up with the phrase? Was 'canteen culture' another dying metaphor?

Was there a canteen culture here? None of the senior management ate in the canteen, which had changed enormously over the years since Laurie had joined the paper.

In the early days, the main luncheon offer would be a plate of liver and bacon with some overcooked tomato and a mug of sweet tea followed by a quiet, reflective cigarette. Now, each dish had a handy guide to the number of calories in it and there were skinny lattes and Americanos and espressos where once the coffee had been doled out reluctantly by Madge, the canteen manager, in modest spoonfuls of instant Maxwell House. The canteen staff were all either from west Africa or eastern Europe. There was, of course, no smoking.

'Is it just me,' asked Guy, who was standing in front of him in the line for coffee, 'or is someone smoking a cigar in here?'

Guy was a born-again non-smoker. Having spent his first decade at the paper cheerfully fighting his way through a packet of Disques Bleus a day, he had given up all tobacco with a flourish one New Year's Day and his finely attuned nostrils could scent any hint of tobacco in the air. Any of the dwindling number of smokers who shuffled past Guy's desk after their smoke break in the street still trailing the evidence of their addiction could expect a sharp sideways glance, freighted with disapproval. Guy had made the mistake of writing a long first-person article in the paper about how easy it was to give up, how only will power was required and how the received wisdom that nicotine was more addictive than crack cocaine was nonsense. This made it impossible for him to have even the slightest fall, a guilty puff of a King Size late at night at the end of a party.

Laurie seemed to be surrounded by people who had impressively conquered their addictions. Vic rarely talked about how he managed to abstain when he was surrounded by boozers, not least at the quiz nights in the Dirty Dog. They had to beat those bastard schoolteachers one time. It was getting embarrassing now; the teachers had started patronising them, dropping loud hints of answers when they clearly reckoned they had built up a substantial lead. Vic was quite hard line on drink, censorious of those with alcohol problems who did not address them, religious in his observance of his regular twice-weekly AA meetings. He had been scathing when Laurie told him about another alcoholic friend who had what he described as a very occasional 'fuck-you' beer. Vic said he had once thought, on a hot midsummer London day, a couple of years after he had given up, that a quiet pint of lager and lime should be fine. It had tasted 'like nectar', he said, and had been the start of another three months' worth of benders, a court appearance and the end of a new relationship.

'Cigar?' said Laurie. 'Oh, Christ.' He reached into the pocket of his jacket. He could feel the stub of the Romeo y Julieta there. He'd transferred it from his dinner jacket last night with the vague idea of waving it under the Vicar's nose next time he blew his Hamlet smoke at him. He extracted it now and held it up for examination. 'You're quite right, Guy. Your sense of smell is phenomenal. You could always get a job as a sniffer dog when the redundos come through.'

Guy had secured his de-caf latte.

'I wanted to ask you about sniffer dogs, as it happens,' he said. 'I heard something about how they were trained. Do you think it's cruel?'

'What, being made to sniff marijuana every day and being rewarded with a tasty snack whenever you recognise the smell?' said Laurie. 'Doesn't sound too hard to me.'

They edged their way to a free table and sat down.

'What about the ones who have to smell explosives? That can't be so much fun. Do you think other dogs look down on them for working for the Man?'

'I expect so. Except for the Alsatians. You know pigs and mice are just as good as dogs at sniffing stuff out but the police don't use them because no handler wants to walk around with a pig or a mouse.'

Guy nodded, sipped his coffee and surveyed the canteen.

'How come you've been smoking expensive cigars?'

'Well, what would be the smoker's equivalent of drowning your sorrows?'

'I dunno. Suffocating your woes?'

'That'll do. I was at this Flying Squad charity do last night and one of the detectives on the Hook case gave me a cigar.'

'Have you declared it?'

'What, one cigar? Or to be more accurate,' Laurie pulled the remains from his pocket again, 'one half cigar. Do you think I'm that cheap?'

'"You cannot hope to bribe or twist, thank God! the British journalist. But, seeing what the man will do unbribed, there's no occasion to."'

'I know Humbert Wolfe wrote that but what else did he write?'

'No idea.'

'We know nothing,' said Laurie. 'We just churn out those old quotes. What's the word on the redundo front anyway? There was a chapel meeting while I was in Thailand. How many of us are they trying to get rid of now?'

'God knows,' said Guy. 'I think they'd like to get shot of

everyone who can remember typewriters and who can't edit films online and who doesn't like to pod-cast. Can't you get a job as a consigliere – isn't that what they're called? – to one of the criminal families? I've always thought you would be quite good at that.'

'Thanks a lot. They're still trying to do me on expenses. Had a rather grim little session with one of the accounts people.' Laurie pondered on whether he should share with Guy his experience with Flo in Pattaya. Maybe better not. If he ever got back with Caz again, he might want to cast that episode into history and it would be better to have no witnesses. But he wondered if Flo was still in Thailand. Was it just a holiday fling? Would it be different with her dressed as a member of South Yorkshire's social services department in the rain rather than lying naked in a warm, sunlit, unmade bed?

'By the way,' said Laurie. 'Any clues on the soaking trouser saga?'

'You tell me. I gave you two suspects.'

Laurie looked under the table to see what trousers Guy was wearing. It was his familiar red moleskin pair. 'Well, I suggest that you leave those same offending trousers there today at lunchtime and I guarantee to unmask the guilty trouser-flusher.'

'Guarantee?'

'Sure.' Laurie felt light headed. What had he to lose? 'What's my fee?'

'We'll work something out. I just want to nail the bastard who did it.'

'Revenge is not as tasty as everyone imagines it to be.'

'How do you know?'

Eva-Marie had picked up her morning smoothie and was sashaying through the canteen, sunny smile on her face. She had a photographer in tow, a tall woman, about sixty, good looking, in cowboy boots. Eva-Marie spotted Laurie. He responded with what he hoped was a suitably avuncular smile.

'Oh, hi, Laurie,' she sparkled. 'I've told Joe and he's thrilled. He's so looking forward to working with you. He's got lots of ideas, too. I'm sure you'll like him.' Laurie kept his grin fixed. She gestured at her tall companion. 'By the way, this is Britt. She did that spread on the Californian maximum security prisons for the magazine last week . . . I'll make sure Joe is on time on Monday!' And she was gone.

'What's she on about?' asked Guy.

'Her boyfriend wants to do his work experience with me,' said Laurie. 'Just what I bloody need, some keen little smartass who knows how to work all the gadgets.'

'You can't be an analogue man in a digital age for ever, Laurie.'

'Don't you start.'

'I thought she had the hots for you.'

'Of course she didn't. She's half my age.'

'That doesn't mean anything these days. Fifty is the new forty or is it the new thirty-five?'

'Does that mean that thirty is the new fifteen?'

'Good point. So if Eva-Marie is only thirty, that would make you a paedophile if you had a scene with her. Lucky escape.'

'Exactly. I could have ended up in the nonces' wing, couldn't I?'

There was a double bleep from his mobile phone announcing a text message.

'R U in? Plse cntct urgnt. GBS.'

Laurie looked up from his message. 'Do you think that Stark knows he has the same initials as George Bernard Shaw?'

'Do you think he knows who George Bernard Shaw is?'

'I guess I'd better get up there and face the music.' Where did 'face the music' come from? Was it a dying – dead even – metaphor? Could he use it in a story if he could guess the context? Would George Orwell allow that?

'Do you think that George Bernard Shaw and George Orwell knew each other?'

'I'm sure they did. It was a smaller world in those days. In fact, I think Orwell disapproved of Shaw.'

Laurie elegantly binned his paper cup.

'Good luck,' said Guy.

Stark had omitted to slap on the Homme Sauvage that morning. Was this a sign that he was starting to fall apart? Perhaps he would be more vulnerable.

'Hi,' he said. 'How's tricks?'

Where did 'how's tricks?' come from? Laurie wondered. Would George allow it? Probably not. Could it be a circus expression? Or something from vaudeville days?

'Fine, fine,' said Laurie. 'Had a very interesting night with the Flying Squad last night.' Laurie knew that Stark would be in awe of the Flying Squad and would, with a bit of luck, be impressed that he was spending his evenings rubbing shoulders – now where did 'rubbing shoulders' come from?

'Look, a couple of things,' said Stark. 'The accounts people were on to me again today about, I gather, a bit of snafu' – where did Stark come up with 'snafu' from? – 'over them checking your expenses. I hope we can work it all out amicably but there are certainly . . . issues . . . to be addressed. The other thing is that the guv'nor' – Stark's respectful shorthand for Max, the editor-in-chief – 'has heard from a chum of his at the Ministry of Justice that we may have been responsible for putting old Vladimir Petrov at risk by splashing him all over the front page and apparently the Russians are kicking up a bit diplomatically. Seems he was quite well placed with some of the embassy people here.' Stark gave him his fresh-faced look.

'What are you saying?' said Laurie. The late night, the nightcap of a double brandy with Kevin Yu, Mo, the Vicar and a recently retired commander whom they had half carried to a taxi – 'He's ex-Old Bill so make sure you get him home OK if you want to keep your licence, sunshine,' the Vicar had instructed the driver – was starting to kick in. 'That I'm responsible for Petrov being murdered because we suggested that he was under investigation by the police?'

'Look,' said Stark, loosening his collar symbolically. 'No one's making any accusations. It's just that the guv'nor is being asked what sort of evidence we had to back up Petrov being under suspicion.'

'I thought Max was pretty pleased with the story on the day.'

'On the day,' said Stark archly.

'Well, I would have thought that Scotland Yard finding the murder weapon in Petrov's garden might have something, just the tiniest bit, to do with him doing a runner to Thailand. Or did I miss something?'

'Look, I'm backing you one hundred and ten per cent on this,' said Stark. 'But the point is that Petrov had connections with the Russian government, they are unhappy that he seems to have been virtually convicted of a murder here and even unhappier that he has now been whacked to death in Thailand.'

Stark's eyes slid from Laurie to his BlackBerry to his screen and back again, like a CCTV camera in a cash depot.

'The thing is, Laurie,' said Stark, worrying his collar again, 'that I am having to fight for your job at the moment and you're not making it easy for me. You haven't had another thought about the motoring correspondent's post, have you? You'd keep the same salary. Less deadlines.'

'Fewer.'

'That's what I said.' Stark's corporate attention deficit disorder had got the better of him. His eyes were now flashing between BlackBerry, screen, Laurie and a new entry to the equation which was a dizzy graduate trainee called Miranda whom Stark was trying to impress. 'Anyway, see what you can come up with by the end of the week. I think we need some sort of resolution by Monday.'

'Revolution by Monday?'

'Resolution, Laurie, resolution.'

Laurie picked through his emails. Russian lady seeks husband. Nigerian fraudster seeks sucker. Penis enlargement. Who actually went in for that kind of surgery if you found it over the internet? People used to say that Old Man Hook had a legendarily large dick. Had that fuelled his gangster ambitions? Wasn't it meant to be the other way round? That men with erectile problems became killers. Wasn't that what Clyde Barrow had been afflicted by? What about Al Capone? No, he had had syphilis. Had that made him more inclined to break the law or less? Leaving party. Police Federation statement on pay. Funny photo of a turtle that had bonded with a rhinoceros from Violet. ACPO statement.

The phone rang.

'Hello,' said a deep female voice. 'This is Beth Plimsoll. We met briefly, if you remember. I wondered if you might want to pop by for a little chat. You remember the address, do you? When? No time like the present . . . I shall see you shortly then.'

Where did 'no time like the present' come from? Obviously there was no time like the present as the present differed from both the past and the future. Or did it? Sometimes it seemed depressingly like the past. He must stop doing this. It was preventing logical thought. He took a new notebook from the stationery cupboard.

'Ah, do you mind signing for that?' asked Linda, the newsdesk secretary.

'God, when did that come in?'

'I know, I know,' said Linda, rolling her eyes. 'Management's latest wheeze. My ex would turn in his grave if he knew how regimented this place has become.'

Laurie only dimly remembered Hugh Dunn, Linda's ex, although he had gone with Linda to the funeral. He was best remembered at the paper for having been in Death Valley and out of contact on 9/11, on what should have been the biggest story of his life. Laurie recalled Max's slightly ambiguous eulogy at the eventual memorial service in St Bride's, complete with coded reference to the 9/11 cock-up. There had been an unseemly drunken brawl in the Bell afterwards for no good reason.

Laurie shoved the notebook into his jacket pocket. It still smelled of cigar. He went to the gents. Once you have passed fifty, his father had once told him, never run for a bus or pass a public toilet without using it. His father had barely made it past sixty himself when, worn down perhaps by all his failed little dodgy business ventures, in Oban and Welshpool and Nottingham, he had politely died in his sleep one night, while Laurie was off at Rosemary West's trial in Winchester. A year later, his mother had, equally politely, succumbed to cancer.

Someone was in the shower. Laurie took the cubicle furthest away from the door. There was a copy of the morning's paper discarded on the floor. Why did people leave the gents in such a mess? he wondered. They were like little boys. Was the ladies as untidy? He would never know. He read his own story again. They had cut the last paragraph. Of course. He turned to the obituaries pages and checked the ages of the dead. Two in their eighties. One, a television presenter, of only fifty-two. Heart attack. Younger than Laurie. That was strangely cheering.

Ralph, the health correspondent, had told him once that more than a thousand people died of heart attacks while having a crap every year but no one wanted to publish the information in the *British Medical Journal*. What a way to go. Better have your face eaten off by a Staffordshire bull terrier – oh, no, he still had to talk to the reader's editor about having a face-to-face meeting with the Staffordshire Bull Terrier

Owners Society over his allegation that one of their chums had bitten off Petrov's face. Laurie had said that he thought, in the circumstances, that a 'face-to-face' meeting was not appropriate. As he checked the other death notices to cheer himself up, he heard the sound of a toilet flushing and then of someone's feet scurrying out. A few seconds later, he noticed, to his horror, a slow flood of water coming under the cubicle door making its inexorable way towards his half-mast trousers.

Chapter Thirty-seven

BETH PLIMSOLL WAS standing at the front door ready to greet Laurie as he arrived. She looked as though she should have had a cigarette holder in one hand and a dry Martini in the other but, in fact, she was carrying a dustpan in one hand and had a copy of the *London Review of Books* under her arm.

'Good afternoon,' she said. 'Come in. How's the crime beat?'

'Can't complain. Never any shortage of work.'

'I thought the crime rate was meant to be going down.'

'It's always meant to be going down but it's all a case of smoke and mirrors. They just invent new crimes they can solve.' Smoke and mirrors? Now that was a conjurer's trick, wasn't it? Maybe the same conjurer to whom one would pose the question: how's tricks?

'That's a very cynical attitude,' she said, gesturing to an armchair by the fireplace. 'What can I get you? Tea? Coffee? Something stronger?'

'Bit early in the day for me.'

'Yes, I seem to remember. Can't drink while on duty. Or is that just the police? Sometimes I can't tell the difference between the police and the press. They're all as nosy as each other. Usually the ones with the shinier shoes are police.'

'Tea, thanks,' said Laurie, sinking into the leather and glancing down at his scuffed Doc Martens. He leant back. Then forward. Dog hairs. That Chihuahua.

'I've never had so many people ringing the bell and asking if they can just have a very quick word. Do you ever get troubled by your calling?'

'Who said it was a calling?'

'Oh, you all do, don't you?' She left the sitting room and went into what Laurie presumed was the kitchen. She returned with his tea and a large glass of white wine. 'Still, it's a business. Crime sells, doesn't it?'

'Oh, I'm not so sure it sells any more. In the old days, before they abolished capital punishment, the London evening papers used to sell more than a million and a half copies every day. Everyone wanted to know if someone was going to be topped and liked a nice gory murder. If it bleeds, it leads. That was the old credo. And in those days, all the papers had crime bureaux, not just a single crime correspondent. Now everyone's chasing celebrity stories. Every paper's got a showbiz this and a showbiz that. No one's that interested in the twists and turns of trials any more.'

'And you don't have the Krays to write about, do you?'

'No, that's true. Did you ever come across them?'

'Do I look that old? I was about ten when they were locked up. Don't you ever feel guilty that you're encouraging young men to imagine that crime is glamorous?'

Laurie sank deeper into his armchair. When was she going to come to the point? Where was Mr Plimsoll? She sat down opposite and crossed her legs. One shiny red high heel hung over the tip of her toe. She returned his gaze.

'Dickens got accused of making crime glamorous with *Oliver Twist*,' said Laurie. 'People said then that he was creating a seductive world for young boys that would entice them into criminality for the sheer pleasure of joining a little gang. And Dickens defended himself by saying that John Gay had made crime glamorous with *The Beggar's Opera*. You know, Polly Peachum and Macheath . . . Mac the Knife. Did you know that "Mack the Knife" was Ronnie Kray's favourite song?'

'Was it really?' said Beth Plimsoll. She was sucking her cheeks in. Laurie could not decide whether this was because her Pinot Noir was dryer than anticipated or so that she could stop herself laughing.

'And he used to do a mean version of "Knees Up, Mother Brown",' said Laurie.

'I'm sorry I missed that,' said Beth Plimsoll.

'Anyway,' said Laurie, 'I don't think young men pick up a copy of my paper and read about someone having their head blown off and think that they'll start a career in crime rather than, I dunno, starting their own restaurant. In fact, I don't think young men pick up papers very much any more. But doing the forbidden has always been glamorous, hasn't it? Look at Robin Hood and Dick Turpin and Jesse James. Turpin was a little toerag who tortured old ladies to get their money and Jesse James was a pro-slavery racist who got his just deserts. Look at *Pirates of the Caribbean* – pirates are essentially robbers and rapists yet they're seen as something jolly to take the kiddies to enjoy.'

'Is this your little set piece?' she asked, setting her glass down on an antique wooden coal scuttle. So it must be a real fire. 'The justification?'

Laurie felt a slight cramp in his left calf. He grimaced.

'Oh, don't take it so personally,' said Beth Plimsoll. 'No need to wince. And I promise you that you don't need to tell me that doing the forbidden is glamorous.'

'Oh, don't worry. I don't take it personally at all. I think the new generation of criminals couldn't give a hoot about what's said about them in the papers. They're not like the Krays, giving interviews and having their wedding photos taken by Bailey. It's a whole lot of other things now, isn't it? I blame their diet, all that fast food. None of them can concentrate on anything any more. And all those video games. They can't tell what's reality and what's a game. They think when they shoot someone that they're going to get up afterwards and the game is going to go on.'

Beth Plimsoll stood up and fished a cigarette from the silver box on the mantelpiece.

When did I last see a cigarette box? wondered Laurie. He felt surreptitiously in his pocket for the half-cigar. Would it be cool or not to take out a half-finished cigar and smoke it? Probably not.

'That's not a tape recorder in your pocket, is it, Mr Lane?'

'No – just pleased to see you,' said Laurie. He regretted it immediately. She shot him a fierce look, lit her cigarette and blew the smoke towards the fireplace. Where was her husband? Was this a marriage in name only? His tea was weak and cold. He sipped it. Time to change the subject.

'So how are things here now? Has it all quietened down since Mr Hook went to a better place?'

'Ah, you think he could find a better place than here, do you?' Mrs Plimsoll finished off her glass of wine with a flourish. 'You'd better tell our estate agent. They believe it's one of the most desirable areas in Britain. Have things quietened down? I think for some people they have. That was what I wanted to talk to you about, as I am sure you gathered.' She lowered her eyes at him and looked at him through her eyelashes. Did women start doing that only after Princess Diana or have they always done it? he wondered.

'Excuse me a moment,' she said. She picked up her glass and left the room. A few moments later she was back, her glass filled.

'Refuelling stop,' she said. The legs folded again. Quite muscular calves. Like Sandra King's. Had the genetic make-up of British women changed? They were more muscular than forty years ago. But they can't all run marathons, can they? Diet, probably. Protein. She was an attractive woman. What was she going to tell him? She butted in to his thoughts.

'Now, just to clear up one fantasy,' she said.

God, she could read his mind.

'Er . . . yes?' said Laurie.

'Hook was not the old-school villain portrayed at his funeral. I know the boys, Crispin and Ashley, tried to make him sound like a combination of Marlon Brando and Dr Barnardo, just looking after his boys and doing the best for everyone. But the reality was a bit different . . . Why are you looking at me like that?'

Laurie shifted in the armchair.

'I don't think any of us really thought that he was Mrs Tiggy-Winkle,' he said. 'I mean, we didn't give that impression, did we?'

'I read all the reports of the funeral and it was as though some cuddly old footballer or boxer had died, not someone responsible for – how many murders? How many beatings? Not quoting Charles Dickens at me now, are you?'

'Any chance of another cup of tea?'

Beth Plimsoll stubbed her cigarette out and headed for the kitchen again. Laurie stood up and checked out the mantelpiece photos. A younger, darker-haired Beth marrying a more upright, more self-assured-looking Mr Plimsoll. Baby photos of what he presumed was their daughter. An awkward formal photo of the three of them together, a good few years ago, Laurie guessed. He thought of his own mantelpiece photos and realised that he did not have a mantelpiece. The family photos were stuck by magnets on the fridge. Caz used to remove his relatives from the display but tried to remember to replace them when they were coming into London for a visit. He had not got round to removing the big publicity picture of Caz taken in Nashville two years earlier, during her last bid for stardom. It had been badly retouched so that her chin looked as though it had been chiselled to a point. She still looked great. He missed her.

Beth Plimsoll returned with the tea and a plate of Jaffa cakes. When did I last see Jaffa cakes? Oh, the gatherings from Hook's rubbish that Gustafson, the binologist, had brought in. But what did that prove? Maybe Beth dumped her rubbish in the Hooks' bins when her own was full. Maybe the whole of this little close were Jaffa cake addicts.

'You see, Laurie, Charlie Hook was used to getting his own way,' she said. 'Look at the way he brought the boys up, making them go to public school so that they speak in that ridiculous half-posh, half-common way. But we also watched the way he felt he could exercise his own little droit de seigneur over everyone. Everyone.'

What was she trying to tell him? That Old Man Hook had put his hand up her skirt? He hoped that his expression conveyed understanding, curiosity, trust and wisdom in equal measure. Would he have to prompt her? He would.

'Did he . . . er . . . are you saying that he . . . er . . .'

'Did he try to fuck me? Please. I can look after myself. Anyway, he was interested in much younger members of the species than me.'

Laurie wondered if he should make some chivalrous remark but it might have come out wrong. He did not want to give the impression that Old Man Hook had made a serious error of judgement by not trying to grope Beth Plimsoll, while at the same time expressing surprise that anyone would not find her attractive. He settled for what he hoped was an enigmatic look.

'If you know what I mean,' she continued.

'You mean your . . . er . . . your . . .' Laurie struggled to remember her daughter's name.

'Oh, not my daughter, she wouldn't have given him the time of day. Apart from anything else, he had dreadful halitosis. Never a great aphrodisiac, is it? I told him myself that his breath smelled like a dead badger. Not that I've smelled one. No, he was interested in girls even younger than my daughter. I don't know if you caught that very moving reference at the funeral to the local cheerleaders group that he so generously donated money to and—'

'Oh, the Mile End Majorettes, I wondered what that was all about.'

'Minor-ettes more like. I'll think you'll find that his contribution became, shall we say, outstandingly generous in the last few months of his life.'

'You're going to have to decode this for me,' said Laurie.

'I am, aren't I?' she said with a sigh. 'You journalists are terribly slow on the uptake, aren't you? Let me spell it out. Old Man Hook liked girls in their teens, some just over the age of consent, some just under. About three months ago, he went just a little too far with one of them who, quite rightly, reported what had happened to her father. He, quite rightly, reported Old Man Hook to the police. And I think you will find that he was accused of indecent assault and indecent exposure.'

'Are you sure?' said Laurie. 'I think we would have heard about that. Old Man Hook charged with a sex offence? That would have been everywhere. One of the agencies would have picked it up, someone would have tipped off the nationals. Are you sure he was actually charged?'

'I didn't say he was charged,' said Beth Plimsoll. 'But he was accused of it.'

'So are you saying that the girl's family may have . . .'

'Taken revenge? Oh, I don't think so, Mr Lane.'

'Please call me Laurie. You don't think an outraged dad would have—'

'Oh, please, this is Highgate, not Karachi.'

'So what are you saying?

'Well, let's put it this way. I don't think the Hook family, with all their nice little businesses, wanted the old paterfamilias to be shown to be a paedophile, do you?'

'So you think one of the boys . . . ?'

'I'm not saying anything, Mr Lane – Laurie . . .' She enunciated his name as though it was a vehicle in the cab of which unspeakable things might occur. 'Except that I think you might well choose to explore an avenue the name of which is not written in Cyrillic. I am sure you must have already reached the conclusion that the Russian was a red herring. Or, to be more accurate, a dead herring.'

She allowed herself a small smile and stood up, her head cocked to one side.

'That's my husband's car. He's back a little earlier from his massage than usual. I'd be grateful if you said that you came here on your own initiative rather than mine and that I was my usual unhelpful self.'

'Happy to oblige.'

Laurie stood up and shook hands with her.

'By the way,' he said. 'The *London Review of Books* – is that your regular reading?'

'Don't I look intellectual enough? You think I should just read *Hello!* and *OK*!? Have a look at the personal ads, Laurie. They offer just a tiny bit more variety than the Edmonton golf club members' bar.'

She saw him to the door. Laurie glanced over the road at the Hook mansion. The curtains were all closed. A few pizza delivery leaflets had spilled from the letter box on to the front step. The house must still be empty. Would they be putting it up for sale? Laurie had read somewhere that, if a violent death had occurred on your property, you were required to inform a potential buyer. Must take a few grand off the value.

As he pondered this, a tall, broad-shouldered man in a black baseball cap and a leather coat emerged from the alleyway beside the house. What was there about his gait, the hunch of his shoulders that seemed so very familiar? Laurie stared at the man and the man stood motionless and briefly returned his gaze before pulling his coat collar up and striding away in the direction of Highgate Cemetery.

Chapter Thirty-eight

LAURIE TOOK A blue shirt off its hanger. Old habit. When going to confront someone, never wear a white shirt. A white shirt said officialdom: police officer, council official, lawyer. A white shirt immediately put people on their guard. Not that it would make much difference to the person Laurie was about to visit whether he was wearing a white shirt or a pink burka. Violet was still asleep when he left the house. Foxes had ripped open a neighbour's rubbish during the night, spilling a used condom and some chicken bones on to the pavement.

The office he sought was easy enough to find. A couple of minutes' walk from Liverpool Street station. 'I'm looking for Mr Mulgrew,' he told the young, unashamedly bored receptionist. 'He's head of security, I think.'

'Who shall I say is here?' she asked sweetly.

He watched her as she communicated the information over the phone. She had to repeat herself. Maybe Mulgrew was going deaf, or maybe he couldn't believe that Laurie would arrive unannounced at his new workplace.

'He said he would be right down,' she smiled at him. 'Please take a seat.'

Laurie skimmed the copies of the *Financial Times* lying on the low glass table as he waited. The lift opened and a purposeful Mulgrew walked out. He was old now, the hair more white than ginger, the knees a bit dodgy, but the back was as stiff and straight as when Laurie had first seen him, cheerfully and convincingly lying under oath in some Old Bailey robbery case. Dark suit, grey shirt, regimental tie. His gaze swept the foyer before settling on Laurie. Did Laurie detect a barely suppressed sigh?

'Hello, Laurie,' said Mulgrew, shaking hands. 'Saw you at the boxing. What's going on?'

'I was hoping you would tell me. They want a bit more on this whole Hook thing.'

'Done and dusted, isn't it?' said Mulgrew, meeting Laurie's gaze. 'Why are you asking me, anyway? I'm out of the loop. All my info's second-hand these days. I rely on you chaps to tell me what's going on.'

Mulgrew sat down beside him on the black leather couch. Their knees touched. Mulgrew shifted his weight and leant back. An inch of pearly white calf showed above the elasticated top of his sock.

'It was just that I know that you had . . . um . . . come across Charlie Hook over the years and wondered if you could throw any light on something I had heard.'

Mulgrew stared at him. His eyes were unforgiving. Laurie tried to imagine what it would have been like to be a criminal confronted by him. Mulgrew was a survivor. He came from a time when many of his fellow detectives had been corrupt: 'bent for yourself' or 'bent for the job'. 'Bent for the job' was now known as 'noble cause corruption'. Framing guilty men.

Fitting up criminals to get them off the street. Playing the slippery defence lawyers at their own game. 'Bent for yourself' meant taking bribes, pocketing the stolen goods you found. Mulgrew had always been doubly bent, according to Vic and Mick. If there had been a third way to be bent, he would have had a shot at that, too. No one really knew how he survived all the purges at Scotland Yard.

'So what is it you have heard, Laurie?'

'There is a suggestion that Hook had been . . . I don't know how to put this—'

'I'm sure you do, if you try, Laurie. It's your job, isn't it, expressing things.'

Laurie looked at Mulgrew's neatly clipped nails. The hair on the back of his hands was still ginger. There was a wedding ring. He tried to imagine a Mrs Mulgrew. Did she know that her husband had been on the take?

'Yeah . . . Anyway, I heard that Charlie Hook had been behaving inappropriately with a young woman and that her family were going to press charges . . .'

He could sense Mulgrew stiffen.

'Who told you this?'

'Oh, I just heard it on the . . . through the grapevine . . .'

'Don't play silly buggers with me, Laurie. Did DCI King tell you this? I saw you having a chat with her at the boxing.'

'No, it wasn't her. Honest. But you must have heard about this. It seems that the whole neighbourhood knew . . .'

Mulgrew smiled and leant back.

'You've been talking to Beth Plimsoll, haven't you?'

Laurie tried to fake puzzlement.

'Who?'

Mulgrew smiled more broadly. He was in charge now. 'You forget, Laurie, I've made my living for nearly forty years spotting when someone's telling the truth and when they're fibbing. Journalists think they're so clever but they would never make it as a thief – or a detective. Do you know why?'

'Tell me.'

'Because they always think they're cleverer than the person they're talking to. If you want to be a good detective – or a good thief – you have to assume that whoever you're dealing with is smarter than you and think what their next move might be. Most reporters are too lazy to do that. For years and years, I've had people like you, clever chaps with degrees, trying to prove that I was a corrupt officer. But they never did, did they? So maybe you have to ask yourself – was it because he was so clever that he never left any trace behind him or was it because a lot of little toerags – some of them in uniform – spread the word that I was bent for their own reasons? If I had been really bent, Laurie, do you think I would be doing this soppy job? Of course not, I would have made my pile and moved on. Think about it, Laurie.'

That stare again.

'OK . . . OK, but that doesn't answer my question, does it? Was Hook about to be investigated for—'

A tall motorcycle messenger in leathers and helmet pushed his way through the revolving doors and into the reception area. Mulgrew leant forward to address the newcomer.

'Excuse me – do you mind taking off your helmet? Like it says on the sign there.'

The messenger sheepishly obliged. Mulgrew turned back to Laurie.

'A head of security never sleeps,' he said. 'So. Was Charlie Hook about to be arrested? No. Was he shot because he'd been misbehaving? No.'

Mulgrew stood up. Laurie joined him. They were almost exactly the same height.

'Look, Laurie, I know you like to think the worst of people. Think the worst of me. Think the worst of Hook. Dig as much as you like. In the end, you will discover that Charlie got shot for a very simple reason. He crossed another villain. Amazingly enough, Laurie, for once you got it right. You should be really pleased with yourself. By the way, I always meant to tell you – I really liked your wife's last album. Ron – the Vicar gave it to me for my birthday. Marvellous.'

He stuck his hand out, the palm firm and flat, as though he was challenging Laurie to a game of paper-scissors-stone.

'I will bid you good day.'

Chapter Thirty-nine

'I'M SO GLAD, Dad,' said Violet when she found him perusing the small ads section of the *London Review of Books* at the kitchen table. 'That's a real sign that you've moved on in your life. It means that you're going through the bereavement stages really quickly.'

'Look, Violet, I'm not reading them for me. It's . . . it's something to do with work.'

'Of course it is, Dad. Look, I think it's great. Do you want a hand?' She pulled up a seat beside him. 'I'm sure I can find the right one for you.'

'I thought your mum was the right one for me.'

'Don't be morbid. She was once but she's moved on.'

'God, you sound like one of the chief constables at a conference. They're always talking about how things have "moved on", how there has been a "step-change". What's the difference between a change and a bloody "step-change" anyway?'

Violet was taking her new task seriously.

'Oh, look at this one – "Being remembered as the blind date who stabbed himself in the back of the hand if I carried out my threat to leave the restaurant unless the crying stopped". What is that about? This sounds a bit better – "I am

Melinda Mercouri on fur rug in Phaedra. Would you like to be Anthony Perkins?" What does that mean? I thought Anthony Perkins was the one in *Psycho*. Does that mean she's looking for a psycho or something? And are you drinking already? It's only six o'clock.'

'I'm sure she's not looking for a psycho, whoever she is. It's a famous scene in an old film so what she's looking for is someone who is old enough now to have been young enough then to remember it when it came out and to have thought that making love on a fur rug in front of a roaring fire was the sexiest thing you could possible imagine.'

'Well, it is pretty sexy, isn't it – apart from the fur.'

Laurie did not want to hear his daughter describe to him what she regarded as sexy scenarios.

'And yes,' he said, 'I am having a drink. It's been an odd day.'

'Oh, that's a bad sign.'

'Is that another of the seven ages of—'

'Stages, stages of bereavement. No, it's one of the signs of addiction. In fact, it comes from your own paper. They read them out to us in our citizenship talk just before A levels because they thought some of us might be drinking too much because of worry about the exams. And alcoholics always give themselves excuses, like they're having a little drink because they've had an odd day or they're depressed or they're only having a little drink because they're celebrating.'

The beer tasted warm and unappetising. Violet had not finished her search.

'How about this one? She sounds about the right age. "Ever wonder what it would be like to go to bed with Lady Macbeth? Now is your chance!" She sounds fun, don't you think?'

'Sure.'

'And here's one that sounds perfect for you – "Please don't try comparing me to a summer's day. I am more like a late autumn evening that could turn into night: mellow and full of light and shade. I'm a blonde, voluptuous and certainly not your average catwalk shape but friends tell me I'm attractive. GSOH. Maybe we could winter somewhere together while I put that spring back in your step." She sounds nice, don't you think? D'you like voluptuous? It just means big breasts, doesn't it?'

'Please,' said Laurie. He opened the fridge and peered inside. Since Caz had left, it had become emptier and emptier. While she operated a policy of consolidation in the fridge – every item of food a wanted item – Laurie preferred the slash and burn approach, binning any malodorous leftovers with abandon. Now all that was left inside were a few bottles of Budvar and a sad little container of unfeasibly pink taramosalata. He sighed.

'Don't sigh, it's so depressing,' said Violet. 'People are not attracted to depressed people.'

'You don't say. Do you get an A grade in psychology for coming up with that one? Which reminds me, when do you get your results? Have you thought about what happens if, heaven forfend, you fail?'

'Well, at least if I fail I won't have to appear on the front of your paper jumping in the air like a pony and pretending to be excited. Why do you always put white girls on the front page with their A level results? It's so gross.'

'You'd have to ask the picture editor.' Laurie felt a momentary shudder as he recalled the scene with Eva-Marie.

Well, if he was sacked, he would not have to worry about bumping into her again in the canteen. 'And why do you think I'm suited to a late autumn evening? You make me sound like a bloody cardigan.'

'Yeah, but look – "that could turn into night". You know what that means? Hot sex with an older woman.'

'What makes you think that's all I'm interested in?'

'All men are.'

'Did you get that in your citizenship class too? What are you doing for supper, by the way? Shall I order some takeaway or can you handle another pasta?'

'Oh, I ordered a pizza on the way home. It should be here soon. And I forgot to tell you, Mum's on at the Goblin again tonight. Someone cancelled. She said to tell you. Godfrey won't be there.'

'Did she tell you to add that?'

'Yeah,' said Violet. 'But you're going to have to meet him soon. You have to be adult about it.'

'Is that what your mum says? That I have to be "adult" about it? She has devoted her entire singing life to telling people not to be adult about the end of relationships, hasn't she? "Now and Then There's a Fool Such As I". "A Little Bitty Tear Let Me Down". "It Comes and Goes". God, half her songs are about wallowing in self-pity and refusing to "move on". When did she ever sing a song about "being adult" about someone breaking your heart and "drawing a line under it"?'

'Oh, this is getting morbid. Which reminds me, what does "morbidly obese" mean? Becky called Erica "morbidly obese" yesterday and Erica said, if she really was morbidly obese, she would be dead. Your paper is always going on about it, you know.'

'Do we have a ten-part test to see if we're morbidly obese? Or are there seven stages of morbid obesity?'

Violet was busy texting someone but seemed able to conduct a conversation at the same time.

'And what's happening about that murder case?' she asked. 'People at school were asking about it. Is there going to be gang warfare?'

'Who knows?'

'I thought you were meant to know everything about crime. And don't sigh again. It's really depressing.'

'Do you think it would put Miss Autumn Leaves off?'

'Absolutely. So what is happening? Did that Russian guy get killed because of you? That's what Erica said. And her dad's in the Crown Prosecution System.'

'Service. The Crown Prosecution Service, it's called.'

'Whatever.'

Laurie surrendered to the remains of the taramosalata and some stale water biscuits. He tapped one.

'Did you know that sailors used to tap their ship's biscuits before eating them to get rid of the weevils? No?'

'What's a weevil?'

'An unpleasant little worm. Which reminds me, did your mum say that Godfrey was definitely not going to be there?'

'You are really not coming to terms with this, are you? So what is happening about the murder? Was Old Man Hook really like the Godfather? Did he have jowly cheeks and talk out of the side of his mouth?'

'He was rather handsome but he looked like what he was, a

very ruthless businessman. But who killed him? God, I wish I knew. It's so confusing. I saw this woman this afternoon—'

'Oh, great, so you are dealing with it!'

'Violet, it was work. This woman who lives next door to the Hooks rang me up because she wanted to tell me that Hook had been chasing after teenage girls. She said that he was in trouble over that.'

'Hey, maybe one of the girls killed him. That would be a story, wouldn't it? Maybe he had a girl in his house and he grabbed her and she grabbed his gun and blew him away. That would be cool, wouldn't it? She wouldn't go to jail for that, would she? That would count as a crime passionel, I think. Yeah, if it's passionate, you don't have to go to jail. That's right, isn't it?'

Laurie coated a water biscuit in pink and popped it into his mouth.

'No, that is not right,' said Laurie. 'That was an old law in France when it was possible for a husband who caught his wife in flagrante to kill the lover and his wife and not go to jail.'

'What's in flag-whatever?'

'In flagrante means "in the act".'

'You mean you would have to catch them with their clothes off actually having it off?'

'Well, in a compromising situation, I suppose. But if a woman – a girl – killed her attacker, then she could plead self-defence and she might not even be charged, provided the CPS were satisfied that she really was protecting herself.'

'That would be real girl power stuff, wouldn't it? She would be like a heroine – she would have her own TV show. I bet that's what happened. Why don't you suggest that as the real reason he was killed? They seem to believe anything you write.'

'How do I attribute it? A source close to my kitchen table suggested that it would have been really neat if Old Man Hook was killed by an abused teenage cheerleader.'

Violet examined the lid of the taramosalata container. 'Do you realise that this is soooo past its sell-by date? This is more than two weeks past the time when you're meant to have eaten it.'

'Didn't your mother explain that those dates are bogus, they're just put there to make you throw away perfectly good food and buy a replacement.'

'Oo, I wouldn't be too sure. We did taramosalata in biology with Mr Schwarz and he said that it is one of the prime causes of . . . God, what was it? Brucellosis or something. Or was that doner kebabs? Still, it's your insides. Do you think Mum would come back to you if you were dying?'

Laurie binned the remains of the taramosalata.

'What do you think?'

'She would almost certainly write a song about it,' said Violet. 'Did you know that the song about the stranger in the rain is about you?'

'Of course I do.'

'Oh. Mum said that it was a secret.'

'Did she tell you a lot of secrets?'

'A few. Is it OK if I have one of your beers? I'll be eighteen next month.'

'I suppose so. So what secrets did she tell?'

He watched his daughter place the lid of the bottle of Budvar against the side of the kitchen table and remove it expertly with a swift blow from the heel of her hand. She gulped down about half the bottle, belched and apologised. Laurie helped himself to another bottle from the fridge.

'They wouldn't be secrets if I passed them on, would they?' Violet was a little unsteady on her feet. Laurie realised that she must have been drinking before she came home. He sighed.

'Don't sigh! Look, I'll tell you one. I don't think she'd mind.'

'As long as it's not going to be—'

'Oh, don't worry, it's not about how many orgasms she has with Godfrey. I promised I wouldn't pass that on to anyone.'

'Great.'

Violet polished off the rest of the bottle with one long swig.

'No, it's about her leg.'

'What, the motorbike crash?'

It had been just after they met, maybe even that first night in bed together, when Caz had explained why she walked with a limp. She had been coming home from a gig and sitting on the back of the fiddle-player's motorcycle. He had tried to overtake a sports car on the Brighton–London road and they had skidded into a tree. Her leg had been broken in three places and the doctors had never been able to patch it up properly. He remembered stroking the scars on her long bare leg.

'It wasn't a motorbike crash at all.'

'So what was it?'

Violet eyed the fridge.

'Since you've had a second beer, can I too?'

'I suppose so. So what is the secret?'

'There was no motorcycle crash. She was drunk one night

at a gig somewhere and she missed the step coming out of the ladies and fell down a flight of stairs. But she couldn't tell her parents that so she made up this story about the crash and she said that once she'd told people, she couldn't take it back because it was too embarrassing. I mean, her career was just starting off and the Goblin even had a benefit for her so she couldn't say she'd just been pissed and fallen out of the ladies. It wouldn't have had quite the same aura, really, would it? After that, there was no way she could tell anyone, even you, the real story.'

'Poor Caz, I wouldn't have minded.'

'That's what I told her. But she said she had told you the first night and she was frightened you would leave her if you found out she was a bullshitter. Anyway, since you're not together any more, I think it's OK for me to tell you that.'

There was a banging at the front door.

'Pizza time!' yelled Violet, hurrying downstairs.

A moment later there was a high-pitched scream.

Chapter Forty

CAZ WAS TUNING her guitar as she spoke.

'I can't believe, Laurie, that you left our daughter alone after something like that happened,' she said. 'Someone sends you a human tongue with a hook stuck through it?'

'I don't know if it was a human tongue, it was just a tongue. It could have been a small cow's tongue or a big dog's tongue or—'

'That's even more disgusting!'

'Look, we used to eat tongue when we were kids. Didn't you? It was lovely with salad dressing and a bit of lettuce. Or with a little Coleman's mustard in a nice brown bread sandwich.'

'I can't believe you're here. Have you told the police?'

'They probably sent it.'

'God, really?'

'Look, I don't know, Caz. I heard Violet scream, I went down and someone had nailed this little packet to the door and Violet opened it. There was just a tongue and a hook through it. The whole thing is fucking bizarre. What am I meant to do? Obviously, I wouldn't have left her on her own but she had other plans for the night anyway. She said she was going to a film with Erica and she would be staying over there. Nothing bad is going to happen to her, I promise you.'

'It had better not,' said Caz, looking up from her tuning. 'I don't want Violet getting involved with all your low-life chums. I had that reporter friend of yours round here last week, the one with the clashing shirts and ties.'

'Oh, the Vicar.'

'Yes, and he was with a very creepy guy who had been a cop who wanted to find out if I knew what you were up to. Creepy.'

She had a new outfit on. A long straight black leather skirt that came down just below the tops of her cowboy boots. They were new, too, with some fancy stitching design down the outside. The white blouse with pink and green cactuses sewn into it was also new. Was this what Godfrey liked her to wear?

'All my low-life chums?' said Laurie. 'What about this little lot?'

He surveyed the Goblin. It was not having its busiest night. There was a trio of elderly, beer-bellied men in check shirts at the bar staring lugubriously over the barmaid's shoulder at the whisky-sponsored mirror before them and sharing an occasional desultory word. In the corner, a fat man with a bandanna round his neck, cowboy style, slept with his mouth open and a half-pint of Guinness on the table in front of him. A posse of male smokers stood at the pub entrance like reluctant sentries. Two women sat silently at the table closest to the stage, each wearing denim skirts and grey T-shirts carrying the image of Willie Nelson and suggesting that they were the property of Lukenbach County Jail.

'It's hardly the fucking Algonquin round table, is it?'

'Have you been drinking, Laurie?'

'Well done. I always said you should have been a forensic scientist.'

'Why would they send a tongue, Laurie?'

'I dunno – they were out of Spam. Your guess is as good as mine. It could have been some sort of warning about wagging tongues. Who knows? If they send a human ear, I'll know they're serious.'

Caz grinned at him, the old smile. She tossed her hair back. He took her hand and squeezed it. She did not withdraw it.

'Ow,' he said. 'You haven't cut your nails since you left me.'

'It's a plectrum, dummy. Now I have to go and sing for my supper for the next half hour. You're not going to run off on me this time, are you? You're not going to be tracked down by a hitman here, are you?'

'Amongst all this crew? They would take one look in here and think they'd stumbled across the living dead and there was nothing left for them to do. You can't kill zombies, according to Violet. They are the undead.'

Caz shrugged. 'Want me to do any requests?'

'Oh, sure,' said Laurie. 'How about "You're Right, I'm Left, She's Gone". Or, maybe, "Tonight the Bottle Let Me Down"? Oh, I know – "Snowbird . . . the one I love forever is untrue . . ." '

'Morbid,' said Caz, shaking her head.

'That's what your daughter said.'

Caz shouldered her guitar and scanned the room for her band. They were already on stage, fiddling with microphones and drum kits. She nodded at them. Laurie watched her limp towards them, exchanging smiles and handshakes with familiar faces at the tables near the stage. Should he shout out that he knew how she came by that limp? Did it matter? He checked that his phone was switched off, fearful of the wrath that Caz delivered from the stage towards anyone unwise enough to let their ring tones interfere with a ballad.

She had not added anything new to her repertoire since she had left him. There were a couple of Townes Van Zandt songs, an old Emmylou Harris, a brace of John Prines and a couple that Caz had written herself, including one that she had once dared hope would be a hit, called 'Too Bad'. It had not been and Caz had gone into a long depression. Was that when she had started seeing Godfrey? He bought a drink while Caz was consulting with the boys in the band as to whether to do a Bob Wills or a Bill Monroe as their encore. Three minutes later she was sitting by his side at the bar.

'So what's happening, Laurie? You go to Thailand and you find a body. You come back here and someone sends you body parts in the post.'

'Now that would be a good title for a song: "You sent me body parts in the post but all I wanted was your heart". They weren't in the post, someone dropped 'em off. I wish I knew what was happening, Caz. I don't know any more who's lying, who's manipulating me, what's coincidental and what I should be frightened of. The great thing about you leaving – apart from the fact that I can watch the late-night football without you asking who's playing – is that I don't care too much about other things.'

'I can tell that,' said Caz, smiling over her shoulder and shaking her head as a fan in a suede, fringed jacket offered to buy her a drink. 'When did you last have a bath?'

'That's the smell of fear.'

'It probably is but you would never admit it, would you? Always playing the clown.'

'I thought that was why you went out with me.'

Caz smiled at him. The new band on stage had already played their first number. The lead singer held the mike stand in one hand and gestured at the accordion beside him on the stage.

'It is one of the rules of stagecraft,' he said, 'that you never bring an accordion on to the stage without using it.'

'He got that line from the Household Gods,' whispered Caz. Laurie surreptitiously switched on his mobile phone in his pocket. They listened to the song together.

'Just like old times,' said Laurie.

'Why don't you get out of this whole crime thing?' said Caz.

'You sound like a probation officer.'

Caz shook her head. They talked about the house, their daughter, their joint bank account and their CD collection. They listened to a bad version of 'The Night They Drove Old Dixie Down' and parted on the street outside. Caz flagged a black cab down and kissed Laurie on the cheek as she said farewell. Laurie walked all the way home. It was just after midnight when he put the key in the lock of his front door.

'Hello, my friend,' said a half-familiar voice behind him on the street. 'Had late night, have we?'

Chapter Forty-one

'WHO WOULD HAVE thought we meet again, hey?' said the now slightly more familiar voice. 'Weather not so good as Thailand, no?'

Laurie felt his heart flutter and realised that his mobile phone was in his pocket so it really was his heart that was wobbling.

'Jesus Christ,' he said. 'Am I seeing a ghost?'

'Sure. Tam O'Shanter, perhaps,' said his visitor, pulling his baseball cap down further over his face. 'Not ghost, no. Same person you see before but different look, different name.' There was a pause. 'Different mood.'

'Jesus!' Laurie surveyed the street. There were a few lights on in houses. A solitary dog walker on the other side of the street was calculating whether he could get away with leaving his Labrador's mighty turd on the pavement without anyone noticing; Caz had been famous in the neighbourhood for outing such offenders, on one occasion scooping up a golden retriever's gross offering and depositing it on its owner's doorstep. The neighbourhood was well practised in ignoring the noises of conflict on the streets, at least until they heard the reassuring sounds of the police siren. No one would hear him scream.

'Can we go somewhere for talk?' asked the voice.

'I'm not sure where is open,' Laurie heard himself say. He sneaked a look at his midnight visitor. He seemed both familiar and unfamiliar.

'I thought London was twenty-four-hour city, capital of world.'

'Well, there is a kebab place round the corner.'

'Fantastic,' said the voice. Even with a foreign accent, the sarcasm was apparent.

They made their way to Green Lanes. A night bus shuddered past.

As the only patrons of Kyrenia Top Kebab House, Laurie and his visitor sat opposite each other. A waiter in a green velvet waistcoat offered them a menu.

'I'll have just coffee,' said the voice. 'Doner kebabs not so good idea. Salmonella.'

'Don't you start.'

'I read it in your paper.'

Laurie ordered a pita bread, some hummus and a beer and looked up from the menu at the man opposite him.

'Surely you know who I am?' asked the man.

'Well, you sound just like—'

'Just like who?'

'The late Vladimir Petrov . . . Oh, my God, outside the Hooks' house, when I was seeing Beth Plimsoll . . .'

'Very good. But Petrov is dead, isn't he? I read in your paper. Online edition. Very good. I like new interactive options. Good Moscow blogger you have, too. No, Vladimir Petrov is dead. No question. He was certified dead in Bangkok. His ex-wife came out from Moscow and identified him. Body cremated. And your paper said he had been killed in revenge attack so it must be true.'

'Maybe we're more accurate when it comes to writing about salmonella.'

'Maybe.'

The visitor sipped his coffee. There was a long silence. A drunk ordered a takeaway doner kebab with no salad but more spicy sauce. Laurie picked at his pita and hummus and shook his head.

'OK,' said the stranger. 'I stop play games. You are right. I am Vladimir Petrov.' He looked sideways to see if anyone was watching them. He pulled off his baseball cap. His hair had been shaved off. He looked very different.

'But you looked so . . . dead. I mean, that dog was eating your face. There was no way you could have come back from—'

'Look, that wasn't me, my friend. My clothes, my shoes, my ring, my – what you say? Crucifix. Little star tattoo on hand. Easy. Anyway, you spot them all. I read. Very observant. But if you look closely, shoes don't fit on feet, ring doesn't fit on finger. Star not real tattoo. What you see was one of your countrymen.'

'You mean you killed—'

'No, killing not so simple. Every month or so, one of your countrymen die there. Drink too much, fall in water, have heart attack while fucking bar girl. No shortage bodies. No one come looking for them. Who cares? Lots of football hooligans there. No one misses them and all have false identities so no one knows who is really missing. This man, English drunk, fall in sea. A little bigger than me, not much. Same colour hair. We keep him one week in deep freeze. We had to close kitchen at Henri's. Bloody nuisance. Deep freeze turned up too high. We had to scrape him off floor with spade, then defrost him. Have to hit him round head with baseball bat but, you know something, when you're dead you don't mind too much if someone hits you with baseball bat.'

'But . . . but . . . why?'

'You ask that? I have argument with Hook but not enough to kill him. He is silly old man and he make no sense. He promise to invest in property. Then when I see him he says he never made any agreement. Then Hook killed. Gun found in my garden. In my garden? You think I am so stupid? Then you – your paper – make me look like killer of Hook. What happens if they arrest me? I know British justice, best in world. But for Russian man? Or Muslim man? Maybe not so good. So I need to die. Yes? Now I'm dead. No one look for me any more. I have new name, new passport. I am new person.'

Laurie studied his face.

'Yes,' said the stranger. 'Good, yes? Easy now. Latex, little make-up. Just like movies. No? You report Securitas robbery trial, didn't you? All robbers in that have such faces. All you need, good make-up artist. My niece, beautician, that's what she does. No problems. You like it?'

'But why come back here?'

'Unfinished business.' He stared at Laurie. 'I want to see someone. Maybe that's why I am at Hook's house. I am not staying long.'

'But why . . . why bother seeing me? I would never have known you were still alive.'

'You saw me at Hook house, didn't you? Yes?'

Laurie paused. The man in the alleyway. The broad

shoulders. The familiar gait, yes, that rolling walk. 'But I would never have known if . . .'

A sudden look of – what? Disappointment? Frustration? Annoyance? – flashed across Petrov's handsome face. He looked hard at Laurie.

'You stare at me. Yes? I think you knew it was me. I cannot take risk. If anyone claims that I am alive, I am back in trouble. I have things to finish here. Maybe you tell police you have seen me still alive at Hook's house. If people come asking if you sure that was Vlad you saw lying dead, I need you to swear that it was me for sure. For sure! I need you to swear on your child's life.'

An image of Violet screaming.

'God, is it you that's been sending me the hooks and the tongue?'

'The what?'

His puzzlement seemed genuine. A drunk at the counter buying a takeaway had dropped the chilli pepper off his doner kebab on the floor and was scrabbling for it. A fluffy marmalade cat emerged from the kitchen and joined him in the search.

'Oh, nothing, just that I've had some weird deliveries of late and I couldn't work out who might be sending them.'

Vladimir Petrov sipped his coffee. He wrinkled his nose.

'No, I deliver messages personally. But you should know that I was not responsible for Hook's death though I am glad he is gone. I think his sons kill him. Not a good man. Was he your best gangster? No wonder this country is a mess and you have to bring in foreigners to do everything for you – foreign footballers and foreign plumbers and foreign waiters and foreign security guards. And now foreign gangsters. You can't even run a decent gang now because you are soft and envious. I am not staying long. Not in this café and not in this country. But remember what I tell you, my friend. When they ask you sure that I am dead, you tell them yes. And you never tell people you saw me alive in London. OK?'

'But why . . .'

'Why should you lie for me? Good question. I think about that. I think – I know where you live, I could threaten to hurt your family but that is not my way. That is stereotype way, the way you think I would behave. But then I think, better reason. You already say in your paper that I am dead. I think maybe not so good for journalist to look too foolish? Another reason.' Petrov smiled and pulled a Jiffy bag from his pocket. He placed it on the table and rose to his feet. Laurie joined him. They shook hands.

Vladimir Petrov walked out, pulling his collar up as he left. That familiar, athletic, rolling walk again. Laurie watched through the window of the restaurant as a black saloon car pulled up alongside him and he got in. He opened the envelope. Inside was a book called *A Night Out With Robert Burns*. And inside the book was a bundle of new £50 notes. At the page bookmarked by the money, someone, presumably Petrov, had asterisked a verse which Laurie was clearly meant to read.

> Pleasures are like poppies spread,
> You seize the flower; its bloom is shed,
> Or like the snow falls in the river,
> A moment white – then melts for ever . . .

Chapter Forty-two

'YOU CAN BUY me my coffee,' said Laurie to Guy as they stood in line at the canteen. 'I have solved the mystery, I have cracked the biggest case of my career.'

'You're having me on!'

'No, I'm serious,' eyeing a temptingly fresh croissant and succumbing. 'The perpetrator has even confessed to me.'

'Wow, that's great! That should shut Stark up. Were the police there when he confessed?'

'No and I'm not planning on telling them. I'm not sure they really need to be involved.'

'Christ! A double murder and you're not going to tell the cops. That's cool for you. Shall I make that a double latte?'

'Oh, I haven't solved the murder. No, I thought you'd be much more interested to know that I'd solved the trouser-flusher case.'

Guy turned to face him and beamed.

'Now that *is* impressive,' he said. 'So who was it?'

'Guess!'

'That bloke in accounts.'

'Wrong. He was eliminated from our inquiries quite early

on. For a start, he doesn't use those loos and he didn't really fit the profile of a suspect. He might have done it once but we were looking for someone with a genuine grievance or alternatively—'

'A sociopath?'

'Exactly,' said Laurie, gathering up his croissant and coffee and joining Guy at the counter.

'Well, that means about fifty per cent of the people working here.'

'At least,' said Laurie. 'Guess again.'

'Not Stark, surely? Trying to harass me into taking redundancy, perhaps?'

'No, Stark was also eliminated quite early on too. I decided that he had ample ways of getting rid of you without resorting to shoving your breeks down the lavvie.'

'So was it Henderson? Still pissed off that he didn't get my job? I guess we have to work out a suitable punishment. What do you reckon?'

'Oh, it has to be the trouser press, doesn't it? Break their fingers in a trouser press until they squeal for forgiveness. And no, it's not Henderson. You're thinking in too linear a way.'

'Wow,' said Guy, licking the froth off the top of his cappuccino. 'Thinking too linear . . . So, let's be a little more . . . Heh! A woman disguised as a man going in there – surely not Linda because she's pissed off that I said something nice about her ex-husband?'

'So she would get a deerstalker and a man's overcoat and sneak into the gents on the off chance that you might leave your trousers in there? Anyway, Linda's not spiteful.'

'Well, you told me not to think in too linear—'

'I'll take you out of your misery. It was Geraldo.'

'Geraldo? Who's Geraldo?'

'Exactly. No one knows who he is.'

'So?'

'He's the guy who cleans the loos.'

'So he flushes my trousers down the lavatory. Isn't that taking the cleaning thing a bit too far?'

Laurie nodded at Linda and Eva-Marie as they went past.

'You know it was always those red trousers of yours that were the victims?' said Laurie. 'Well, I always said that those red trousers were a mistake, that they sent out the wrong message to people.'

'Yeees . . . Are you saying that I have been the victim of – what would it be called? Redism? Redophobia?'

'No, I'm afraid you were the victim of mistaken identity. You know Fowley, that rather odd bloke in City, little beard, specs, going a bit bald, rather up himself, talks in conference about the bear market all the time?'

'Hmm, I don't think I've ever spoken to him. Why would he—?'

'No, it's nothing personal and he didn't do it but Fowley is like a little boy and he always reads a paper in the loo and leaves bits of it lying on the floor of the cubicle. Well, as you might imagine, anyone cleaning the loos has to deal with all that and after a while it can make them really pissed off. Well, wouldn't it you? Now Geraldo is a bright guy, political refugee, he was a teacher in Colombia and had to leave because his brother had joined the FARC and he was fingered by someone. Anyway, he does his job here, swallows it, as it were, but you can imagine that after a while, clearing up after all these snotty creatures who can't even be bothered to pick up the paper they're reading gets to be a bit of a drag and—'

'But I'm always very, well, meticulous, Laurie.'

'That's what I'm saying, Guy. It was mistaken identity. Fowley is the only other person in this building – in London, probably, possibly even the world, who wears red moleskin trousers. So a couple of times Geraldo has been in there when Fowley walks out leaving all this mess behind him. He just sees this guy with a little beard and these red trousers. So when he sees red moleskin trousers hanging up in the cubicle, he can't resist striking a blow for the oppressed of the world.'

'How do you know?'

'Well, remember when you gave me the decoy trousers to leave? It worked. I was in the loo the other day when he did it again. And I caught up with him and he told me – he didn't say it was Fowley he was targeting but he described him – the little beard, the specs. And he said he always, always left the paper on the loo floor, and he does have those red trousers. So I've told him that you are the salt of the earth.'

'You told him all this in Spanish?'

'I told him you were *buena gente* – good guy. So your trousers are now safe. Does that make you feel better? Don't tell anyone or Geraldo will get the sack. He offered to buy you a new pair of trousers but I told him not to worry.'

'Great. Well, well, well. So how are things on the murder front?'

'Weird. I saw a ghost last night.'

Laurie felt a tap on his shoulder. It was Stark.

'We need to talk,' he said. He nodded at Laurie and was gone. Laurie looked at Guy and stood up.

'We who are about to die salute you,' he said.

In Stark's office, he found John from Accounts and Marcia from Human Resources. Where did 'human resources' come from? George Orwell might have wondered. Could you use that phrase without knowing its origin? When did that title take over from Personnel? Was Personnel seen as a weird idea when it was first introduced? Should he ask Marcia this, as a way of breaking the ice? Probably not. They would think he was cracking up and make him undergo a medical.

Stark nodded at Marcia. Stark was clearly playing the role of judge. John was the prosecutor who had already successfully convicted Laurie. Marcia was to be the executioner.

'I should make clear that this is a "without prejudice" meeting,' said Marcia. 'That is to say, we have an offer on the table which we hope will be found acceptable but should you choose to go to dispute, as I understand you have suggested you might, then we will, of course, move to a more formal situation and, of course, our offer, which we believe is a generous one, recognising everything that you have done for the company, will have to be withdrawn.'

Laurie felt strangely serene.

'What about my union rep? Can I get Rosie?'

'Rosie is out on a story,' said Stark, with a little too much satisfaction. 'In Hartlepool.'

Maybe this was how condemned men felt as they stood on the scaffold and the prison chaplain droned on with a few homilies about the life everlasting before the trapdoor opened and the noose tightened. He had written a couple of articles over the years about Albert Pierrepoint, the busiest of Britain's official hangmen, and he remembered what professional pride he had taken in getting the drop exactly right. Did the people in Human Resources have training in sacking people? Like, bring a box of man-size tissues, pass on the number of the Samaritans? Would one of them explain about the ten stages of grief? Or was it the seven stages of grief and the ten indicators of alcohol addiction? Marcia was still speaking.

'. . . your situation has been carefully analysed and, in light of your earlier refusal to take on the post of motoring correspondent and your stated reservations about the company's commitment to good practice vis-à-vis the merging of the newspaper and the website, we would like to offer you a redundancy package that reflects your service and the company's gratitude for it.'

She pulled a sheaf of papers from a pink folder and laid them with a flourish in front of Laurie. He skimmed through them until he came to the money. They were offering him two years' worth of salary to leave. He looked up. All three were swapping glances apprehensively, as if they feared he might explode. He imagined sinking his teeth into Stark's neck and hitting a vein. He pictured himself more in the role of a zombie than Count Dracula. Marcia had a long pale neck. He would have happily sunk his teeth into it. John's neck was short and bore the bristles of a bad shave and the aftershock of a boil; he would spare him.

'It's all right,' said Laurie. 'I'm not going to bite you or something.' He looked at Stark who had his switch-on smile operating and had not spared the Homme Sauvage. 'I guess this means that you don't want anything more on the latest developments in the Hook murder?'

Stark flashed a sideways look at his two fellow conspirators. Their mute response was clear: don't rock the boat. (No need to wonder where 'don't rock the boat' came from, thought Laurie.) Laurie flashed them a smile which he hoped would disconcert them, swept up the papers and left the room.

Guy looked up from his screen as he returned to his desk.

'You look cheerful,' said Guy.

'The condemned man ate a hearty breakfast,' said Laurie.

'What does that mean? Did you get the sack?'

'Since you ask, I did,' said Laurie.

'I'll miss you,' said Guy.

'Is that all you can say?'

'What would you like me to say – we'll always have Blackfriars? Look, don't let the bastards get rid of you. We can organise a strike. Well, maybe not a strike but perhaps a ten-minute stoppage. I'm sure we can do something.'

'Don't worry, Guy. I think I've already decided I've had enough. They're giving me a fat pay-off. I think I'll go and live somewhere hot and get a job in a bar and read all the books I never got round to.'

Guy shook his head at him. 'Who's going to track down the trouser-flushers after you've gone, for heaven's sake?'

Laurie shrugged and started looking through the drawers on his desk and binning ancient notebooks and business cards.

'What are you doing?'

'Emptying my drawers – if that doesn't sound too risqué.'

'Aren't you meant to hang on to your notebooks for at least a year in case someone sues you for libel?'

'Exactly. The paper will now have no defence against an

expensive libel action. God, it's odd looking at these notebooks. I have no idea what some of those stories were about. It would be more satisfying to burn them but I guess health and safety might object.'

'Are you going to have a leaving do?' asked Guy, as he watched Laurie dropping files into a tall waste-paper bin. 'You could have a joint party because I think there are at least another five redundos on the cards. Half of the foreign subs are going. End of an era.'

'No, I don't think so. I went to one of those parties at *The Times*. There were six of them being weighed off, I think. The editor gives a little speech for every one, which lasted about forty-five seconds each, which must work out at about two seconds for every year served. It reminded me of those old cowboy films when they have six outlaws being hanged at the same time.'

'God, you're getting a bit morbid, aren't you?' Guy looked at his watch. 'It's nearly noon. Why don't I take you round the corner for a swift noggin, just like journalists used to do?'

Laurie pulled his jacket on and he and Guy started walking down the corridor, past the newsdesk. Stark did not look up but Linda, the newsdesk secretary, did. She blew Laurie a big sexy kiss. He blew one back.

As they reached the lifts, they bumped into Eva-Marie.

'Ah, Eva-Marie,' said Laurie. 'I'm afraid I'm going to have to let your boyfriend down. I won't be around to act as his work experience person after all. I've got the tin tack.'

'The tin what?' said Eva-Marie, puzzled.

'The tin tack – the sack,' said Laurie. 'You are looking at a dead man walking.'

'Oh, no,' said Eva-Marie. 'I'm soooo sorry. That's awful. And I was just coming to tell you that Joe wouldn't be doing his work experience here because we broke up anyway.'

Guy shot a sideways glance at Laurie and nudged him surreptitiously in the ribs.

'I'm sorry to hear that,' said Laurie.

'Well, it all came to a head over you, as it happens,' said Eva-Marie. 'You had very kindly agreed to have him and that's what I thought he wanted and then when I told him that it was all fixed he said that he'd arranged to go to the *Standard* and – the ungrateful little sod – he had the cheek to say that he'd heard that you were over the hill anyway.'

Guy put a hand on Laurie's shoulder.

'Time for that drink, I think,' he said.

Chapter Forty-three

'AND THE FIRST question is – who was Henry the Eighth's second wife, his second wife?'

'Where's Vic?' asked Laurie. 'He's always on time.'

Mary shrugged and looked at Mick.

'Beats me,' said Mick. 'I spoke to him this morning. He seemed a bit distracted but he said he'd see us tonight. We need him for these bloody history questions, too. Maybe his motor's packed up on him again or his AA meeting has overrun. By the way, Laurie, isn't that your little girl behind the counter?'

Laurie nodded. Violet had got her job. She was, she had told him, being paid £2 more an hour than the minimum wage and could keep her tips. No one tips in the Dirty Dog, he told her. This was her fourth day and she seemed to be enjoying it. She got on well with Cliff and the other barmaid, a cheery Australian, called Tuesday, who greeted all the regulars with a 'G'day' which they had taken to repeating back to her so that the air was constantly punctuated with a series of 'G'day-G'days.'

'I think it's Jane Seymour, isn't it?' said Mick.

'No,' said Mary. 'It's Anne Boleyn. Betcha.'

'You sure?' asked Laurie.

'Yeah,' said Mary. 'You look well. Being sacked must suit you.'

'I wasn't sacked, I took advantage of a generous redundancy offer in order to spend more time on special projects,' said Laurie. 'That's what it said on the online noticeboard at work anyway. In fact, I still have the bloody office mobile phone. My news editor keeps texting me to hand it back. Small-minded bastard.'

'Well, you don't look so stressed,' said Mary. 'All we have to do is find you a nice woman.'

The teachers' team was in boisterous mood. They had won the quiz for the last three weeks and were wearing new T-shirts bearing the legend 'The Invincibles'.

Laurie provided Kirkaldy as the town where Raith Rovers came from and Roy Jenkins as the home secretary when hanging was abolished. Mary came up with Brian and Michael as the duo that had had a hit with the song 'Matchstick Men'. Mick knew that the longest river in Asia was the Yangtze.

By the time Cliff announced that they were halfway through the quiz, the team was satisfied that they had maximum points. Traditionally, the questions in the second half were more difficult and Mick kept eyeing the door for new arrivals to see what had happened to Vic. The doors opened frequently but the newcomers were almost exclusively young Polish men, who had now entered their own team. Then the door swung open wide and Vic came in.

'Bloody hell,' said Mick.

'Oh, dear,' said Mary.

Vic had been drinking. He was having difficulty focusing on the room and was frowning. He did not seem to notice his teammates but went straight for the bar. Violet greeted him with a sweet smile.

'Bloody hell,' said Mick again. 'Trouble.'

Vic was fumbling in his pockets, looking for money. He pulled out a crumpled £20 note which he thrust across the counter at Violet as Laurie approached him.

'Hello, mate,' said Laurie. 'You OK?'

'Oh, yeah, just having a little one, you know, just the one,' slurred Vic. 'Make that a double, darling,' he told Violet. 'Don't I know you?'

'It's Violet, Vic.'

'I knew that,' said Vic. 'You're looking lovely, darling. Good job you didn't take after your dad.' Vic fished in his pockets again and pulled out a packet of Marlboro.

'You can't smoke in pubs any more,' said Laurie. 'Why don't we go outside, you can smoke there. Violet will look after your drink.'

Vic was remarkably acquiescent. They stood outside along with a couple of young Poles smoking roll-ups. Laurie found the ancient half-cigar still in his pocket. It was dry and cracked. He took a light off Vic who got through four matches before he ignited one properly.

'So what's up?' asked Laurie.

Vic stared at him with a look of pain and bewilderment. Laurie thought he was about to burst into tears but instead his face broke into a mad, desperate smile.

'Oh, Laurie. Oh, fuck. I've fucked up. I don't know what to fucking do. I—'

'Well, don't get maudlin, whatever you do. What is it, Vic? What happened? Is it about the Hooks?'

'You know! You know! Who told you?'

'I know nuzzin,' said Laurie with a bad Italian accent. 'Tell me. Whatever it is, I'm sure it's OK. Blimey – you didn't kill him yourself, did you?'

Vic gazed at him in a silence for almost a full minute. He took an enormous drag on his cigarette, as though he was a diver about to descend many fathoms, and launched into a speech.

'I didn't kill him,' said Vic. 'But nor did the Russian guy and now the Russian guy's dead and I—'

'Well, hang on a minute, I may have some reassuring news on that front,' said Laurie.

Vic looked at him in bewilderment for a moment and then carried on.

'The night Old Man Hook died, I got this call from Crispin,' said Vic.

'God, it was Crispin then?'

'No, no. You see Crispin rings me. He says the old man has shot himself.'

'Shot himself? But there was no gun.'

'Listen to me, listen to me,' said Vic. 'Crispin says the old man topped himself. He had Alzheimer's, you know. His memory was shot. The family was embarrassed and was keeping it a secret. They thought once it got out, there would be no respect for the old man. All their deals over the clubs and the casinos would fall through because there would be an argument about whether he was compos mentis. You know how old school they are. First he's just a bit barmy – buys a bottle of mouthwash every bloody day because some neighbour told him his breath smelled. Then he starts misbehaving himself. I shouldn't tell you this but he had groped some girl and the police were about to be on his case. Said that they were going to bust him and do his wife for being an accessory because she was trying to pay the girl's family off. So he decided he would do himself in. But he doesn't want to look like a loser – you know how hard it was for Mousey's wife when Mousey topped himself. And it buggers up the insurance payments, doesn't it? So he rings Crispin up just before he does it. He says, "I'm about to shoot myself, I'm not going inside as a fucking nonce but I want to go out with my boots on so come round in ten minutes and take the fucking shooter away," and then – bosh, he shoots himself.'

'Are you sure? Or is this just what Crispin is telling you?'

'I know for sure. You know how the Hooks taped everything? That was how they got people over. Well, Crispin tapes all his calls. He's got it on tape. He played it for me.' Vic took another deep draw on his cigarette. It was down near the filter. 'So Crispin hears the bang and he goes round. There's the old man. He takes the gun and he's off at speed.'

'That was the noise the neighbours heard,' said Laurie. Vic was not listening to him. He was in full flow.

'Crispin now has the gun. He wants the old man to have a heroic end. Go down in legend like Jack Spot or Billy Hill. You know, draw his line in the sand kind of thing. So he thinks – oh, there's the uppity Russian bloke who's trying to pull strokes on the club front. He knows where he lives. He knows the back garden is next to the Heath. Of course, he's got security but . . .' Vic shrugged. A shrug that indicated that his old skills as a career criminal had not deserted him and that security cameras presented no real problems. 'So this is where I come in.'

'But . . .'

'Why am I involved? Good question. Well, you know about all my addictions. Addictive personality. The lot. Alcohol. Nicotine. Gambling. Before I got into AA and GA – Gamblers Anonymous – I ran up nearly a hundred thousand in debts. I'm still paying it off, still owe more than fifty thousand to the Hooks. And on top of that . . .' Vic's face crumpled. 'On top of that, well, you know how I only got a five on the Midland Bank job back then?'

Laurie shrugged.

'Well, there were rumours at the time I must have done a deal. Someone even suggested that at Xanadu. I always denied it. The only person who knew was Bill Beirce, my brief. He's also the Hooks' brief. For good reasons. They know all about his love of spanking. Anyway, he tells them about me cooperating with the Old Bill, telling them where the money was. So Crispin says, if I dump the shooter on Petrov and do something else very small for him, the fifty grand will be wiped off and he'll never tell anyone that I grassed people up on the Midland Bank job.'

'Blimey,' said Laurie.

'Blimey, all right,' said Vic. 'Well, the something else I had to do was this.'

He paused. His handsome face crumpled again and then he seemed to compose himself.

'I had to tip you off so there would be the story in the papers and the police would look into Petrov. Then they find the "murder weapon" there and, hey presto, you've got a suspect who goes on the run and Old Man Hook has died a hero's death. And that's just what happened. We couldn't believe it would go so sweet.'

'Blimey,' said Laurie. 'But how would he know that the Old Bill are going to swallow that? It's a bit bloody obvious that someone must have planted it on Petrov, isn't it?'

Vic sighed deeply again. 'Crispin had everything figured, Laurie. Of course, the police thought it might have been an inside job so they planted a bug in Crispin's house, the day after the murder, to see if they could find out what the Hook family were saying. So what happens? Ginger Mulgrew still has a mate on the squad that's doing the investigation—'

'Not Sandra King?'

'No, she's straight. One of the older blokes, can't remember his name. Anyway, Ginger finds out there's going to be a bug in there and he tells the Hook boys. Hey presto, you get the two of them having this moody conversation – purely for the benefit of the bug, of course – about how they had been warned that Petrov was planning a hit and had been boasting about how the British police knew nothing about him. Anyway, in this phoney conversation, they go on about sorting it out themselves and getting Petrov so that's why the police stepped in so bloody early and that's why the police were so sure it was Petrov! Crispin even got some bloody Russian waiter from Xanadu to write something in Russian on a wreath at the funeral for the police to see.'

'Blimey.'

'Don't keep saying "blimey",' said Vic. 'But how was I to know that Petrov would be bumped off in Thailand? That was never meant to be part of it. And at the time I thought I was even doing you a favour. You'd been saying you were short of a good story and, well, for a while it was a good story, wasn't it? The police bought it and everyone else, all the other papers followed it up. And even now, Laurie, even now, it still stands up as a story, doesn't it?'

There was the sound inside the pub of Cliff tapping the microphone in readiness for the second half of the quiz.

'It's all a bit academic now, anyway, Vic,' said Laurie. 'So don't worry about it.'

'I do worry about it, Laurie. I hated fucking lying to you. But it was that or Crispin telling everyone I was a wrong 'un. I couldn't live with that. You understand, don't you? And he said he would stitch you up, too. Said he had photos of you and one of their lap dancers at the club that your daughter wouldn't like too much and that he was going to send them to your editor if you didn't play ball. Anyway, now I'm back on the fucking juice . . .'

Laurie put a hand on his shoulder. 'So was it him that got the drugs put in my suitcase in Thailand?'

'Well, that was it, Laurie. While you were away in Thailand, your name came up. And Horace said he didn't think we'd be seeing you for a while. Then when you said about the drugs in your case and I know the Hooks have got lots of people in Thailand, that's when I—'

'Jesus. So Old Man Hook was really just a suicide? Nothing to do with Petrov? Nothing to do with Barney Quick even? Or that Asian minicab driver?'

'Well, all the Quicks are gone now. There's only his old sister left and all she ever did was send photos of Barney to

Old Man Hook every year on the anniversary to spook him out. Game old bird but she could hardly organise a hit, could she? The minicab driver was squared years ago. No, the only problem was that neighbour—'

'Beth Plimsoll?'

'Yes. She woke up the night it happened. Crispin's having to pay her off and all. Oh, God, Laurie, I had no fucking idea what was—'

'Don't worry, don't worry.' Laurie gripped Vic by his unsteady shoulder. 'If you help us beat the bloody teachers, all will be forgiven.'

Vic looked unconvinced but followed Laurie back into the pub. Mary and Mick both looked up from the table as Vic made his slightly wobbly way to join them. Laurie noticed that Mary had just bought a round which included a bottle of ginger ale for Vic.

'Just to let you know, ladies and gentlemen, that the prize money tonight stands at one hundred and ten pounds,' said Cliff. 'And the first question of the second half – and remember, there's no calling a friend in this quiz – is question number eleven: who won an Oscar for best actress in a supporting role for her part in the nineteen ninety film *Ghost*?'

'Bloody hell, it was Whoopi Goldberg, wasn't it?' said Vic. 'I remember it. It must have come out then because we were in Maidstone.'

'We were never in Maidstone in nineteen ninety,' said Mick.

'I was,' said Vic, talking with the exaggerated pronunciation of a drunk.

Mary correctly answered the next three questions – on Lily

Allen, Shameless and the leader of the Burmese opposition –
and Laurie knew the name of the Brighton hotel bombed by
the IRA during the Conservative Party conference. The
teachers also seemed confident that they had got all the right
answers. Then it was time for 'double or quits'.

'Just to remind you all of our next section, double or quits:
there are five questions in this section and you get two points
for each one answered correctly but – BUT . . .'

'BUT!' echoed the competitors across the pub.

'But if you get any of the questions wrong in this section,
you lose all your marks in that section. Is that clear?'

'Yes,' came a mumbled general response.

'IS THAT CLEAR?' boomed Cliff, warming to the task.

'YESSSSS!' came the response.

'He thinks he's bloody Billy Graham,' said Mick.

'I think he's sweet,' said Mary.

The questions were harder than the rest of the quiz: the
capital of Togo, the name of the main character in
Trainspotting, the location of the tallest building in the world,
the date of the Battle of the Bulge, and the name of the
American punk band who made an album called *Milking the
Sacred Cow*. Between them they were fairly sure they had got
the first four right. But no one had a clue about the fifth.

'Who's meant to know that kind of stuff?' asked Mick.
'That's just trivia. Bloody trivia.'

'Well, we just have to not fill it in and hope no one else
knows,' said Mary.

'Someone else will know,' said Laurie. 'I know, I can ask
Violet. I'm sure she did American punk music in her media
studies.'

'You can't do that,' said Mary. 'It's cheating.'

'In the great scheme of things,' said Vic, making his first proper contribution to the conversation and still speaking in the convoluted manner of the drunk, 'that does not seem to be the greatest of my offences.'

'No, come on,' said Mary. 'If we don't know, we don't know. Leave it.'

The last two questions were easy. Cliff called for the papers to be handed in. The teachers seemed disturbingly confident. Violet came round to collect their glasses and see if they wanted another round. Vic made an attempt to ask for a tequila but Mary shook her head.

'I'm going to call your sponsor in a minute,' said Mary.

Laurie went to the bar to pick up the drinks that Violet was pouring.

'Does Vic really have a sponsor?' she asked. 'Like Nike or Puma?'

'No,' said Laurie. 'Not like Nike or Puma. It's someone in Alcoholics Anonymous. It's like a sort of buddy, you know, someone you can call when you need a bit of support. And can we have some of those spicy crisps.'

'They're bad for you, you know that,' said Violet. 'Full of salt.'

'People come to the pub to escape from all that judgementalism,' said Laurie. 'Didn't they teach you that in citizenship class?'

'No,' said Violet.

Vic was silent now, staring at the table, frowning deeply. The quiz papers were being passed between tables for marking.

'So what are you going to do now, Laurie?' asked Mick.

'Dunno. Any smart ideas?'

'He could be a private detective,' said Mary.

'Yeah, I'd be great at that, wouldn't I? No one would ever get one over on me, would they?'

Vic looked up mournfully at him.

'You're right,' said Mick to Mary. 'He would be a perfect private eye. He's got all the right attributes – a fucked-up marriage, an incipient drink problem and burgeoning self-pity issues. All he needs is a fucking hat.'

'Thanks a lot for that,' said Laurie.

Cliff had taken the microphone. The marked answers had been handed in.

'And now, my lords, ladies and gentlepersons, the results. I will announce the winners but first I would like everyone to give a big hand for the Krakow Bloody Plumbers who scored nine points. A big hand, please!' A beaming table full of Poles acknowledged the applause. 'And now the top three teams in reverse order. At number three . . .' Cliff paused for dramatic effect.

'He thinks he's doing the bloody Oscars,' said Mick.

'Well, I hope we were right about Whoopi,' said Mary.

'At number three,' intoned Cliff, gesturing at a quartet of forty-something, shaven-headed men demolishing pints of Guinness. 'The Einstein family – with eighteen points.' The men toasted themselves noisily with raised glasses.

'In second position,' said Cliff.

'This is going to be bloody us again,' said Mick.

'In second position, on twenty points, with a perfect score until they lost all their ten points through one wrong answer on the double or quits round, is our old friends – School's Out Forever. And the winners . . . roll of drums . . . is another old friend, with twenty-five points, the Long Lartin Old Boys Club who pocket this week's bumper harvest of one hundred and ten pounds – yes, ladeeeeez and gentlemen, one hundred and ten pounds!'

Mary threw her arms round Laurie. Vic accepted a hug from Mick. The teachers were in the midst of a post-mortem. Violet gave Laurie a distant wink and smile. At that moment his phone rang. It was a woman's voice at the other end. He could not hear what she was saying amidst the hubbub. He went out into the street and joined a couple of young Poles who smiled at him.

'Well done with quiz,' said one. Laurie nodded back at him.

'Hello,' he said into the phone. 'Who is that? Sandra? Oh, Sandra King, hi . . . What are you saying? You're giving me that tip-off you always promised me? But . . . What? You're kidding me. Crispin? Dead? I don't believe it. Where? What happened? God, I can't believe that . . . In a latex mask? Amazing! When is all this going to come out? A press conference tomorrow morning.' Laurie shook his head. 'It's great of you to do this but the awful thing is I no longer work at the paper . . . Yeah, I'm afraid so. But I do really appreciate it. Thank you . . . And you. What did you say? Lunch sometime? Well, as long as it's not that dreadful steakhouse round the corner from the Yard . . . Yeah, OK . . .'

Laurie returned to the pub. Vic was being persuaded to have a cup of coffee which Violet had conjured up from behind the bar. Mick was graciously accepting eleven £10 notes from Cliff. Mary was beaming.

'Important call?' asked Mary.

'Well, here is the news,' said Laurie. 'Ready for this?' He waited until his table had quietened down.

'So, what's the big news?' said Mary.

'Crispin Hook has been shot dead in the car park behind Xanadu.'

'You are fucking having me on,' said Mick. Vic stared open mouthed.

'You'll enjoy this, Vic, and I mean that sincerely,' said Laurie. 'Unfortunately, for the alleged assailant, an ARV—'

'A what?' said Mary.

'Armed response vehicle,' said the three men in unison.

'An ARV which had been told there was a large suspect package in the Holloway area left by some bloke who ran away – false alarm, as usual – was driving past a couple of minutes after the shooting. They see the bloke who did it with a weapon still in his hand. Desperate guy. He opens fire at them. They shoot back. Bosh. Another dead body.'

'Who was it?' asked Mick. 'Barney Quick's big sister in drag?'

'Better than that,' said Laurie.

'Come on,' said Vic.

'The police don't know this yet, but it was Vladimir Petrov himself,' said Laurie. 'Back from the dead.'

'I don't get this,' said Vic.

'You're not exactly alone on this one,' said Mick. 'Back from the dead? What are you talking about?'

Laurie picked up his phone and handed it to Violet.

'Now, if you'll excuse me, I must just text my erstwhile boss,' he said. 'Violet, can you translate this into textese and send it to Stark, who you should find on my address list. Ready? Right, here's how it goes: "Exclusive. Another Hook murder. Ghost also killed. Alas, can't get it into paper, can I? So you'll miss the scoop of the year. Bye bye. Laurie."'

Mary was calling for a minicab for Vic. Laurie went for a pee. Two of the teachers were standing at the urinals, looking aggrieved.

'I don't understand why we put down an answer for that American punk band,' said one. 'That's what screwed everything up.'

'Well, Zoe was adamant about it,' said the other.

'How did she know?'

'She said the barmaid, that new young one, told her in the ladies, said she was a hundred per cent sure it was the New York Dolls. Said her dad had the album.'

'Bloody hell,' said the first teacher. 'Bloody hell. So how come it turned out to be the Dead Kennedys?'

Laurie stared ahead and contemplated the paleness of his urine. Was that good or bad? Did yellow mean a healthy liver or the reverse? He could not remember.

He rejoined Mary and Mick. His phone rang. Vic picked it up. He looked at the screen.

'Somebody called Stark,' he said.

'I'm busy,' said Laurie.

Vic dropped the phone delicately into Mick's pint of Adnams. His minicab arrived. He gave Laurie an awkward hug. Laurie said his farewells to Mary and Mick and waited while Violet cleared away the glasses with Daffyd. On their short walk home, she slipped her arm into his. 'Well, you're well set up now, Dad. All that prize money and – I have to confess I saw how much you got as your pay-off from the paper.'

'How d'you mean?'

'Well, that big fat wodge of money – it was in a book about Robert Burns on the kitchen table. I didn't know they just gave you the dosh in notes. They must have really appreciated you after all to give you that much.'

Laurie said nothing. The light was on in the house.

'Did you leave it on to scare away these people sending us hooks?' he asked Violet as he fished for his keys.

'Oh, God, I meant to tell you, I completely forgot,' said Violet. 'A funny little old skinny bloke with straggly hair and teeth and a tie that didn't match his shirt came into the pub before you lot all arrived. He said he couldn't wait for you but he'd see you later in the week at, what was it, the CRA meeting? Is that like AA? He said that he heard that you'd been sacked and he was very, very sorry and he felt bad about pulling your leg by sending you a tongue with a hook in it.'

'You're kidding? What did he say his name was?'

'He said he was the vicar but I think he was lying,' said Violet. 'He didn't look at all like a vicar.'

'The Vicar,' said Laurie. 'The bloody Vicar.'

'I'm telling you, he didn't look like a vicar,' said Violet. 'He said that, if you hadn't thrown the tongue away, it was OK to eat. He said it wasn't past its sell-by date.'

Laurie opened the front door. There was a letter on the mat that had been forwarded from work. He recognised Linda's handwriting on the envelope but not that of the original sender. He opened it.

'Hi,' said the letter. 'I'm back in Sheffield now. No probs if it was just a holiday fling but now that I gather you have a bit of free time, why don't you come and discover the joys of the Yorkshire Dales? Can't promise that it will be as exciting as Thailand but nicer walks and fewer dead bodies being eaten by dogs. Love, Flo.'

'Who's that from, dad?'

'Just an old friend,' said Laurie.

'So what's that big grin for?'

Violet put on a CD. It was a David Allen Coe song. 'Ride 'Em, Cowboy'. A song Caz often sang. Laurie sat down to listen to it. There was a line in it about only riding wild horses in your dreams. He dozed off. When he awoke, Violet had gone to bed. He looked out of the window. There was a fox nosing its way casually through a neighbour's overcrowded dustbin. He drew the curtains. In the distance, there was the sound of a police siren.

Acknowledgements

Many thanks for different reasons: especially to Pat Kavanagh (1940–2008), and also to Martin Fletcher, Jo Stansall, Jane Heller, Helen Norris, Peter Lyon, Yoni Gottlieb, Oxana Gottlieb, Lorna Macfarlane, Niyaz Laiq, Amber Marks, Matt Sinclair and Ruby Crystal.

DUNCAN CAMPBELL

The Paradise Trail

Calcutta 1971. A city in black-out as India declares war on Pakistan. Even so, the backpackers who end up in the flea-pit Lux Hotel are determined to have a good time. That is, until two mysterious deaths amongst them change their lives for ever.

Thrown together in the city are Anand, the jazz-loving insomniac hotelier; Gordon, one of the hotel's dope-smoking guests; the philandering journalist Hugh, covering his first war; Britt, a Californian photographer with a jealous boyfriend; and the enigmatic Freddie Braintree, who interprets life through the lyrics of Bob Dylan and the Incredible String Band.

Is it possible that one of them is behind the deaths? And why will it take more than three decades and three continents to find out?

'A hugely enjoyable, ambitious and unusual story, told with wit, humanity and an attractive sympathy for his characters and their flaws' Ronan Bennett

'A marvellous evocation of the glorious madness which was the 70s hippy trail' Felix Dennis

978 0 7553 4247 1

headline
review

JED RUBENFELD

The Interpretation of Murder

Manhattan, 1909.

On the morning after Sigmund Freud arrives in New York on his first – and only – visit to the United States, a stunning debutante is found bound and strangled in her penthouse apartment, high above Broadway. The following night, another beautiful heiress, Nora Acton, is discovered tied to a chandelier in her parents' home, viciously wounded and unable to speak or to recall her ordeal. Soon Freud and his American disciple, Stratham Younger, are enlisted to help Miss Acton recover her memory, and to piece together the killer's identity. It is a riddle that will test their skills to the limit, and lead them on a thrilling journey – into the darkest places of the city, and of the human mind.

'[Rubenfeld's] portrayal of New York's social divisions, its louche, rumbustious energy, and its skyscrapers reaching higher and higher, have a vivid authenticity . . . an unusually intelligent novel which entertains, informs and intrigues on several levels' *The Times*

'A thrilling, heart-in-the-mouth read . . . Once you start reading, it's impossible to put down' *Scotsman*

'Rubenfeld writes beautifully . . . an intriguing mystery' *Sunday Telegraph*

'Rubenfeld's brilliant conceit is to weave this real-life event into an accomplished thriller . . . a dazzling novel' *Independent*

978 0 7553 3142 0

headline
review

Now you can buy any of these other bestselling **Headline** books from your bookshop or *direct from the publisher*.

FREE P&P AND UK DELIVERY
(Overseas and Ireland £3.50 per book)

TO ORDER SIMPLY CALL THIS NUMBER

01235 400 414

or visit our website: www.headline.co.uk

Prices and availability subject to change without notice.